In a sequel to the successful *Three Naughty French Novels*, here is a second volume of classic erotic works by French literary figures. *Les Libertines*, four stories of upper-class decadence by Adolphe Belot, begins with the tale of a French gentleman who wiles away his time at a special Parisian house of pleasure. Belot (1829-1899), author of many "naturalist melodramas," also wrote works of pornography like *Les Libertines* on the side.

Octave Mirbeau's *Diary of a Chambermaid* follows the arousing adventures of Celestine R., a fisherman's daughter who leaves home and discovers she likes to have men around—lots of them. The anarchist journalist Mirbeau (1848-1917) turned to fiction and drama after marrying well, and at first denied authorship of *Diary of a Chambermaid*, admitting only to be its editor because of the racy content.

Irene is the infamous surrealistic tale of voyeuristic obsession by "Albert de Routisie" that Albert Camus called "the finest erotic novel ever written." The author is almost certainly Louis Aragon (1897-1982), the beloved communist "Poet of the Resistance," who was a prominent Surrealist and proponent of automatic writing when *Irene* was first published in 1928.

Three More Naughty French Novels

Three More Naughty French Novels

Les Libertines
by **Adolphe Belot**

The Diary of a Chambermaid
by **Octave Mirbeau**

Irene
by **Albert de Routisie**

QUALITY PAPERBACK BOOK CLUB
NEW YORK

Les Libertines

by Adolphe Belot

Contents

Some More About "My Little Cousin"

A lady, young, fresh, extremely pretty and stylishly though quietly dressed, tripped daintily along a street in the neighborhood of the Madeleine, in Paris, then disappeared into a respectable house, ran quickly up the stairs to the first floor and nervously pressed the button of the electric bell.

The tinkle had hardly ceased when the door was opened by a neat maid who ushered the visitor into a handsome drawing room in which were assembled sundry other ladies, all young and fashionably dressed, but all wearing the preoccupied air of persons about to have an interview with, say, their doctor or their solicitor.

Presently, as if awaiting the newcomer, the mistress of the house appeared—tall, slender, exquisitely attired in black silk with a dainty headdress of the style adopted by many English ladies of a certain age, possibly because of the undoubted air of distinction it confers. She smiled pleasantly at her young visitor as she shook hands with her; then with a murmured apology, she turned towards two of the other ladies and said: "Your friends have arrived and are awaiting you"—and whereupon they rose and retired, smiling their thanks.

Turning again to her young visitor, she said affectionately, "My dear, someone is waiting also to see you, a
gentleman, one of my best friends. If you are willing to
let him make your acquaintance, I shall be happy to
introduce him to you."

This "good friend" was none other than myself! The
house belonged to Madame de Saint-Edme, the most
obliging of women and also the most tactful of her sex in
the delicate mission of creating and establishing the most
intimate of relations between persons of opposite sexes
who desired to avail themselves of such services. To pretty women pressed for money or inconvenienced by their
sexual appetites and desires, to mistresses *en titre* seeking
to increase or supplement their alimony, and to married
women who found their allowances insufficient or their
husbands' powers not equal to the marital duties desired
from them, Mme. de Saint-Edme's discreet chambers
offered the safest and pleasantest of opportunities for the
acceptance incognito of financial or other assistance
from gentlemen. Similarly she was ready to provide for
gentlemen of amorous proclivities satisfactory opportunities of satisfying their carnal desires by the favors of
impecunious ladies—thus avoiding on one side a lengthy
pursuit and on the other resistance before surrender.

Further again, those who loved to indulge in Lesbian
practices found at her house a convenient rendezvous
where they could revel in the enjoyment of their sweet
fantasy with the wished-for object of their desire, or (in
her absence) they could there without difficulty come
across girls who understood and shared their tastes, and
who desired nothing better than to either bestow or
receive the lingual caresses so dear to tribades, lending
themselves adorably to either of the two functions.

To old and trusted habituées (the younger set being absolutely debarred unless there was not the slightest doubt as to their fidelity and discretion) she allowed the privilege of assisting at Lesbian-Priapus fetes and representations to which were also invited such ladies as wished to be present and whose discretion was assured —the lively feminine contingent knowing they had nothing to fear on such occasions where modesty was conspicuous by its absence.

She for who I was waiting was, according to Mme. de Saint-Edme, a debutante in libertinage who had so far honored her house once only with her presence. Said Mme. de Saint-Edme to me: "I wanted you to be first to enjoy her, but you were unfortunately in the country when she finally plucked up her courage to visit me, having disappointed me twice previously. I wished very much that one of my good friends had been then on the spot, but alas, there were none! And from fear of letting her slip away again, I introduced a casual visitor to her and she let him enjoy her! It was a rare good piece of luck for him, but now, at all events, we have caught our little bird."

Despite her cynically immoral principles, this excellent woman had the considerate delicacy to let her female clients have a peep in secret at their respective proposed male companions, to decide whether they were pleased with them. Some fancied dark men, others fair—some admired beards, others preferred the simple moustache. Hot-blooded and passionate women sought for muscular strength coupled with distinction; cold-blooded ones were more solicitous about the price they would receive for their favors. To these latter, the preliminary peep was only a formality of secondary importance.

It is no use to run counter to tastes—to clash with caprices. The ladies that were satisfied by their preliminary peep were forthwith conducted to the destined chamber and the introduction effected, a similar privilege and opportunity of inspecting his proposed female companion having been accorded to the male client.

But as a rule these preliminaries were purely formal—thanks to the care that Mme. de Saint-Edme took to bring together suitable partners—thanks also to the skill with which she described to each in turn the charms of the other. And when the happy man was conducted to the allotted chamber (carefully furnished with every requirement a loving pair could desire) and introduced to the lady (who invariably made a pretense of doing needlework or reading when he was ushered in), Mme. de Saint Edme would disappear, the sequel not concerning her.

But when it was a case of a debutante she took care never to be far away!—for it was at the critical moment that the courage of the former failed them. "No! no!—not now!—not today!—" they would not infrequently exclaim—and run out of the room. Then Mme. de Saint-Edme would intercept them in the corridor, and by means of her soothing caresses and persuasive words, she could convince them to stay. Then she would take them to another room and induce them to undress, then whisper soothingly and encouragingly, "Now dear, you are all right, I will go and bring him myself to you!" and the episode would terminate with a bout of love made all the more delicious by the ardor imparted to the lover by a resistance that could only indicate that the girl he was about to enjoy was a novice in such matters!

But it must not be supposed that all the debutantes gave this trouble. After their second—and very often on their first visit—the majority of girls would not make any serious resistance to even the most audacious and libertine actions of their male companions. Very often indeed, instead of resorting to airs of startled innocence in order to stimulate their partner's lust, they would endeavor to attain to the same end by arraying themselves in the most provocative and décolleté costumes! Among her other virtues, Mme. de Saint-Edme was able to give the best of advice as to the toilette to be adopted towards this end. It was not for nothing that she had been for years in one of the leading Parisian modistes establishments. In this situation, she had amassed much by pecuniary gifts from the clientele, both for her suggestions and still more for her services as a "broker-in-love," and the friendly relations she thus inspired invariably remained unimpaired.

On this occasion the lady whose favors had been retained for me had simply removed her hat, and I held mine respectfully in my hand while being introduced to her in the following words—"My dear, let me introduce to you the gentleman and friend regarding whom I have spoken to you!"

She turned to greet me, when—good heaven!—I recognized a young cousin of mine! In our preliminary peeps we had seen each other but imperfectly—her face had been in a great measure hidden by her matinee hat while it was no doubt my beard that made her fail to recognize me, for many years had passed since we had seen each other.

"Why?—it is you, Gilberte!"

Mme. de Saint-Edme at once saw that she had unwittingly created an awkward situation—that she had "put her foot" in it! She stood dumbfounded! I begged her to leave us to ourselves.

The situation was piquant! This cousin was the *"petite cousine"* of authors, the *"petite cousine"* of youthful amorous indiscretions and yearnings that had not come to anything owing to her early marriage and the subsequent impossibility of rendezvous—and further, at such a time a woman does not lend herself to amorous adventures. I now found her grown into a beautiful woman, and under surroundings that (to me, at least) afforded an opportunity of reviving our youthful mutual passion and of carrying it to a satisfactory denouement.

She dropped her eyes in confusion! I took her hands gently in mine, and while assuring her that she could absolutely rely on my discretion I added that if she would like to go away she was at perfect liberty to do so and that I would never breathe a single words as to this meeting. But as my noble and chivalrously virtuous declaration did not produce any response, the mere man in me began to assert itself—and imperiously, too!—as I contemplated the tumultuous heaving of her breasts under her dainty corsage and the betrayal by them of her emotions!

"Speak, Gilberte!" No answer. "Would you like me to go away?" Still silence.

I was puzzled to know what to do. Would it be advisable straightway to respect her and give up any attempt to induce her to accord to me favors she had evidently come prepared to accord to a stranger? Or should I treat her as if she was of easy morality, and without circumlocution address to her proposals that I would have made to any other woman I met under similar circumstances, and which I was justified in assuming would not be unwelcome to her? But women are so odd, their ideas of morality so extraordinary, and some who would on occasion submit themselves without hesitation to the grossest lubricity would on other occasions resent the least attempt at a liberty! At all events women that came to Mme. de Saint-Edme's chambers could hardly expect to be considered as strictly virtuous—and Gilberte must rank herself with them! But our cousinly relationship—which at an ordinary society function would have assist-ed me—here was a positive handicap to both of us: I rep-resented to Gilberte her family, her respectability, her past life, her girlish days.

I must confess that the memories of these latter were such as afforded to both of us a pretext for reviving the past in the present. In our youthful amusements we had not troubled to respect our mutual modesty! Stolen kiss-es, caresses of tongue against tongue, indiscreet ram-blings of inquisitive hands under clothes, all had brought us to the very threshold of the supreme pleasure. One day, when hidden in a barn with her, my hand had found its way to her little girlish cunny that it strove to excite by an active finger, while her little hands were amusing themselves with my prick as it stood rampant and stiff in her honor. But nothing else had transpired, and we had not met again, until now.

I reminded her of this; she smiled, and little by little let fall her constraint, whether real or simulated.

"Don't speak of it!" she said. "We were sillies!"

"We certainly were, because we did not take advan-tage of our opportunities! But now that we have so unex-pectedly met? . . ."

"Tell me—didn't you know who I was when you came in?"

"Honestly, I did not."

"Well, suppose that you had made me out, would you then have come in?"

"It is possible that I might have considered it better in your interests to disappear, but I should have done so with great regret, for you were looking so lovely! And you? If you had recognized me?"

"I should have run away!"

"But why? Do you think I cannot appreciate your charms as well as anyone else?"

"Oh! . . . But you and another man are two very different things!—you are a relative—and I had not come here for the purpose of meeting my family."

"I don't suppose you did!" I replied laughing. "But it is so easy for us to forget that we are relatives. I have only to think of you as a charming young lady I have for the first time met, and you have only to allow me to make to this charming young lady declarations and proposals to which I am sure she would like to listen much more than to remonstrances she might fear!"

"It seems to me so strange that I should be here at all with you! I feel my presence here is so extraordinary—so upsetting!"

"Then, if we were to go on with our last meeting in the old barn, the sin—if any—would seem to you to be less grave and less piquant, in fact almost allowable, as in marriage?"

"You're talking nonsense . . . Of course not! . . . But to be seen by you here makes me feel as if everybody I know is also looking at me!"

"Then you don't care about doing this sort of thing before the world?"

Gilberte laughed frankly. I saw at once to what extent I should have adopted a false policy and how weak I should have been had I treated with an excess of respect a girl who, although my cousin, had of her own accord come to a house resorted to only by those who wished for a gratification of their sexual passions and desires. In fact, with anyone else but her, I would before now have put myself in possession of charms that would have been surrendered to me kindly, while had she been with anyone else but me, she would not have concealed them from the eyes and no doubt the kisses of her happy companion.

"Well," I continued, "I don't know who you are. It is the first time I have seen you. Mme. de Saint-Edme told me that she would introduce me to a charming girl who was visiting her for the first time, who proves to be even prettier than I could have anticipated, and who will, I trust, prove not less unkind than the others to whom Madame has introduced me and who have been good enough to amuse themselves with me here. May I ask what is your Christian name?"

"Gilberte," she replied laughing.

"Gilberte! What a pretty name. Well now, Gilberte, let me help you to take off your hat and cloak."

When I had hung these up, I passed my arm round her waist and kissed her on the mouth clasping her to me as I did so.

"You come here very seldom, I understand?" I said. "I have not had the good fortune to meet you before."

"This is my first visit, Monsieur," she replied, entering into the spirit of the game.

"Really! But I think it cannot be the first time that you have left your husband in the lurch, for you look to me like a young married woman?"

"You are indiscreet, Monsieur."

"Well—I won't press my curiosity any further. At all events it is very sweet of you to allow others to share with him in enjoying your charms."

Seating myself on a sofa, I drew her gently onto my knees, and repeated my kisses on her mouth while my hand wandered inquisitively over her corsage. She laughed, then exclaimed "Oh! Monsieur!" in the most natural way.

Then my hand descended a little, and pressed against and between her thighs over her dress. Her hand tried to push mine away. I yielded, but only to pull up her skirts, in order to touch the bare flesh of what I had been feeling over her clothes. Gently I groped her calves, knees, and thighs.

"Oh! . . . what are you doing, Monsieur?"

"Only trying to learn if you wear your garters above or below your knees."

"Above, always!"

"You have such sweet calves." My hand climbed a little higher—her skin was so soft and sweet.

"Oh! . . . oh! . . . you're tickling me! . . . No! . . . no! . . ."

"Why! . . . your drawers are closed in front!"

"Ha! . . . ha! . . . oh! . . . take away your hand! . . . you're tickling me!"

"Oh! . . . now I've got to it! . . . oh! . . . what a lot of hair you have. Ever so much more than you had in the barn!"

"What barn?"

"Ah! . . . pardon me! I was forgetting!"

In spite of the reappearance of the cousin under the lover, she did not stop or even hinder my delicious rovings among and over her most secret charms. This proceeding no doubt pleased her better than any sentimental modesty on my part—it also pleased me better!

Arranging her comfortably on my knees, my hand set to work to explore the delightfully rounded contours of her bottom, which I found plump, firm, and springy.

"Madame," I said, "what lovely globes you have— real Maps of the World! Very few girls have anything like your bottom, so hard and elastic!"

"What a comical name, Map of the World? Why?"

"Because there are there the two half globes of the world. Do let me see them. Let me take off your corset. Oh, what a troublesome corset! Ah! Now it is off. Oh what lovely breasts! So nice and firm, as firm as your bottom."

"Hush! You mustn't talk like that!"

"You are simply charming—delicious. I am charmed to make your acquaintance! No woman has ever inflamed me with desires to such an extent."

I seized her hand and placed it on the unmistakable proof of the desires with which she had inspired me. She called me "*polisson*," which in the mouth of a woman is an encouragement to go still further, and declared that I had not improved, I whom she had considered sentimental! I confessed to her that I was no longer so, that sentiment between men and women only tended to waste time and delay the pleasures of love.

"You then are no longer sentimental?" I asked.

"As you find me here you can see for yourself. Anyhow, all women sentimental or not, who talk about it, manage to finish in the same way, either sooner or later."

"You are making nice distinctions. You make me think you are a little student in love matters."

"Well, as to that, I fancy I shall be still more so as soon as I escape out of your arms. You have a way of effecting this. I shall emerge from this truly accomplished."

This phrase spoken with a delicious smile, with that look that a woman knows how to use when she wishes to undress a man with her eyes and say to him, "Now come, let me see your—" This passage of words transported me with desire in indicating to me a horizon of endless pleasures with my lively cousin. I clasped her lovingly in my arms, exchanging tongue kisses with her, then prayed her to undress herself.

I assisted her, seizing every opportunity for deliciously touching her bare flesh, intoxicated by the sweet fragrance emanating from her undergarments that she had carefully selected—for every woman knows that the charms of her person are a treasure to be placed in a suitable frame to fairly show its beauty to the eyes privileged to view it.

Very soon she only had on her chemise! In a jiffy I was in a similar costume. Then after the necessary toilet we laid ourselves on the bed, closely clasped in each other's arms, and abandoned ourselves to the sweet preliminaries to bliss.

"You will be discreet, eh?" said my cousin as she surrendered herself to me. To be so was of course as much to my interest as to hers.

Very soon she allowed herself to be invaded by symptoms of pleasure. Her lovely breasts began rapidly to heave, her eyes half closed languorously. Was it real, or was she only pretending as part of her assumed role of a woman of pleasure? As she afterwards admitted that she had perfectly recognized me at the first and had allowed me to be introduced to her fully knowing the reason of my presence, it is quite possible that my handling and fingering of her naked body had the same rapid and sweet effect on her as when we indulged in our youthful escapades. As a matter of fact, it is the restless women who feel most sensitively the hand that caresses them. Gilberte, I recollect, used to go off at once, like a thoroughbred to the least pressure of the bit, and now she had become a woman, she evidently had preserved this precious quality. Anyhow, on my part, I was soon burning with the hottest lust. The girl I held in my arms inspired me at one and the same time with a craving for orgies such as one would indulge in with ladies of professed easy virtue, and the rage for such forbidden fruit gained additional piquancy from the fact that she was my cousin.

At my request she took off her chemise and displayed herself to me, naked, her lovely body relieved by the thicket of silky hairs that formed a triangular shadowing at the extremity of her rounded stomach, her nakedness being emphasized by her shoes and stockings, which she had kept on, by her garters that she adjusted above her knees when pulling her stockings tight. The little coquette knew well how a naked girl can heighten the effect of her nudity.

Then I felt and handled her all over. I kissed and sucked her breasts. I thrust my nose under her armpits, diving amid the tufts of hair. There is nothing that imparts to one's desires so alluring a frenzy as the breathing of the "odor di femina" of the sweet body that has surrendered itself to you. My fingers nevertheless employed themselves in curling and twisting and playing with the mossy covering of her plump cunt, one of them caressing the delicious slit into which it soon forced its way, for the first time since our adventure in the barn. At that time, this cunny and slit were virgin but my pleasure lost but little through this detail for then her breasts were not so sweet a handful, her thighs were not so fat and round, her hips were not so full and plump, while the little hand that I had taught to play with my prick (oh so timidly) was not so clever and soft. Her mouth then was not so skilled in the art of kissing, while her chaste little ears would have closed themselves if I had whispered to them all that I was now softly murmuring to them while I gently agitated my finger over her clitoris.

"And what about this little pussy, this sweet little pussy? Does it love catching and eating mice? I will gladly give it mine!"

"It is a very big mouse, this one!"

"Girls like large pricks in their cunts! They are also charmed when a male tongue is applied. I want to apply mine to your cunt—I want to do *minette* to you! You know what that is?"

She answered me simply with a smile. Promptly I placed my mouth on her closely clustering hairs (Gilberte was a lovely brunette)—and I nibbled them with my lips, inhaling delightedly their fragrant perfume tempered with rice powder and Eau de Lubin. Even as a young girl, this was her favorite scent, but then she did not apply it to this part of herself, no doubt in ignorance of the arts of provoking and spicing the audacious kisses that make the coldest girls faint with pleasure. But cold she never was, and when my mouth settled itself on her cunt, when my tongue insinuated itself gently between its lips in search of the little spot in which a woman's sexual pleasure is concentrated, unmistakable symptoms indicating the most exquisite delight gave me to understand that she knew well how to taste this caress. One of her legs was thrown across my back and held me firmly to her, and I could feel the little heel of her dainty shoe dig into my ribs like a spur. The other foot she extended right down my front and against my prick and I could feel the soft leather that was rubbing against it.

Oh, what ecstasies! I could hear the broken breathings of my voluptuous companion, I could feel her body quivering under the thrusts of my tongue, and the cheeks of her bottom wriggle in my hands as they gripped them. I felt her frenziedly press down my head between her thighs so as to let her taste every tongue-thrust. And I, twenty times was I was on the point of flooding my cousin's shoe with the torrent of my discharge, but I preferred to dispose of it otherwise. So at length, I released myself from her sweet clasp and placed myself again alongside of her on the sofa.

"Was it good? Did I do it properly?" I whispered to her.

"Very sweet indeed, you naughty man! It is very evident that you were not doing it for the first time!"

"And you? Is it the first time that you? . . ."

"You are horrid!"

"Ha! ha! Then you like having it done to you, eh!"

"All women do! But what do you think of one of my friends who declares she commits no infidelity towards her husband when she lets a man do her in this way?"

"I think I know her. Is she not a tall fair girl called Angela?"

"Yes. So you know her?"

"She comes here!"

"But how do you know that she is the one I mean?"

"Well, it is the same name, and she won't let a man do anything else to her but this."

"And have you then done it to her?"

"Yes—I must admit it—and it was well worth my while! But did she not also tell you that she confines her ministrations to her husband to this same one way?"

"Which way?"

I placed my finger softly on her mouth. Gilberte broke into laughter and asked if I had let Angela do me in the same way.

"Of course—and what's more I begged her to do it as she did not do any other way."

"Oh you men!—you dreadful men! Monsieur Henri!" (my Christian name). "I would not have believed you to be so . . . so . . ."

So naughty? But in love many things that are naughty are also nice. But tell me—has no one ever asked you nicely to do it?"

"If I could say that no one had ever made such a request of me, I would not be able to say so for long— for I can read your intention in those eyes that are sparkling with lust!"

"Ah!—so I have missed also the virginity of your mouth! And so you have already committed this sweet sin! Was it in this house? Tell me all about it?"

"I don't remember!"

"Oh yes you do!—now do tell me—whisper in my ear as if you were with your confessor!"

"You're a fine confessor."

"At all events not a cruel one! Listen:

> *Ma fille pour pénitence,*
> *Et ron, ron, ron, petit patapon,*
> *Ma fille, pour pénitence,*
> *Nous recommencerons.*

"Come, I'll give you a start! You've done it once,

twice, thrice, the first time out of curiosity, the second . . ."

"Oh! Once will do . . . I think I was made that day!
. . . A girlfriend had invited me to supper with her and
her lover, and after dessert we all were a trifle squiffy!
They told me all sorts of naughty stories, and they didn't
mind what they did before me! In short, I watched them
do all sorts of things till I was completely upset and excited beyond my self-control until I was unable to stand
their teasing and challenges. I let myself go in rivalry of
my friend's libertinage and let her see me do with her
lover all that she herself had just done with him!"

"And your friend was not jealous? And this is how
you learnt this sweet little vice?"

"Alas, yes, I must admit it."

It is a well established fact that it is by their own sex
and not by men that women are initiated into the most
ingenious refinements of lust, and Casanova correctly recognized the fact when he maintained that a gallant who
could manage to bring to one and the same rendezvous
two girls hitherto enjoyed by him separately, would realize with the two together the most erotic of debauches.
But as far as I was concerned, I was going to take advantage of what I had so happily found out, and so continued to play my part as Gilberte's Father Confessor.

"Very good, my daughter!" I said to her. "And since
then, how often?"

"I haven't done it since, Father," she replied laughing.

"My daughter, you must be nearly a saint! But nevertheless you must do penance!"

> *Et pour pénitence*
> *Nous recommencerons, ron, ron,*
> *Nous recommencerons.*

She resisted a little, saying that she was not worked up as on that occasion, that she didn't wish to do it again, that she had promised herself not to repeat the perform-ance . . . But the example of her friend that I recalled to her soon overcame these feeble hesitations—coming as they did from her head and not from her inclination.

"Oh!" she exclaimed, as she bent down towards the object that stood rampant and stiff, burning to receive her caress. "I don't think Angela would have waited till she was asked twice! She loves doing it! Say," she added with a malicious smile, "when we were in the old barn we didn't get as far as this, eh?"

Her soft hand guided my pego towards her lips and I felt it enter into her mouth, the moist warmth of which caused a delicious quiver of pleasure from my thighs to my loins. For a beginner she acquitted herself divinely: she took my prick well into her mouth, and with the rec-ollection of her friend's methods in her mind, she set to work to give me the most intense pleasure in her power. Oh, my exquisite bliss! . . . my delirious sensations! Twenty times I was on the point of spending! . . . twenty times did I make her moderate her sweet suction so as to avoid spending, to postpone for the moment the ecstatic crisis. Twenty times did I ask myself in my rapturous transports whether I might let myself go, whether I might not expire deliciously in the mouth of the sweet girl whose fair head I could see as it rose and fell in cadence with the agitated movements of my body!

When a man is being thus blissfully ministered to by a woman who has a taste for this method—a taste that is more common than people believe, and which sometimes betrays its votaries when they are in the act of eating thick asparagus—and has reason to guess it, he can fairly let the sweet operation pursue its natural course and deposit his spermatic nectar on the pretty lips or in the dear mouth that has extracted it from him. But it is not less delicious to pour it, tripled in quantity by such a caress, into a cunt prepared by a similar caress and burning to receive it! And I shrewdly believe that while women may be willing on subsequent occasions to receive in their mouths the tribute of their lover's ardor, they are reluctant to do so on the first occasion on which they consent to effect this sweetest of ministrations!

Accordingly, placing my hand softly on her forehead, I reluctantly arrested the up and down movement of my cousin's head as she sucked my prick with a frenzy that seemed to indicate that she was fully sharing the pleasure she was giving me!

She looked at me in surprise, as if astonished at being stopped before the appearance of the unmistakable indication that her sweet duty had been accomplished!—the fact being that her friend (whose performance she had witnessed and was now following) never stopped her sucking until the "situation had been liquidated!" as good Mme. de Saint-Edme put it. And possibly on that memorable evening Gilberte also had! . . . Not having the skill of her Father Confessor, my interrogatories on this point had not been sufficiently direct and her confession remained incomplete.

So Gilberte, with a flushed and rosy face and moist lips, got up, and placing herself by me asked me if she had done it properly.

"Most charmingly, dearie—quite as well as your friend!" I murmured as I kissed her on the mouth and passed my tongue over her lips all wet and humid! "Now darling, come! . . . on me, eh!"

Without a moment's delay, she placed herself on top astride of me, and quickly I shoved into her cunt my prick all moist with her kisses!

Suddenly, while lying on me thus transfixed and clasped in my arms, quivering with pleasure and jogging herself up and down in rhythm with my movements, she whispered, "But when you were . . . with my . . . friend . . . how . . . did you . . . do it . . . for she won't do . . . what we . . . are now doing? . . ."

"You must know! A pretty woman . . . is . . . all cunt! . . ."

"You dreadful man! . . . So . . . it was in her . . . mouth . . . always? . . ."

"Well . . . yes . . . but you . . . are forcing . . . secrets . . . out of me."

"Then why . . . didn't you do so . . . with me? . . . I . . . was doing . . . the same thing . . . to . . . you?"

"Are you . . . sorry . . . I didn't? . . ."

"No! . . . I only . . . wanted to know!"

"Well, because . . . I fancied . . . you didn't care . . . only . . . for this . . . like Angela!"

"That was very kind of you! . . . Well . . . one won't get . . . children . . . that way . . . that's something!"

"So . . . next time . . . you wish me to . . . to . . . spend . . . in your mouth . . . like . . . Angela does?"

She smiled, nodded her head slightly, then closed her eyes voluptuously as if not to lose a single particle of the pleasure that was now thrilling through her whole person. For a moment I had an idea of resuming the sweet exercise we had just abandoned, but the keenness of my present pleasure retained me at my delicious post beneath her. For the most exquisite of crises was approaching! Our tongues intertwined, our lips met, our

movements accelerated! . . . oh! . . . now! . . . now! . . .
"Oh!"

Just at the critical moment, I took the precaution to
swing Gilberte from the danger of presenting me with
more cousins. I spent wildly outside her, my discharge
shooting up into the air and falling like hot rain on her
bottom and loins.

We had half-dressed ourselves again when we heard a
knock at the door. It was Mme. de Saint-Edme, who had
come to see if we wanted anything. We asked her to bring
us some refreshments. She seemed delighted and relieved
to note from our deshabillé that not unpleasant sequel
had followed her mistake in introducing us to each other.

In due course my cousin, now fully dressed and
gloved, gave me a parting kiss through her veil—and
before leaving me arranged with me a further rendezvous—at which I promised myself (with a thrill of
concupiscence) the pleasure of treating her as I did her
friend Angela. I then called a carriage for her, a concluding attention that a woman appreciates after an amorous
escapade.

"Well," said Mme. de Saint-Edme to me after Gilberte
had gone, "so you are satisfied! I was terribly afraid of
scandal when I saw you knew that lady! Is she a relation
of yours?"

"No. I used to know her when she was a young girl!"

"Oh! Well, I was very afraid of a scene!"

"Thanks to me, dear lady, there wasn't one!"

"I do thank you, but somehow I felt sure that you
would arrange the matter without any scandal. Another
thing that reassured me was the air of distinction the lady
had—a woman of that caste hates a row. I feel the same
also; do what you like, amuse yourself as you may wish

with ladies—all this concerns nobody else, and does harm to no one!"

"Rather the contrary," I rejoined.

"But do it in the proper way—maintain appearances."

"Pleasure coupled with discretion. That's my rule."

"Oh, I'm not referring to you—it's a pleasure to do anything for you! But all the same, when you asked me to leave the room, you looked a little afraid!"

"But now, you are reassured?"

"Oh, now she has once passed through your hands, she will be all right."

On the day arranged between Gilberte and myself, I arrived at Mme. de Saint-Edme's house. She escorted me to the chamber she had got ready for us, where she left me alone. I was the first at the rendezvous, and I must have waited some little time when she came in to tell me that my fair cousin had just arrived but that just at that moment a lady "habituée" had stopped her in the corridor and was expressing surprise at meeting her here.

"Why, Gilberte," she had exclaimed, "I never thought of meeting you here! You always used to say you dared not come! Have you come then to meet somebody?"

As Gilberte, surprised unpleasantly, hesitated—not knowing what to say, Mme. de Saint-Edme came up and told her that her visitor had already arrived—whereupon the other lady had remarked that it was a pity, but nevertheless continued her conversation.

This lady (I had very little doubt) was the blonde friend of Gilberte, Angela de Valençay, an adopted name, as I learnt later on, without my having done anything to pierce the veil of anonymity with which she (like the rest) strove to hide her visits for the purposes of satisfying and gratifying her secret passions.

"At all events, she does not seem to be jealous?" I asked Mme. de Saint-Edme.

"Not in the least. She would not mind lending her lovers to her friends. But she objects strongly to anyone being jealous of her. That seems fair enough."

Gilberte had not yet appeared.

"If she lets herself begin chattering with her friend, you may have to wait a long time," said Mme. de Saint-Edme. "But it is all right—here they come, both of them. Ladies you are being anxiously waited for!"

"Oh, no one's waiting for me!" exclaimed Mme. de Valençay. "All have made their arrangements for their fuckings and fun, for I notice the refreshments all over the place."

She indicated a table on which stood afternoon tea already laid out, which I had ordered in anticipation of Gilberte's arrival. I invited her to join us.

"But shan't I be in the way?" she replied. "Two turtledoves like best to be alone! Very well. If I shall not be in the way, I will join you with pleasure, only you must tell me when I am to disappear. You will respect my modesty, I am sure!"

But as she spoke she looked at me in a way that sufficiently indicated that her wishes were the very opposite of her words: Her ardent glances seemed intended to recall to me past pleasures shared together and to invite me to the further joys she was evidently ready to give me. Dressed simply in a black costume, and carrying herself in a quiet manner but with an air of distinction, there was nothing about her to betray the lascivious desires that had brought her here, or the lecherous fashion in which she was ready to conduct herself—unless it was that peculiar glance that allowed one to detect, beneath the woman dressed, the naked woman, and behind perfect Society manners the intimate familiarity with the most daring libertinage.

While she was apologizing to Gilberte for the liberty she was allowing herself to take, I had called for another plate and had dismissed her cab. She had said that she hesitated to rejoin a cab that had been waiting at the door so long, a feeling and accession of shame that a woman on an amorous escapade will well understand and which is often experienced when the time comes for her to quit the sweet seclusion in which she has been surrendering herself to her lust.

Then when the ladies had removed their hats and mantles we sat down at the table. Thus I found myself between two pretty women, one a blonde, the other almost a brunette, a charming contrast! Each of them had been enjoyed by me separately—but this fact did not in the least diminish the power of their charms over me—and their joint presence, the sweet proximity of these two appetizing feminine bodies to me aroused in my flesh the wildest lust that I hoped in turn to communicate to them.

The idea that each of them had been previously enjoyed by me made them both somewhat constrained at first, especially Gilberte, who seemed almost jealous. But very soon, under the soothing influence of "five o'clock tea" skillfully prepared, snatched kisses, and licentious handlings, this slight constraint disappeared like dew under a morning sun. My mouth hotly attacked theirs alternately; my tongue greedily sought theirs in turn, finding them only too ready to respond. Finally, when I was busily occupied with Gilberte, sucking her tongue while my hands actively wandered all over her, unbuttoning her dress and stealing up her legs under her clothes till it reached the silken-haired center of attraction that my finger then sought to inflame, I felt Mme. de Valençay's hand pass over my trousers and attempt to drag into the air my torch of love, now fully alight and getting stiffer and stiffer in her fingers! Then away went all reserve! I begged them to undress or at all events to throw open their clothes so as to let me see, feel, handle, and kiss more at my ease the two pairs of lovely breasts of which now I could only get a glimpse.

"But I say," exclaimed Mme. de Valençay laughingly, "if you're going to ask your guest to undress herself, your invitation in place of being a simple one to lunch will be one including a dance!"

"When a lady is invited to a dinner," I replied, "she naturally expects to stay and see the fun that is sure to follow."

"Ah! A play for three, eh" she rejoined gaily, "but not arranged by the ballet-master of the Opera! Well, there's no reason why it should prove any the less entertaining, is there Gilberte?"

Gilberte smiled, half-pleased, half-vexed, not from any sense of offended propriety but from a sort of feeling that as a comparative novice in amorous orgies she might have to play second fiddle to her friend! But her semi-hesitation only added a piquancy to her final surrender of herself, and did not hinder a woman of my cousin's disposition from letting herself go freely to learn fresh experiences in lust.

Mme. de Valençay was already busy (in accordance with my request) to release from their confinement the two prisoners whom I had begged her to set at liberty. To effect this she had taken off her light blue silk stays, and my lady readers will fully comprehend how the removal of a corset causes the dropping of petticoats unless held up by the hand. Mme de Valençay did not bother to do this, and so when the exciting rustling noise made by feminine garments being hurriedly taken off and thrown on a chair had ceased, she had on only a half-transparent chemise when she returned smiling to my side. Gilberte, after a little pressure, followed suit and soon was similarly attired. As for me, I rapidly divested myself of all my clothes, and Mme. de Valençay's hand—Gilberte's also—was able to learn without hindrance the state in which I had been driven by the sight of the charms they were now exposing naked to me!

Then we set to work to play the fool, to commit a thousand erotic follies! We took chocolates from each other's mouths; with my lips, I set to work to nibble one balanced on the nipple of one of their breasts, tickling her delightfully in so doing. Then I made a minute and close inspection of my companions' breasts, of the hairs under their armpits, also of what grew on their hills, light and golden on Mme. de Valençay's, auburn and plentiful on Gilberte's. They both lent themselves to these games with a grace and freedom that was simply charming. At each fresh indecency that she found herself committing, Gilberte blushed shamefacedly, her bashful modesty being increased by the presence of a witness. Having kissed with ardor all the charms that I had been comparing, dividing my admiration and tribute equally between my fair companions, I proceeded to cover with kisses the two mossy hills of Venus they were exhibiting to my delighted eyes. Kneeling in turn before each one and between her legs, my mouth played lovingly with their curling hairs, every now and then touching with my tongue the sweetly hidden slit, and eliciting from them little shrieks of pleasure. Suddenly, under a libertine inspiration, I took from the table two chocolate creams, and having slipped them into each of their cunts to their great surprise, I announced my intention of eating them there, and proceeded to do so taking Gilberte first.

"Oh, what an ideal," she exclaimed, quivering and palpitating with pleasure as my tongue discovered the fondant between the lips of her cunt and having dislodged and rolled it over her clitoris.

"Oh! make haste! make haste!" cried Mme. de Valençay, "mine's beginning to melt!"

And truly, when I planted my mouth between her thighs on the lovely slit that she impatiently presented to me, my tongue had really to hunt for her chocolate, to dive and burrow deeply in the charming cleft, only to find a trace or two and the aroma of the flavoring. Oh, how delicious her flesh tasted, thus sugared!

With such erotic pranks and antics our desires increased and grew stronger. Mme. de Valençay, now quite wild with lust, took a candied cherry in its paper covering, and having removed the envelope she made me sit down—then kneeling before me she pulled up my shirt, seized my priapus with one hand, and with the other balanced the cherry on the cherry-colored gland that was rivaling its complexion. With smiles of delight she contemplated the result, then suddenly, with sparkling eyes and heaving breasts, she moved her mouth forward and engulfed the cherry—and with it the head of my member, thus bestowing on it that most delicious of caresses that makes the happy recipient long to employ his mouth in a similar fashion and that impels the loving pair to satisfy their mutual cravings in a sweet "soixante-neuf." Burning with this desire, I clutched hold of Gilberte who was busy kissing me and sucking my tongue, and was just going to propose to gamahuche her when she exclaimed: "Come, it's my turn now, Angela!"

Forthwith Mme. de Valençay rose reluctantly, her lips moist, her face flushed. Gilberte immediately slipped into her place, and had already put my pintle (still wet with her friend's kisses) into her mouth when the latter cried out, "Why you've forgotten the cherry!"

Quickly Gilberte blushingly repaired this omission, and then I felt my prick again put into her mouth and sucked with ardor. Mme. de Valençay had come back to her old place at my side, and while she finished eating the cherry she had taken, she watched with curiosity, whose pretty head was now bent down between my thighs. I slipped my arm round Mme. de Valençay's waist; our lips and tongues met in kisses into which I strove to put the burning pleasure that I was tasting from Gilberte! But I wanted something more! I wanted with my mouth to pass on to her exquisite sensations that were thrilling through me.

"Do let me do *minette* to you!" I murmured.

"All right," she replied, "but not here, as we now are! Let's go to the bed!"

This forced Gilberte to interrupt her ardent suction, and when she had risen from between my thighs, I lovingly kissed her lips still fragrant with the scent of the fruit she had just eaten. And so we moved towards the bed. As we reached it, I begged the ladies to take off their chemises.

"No!" replied Mme. de Valençay, "but this will be better still!"

Cognizant of Mme. de Saint-Edme's forethought in

matters erotic, she opened a drawer and took out two dressing gowns made of the thinnest and most transparent material possible to imagine, one black and the other rose tint.

"The black one will suit me as I am blonde," she said. "Don't look!"

She let the chemise slip down and replaced it by the dressing gown, the transparency of which seemed to heighten the brilliant hue of her skin without in any way veiling the nakedness, but making it more piquant still. Moreover she did not fasten it in front—but on the contrary she allowed it to float open on each side of her— thus displaying her lovely body naked from her stockings to the velvet ribbon round her throat. In this adorable costume, she placed herself in front of me and saluted me in military fashion.

"All in order, Monsieur!" she said. "See, I'm naked— yet I'm—not!"

My cousin slipped on the rose-tinted dressing gown.

"I'm absolutely naked in this!" she exclaimed laughing.

"That is exactly as you ought to be!" I replied smiling.

Being then stretched out on the bed between my two pretty guardians whom I kissed and felt all over while their little hands contended for the control over my member, I was trying to decide which one of them I would choose in which to extinguish the fires of my concupiscence when Angela, who was then holding my prick tightly with her fingers, said:

"Who is to have this first?"

"Better draw for it!" I replied. "Guess how many?" And I took in my hand a lot of hairpins. Gilberte's guess was the nearest.

"Don't forget me, Gilberte!" said her friend. "Leave a little for me!"

But as I began to place myself between Gilberte's legs so as to put my prick into her cunt and fuck her, she appeared surprised, then declared that she understood that she was to do what she had been doing to me on the sofa, viz, suck my prick!

"For you know," she explained, "Angela won't do anything else."

"Oh! don't give me away like this, silly!" exclaimed her friend.

"Do you know that you are a charming and ravishing naughty little girl, just as she is?" I said, kissing her lovingly. "Well, do you also prefer? . . ."

Her response was to gently slip out from under me and to lay me on my back in her place, and as soon as she had got me properly extended on the bed, she, without loss of time, lowered her face towards the God Priapus. I felt her lips kiss the burning head, then her mouth envelop it, engulfing it deeply! Then I took up the thread of my caresses with Mme. de Valençay; I drew her to me, kissed her lips, and let her tongue play on mine.

"Let me do *minette* to you," I murmured.

"Yes, dear."

Smiling lovingly at me, Mme. de Valençay placed herself in position by straddling across my upturned face, arranging herself so that her cunt rested on my mouth, her face being turned towards Gilberte who had not stopped her sweet employment and who she watched at work intently. My tongue attacked her cunt eagerly, plunging deeply into it. I sucked her excited clitoris. I licked passionately her warm and throbbing slit from end to end. Many times before this had I enjoyed this privilege and pleasure, but always without the accompaniment of the spicy sucking that was doubling my transports and was impelling me to pass on to her the delicious fury that was agitating me.

Oh! the indescribable ecstasy—to be sucked by one lovely woman while sucking another! Oh, the delightful postures of this doubled soixante-neuf, which permitted my lascivious fair friends to taste the most piquant voluptuousness equally with myself! But soon I felt that the torrent of my sperm would overcome my efforts to restrain it so as to prolong my present bliss!

"Gilberte! Gilberte!" I gasped brokenly, ceasing for the moment my sweet attentions to Mme. de Valençay's cunt, my tongue resumed its voluptuousness occupation with an ardor now unfettered by my efforts to retard my pleasure. Then came the ecstatic crisis. In my paroxysms of rapturous pleasure, my hands closed on my cousin's head, stopping the movements of her mouth. I thrust my prick wildly down her throat! My tongue madly darted deeply into Mme. de Valençay's quivering cunt. Oh! . . . Oh! . . . I spent! . . . I spent! . . .

My boiling discharge shot in jets into Gilberte's mouth, making her retire in the middle of the eruption. Mme. de Valençay, half fainting with pleasure, dropped limply on me. We lay motionless till our energies revived. Then Gilberte wiped her mouth with her dressing gown.

"I believe I've swallowed some of it!" she exclaimed laughing.

Mme. de Valençay's head happened to be close to Gilberte at the moment when the latter drew back with filled mouth in the middle of my discharge, and she got the rest of it on her face, which made her laughingly tell Gilberte that the latter had kept her promise to leave a little for her. Then she slipped off the bed and hurried off to the dressing room, picking up her dressing gown and holding above her waist as a woman does when she fears that her chemise may get compromising traces! Of course in this case there was no such fear, but the result was to exhibit the most charming contours! Gilberte in turn went off also to wash off the traces of her recent occupation, for which purpose she did not require to use the bidet. I also imitated them, for my mouth, my lips, my moustache, all bore evidence of Mme. de Valençay's warm feminine essence.

While I was thus occupied, Gilberte returned and lay down carelessly on the sofa. Mme. de Valençay went to her, and placing her hand laughingly on her pretty calves began to amuse herself by running her fingers softly up and down Gilberte's legs. But when she got above the knee, Gilberte stopped her.

"Chut! . . . Not here! . . . Not before everybody!"

"It isn't before *everybody*!"

"Please don't trouble about me!" I said.

This little gust of passionate affection concluded for the time with a kiss from Angela to her friend, which clearly meant a great deal. There was no doubt about it!—my delicious companions were worshippers at the shrine of the Lesbian Venus! This revelation did not surprise me as far as Mme. de Valençay was concerned—to so voluptuous a woman nothing that was connected with sexual pleasures would be unknown to her—but I never imagined that my naughty little cousin also had this fantasy. I was far from being displeased at this discovery, and I had the curiosity to ask since when they had mutually enjoyed each other. Then to my surprise, I learnt that it was Gilberte who had in the first instance seduced

Angela! As girls they were great friends, and one day, or rather night, an overflow of guests at a country house at which they were staying compelled their hostess to ask them to share the same bed. And oddly enough, it then came out that I must also have been a guest on that very occasion! Among my dancing partners was a certain Mlle. B——, the fiancée of a happy mortal introduced to me as Monsieur R——, a colonel in civil employ in the War Office. This girl had become Madame R——, and her husband having obtained rapid promotion (as well may be imagined) was now one of the pillars of the Administration. As for her, after that valse with me, she had under an assumed name executed dances of quite a different nature, and I had often had the pleasure of being her partner without either of us recognizing the other.

"So after all, there is no reason why you should be so particular today, Gilberte" I said, as I played gently with her bottom and her pretty white breasts. She only laughed and hid her face in her hands. We asked what was the cause of her merriment.

"Now, I come to think of it," she replied, "it must have been the very night on which you danced with Angela that she and I did! . . ."

"Of course in honor of myself and of all the partners that had pleased you!"

"But my dear," exclaimed Mme. de Valençay, who continued to use this name, "you really are very indiscreet to tell Monsieur who I am. Fortunately he is your cousin instead of simply one of your lovers, and so the knowledge will not go any further. However, Monsieur, you must allow me to continue to be an entire stranger to you, should we ever happen to meet anywhere outside.

Here I shall be delighted to continue on our old footing, and to place at your disposal myself and any talent I may have."

I promised, I swore to obey faithful all her wishes, and this little interlude did not divert the ardor that began to assert itself in our senses.

The thought that my cousin's friend, this lady whose naked charms I was enjoying, was really Mlle. B—— and now Mme. R——, the wife of a man high in office, and that she came to this asylum of elegant immorality and discreet prostitution as a habituée, to yield herself to the most unrestrained demands of her lust, to the most erotic fantasies, this thought did not tend to allay my concupiscence! Every sensation is heightened by contrast. A fair valley is doubly delicious after a painful toiling along burning rocks. The possession of a woman outwardly of rigid virtue seems to some preferable to having a beautiful courtesan. It is simply the idea of contrast that makes certain lovers dress their mistresses as nuns before rogering them! So with this woman, already so desirable while I thought she was simply a fast member of good Society (an opinion quite justified by her bold ways, her science in provocative arts, her freedom from prejudice as to the ways of enjoyment), what additional piquancy her favors acquired now that I knew that the lovely body she delighted to surrender to my licentious caresses was that of a well-bred and beautiful member of Society, respected in her circle, but who knew how to become debauched, naughty, almost as if she wished to make up for the time she was compelled, under the dictates of polite society, to behave as a "virtuous and godly matron!"

It was an agreeable sequel to my surprise when Gilberte, instead of manifesting by tears, refusals, etc., her dislike to seeing her position as a woman of respectability compromised in the eyes of someone that knew who she was, did not hesitate to be persuaded by the calls of her flesh and blood, and resolving to see in me only a lover, lavished on me the pleasures of her person with an ardor and abandonment I could not have dreamt of!

So I renewed to both my fair friends my vows of discretion, etc., adding that I swore on what I considered to be my most precious possession, viz, my prick, which now was asserting itself boldly under the caresses of their delicate hands.

"Egoist!" they exclaimed, "so what we have is not so precious according to your ideas!"

"What you girls have is to me the dearest of possessions and what I have to enable me to enjoy yours is to me the most precious."

"That is sweet of you! But I'm afraid that we are wasting good time!"

"And in a costume that in itself makes one wish to employ the time more sweetly!" added Gilberte.

"Just listen to her!" exclaimed Mme. de Valençay.

"Who loves me will follow me!" cried Gilberte, throwing herself on the bed.

And very shortly there raged between the three of us a storm of kisses, interspersed with exciting touchings and gropings and all the delicious preludes to a fresh bout of love! My hands wandered over two pairs of bubbies, two pairs of thighs; my mouth and my tongue played on theirs, deserting them at times in favor of two other mouths lower down and sweetly hairy—desertions which their charming owners did not seem to mind if I might judge by the sweet murmurs that came from the former as I licked and tickled the latter! Oh, if I only had two tongues so that I could gamahuche them both at the same time!

When at length I ceased and rose, I saw they both were on fire from the ardent way in which they kissed each other! Thereupon, I passed my arms round them, and drawing them close to me so that their lips and mine were touching I murmured, "Oh!, you two darlings, what a delicious and adorable pair of *gougnottes* you would make!"

A gentle cuff on my head told me that the word was not strange to my fair friends—but the smiles that their faces wore showed me that they were not displeased by my audacity.

"Won't you then do it before me?" I whispered. "Do let me see you!"

"Oh, what a mad idea! Well, what do you say, Gilberte?"

"Oh, I daren't. I really couldn't. See, we aren't by ourselves!"

"He won't look at you! Come, I want it. I'll do it to you!"

Mme. de Valençay slipped across me and gave my cousin several long clinging kisses, then quickly placed her head between Gilberte's thighs, and soon the latter began to quiver under the action of the former's tongue! Leaning over my pretty cousin as she lay deliciously happy, I kissed her rosy lips, introducing my tongue between them as I reveled at the sight of these two naked lovely women surrendering themselves to their lesbian passions before me. Suddenly, Mme. de Valençay stopped, raised herself, then flushing with delight, turned herself round and straddling across Gilberte, she placed herself on Gilberte, reversing herself. Her lovely backside sank down and hid her friend's face, then settling herself down with a movement or two she placed over Gilberte's mouth the cunt that sought the lingual caresses which she recommenced on Gilberte's cunt! As for me, I delightedly contemplated the curtain of flesh which masked my cousin's face, the two plump and white buttocks that already had begun to agitate themselves in sweet tremors under the caress that had commenced. My hand passed lovingly over the rounded contours—my lips deposited a hundred kisses on them—and my tongue passing along the valley that separated them, traveled downwards till it nearly met Gilberte's, now in full operation on Mme. de Valençay's cunt. But by this time it was not only a gentle tremor that agitated those charming globes of flesh, it was a veritable storm of quivering heavings that indicated the approaching burst of her voluptuous discharge. I also, horribly excited, felt myself ready to spend, but with a desperate effort I restrained, and eagerly watched my sweet pair of lesbians in the spasms of their spending, waiting impatiently for the finish of their ecstasy to beg one or the other of them to put out the fire that was blazing within me.

But no! They continued in their charming posture . . . were they going to begin again? Oh, the naughty darlings!—they started afresh! I bent down towards Mme. de Valençay, whose lips were playing on the lowest portion of the dark silky fleece on Gilberte's cunt. On seeing me she discontinued for a moment her charming employment.

"Are you going to do it again?" I asked eagerly.

"Well . . . yes! It's all your fault, you know. You've so excited us!"

"You naughty girls! Oh you're a pair of naughty, naughty girls!" I exclaimed—then kissed her luscious lips all moist and impregnated with Gilberte's spendings.

Before allowing her to resume her duties, I amused myself by playing with the hairs on my cousin's cunt. She began to do the same with one of her delicate hands!

"What lovely fur Gilberte has!" she murmured, "and pretty thighs!" she added as she passed her hands lovingly up and down over the satiny skin from the top of Gilberte's cream-colored stockings right up to the sweet junction with her abdomen. I in turn did the same.

"Now, I begin to understand," I remarked, "why one loves to get one's head between a girl's thighs even though one should be a girl!"

"Rather say because one is a girl!" she replied laughing, "for it is all that a girl can do unfortunately!"

"Now tell me," I continued seriously, "which gives a girl the intensest pleasure—to be sucked by a man or by a girl?"

My pretty companion laughed amusedly, tickled at the idea of such a conversation being carried on in the silent presence of Gilberte's cunt. But at all event, she recognized that here was a chance to test the pleasing experiment.

"Gilberte!" she called out, "we are both going to do it to you—tell us who does it best. You go on!" she whispered, pointing to Gilberte's cunt lying temptingly ready.

Her increasing agitation as betrayed by her voice clearly indicated that the fair judge was getting impatient and had recommenced her sweet ministrations to her friend's cunt. Quickly I thrust my tongue into the charming slit so impatiently awaiting it, my salute being received with violent and rapturous transports! After a few moments, I made way for Mme. de Valençay, who before long stopped for Gilberte's verdict. But the latter remained silent!—her tongue was too much occupied with Angela's cunt and the fair owner, no longer able to restrain herself, stopped talking philosophy with me to give herself up to the imperative call of fast increasing pleasure. Thus the interesting experiment remained unsolved, ample opportunity being now available for some fair seeker after truth to test the efficiency of the male and the female tongue on her cunt! But I felt I could no longer remain an idle spectator of so voluptuous a combat. I must cut in somehow!

"Would you like all you can get now?" I whispered in Mme. de Valençay's ear.

"Yes! . . . yes! . . ." she answered, her tongue hard at work.

"You would? Oh you naughty thing! . . . You would like . . . *feuille de rose?*"

"Yes! . . . yes! . . . yes! . . ." she murmured with difficulty.

Promptly my tongue commenced to wander up and down between the firm yet elastic twin globes of her bottom, traversing the depths of the mysterious valley that separated her buttocks, thrusting, tickling, and working her into erotic fury. The naked bodies of the two girls plunged and twisted to the accompaniment of broken murmurs and inarticulate ejaculations! And I? Their lascivious transports sent me into a state of lustful excitement impossible to describe—it was veritable torture! I could stand it no longer! I must have something, some hole, a mouth, a cunt! I rushed behind Mme. de Valençay as she lay astride across Gilberte's face—I caught a glimpse of the cunt the latter was licking and sucking—I slipped my rampant and furious prick between her nose, her lips, and the grotto of love. I drove her tongue away, and rammed myself in! Oh the exquisite pleasure! Oh the cunt, so soft, so deliciously warm and moist, so exquisitely lubricated by my cousin's ministrations! But I was soon forced to beat a retreat! It was contrary to the principles of my voluptuous partner to allow her cunt to be invaded in this way, and in spite of my endeavors to the contrary and the grip of her posteriors I had effected in my desperation, she managed to dislodge me.

"Oh, you are very disobedient!" she exclaimed, shaking her finger at me. "We must bring you to order. Oh, look at it! How angry it is, poor thing!" It was my raging prick that she was addressing. "Come! We'll soon calm you, sir! Lie down!"

I released Gilberte, whose head had been imprisoned between my legs.

"You were in a funny position!" Mme. de Valençay said to her.

"You at all events cannot say that he didn't have you, dear! At all events I could see! He went into you up to your hair! Oh yes, you were properly had that time, my love!"

"As a matter of fact, you ought to have kept him out!"

But by now, I was on my back. Mme. de Valençay, after some tender kisses, directed her mouth to where a different function was eagerly awaiting her. "After the cunt of the girl cousin, naturally comes the turn of the male cousin's prick!" she said, laughingly. I suggested to Gilberte that she should let me suck her, and although she had already spent plentifully with her friend, she was none the less ready to commence anew! "Gladly, gladly!"

she exclaimed, as she slipped across my face and adjusted her cunt so as to rest on my mouth!

I plunged my tongue wildly into it, though I was almost swooning with ecstatic rapture as Mme. de Valençay devoted herself to my prick—kissing, sucking, and tickling the gland with the tip of her warm tongue and her burning mouth, then allaying the poignant sensations thus excited by ardent and passionate suction. Then she would remain passive, retaining my prick in her mouth and letting me work it up and down deliciously between her lips and when I stopped, she would resume the entrancing motion. It was a taste of Paradise that I would gladly have prolonged indefinitely. But this was impossible! I simply couldn't contain myself anymore! My tongue redoubled its activity on Gilberte's clitoris, my hands clenched Mme. de Valençay's head, between her delicious lips my prick worked itself faster . . . faster! . . . with a frenzied upward heave I shoved it into her throat! I surrendered myself wildly to my pleasure then spent . . . spent . . . spent . . . nearly swooning as I shot my three burning discharges into her mouth!

Without the least flinching, Mme. de Valençay received and retained in her mouth this unceremonious homage to her charms, and also held as a prisoner the object that had caused the deluge, till its last spasm, while Gilberte (who had spent equally deliciously on me) fell breathless and panting on me with a gasp of pleasure, and thus we rested for some instants in rapturous oblivion.

69

"What's the time?" asked Mme. de Valençay, who had

slipped on her chemise again and was engaged before the mirror with a powder puff.

"Six o'clock."

"Heavens! And I have to dine out tonight! I shall hardly have time to get back and dress! My husband will be cross!"

"The same with me!" exclaimed Gilberte. "My husband will scold me."

Quickly and hurriedly, the two ladies picked out their belongings from the mass of garments lying all over the room, and soon put on their drawers (the most useless things where love is concerned), corsets, skirts, etc., and very soon were fully attired and ready to appear in public. I called carriages.

Just then Mme. de Saint-Edme asked for a word with Gilberte and whispered something to her.

"Not this afternoon!—I've no time," she replied.

"Only tell me if you would be willing and when."

"I would like it, but I'll write."

Mme. de Valençay caught her arm and asked what it was all about. Gilberte whispered something. I in turn asked for information, but the two ladies went off in fits of laughter.

Later on, I learnt that what had been asked of her and what she had accepted was to be introduced to a young and pretty actress who was well known as a high priestess of Lesbians, and who had desired to make my cousin's acquaintance and to cultivate her in the charming intimacy necessary to the cult. I venture to say that she will not be disappointed.

Mme. Germain "At Home"

"Well? And your loves? Have you brought your last conquest to a successful termination?"

The person who was thus questioning me was Madame de Liancourt, who I was about to accompany in her carriage at the close of a Charity Ball given at the Hotel C——.

"What new conquest?" I asked.

"You know! The lady with whom you were seen in the Bois the other day! It was most imprudent on your part to thus compromise hers. Now, was she not the wife of Maitre B——, the lawyer?"

"What? Did you really see us? Do you know her? I assure you . . ."

"My dear man, you are defending yourself very badly! But otherwise, my compliments to you! She really is very nice! And has she been . . . kind? She has the air of being a trifle too unsophisticated for you, but she is in excellent hands and will soon learn . . . eh? Tell me, have you already educated her to humor your . . . caprices?"

"Dear Madame! I assure you . . ."

"Come, come, you needn't tell me this, me, your old pupil! You know I won't be jealous!"

"A pupil who has graduated with honor to her teacher and now possibly exceeds him."

"Be polite, if you please! You men are really too awful. You teach a poor innocent girl all sorts of naughty things, and then you reproach her if she should put your lessons into practice!"

"I reproach you? On the contrary! I prefer you as you now are, so knowing, so charmingly naughty!"

"Then tell me."

"Here comes your carriage. Haven't you changed your coachman?"

"Yes and no. Baptiste drives when I go out in domestic state in the company of my lord and master, my husband. But when I go by myself, I drop the family coachman and the family state and take a hired carriage. It is better in case of any . . . adventures, for then I have nobody's indiscretions to fear. Baptiste, for instance, knows you."

"Without knowing my successors!"

"You rude man! Come, open the carriage door for me."

"May I not have the honor of accompanying you?"

"Oh yes! I know what you mean. You don't deserve to be allowed. But you must behave properly. Tell the man to drive to Rue de Suresnes."

Since the termination of my liaison with Madame de Liancourt, a liaison that terminated without any rupture or unpleasantness, she (so she told me) had been leading a life without restraint and unfettered by any ties. She amused herself by studies in the physiology of Love, selecting her subjects for comparison how and where she pleased. Further, we had agreed to confide to each other the result of our various amatory adventures, and we did

not interdict ourselves from renewing our former intimate relations if we so desired—if our electric currents
should attract us to each other and if their tension should
become such as to make the contact of our naked bodies
bring about a "discharge" (truly, a scientific word, but
one most appropriate for the occasion!).

This evening, we were in such a condition. Speaking
for myself, the act of dancing, the sight of bare shoulders
and breasts emerging from their lace surroundings as if
to challenge men to consider whether what was hidden
was likely to correspond with what was being shewn, all
this had greatly excited me; and it did not make me any
the calmer to be seated beside a lovely woman of about
thirty, luscious and voluptuous to the degree at which a
touch of maturity adds such spice to the charm of youth.

As for telltale eyes (that seemed to say "Do you
remember?" and "Shall we recommence?"), the gentle
friction of her knees against mine as the carriage swayed,
and a thousand other signs, showed me clearly that she
was quite willing to satisfy with me the warm desire, the
longing for a man that a hot-blooded woman feels after
inhaling the masculine odor emanating from her dancing
partners and after having abandoned herself to their
more or less lascivious embrace. We could not but concentrate our ardent desires one for the other, she, with all
the burning longings of an erotically excited woman; I,
with all the lustful ideas that riot through the brain of a
man as he looks at pretty women and mentally undressing them imagines their appearances without clothes.

It was not therefore very surprising that before we
had got halfway to our destination, I threw my arm
around Mme. de Liancourt's waist, brought my face
against hers, and set to work to kiss her on her mouth

and with my tongue to seek hers. My disengaged hand slipped up under the frilly flounces of her ball dress, crept along over her silk-clad legs and over her garters, and little by little reached her drawers and found the opening—through which it passed and commenced to touch and play with the close clustering and mossy forest of silky curly hairs.

"Wretch!" gasped my companion, as she abandoned herself to the voluptuous sensations that my finger was communicating to her as it sought to bury itself in her warm moist slit. In kindly reciprocation, her white-gloved hand traveled over my trousers, till it found the unmistakable proof of my excited condition. Quickly sundry buttons yielded, and then I felt against my sensitive skin the touch of dainty gloved fingers that promptly began their delicious maneuvers, returning service for service, pleasure for pleasure.

Not a word passed!—only the sound of sighs, breathings, gaspings, as fingers and tongues busied themselves in their salacious duties. Oh, why is man not physically able to sacrifice to Venus over and over again with hardly a pause, as women can? Why must there as a rule be a break between one sacrifice and the next? With what delight would I have surrendered myself to the exquisitely maddening sensations communicated to my rampant prick by those gloved fingers and their subtle compression, even at the risk of ruining those white kid gloves! But as I looked and hoped for a more completely satisfactory gratification of my lust before long, I managed to retain my burning ardor and keep it in reserve. More fortunate than me, Mme. de Liancourt, whose soft smooth thighs kept squeezing my hand, let herself go!—gasping, panting, quivering, she clung to me, spasmodically agitating her heaving hips and bottom—then inundated my hand with the creamy dew of her ecstatic discharge.

Just then the carriage stopped. Hastily we adjusted our dress, and after sending the carriage away, we entered the house in which Mme. de Liancourt's suite was located. A dim light had been left burning for her. As she passed the concierge's den she gave her name as Mme. Germain, telling me after we had passed inside that this was the name by which she was known here.

The suite was on the first floor. Mme. de Liancourt unlocked the door herself and ushered me into a handsomely furnished vestibule in which a rose-shaded lamp shed a soft light quite sufficient to illuminate the place. She remarked that she had done the furnishing, and that besides this there were a few more rooms.

"Here's the Temple!" she exclaimed, leading me into the bedroom, the best room of the suite. In it was a bed, large and low with thick curtains, a veritable theatre of Love! In one corner was one of those long and low easy chairs that accommodate so delightfully the form of a woman, especially when she is surrendering herself to furtive fondling and groping under her clothes! Numerous cushions were scattered all over the place; in another corner was a dainty stove; against one wall stood a full-length mirror. A smaller room opening into the bedroom had been furnished as a dressing room and bathroom; here one saw displayed and ready for use the whole of a woman's mysterious toilet equipage, low divans, bidet, douche, basins, jars of essences, bottles of scent; a third room also communicating with the bedroom served as a boudoir, but for the moment fulfilled the office of a supper room, as the table had been laid with a cold supper for two. Thick close carpets covered the whole of the floors, and each room was fitted after the convenient English fashion with gas heating and lighting apparatus, thus enabling the occupant to practically dispense with servants.

"Does your maid Justine attend to you here?"

"No, only the concierge's wife and her sister."

"But what do they think when they see you here?"

Madame de Liancourt smiled with a significant glance from her eyes and a gesture that plainly said that the presence of a gentleman would not occasion any surprise!

"Then they must have queer ideas about you?"

"My dear man, I have made the position quite simple and easy by not attempting to hide anything, but to pass as a cocotte. You see this cuts short all suppositions."

Undoubtedly she had freed herself from traditions since I last had the honor of being entertained in her arms; and her candid admissions constituted in her quite a new attraction for me!

"Then this evening you are going to be my little cocotte!" I replied as I amorously kissed her mouth. She nodded, with a smile.

Then I proceeded to utilize with her to its best advantage her luxuriously equipped installation. I began by taking off her shoes, and under the pretense that her high-laced uppers rendered it necessary, I lifted the frilly flounces of her ball dress and petticoats till the bewitching sight of a pretty woman's dainty underclothing was displayed to me—the neatly shod tiny feet, the delicately rounded silk-covered calves, the tempting garters above her knees, the strip of naked flesh just above them, her semi-transparent drawers with their frills—all framed by the surrounding waves of her petticoats.

"What are you about? . . . Come, do take off my shoes!"

But in spite of protests, I managed to deposit sundry hot kisses on the tempting bare flesh just above the garters; then in reluctant obedience I took off her shoes and helped her out of her ball dress, but not without permitting myself sundry libertine and wanton touches. How delicious it is to feel a girl's naked flesh under its gauzy covering, to pass one's hands over her back and loins, her hips and haunches, her bottom, when protected only by a thin chemise, then turning one's attention to her front, to draw the light folds tightly round her so as to reveal her shapely round belly and thighs, to press the light material well in between her legs! Oh what delicious preliminaries!—and what riotous desires they kindle. And how girls always pretend to try and prevent the taking of such liberties, pleading shame as an incentive to induce the tickling that invariably results and that draws from them the inflaming little screams and wriggles they know so well how to give. My pretty companion did not disappoint me in this respect.

"Wait, wait!" she ejaculated as she freed herself from my audacious hands and ran towards the dressing room, pausing at the door to say softly but significantly, "I have danced a lot tonight, and . . . I have not forgotten your . . . caprices!"

Could one be paid a more delicate attention or be given a more discreet invitation? Promptly I undressed myself, then when Mme. de Liancourt had quitted the dressing room, I passed in, and presently I joined her on the bed on which she had laid herself.

"Let us stay as we are on the top and not under the sheets!" she suggested. "It is warm."

"By all means, and we can also see each other better!"

"You are just the same, or rather worse than ever! You have already seen me all over, you know every bit of me!"

"Yes, but a man can't see too much of a pretty girl."

"You're very complimentary today. Well, if you must . . ."

She had on only a light dressing gown, and nothing under it—not even a chemise. One by one, I undid the fastenings in front, and soon there was nothing to hide her naked beauty from her garters to her neck, round which she had retained a loop of velvet. Her white satin-like skin lay open to my sight interrupted only by the tawny gold patch that covered the lowest extremity of her belly with its clustering curls.

"You have grown a little fatter, my love," I remarked as my hands passed over her naked flesh!

"Too much so?" she asked regarding herself.

"Oh no—you're just perfect, just delicious!"

"And what about you? The same as before?" With her soft hand she began to feel me, and little by little she approached the organ she had already so deliciously honored during the drive, then gently told hold of it.

"How stiff it is," she said softly, "how it swells. It seems quite pleased to meet its old friend! Eh? You're very pleased, old chap, aren't you? . . . eh? . . . eh?" (She spoke as if to her pet dog.) "And you've seen cunts of every shade of hair since you last saw mine."

"As to hair, yes," I replied, "but nothing so adorable as this!" (My readers can guess where my fingers now were!) "What a lot you've got!"

"More than Madame Beaupré?"

"I haven't yet seen hers!"

"Come, come, what nonsense! Haven't you then even touched it?"

"Hers couldn't possibly be more lovely than yours."

After many a burning kiss, many a thrilling tonguing, my mouth in its turn visited and explored all that my eyes had been feasting on—my hands meanwhile playing with her neck, arms, shoulders, haunches, and then her saucy breasts—the nipples of which I playfully bit gently as I watched the lovely owner as she lay pleased and smiling. Then going a little lower, I pressed my lips through her hairs with the intention of working my way along her tender slit, with the result that my tongue was soon inside her cunt. Madame de Liancourt no longer smiled, she was now too much absorbed in the sensations of the moment, as was conclusively evident by her broken breathing and the wriggling movements of her loins, haunches, hips, and bottom.

"Together! . . . both together!" she presently murmured, then disengaged herself for a moment to pull back a curtain and reveal a large mirror in which one could see everything that passed on the bed.

"Isn't it shocking?" she laughed.

Then without further delay I placed myself on my back, my head between her legs, our bodies forming that delightful posture known as "soixante-neuf" . . . Reflected faithfully in the mirror, I could see the back of Mme. de Liancourt, the adorable curves of her loins, her superb hips and haunches, the magnificent globes of her bottom—between which was visible my head framed by her plump round thighs—while my thighs in turn flanked my voluptuous companion's bent-down head, of which I could only see a few of the curls on her neck.

Oh what pleasures we tasted! What ecstatic quiverings thrilled through our bodies as our mouths emulated each other in their efforts to communicate to each other the most poignant and rapturous bliss! Mme. de Liancourt devoted herself divinely to her sweet function! Although her mouth was small, she succeeded in making it large enough to get into it nearly the whole of my swollen and rampant prick, her fingers supplementing her lips as regards the portion left outside and making me feel exactly as if the whole of my organ was buried inside her mouth. On my side, my tongue (admittedly agile and clever by every woman who had allowed herself the experience) excelled itself in its efforts to drive Mme. de Liancourt into indescribable ecstasy, ecstasy shared also by me, for nothing can be more heavenly to the man than to feel the rapturous thrillings of pleasure as they vibrate through the woman to whom he is endeavoring to impart the most exquisite pleasure she is capable of tasting, and who is ready to forgive the immorality of the act so long as she is maintained in a heaven of blissfulness.

Having thoroughly teased, worried, and tickled her clitoris with my tongue and excited it by tender nibbles of my teeth, I attacked the quivering lips of Mme. de Liancourt's cunt, thrusting my tongue deeply between them and arousing in her a hitherto unfelt depth of pleasure, so keen and so voluptuous as to cause such violent agitation of her hips and the globes of her bottom, that although I was gripping the latter with my hands, I could scarcely restrain their plunging movements sufficiently to maintain my mouth on the dear object of its worship!

Finally we disengaged ourselves, and adopting the ordinary position I extended myself on the bosom of my voluptuous companion; she clasped me closely to her with her lovely arms, and in silence we united the parts of ourselves that our lips and our tongues now finding themselves together again sought mutually pardon for the lascivious caprice that had temporarily separated them. Oh, how delicious is the passage into a grotto that one has been kissing and sucking till the sweet interior has lubricated itself by successive spendings! The heavenly up-and-down joggings are so delightfully facilitated, the pleasure becomes doubly sweet owing to the more intimate contact and union of sexual parts, while the girl now provoked into the highest pitch of erotic desire, quivering with unsatisfied lust and deliriously enjoying her position under her lover and the clasp of his arms, abandons herself ecstatically to the sensations of the moment in furious unison with him.

Presently, I saw Mme. de Liancourt's eyes turn upwards and half close as the first spasms of pleasure began to thrill through her.

"Gently . . . gently!" she gasped. "Oh! It's just heavenly! Gently darling! Oh! . . . oh! . . . wait . . . wait . . . I'm . . . just . . . coming! . . . coming! . . . oh! . . . oh! . . ."

Our tumultuous plungings and heavings quickened frenziedly, then ceased in a storm of kisses!

♋

"Oh darling, what a deluge! I'm absolutely full of it!" And she rushed off to wash and purify herself.

After a visit in my turn to the lavatory, we were ready for supper—pâté de foie gras and old Saturne are most excellent auxiliaries to Venus!

Mme. de Liancourt had placed herself at the table with only a dressing gown on. This did not remain fastened for long, and then the spectacle of her naked charms and the sensations excited mutually by our inquisitive and wandering hands quickly put us in train for more erotic scenes, which soon began to be reflected in the mirror.

"Tell me," said Mme. de Liancourt, "have you ever done this with Mme. de B——?"

"No."

"I can hardly believe you! Then for this particular caprice of yours you have come to your old pupil, your present one not yet being educated up to it. But no doubt you will before long gently break her to it, just as if you were newly married husband and wife! I should like to see you at it. You might do much worse than to let me have her for a time to polish and finish her in these matters!"

"You're very kind. Only you would inspire her with desire for girls, not for men. You know you thus seduce all your girl friends in this particular way!"

"Come, come—don't you speak evil of this fancy of mine, you of all people—for except for it, you would never have met me. But don't you know that a woman can and does love to . . . amuse . . . herself with women as well as with men? I can, for instance."

"Yes, that may be—but there aren't many like you! Most girls go after either girls or men. You are essentially a woman of pleasure, devoted to pleasure, loving pleasure for the sake of pleasure, ready to taste it in any form, with complete indifference to the sex of the person that is communicating pleasure to you."

"I am not worse than you, my friend."

"I'm not reproaching you! I'm simply stating a fact, which explains why we understand each other so splendidly. You have learnt how men can induce pleasure and how women can impart it, and so you go from sex to sex audaciously experimenting, without being able to decide which you like the best."

"I'm exactly like you in this respect, my friend!"

"Yes, but with this one important difference—the feminine sex satisfies my exigencies and my curiosity and generally in every direction in which I may be tempted to pursue my researches!"

"Prettily spoken, my friend. Still, had I your present sweetheart as a pupil, I would soon inculcate in her quite as excellent principles only more in accord with my tastes; I would impress her with myself as an example and also to keep her from concentrating herself on any one person, be it male or female. Moreover, unless I am delivered by the look of her eyes, she possesses the right temperament for my teaching, and I fancy it would not be long before your little innocent friend is ready and willing to lend herself to all sorts of salacious variations of carnal love—and who knows?—may becomes the mistress both of yourself and of myself!"

Mme. de Liancourt laughed merrily, then continued, "But I won't ask for so much! I would like just to give her one lesson for your special benefit, and I would even allow you to listen behind the door, so that you can judge for yourself whether I overstep the bounds of what a girl ought really to know."

I fell in love with her fantasy and I agreed to her suggestion. In my secret heart, the idea of having a woman as my rival in the affections of another woman was to me exceedingly piquant, and I gladly left her to carry out her caprice.

Mme. de Liancourt accompanied me one day when I had arranged to meet Martha, and as soon as we discovered the latter she went forward by herself to meet her as from me, while I slipped off to her chambers. Mme. de Liancourt told Martha that the latter's husband was suspicious, and was endeavoring to have a watch kept on her. And this was why I had not come to the rendezvous, that I had asked her to come instead to explain and to bring her to where I was awaiting her. After a little hesitation, Martha consented to accompany her to the Rue de Suresnes.

While I was hiding in the small boudoir, I saw them come in and pass into the bedroom.

"You're quite safe here. You're in my own rooms! Here you can bill and coo as much as you please with your lover!"

Martha colored to the tips of her little ears.

"But Madame, Monsieur R—— isn't my lover! We have never . . ."

"Really? My child, you have done well to tell me this—you need fear no indiscretion on my part, for I also have a lover. The danger you were running has made me take an interest in you, and this is why I gladly brought you here at the request of Monsieur R——. Really it was almost heroic of me to do so, for there are not many women who would go out of their way to bring to a mutual male friend another woman younger and prettier than herself! But it is so, dear, for you are certainly prettier than me!"

She kissed Martha. Then she invited her to take off her wraps and to make herself at home. But when she observed that Martha remained fully dressed with the exception of her mantle, she said to her:

"Don't be afraid, dear. Do make yourself at home and do as I do! You mustn't remain as you are and receive your lover so, for men like to see their sweethearts in some déshabille when they come to visit them. Besides, I have to change my dress for my evening's engagements. It will be pleasant to take advantage of this and see how some of my dresses will look on you—an excellent idea, for should anyone have followed us here and finds us so engaged, it will completely thrown them off the scent!"

I admired the cleverness of this argument!

Mme. de Liancourt rapidly divested herself of her dress, corset, and petticoats till she had on her chemise only; then she proceeded to reduce Martha to a similar condition of undress, in spite of the latter's hesitation especially as to removing her corset, as she alleged that she should keep this on if she was to try on any dresses. This Mme. de Liancourt would not agree to!

"You wear very pretty underclothing, dear! No doubt, you study his tastes in such details?"

This was a good guess, for Martha had put on the corset we had bought together, also the lace petticoats and the delicately trimmed chemise. How delicate is the female instinct in the matter of attracting the male amorous desires!

"I do not know whether my dress will fit you, dear," continued Mme. de Liancourt. "I think I am bigger than you are in the bust."

Under this pretext she threw open her chemise and exhibited her breasts, which she set to work to compare with those of Martha, after having first unfastened and opened the latter's chemise.

"What deliciously white and firm little bubbies you have, dear! I expect you have often been complimented

on them. A very fortunate man is your lover—of course,
I don't mean your husband—for if the latter saw you
thus, I suppose he would trop to spoil these little darlings, whereas your lover would know how to show his
appreciation of them by his caresses."

"Suppose he should suddenly turn up and catch us as
we are!"

"I should rush off into any corner that I could!"
replied Mme. de Liancourt with a smile she endeavored
vainly to repress. She added:

"But at a ball we women show quite as much of ourselves as you and I are now doing! I, at all events, have
my dresses cut low enough to let my nipples be seen.
Besides, it is only a woman with a bad figure that objects
to be found naked or practically so. I'm not one of that
lot—see!"

With a touch, she caused her chemise to fall to her
feet, and stepped forward out of it in all her glorious
nudity, the effect being heightened by the contrast caused
by the triangular patch of tawny golden hair at the junction of her belly and thighs and her black silk stockings
with their rose-tinted garters worn above the knees.

"This is how I meet my lover!" she said.

Martha became scarlet.

"How you are blushing, dear! Is it because of the sight
of me standing naked? If so, you remind me of one of my
girl friends who declares that the sight of a naked man
would do. Every time she comes to see me, she insists on
my undressing myself completely in front of her. And
then you should see how she kisses and embraces me just
as if she was playing with a naked man. Then she will go
and do a thousand and one improper and indecent things
to me that at first used to make me feel horribly

ashamed, but which now I really like—even to the length of paying her back in the same coin. Oh, it's lovely. And mind you, we're not deceiving our husbands. Strange but true, isn't it?"

She kissed the blushing Martha, and continued:

"Ever since, I have had lovers and . . . enjoyed them; I still recollect how delicious those tête-à-têtes with my girl friend were. We used to caress and kiss each other's breasts, like this . . ."

"Oh, you're biting me!"

"Doesn't your lover do this to you? Oh, see how the pretty little nipples are stiffening and standing out!"

"Oh, Madame, you're tickling me! Oh, take away your hand! Oh, what are you doing? . . . No! . . . no! . . . I don't want it!"

Mme. de Liancourt had seized Martha and was passionately clasping her against herself, holding her tightly with one arm round her waist while she slipped her other hand between Martha's thighs. The latter, utterly surprised by this sudden attack, could only struggle feebly!

"Oh! . . . but Madame, what . . . are you going . . . to do . . . to me?"

"Make love with you, darling! I'm gone on you! Don't you know how one woman can adore another? How two women can mutually prove their love for each other? Let me show you! But you surely must know all about it. At school, didn't one of the bigger girls take charge of you, and teach you . . . this? Ah! You're blushing now. Oh, you little humbug! . . ."

"That was so long ago! . . . I quite forget it all! . . ."

"No, one never forgets that sort of thing. Your girl friend must have had a sweet time! Come, dear little humbug, what was it you used to do together?"

"Really, I don't know!"

"Really and truly? Well, I know! Come, you'd like to do it again, wouldn't you? . . . with me?"

"No, no! Suppose . . . he came in!"

"He can't, without our hearing him. Come, you pretty little coward, come. Place yourself against me so! Take off your chemise. You can have a dressing gown if you like."

She gave Martha one.

"No, don't fasten it! Leave it quite open! . . . I want to have a good look at you! . . . Your breasts . . . your belly . . . your hairs! Oh, how they curl and cluster!"

Suddenly she knelt and applied her lips to the dark triangular path that luxuriated at the end of Martha's stomach, the latter still offering a shamefaced resistance.

"No, no!" she cried, squeezing her legs closely together.

It had been however decreed and registered in the Book of Lesbian Venus that Mme. de Liancourt should sacrifice yet another victim on the altar dedicated to tribadic love. I didn't think it was advisable to intervene. I felt sure that my turn would come before long, and in the meantime here was Mme. de Liancourt preparing for my delectation the most charming spectacle one could desire, one which the famous Regent would gladly have had performed before him at the Palais-Royal, yes, and paid cheerfully for it also!

Martha, now half-willing and still half-reluctant, passively allowed herself to be placed on the sofa. Mme. de Liancourt seated herself at Martha's side, passed one arm round her and slipped her other hand between Martha's thighs while she passionately kissed her, darting her tongue into Martha's mouth! Her finger, directed by both art and passion, soon produced the desired result!

Martha's breath began to come brokenly, her eyes half-closed, her bosom and breasts heaved agitatedly. At this moment Mme. de Liancourt, no longer content to play only the part of the communicator of pleasure, caught hold of one of Martha's hands and gently conducted it to her own cunt with a mute demand for reciprocity. And Martha did not draw it back—she recognized the silent request, and her gentle little hand began to do its untutored best.

What a charming picture the pair made—what a glorious group worthy of Fragonard or of Boucher. I would have paid gladly a long price for a series of photographs representing them thus. Both girls intertwining their lovely white thighs and slender legs, then separating them only to interlace them in some other way in the midst of a storm of kisses and broken ejaculations, principally from Mme. de Liancourt, who by now was simply mad with lust, her hips and haunches quivering, her body rapturously becoming more and more rigid.

"Martha! . . . oh, darling! . . . keep on! . . . oh! . . . keep on! . . . You're . . . doing it . . . beautifully! Oh! . . . Oh! . . . I'm coming! . . . Oh! . . . Oh! . . . I'm spending! . . . Ah! a—h! . . ."

A moment of silence followed this ecstatic crisis, Mme. de Liancourt still keeping her hand on Martha's slit.

"Oh, how wet you are! . . . You've also spent, you naughty thing. Darling, we've done it together! . . . Wipe yourself!" She gave Martha a handkerchief.

"Now, wasn't it good?"

"Yes," replied Martha, timidly.

"Then let's do it together!"

"If you like!"

Immediately, our two lascivious heroines recommenced their lubricious caresses. Martha extended herself flat on her back on the sofa, and while her seducer, bending over her, looked her all over and felt and handled her as the spirit willed her, and freshly aroused in her new lust (as was manifest from the agitation of her bosom and breasts), Martha's hand, without invitation, stole to Mme. de Liancourt's cunt and resumed its lovely ministration. She had caught the fancy, she, so timid with me!

Nevertheless, she began to protest when, after having tenderly sucked her breasts, her mistress in lesbian pleasures carried her lips lower down.

"No, no, not there!" she panted, trying to raise herself.

"Yes, yes! I wish it! Let me kiss your sweet cunny with its pretty hair! I'll do it just as well as your lover can."

"But he has never . . . kissed me there!"

"Then he doesn't know his duties as your lover. So much the better for me. I shall now be the first to do it to you. You'll see how delicious it is. I used to be just like you at first, but now I simply adore this way! And you'll always do it this way in the future whenever you get the chance. So, let me arrange you, open wider these pretty thighs."

Then, in the twinkling of an eye, the desire spot was covered with her lascivious and skillful mouth.

"No! no! not there! Not down there! . . ." panted Martha as she felt Mme. de Liancourt's tongue wandering over her cunt still virgin to such treatment and to the accompanying sensations!

For response, she was dragged down to the foot of the sofa, her thighs widely pulled apart, as Mme. de Liancourt falling on her knees between them murmured almost unconsciously:

"Oh, what a lovely sweet fresh little cunny . . . Oh, the beauty!" Then, like the swoop of a hawk on a chicken, her mouth attacked it and remained there as if glued to it. Completely defeated, Martha fell on her back again and resigned herself as best she could to abandon herself to the voluptuous sensations that now were thrilling through her, induced by the ardent tongue of her passionate friend. Some minutes thus passed. At last Mme. de Liancourt raised herself, red, flushed, panting, almost delirious!

"Together? . . . together? . . . will you?"

"What?" gasped Martha.

"This! Let's do it together. Will you?"

"If you wish it. But how?"

"I'll show you, darling. Now watch."

She got on the sofa, turned her bottom towards Martha's head, straddled across Martha, then placed herself astride of her face, her belly resting on Martha's breasts and her cunt seeking the same lingual caress that she was recommending on Martha's one now lying below her lips. Her thighs hid half the face of my sweet little mistress, and I could only see a bit of her forehead and her pretty hair emerge from between Mme. de Liancourt's buttocks. As the latter wriggled and waggled her charming globes of flesh in lascivious undulations, I noted that Martha had accommodated herself to her position, and that her mouth as docilely as her hand comprehended and daintily executed the delicate function demanded from it.

But as for Mme. de Liancourt, she was simply mad with passionate lust. What a strange thing it is that a woman can thus procure for herself such keen and ecstatic enjoyment in thus caressing another woman. I was splendidly placed for contemplating her, and also the object of her delirious worship. I saw her face in profile, her chin resting on the hairs, her mouth poised on the lips of Martha's slit between which her tongue was playing. These secret charms of Martha, hitherto unknown to me, made me envy Mme. de Liancourt both her place and the game she was playing. Time after time I was on the point of bursting out of my hiding place, and planting my mouth on the sweet spot she was attacking, but I refrained! The charm of the spectacle fascinated me.

Sometimes Mme. de Liancourt seemed as if she wanted to get the whole of Martha's cunt into her mouth, then sometimes amused herself by administering little touches to the clitoris with her tongue, then she would pass her tongue right along the tender slit from top to bottom; sometimes she would, with her fingers, separate the sensitive lips and thrust her tongue between them as deeply as she possibly could. Frequently she stopped, inspected attentively the sweet object of her admiration with eyes blazing with lust unsatisfied, then ejaculating frenziedly in her passionate adoration. "Oh, this cunt, this sweet cunt, this delicious darling cunt!" She would shower kisses on it. How Martha must have reveled in bliss. I would have liked to have been able to watch her telltale face. She evidently was acquitting herself most satisfactorily in reciprocating Mme. de Liancourt's attentions, if one might judge by the plungings and joggings of the latter's body as she brokenly ejaculated, "Oh! . . . oh! . . . you do it well! . . . I can feel your tongue! . . . now, do you feel mine? . . . wait . . . I'm going to shove it right inside this sweet cunt . . . as far in . . . as . . . it will go . . . There! . . ."

It is impossible to indicate the accent of these words

as pronounced by a mouth the tongue of which was endeavoring to talk and lick at one and the same moment. What a terrible state of nervous excitement must have possessed Mme. de Liancourt, a woman so reserved and correct in ordinary life, especially in language. But the ecstatic crisis was fast approaching . . . the breathings become more and more broken.

"Martha . . . oh! Martha! . . . oh! darling . . . I'm coming! . . . Ah! . . . Ah! . . . I'm spending! . . . are you? spend together! . . . together! . . . wait a moment! . . . now! . . . now! . . . Oh! . . . I'm spending . . . again! . . . spend also! s-p-e-n-d!!!"

Their bodies stiffened, constricted, I heard a deep sigh of unspeakable pleasures! They had finished.

Mme. de Liancourt slowly slipped off her position and then proceeded to give her pupil kiss after kiss of approbation and satisfaction.

"Darling! Your face is all wet with what you have drawn out of me. And I've drunk you! . . . Use my handkerchief . . . How flushed and red you are . . . Now, wasn't it good?"

"Oh, yes, much better than I could have believed."

Was it not now time for me to put in an appearance? But what could I do with two women whose lust had thus been satiated? Nevertheless I decided to show myself, and opened the door, regretting that I had delayed so long.

Two piercing cries saluted me! Martha leaped on her piled-up garments and covered herself as best she could with the first she could snatch, then hid herself behind the bed curtains. Mme. de Liancourt caught up a velvet mantle trimmed with fur and threw it hastily round her, but it reached only to her fleshy buttocks and did not even cover the fur of her belly.

"What do you mean, sir?" she exclaimed with a fine pretense of anger and outraged modesty. "What do you mean by thus rushing into a lady's room without first knocking? It is a piece of the great impertinence! You are a mannerless brute. You might well have waited. We were changing our dresses so that we might with the greatest safety leave the house. I had forgotten to lock the door, but I really considered you knew better . . ."

"Madame, I humbly and earnestly beg your pardon for having surprised you in this way," I replied, suppressing as best I could the desire to laugh. "But I came in trusting in your promise to give a kind refuge to this lady and myself!"

"Yes, but Madame has been waiting for you for some time now; we had given you up. Is this your idea of the proper way of keeping an appointment? But I will abide by my promise; you can have my room and my bed. Only be prudent. I know your secrets now and if I choose I can be nasty."

She winked at me out of the corner of her eye as if to qualify her menace, then walked past me towards her dressing room.

"Take care about the sheets!" she added with a meaningfully wicked smile.

I watched as she walked her lovely plump and round bottom, quivering and waggling with ever step—I would dearly have liked to have put myself into her! But I went and dragged Martha out of her hiding place.

"What makes you so red, dear?"

"I've been laughing so much. Madame has been telling me the funniest stories."

"You look simply charming in that dressing gown!

But don't fasten it up, it's quite unnecessary!"

"Oh, very well. But wait a minute. Don't look."

She disappeared into the lavatory, and while she was engaged in clearing away all traces of her recent pranks, I undressed myself. Then when she reappeared I took her in my arms and carried her to the bed, on which I gently laid her. Her desires that I feared were by now dormant were quickly restored to life again, having another promise of satisfaction in a different way. Her modesty after so rude an experience had becomes less troublesome, and I did not meet with any marked resistance on her part when after bestowing a thousand kisses all over her body, I did to her what Mme. de Liancourt had so sweetly inaugurated, the deliciousness of which she now fully appreciated as with her two little hands she pressed my face against her slit so as not to lose a single movement of my tongue!

I thought of Mme. de Liancourt, and wished she could see us. But she did even better than that; she stood stark naked by the side of the bed and while I was busy between Martha's thighs, she kissed her lips and squeezed her breasts, while the former, having with her reach her friend's thighs, slipped her hand between them and let it disappear under the plentiful cluster of curling hairs, without interrupting my ministrations.

Excited, inflamed, burning with hot desire, I rose to throw myself on Martha and quench in her the fire that was raging in my veins. But at that moment Mme. de Liancourt carried her hand to the lowest point of my belly and seized the object she found there in a state of furious erection.

"Look, Martha," she exclaimed. "Look at it! Have you ever seen it before? Isn't it splendid? See how stiff it is. That's in honor of you, my dear. Oh, I must . . . I can't help it! . . ."

I was then kneeling on the bed. With a single quick movement she seated herself with her head at the required height, then covered with hot kisses my member that she found just on a level with her lips. She kissed and re-kissed the gland, the hairs, the testicles, murmuring endearments, then she took my prick into her mouth and sucked it madly in front of Martha, who in utter astonishment was watching her.

"Now, Martha, you take it—it's your turn. Suck it! Do as I did!"

"I don't know how to!" stammered Martha. "It's so big!"

Now redder than fire she approached it, kissed the tip and tried for some time in vain to take it into her mouth, when all of a sudden it slipped in, as if in spite of her, completely filling her mouth, and she then proceeded to suck me violently. Oh, my raptures! It was Martha, Martha herself that was sucking me! It was not with the lascivious skill of Mme. de Liancourt, but her inexperience itself gave to her caress a special and indescribable spice of pleasure.

Finally I put Martha flat on her back and let myself fall between her arms and legs, and shoved my prick into her burning cunt—tasting delights hitherto unknown, divine, delirious. Already I could see Martha's eyes slowly turning upwards and half-closing, indicating her approaching ecstasy, when Mme. de Liancourt, no doubt jealous of our transports, put herself astride Martha's face, blindly seeking for her cunt a further caress that it was impossible to refuse to her. Being thus suddenly driven away from Martha's lips and tongue I transferred my kisses to the two luscious globes of flesh that I had at my mouth's command, kissing them, nibbling, and playfully biting them in spite of their squirming and constant agitation.

Dear readers, I will confess that my tongue at times lost itself in the furrow that separated these temptingly superb buttocks, as much did the sight of them and the subtle perfume that emanated from them madden me.

But everything must end. We three spent simultaneously. The blissful ejaculations of sperm calmed us. One by one we came to our senses and rose to purify and refresh ourselves.

"My gracious! I've got it all over me," cried Martha in pretty confusion. "Even on my stockings! They're quite wet!"

"Well, dear," said Mme. de Liancourt to her, "you've done very well for one time. You must be very tired. By the time you get home, your eyes will have dark rings around them, and then what will your husband think, eh?"

"Ah! I'll risk that. That won't stop me from . . . doing it again."

"What, today?"

"Why not? . . . When one has tasted the forbidden fruit, one must bite it well!" she replied, dropping her eyes. "Now I know what it is to be libertine. And I fancy it won't be long before I am nearly as clever at this game as Madame, your old pupil, with whom you evidently have been practicing, eh?"

"How do you know?"

"By this!" she replied, pointing to an article that stood on the toilet table, which she and I had bought together and that I had left at Mme. de Liancourt's.

"But I didn't want this proof after what I have seen today," Martha continued chafingly. "Now if I had been jealous . . ."

"Your jealousy would have deprived us from the delicious time we have had together," replied Mme. de Liancourt.

"I quite agree with you," said Martha with a smile.

Mme. de Liancourt showed herself a good teacher, and rapidly she educated her apt pupil, till it only remained to put her lessons into practice and delight her *amant* and her *amante!* And after the cares of the toilet had been attended to and a few glasses of champagne taken, we arranged that all three of us should meet at Mme. de Liancourt's chambers on the first day that Martha was able to come, and we separated with longing for the time when we should next find ourselves in Mme. de Liancourt's delicious boudoir for a *séance à trois!*

Hunting the "Rat"

On a warm summer morning, a young lady of elegant appearance was strolling in a pretty park, selecting the narrower paths when possible and every now and then looking behind over her shoulder as if she was on the way to some love tryst and feared that she might be followed. As a matter of fact she was being followed by a gentleman who did not lose sight of her for a single minute as he slipped along, hiding himself in the brushwood like an Indian in a jungle.

My fair readers, do I hear you say, what is he going to relate to us? A scene of jealousy? A husband surprising his wife just as she is about to enjoy with the sweet help of her lover a supplement to the monotonous conjugal attentions? Oh no. Please be assured. Should anything drip it certainly won't be blood, and if you should be affected by the fortune of our heroine it will be only with the most delicious of emotions.

The young lady quietly made her way to a sort of summerhouse, then after a final look round she picked up her skirts (thereby revealing prettily shod feet and shapely calves), pressed through the surrounding herbage to the door, opened it quickly and disappeared within.

Sic vos non vobis . . .

For it was no other than myself who was thus taking a share in this adventure, a poacher in conjugal preserves.

Since I first met Mme. de Baisieux in Paris and obtained an introduction to her, and above all at the Chateau de C—— when kind fortune had made us guests together, I had made assiduous siege to her with a certain hope of success as her husband was away on a long sea trip. But up to date I had been frustrated, and now my want of success seemed to be explained—the place I desired was already occupied.

I thought of withdrawing, but I wished first to make certain of the position; and may I confess that I was also seized with the desire of being a spectator of the piquant scene that no doubt was about to take place and that would finally and convincingly show me the uselessness of further pursuit.

"How shocking!" my lady readers will no doubt exclaim. Well, perhaps so, but I ask them to deal not too hardly with me in a matter of curiosity.

Thereupon I sought for the means of seeing without being seen. A little garret window afforded me the desired assistance, and through it I obtained a view of the interior, full of hay, a suitable furnishing to a rustic boudoir. Mme. de Baisieux was still alone; after having carefully closed the door, she seemed to be choosing a suitable spot for the sacrifice. I held my breath in my absorbed attention, quivering at the idea of being able to witness the scene that the principal actress was preparing against the arrival of the leading actor. Only I could not understand why she had so carefully fastened the door.

As soon as she had found a suitable place, Mme. de

Baisieux seated herself, took out of her pocket a little book and hurriedly turned over the pages. At last she seemed to find what she was seeking. Forcing the book open so that she could easily hold it so in one hand, she stretched herself out voluptuously, and supported herself on her elbow, while her disengaged hand . . .

My dear lady readers, have you guessed? Need I draw a curtain over a picture that you all must recognize? Will you not prefer to take a naughty peep at the sin your sister is about to commit?

This hand with a graceful movement raised her dress and the white petticoats beneath it. In consequence of the heat, she had not put on any drawers, and so my eager eyes were able to travel delightedly over all the charms I so ardently coveted but that so far I did not possess. And all I saw only inflamed me all the more, for her charming exterior had not lied and her naked person was all and more than all I anticipated would be found under her clothes. All was rounded, plump. Above the dainty shoe came a slender shapely leg with a delicately rounded calf, a neat knee, than higher up a thigh underlined prettily by her blue garter, the whole issuing from out of a wave of lace frillings. A fold of her chemise had dropped and so hid the part to which her hand had stolen. It was a living representation of Boilly's picture *Midi*, only with all the movement in it.

So far I had never been privileged to witness this solitary feminine pastime. It was therefore with strangely concentrated attention that I followed every movement of her hand, as it first began to rove from one end to the other of her slit, sweetly and caressingly, as if to gently flatter and excite the deity it sought to tame.

She read a few lines, then her movements quickened!

There was a gentle tremble, as if a tremolo was being executed on the charming instrument on which she was playing, then quicker, and still more quickly . . . The book slipped out of her hand. Her body and her head fell back . . . her eyes half-closed, showing the whites . . . while her lips half-opened, displayed her pearly teeth.

Between her widened extended legs her hand continued its tender gymnastics. She jerked her stomach upwards in violent upheavings, which allowed me momentary glances of blond clustering hairs, but not of the dainty tickling finger that had been entrusted with the delicate mission of awaking and exciting the sources of her pleasure. Ah, now it was over . . . the delicious crisis had come and gone.

Mme. de Baisieux raised herself, put the precious book into her pocket, brushed the dust off her garments, inspected herself in a pocket mirror, and satisfied with the result, slipped prudently and cautiously away.

I quitted my peephole in a state of excitement more easily understood than described. My brain seethed with fresh desires and with them the hope of being able to enjoy them in the company of her whom I coveted, all the more so as it was evident now that she had no means of obtaining for herself a more solid and satisfactory way of solace.

I made a long round in the park timing myself so as to meet her on one of the pathways where she was amusing herself with plucking wild flowers. The action was natural enough as was our meeting, nevertheless she blushed, for a woman will betray herself under such conditions. And she was not any more at ease when I remarked that she was looking pale and tired. All the evening I harped on this theme, leading her to think that I suspected her of having kept an amorous rendezvous, a teasing she accepted in good temper in the impression that she had completely thrown me off the scent as to her real occupation of the morning. Nevertheless, it was many days before she went out by herself. Was this the result of distrust, or prudence, or was she able to solace herself in the house? I learnt the truth later on; the poor girl occupied a room that communicated with that of the lady who owned the house, her aunt, and it was a regular schoolgirl's room in which she had no privacy whatever; hence her visits to the summerhouse.

The recollection of my delicious vision was always with me.

I dearly would have loved to have witnessed again the charming scene, to plan so that I could turn up at precisely the right moment, at all evens to get a chance of a talk with her by ourselves.

One day, the owner of a neighboring estate invited the gentlemen of our party to his place for some rabbit shooting. I loved the sport but what were my feelings of regret that I had accepted the invitation when I saw that Mme. de Baisieux, straw-hatted, was on the point of going out by herself while we were filing our cartridge pouches. Hardly had we started, when I pretended that I had forgot mine (as a mere pretense for getting back to the house).

"We'll lend you some," my friends exclaimed.

"They won't do," I explained, "I use No. 12."

"I believe I saw the gentleman place his cartridge pouch in the wagon," said a servant.

The gentleman had carefully taken them out again quietly!

"Shall we wait for you?"

"No, no, I'll follow on foot. Begin without me. You may as well take my gun along with yours, though."

Off they all went. And now for the park.

The summerhouse had its back on the wall of the roadway. I took the quickest cut to it by not entering the park by the side gate, and soon I was at the gable end. Perhaps Mme. de Baisieux had already begun to . . . In a desperate hurry, I scrambled over the wall and jumped down on the other side.

Crack went something Oh, bad luck. A confounded nail had caught in my breeches and had ripped one leg open from waistband to knee. And I wasn't wearing drawers. What was I to do?

Just then, I caught sight of Mme. de Baisieux at the foot of the little slope on which the summerhouse stood, evidently making her way to it. She was leading her little cousin by the hand, from which I came to the conclusion that she did not propose today to satisfy the cravings of sexual desire. I was rather pleased than otherwise, for now I could slip in and hide there till the evening or until I managed in some way to mend my torn breeches.

So in I slipped, and was hardly among the bundles of hay and certainly not full of voluptuous ideas, when the door suddenly opened, and I saw Mme. de Baisieux enter, leaving the little child outside.

"Don't you come in," she said, "I'm going to see if there are any rats here and to kill them. So don't come in, for they may bite you."

"Don't be long, cousin!"

"No, no." And she set to work to find the spot she occupied on the last occasion.

I had taken off my breeches and I had them in my hand, greatly embarrassed. Here was the much desired tête-à-tête, and a stupid accident was preventing me from benefiting by it. But the sight of Mme. de Baisieux looking more charming than ever inspired me with the most voluptuous ideas and reanimated my somewhat chilled desires and gave me the necessary audacity that the situation demanded. The recollection of the charms that I could still imagine under her clothes and that I perhaps was again going to see in their lovely nudity soon produced in me the effect that no pretty woman can help producing on any man worthy of the name. Rather than appear after the conclusion of the little play she was preparing for herself (and that would make her die of shame if she thought I had been a spectator of her actions) I showed myself without further delay.

A cry of startled modesty, quite natural, greeted me.

"What are you doing here, Monsieur? I thought you had gone off with the shooting party."

"I did start with them, but I left my cartridges behind and came back for them, and chose the quickest way; and in climbing over the garden wall I have torn my breeches badly. I saw you coming along and so took refuge here, and was horribly astonished when you came in. Now will you do me a great favor? Can you somehow get me a needle and thread so that I can repair this disaster as far as may be possible, at all events sufficiently to allow of my getting out of my present extremely unfortunate and inconvenient position."

Mme. de Baisieux broke into hearty laughter, no doubt relieved to find that I had not been spying on her; my accident thus saved me from suspicions that would have entirely spoiled my chances.

Briefly, so as not to tire my readers with conversations and explanations, after some hesitation on Mme. de

Baisieux's part, we arranged that I should hide in a corner and throw my breeches over to her; she would then
mend them as much as was possible and throw them
back to me. She had the necessary needle and thread with
her and in a few minutes she completed her work.

"There you are, Monsieur," she exclaimed as she
threw the breeches back to me, and which I quickly
slipped on. "Now good morning."

"Oh please, wait a moment to let me thank you!"

"No, no, goodbye. If any one should find us together
here . . ."

But by this time I was alongside of her and had
slipped my arm round her waist while I begged for a
sweet kiss. I then stole one.

"Enough, enough. No more!" she protested.
"Suppose anyone should come in? And my cousin?"

"Only one word, please. I must tell you."

"Quickly then!"

"I didn't scramble over the wall to get my cartridges,
I wanted to get here without exciting anyone's suspicions, for I saw you on your way here. I wanted to tell
you that you are the prettiest girl I know, that I adore
you." And I rained kisses on her cheek.

"Oh, oh. Monsieur Henri, how can you? I couldn't
have believed it . . ."

"I adore you! You are so pretty, so sweet! Oh, Bertha,
my darling, my love. You will? You will? Won't you? . . ."

"What? You know my name?"

"It's the first thing a man learns about the girl he
loves, and I've known it for a long time!"

All the time I continued to shower kisses on her as I
held her tightly clasped in my arms against me. I could
feel how her flesh was quivering through her thin sum-

mer dress, as I covered her cheeks, the nape of her neck, her throat, her mouth and lips with my ardent kisses. She let herself sink down on the straw murmuring, "Enough . . . enough," then, as if to conceal her surrender of herself now commencing, she fell into a half-swoon, closing her eyes which I kissed, and half-opening her lips, between which my tongue promptly slipped without however getting any reciprocal response from hers. One of my arms supported her body, the other hand crept under her dress and petticoats and caressed gently her dainty calves, then after a pause crept higher up to her garters where when a woman's leg is bent one can so deliciously lodge one's hand between the swell of the calf and the skin of the thigh. From this vantage point, getting bolder, my hand crept still higher. Oh, what a sweet thrill ran through both of us when my fingers touched the soft warm bare flesh of her plump rounded thighs that she was vainly squeezing against each other.

This time also she had no drawers on. From the top of her dainty shoes to her smooth satin belly, the hairs on which I now gently was playing with, there was no obstacle to my full view.

"No! . . . no! . . ." she murmured as she felt my fingers invade her slit, "not there! . . . not there! . . ."

But in spite of this flicker of rebellion, this last effort of expiring shame, my finger settled itself on her tiny clitoris and commenced the ecstatic function that Mme. de Baisieux hitherto had reserved for her own little fingers. Under its sweetly mysterious influence, her body began to stretch itself out, her faintness increased, her tongue began to respond to mine. And then her legs commenced to open out. She was mine! She had surrendered herself to me. I now only had to take possession of her.

In one's first amorous encounter with any new woman, it is always most advisable to go slowly at first, watching her carefully and defeating every attempt at resistance—to pretend to be seized with delirious passion for her—until your sweet combatant yields herself under the repeated thrills of pleasure you have communicated to her. Then you let yourself go and indulge to the utmost your concupiscence and your desires.

I was now burning to look closely at all the charms that so far I had seen from a distance only. Quickly I threw up her clothes so as to get a good look, and as I did I thought of the piquant spectacle we would afford anyone who might have his eye where I had mine on the previous occasion.

All I saw were now mine! Mine, these lovely legs, these slender, dainty calves. She was wearing the same underclothing as on the last occasion—tiny kid shoes, cream-colored silk stockings, blue garters. On her right thigh was a tiny brown mole. Oh, how I longed to kiss everything, that lovely satin skin, that silky chestnut triangular patch of curls that formed so adorable a contrast to her blond beauty. How I would have liked to put my mouth on the delicious little slit that was now beginning to open its pouting lips. But I hadn't the time now. I had to keep holding her clothes up. Another time I would repay myself with interest.

Recalled thus to the sweet reality, I placed myself between her charming legs, I pulled her clothes still higher up, I rapidly undid the front of my breeches and freed my imprisoned member then shoved it still and burning into the sweet opening that was impatiently awaiting its introduction. At the same time I thrust my tongue as deeply as I could into the mouth of my pretty victim.

"Bertha . . . oh, Bertha! . . . oh, how heavenly! . . . you're delicious . . . divine . . . oh, you angel, you angel! . . ."

Women as a rule do not let their lovers who are rogering them for the first time understand how they appreciate the pleasure that is wildly rioting through them all the time, for they love to behave as if they were being violated. Mme. de Baisieux only departed from this policy to murmur as we were approaching the sweet ecstatic conclusion. "Oh, please, please, take it out! . . . not inside me! . . . no, no, please!" Although I was mad with pleasure I had sufficient control of myself to obey her. Unfortunate results might otherwise arise from our pleasure. Oh, mysterious decrees of Providence—without you how much more amiable and obliging women would be—and also how deliciously libertine.

It comes back to me how I was kissing her tiny ear ornamented with a single pearl as I awaited the moment when I must withdraw my prick from inside her in accordance with her prudent request. The moment arrived—everything shot onto her white petticoat.

I offered her my handkerchief.

"But then you won't have a handkerchief!" she exclaimed.

"Oh, yes, I'll preserve it in memory of the delicious use you will have made of it," I replied with a smile. She blushed prettily.

While we were exchanging the loving kisses that follow so tender an encounter, we heard a little voice at the door.

"Cousin, cousin, haven't you finished killing the rats yet?" We had absolutely forgotten all about the child who was patiently waiting outside!

"Yes, yes!" called out my lovely companion, raising herself hurriedly and flushing scarlet. "I'm just coming— I've killed the last I think!"

We couldn't maintain our seriousness at the plaintive trouble in the little voice that had thus interrupted us.

"Here I am, dear, I'm just coming. Don't come in!"

"Goodbye Bertha, my darling," I whispered. "When again?"

"Oh! Never, never!"

"You little humbug. Shall we say tomorrow?"

"No, no! I'll tell you later."

"One last kiss then!" She gave me a delicious one in which her tongue and mine also said goodbye. "Now goodbye! Au revoir."

As she neared the door, she brushed and dusted herself, took a glance in the pocket mirror she had with her, waved her hand lovingly to me, said goodbye again with her eyes, then slipped out.

As soon as I considered she would have gotten to a safe distance, I crept out, hurried off to my bedroom and quickly changed my things, as they carried evident traces of our sweet combat! Then I picked up my cartridge pouch and set off to rejoin the shooting party, my absence being hardly an hour. How one can employ time sometimes!

From that day, for Mme. de Baisieux and me, the term "to kill a rat" became synonymous with "have a turn." In spite of her innocent air, she was full of mischief, and did not hesitate to let herself loose in her love letters to me. In memory of the adventure she adopted the following formula in her billets-doux:

"Mon cher Monsieur, will you give the pleasure of your company at a rat hunt on —— next at the usual place?" She continued to send me these invitations after we had returned to Paris, even when her husband was there; he did not stay there long, but his presence never-theless was a nuisance as it of necessity reduced the fre-quency of our "hunts" and the consequent opportunities of satisfying our desires.

When our liaison had become very intimate I told her that one day I had surprised her in the act of frigging her-self. I was sweetly scolded for thus playing the spy on a "poor lone woman," but I was soon pardoned, and she consented to let me see the book that seemed to arouse the desires that she strove thus to satisfy. She had found it among her brother's papers. It was *The Confessions of a Woman of the "World,"* illustrated in the most lascivi-ous way, enough to excite anyone's senses.

"On the day we first killed the rat, what bit were you reading?" I asked softly.

In pretty embarrassment she pointed out to me the following lines, which we then read together:

"As I lay on my back on my sofa, stretched out at full length with my legs widely parted, my lover fell on his knees in front of me and in the most delicious way sucked me till I spent in thrilling delirium!"

Needless to say we did not read any more that day. And I take this opportunity to express to the amiable author and to his clever illustrator my sincere thanks for having thus aroused a fire that I was able to extinguish in the pleasantest way possible.

The "Maize Porridge"

If from time immemorial the French woman, especially the Parisienne, has enjoyed the reputation of being in love affairs the most agreeable and the most sprightly of her sex, and of knowing how to impart to her favors a piquancy that greatly augments their value, I venture to consider that the Vienna ladies should be allowed to participate in this praise, especially such as have had the benefit of Parisian education. For their elegance, their air of distinction, their coquetry, their talent for being discreetly provoking, in no way ranks behind their Parisian sisters whom often they surpass in beauty of form and figure. Full of curiosity in all matters appertaining to sexual love, they delight to make a study of them and to lose themselves in dream eroticism, in meditations of the most refined lubricity, after which they will resume in the easiest manner possible the outward appearance of the most virtuous and well-behaved woman.

Such at all events was Mme. de Schoenfutz. Transplanted from the banks of the Danube to those of the Seine, she had there found so many subjects for amorous study that she did not long live in accord with her legal lord and master; the latter, like a wise man, avoided any scandal by quietly letting her live as she chose while he in turn did as he also pleased.

It was I who was the privileged mortal with whom she took her first lessons in the Art of Love, with whom she made her first studies, which we did not hesitate to carry on to extremes.

She was a delicious pupil, so full of enthusiasm. I could conduct her and teach her the most outrageous method of unrestrained lust as long as I did so by agreeable and picturesquely amusing paths. And there was little doubt that I had hit off the right way, as very soon she become most expert.

But everything comes to an end, even such delightful refinements of amorous pleasure. She began to put into practice with others the lessons I had taught her, while I passed on to the education of other pupils. Since then we had often met, but our Lady Venus did not receive any sweet sacrifice from us, partly because the occasions were not propitious and time was wanting. Now the attractions of the hunting season had brought us together at the Chateau de V——.

My Viennese charmer had become even more beautiful than before; to the charms of her face and figure was now added a certain trick in the way she looked at you, which under the air of distinction nevertheless indicated she was not wanting either in enterprise or audacity. In short I found myself ready if she should indicate that she was willing. But do not think that I imagined that I had only to ask her to let me have (so to speak) my latchkey again. To have done so would have been both foolish and fatal, for a woman requires to be reconquered by any man whose caresses she has forgotten. Accordingly I laid siege to her in the regular way, but at first all the encouragement I got lay in vague half-promises, such as "Perhaps . . . if you're very good!" But little by little I made progress, now snatching a hasty kiss, now a significant pressure of her corsage, sometimes a hand slipped under her clothes but not permitted to! . . .

One day we went out fox hunting. Mme. de Schoenfutz both rode well and looked well on horseback, having something of the elegance of seat and style of the late Empress Elizabeth of Austria, whom indeed she resembled in more ways than one.

The atmosphere was heavy and thunderous, the heat stifling. The sport was poor. Twice the hounds had to be whipped off a false scent. A state of confusion prevailed, and the riders formed little groups as they watched the proceedings and held themselves ready to gallop off as soon as the signal was given. Presently the sky began to be covered with black threatening clouds that presaged a serious storm. Was it good enough to go on? Wouldn't it be as well to get to shelter? But before any general decision was arrived at, a roll of thunder shook the air and large drops of rain began to fall.

Immediately there was a general skedaddle, a wild rush for the carriages. Several riders galloped off to the kennels not far off, others to the village of T——. The men ceased to chat with their lady friends and with each other, concerned now to make the best of their way to shelter. But Monsieur de Z—— (who I suspected to be in Mme. de Schoenfutz's high favor) remained by her and asked her what she proposed to do.

"I'm going back home," she said.

"You'd much better come to T——. The rain will soon be over and we can then resume hunting."

"Many thanks! In the forest, all dripping? I've had enough for one day already!"

"But really it is not going to be wet."

"Please don't let me keep you from hunting! I'm going off, I hate rain."

"Then let me come with you. You don't know the road and you will most likely take the longest way round."

But Mme. de Schoenfutz had galloped off as he spoke. And now I recognized why old Ovid had included the chase among his Remedies for Love! Monsieur de Z—— did not insist on following. The lady riders all dismounted quickly and crowded into carriages to drive back to the Chateau, while the men unanimously allowed them to go off unescorted while they themselves made the best of their way to T—— to wait there till the rain was over and the hunt could be resumed.

"This is much jollier than with all those petticoats hanging about," remarked F——, a woman-hating sportsman. "Come along to T——. There's a good hotel there, a good stable, and a good billiard table on which we can have a game while we wait."

"Sorry I can't come, old chap," I replied. "I must go off to see one of the keepers about a dog. We'll meet presently."

It had stopped raining, but the sky was more threatening than ever. My intention was not to stop at the keeper's but to get off to the Chateau and try and find Mme. de Schoenfutz, for in such panics it is seldom that an enterprising gallant does not have some luck, because everybody is too busy looking after himself or herself to notice what anyone else is doing. So after a few minutes at the keeper's house, I galloped down a bridle path that was a shortcut to the Chateau and led into the road Mme. de Schoenfutz had taken.

As I joined the road I saw some way down a lady riding slowly by herself. It was she! I soon caught up.

"What, not home yet?" I exclaimed.

"No," she replied. "My horse has a stone in his hoof and I have nothing to get it out with. So I am forced to go slowly."

I had with me the necessary implement and soon put matters right, then remounted.

"Are they all coming this way?" she asked.

"Yes, the carriages are just behind, with all the women inside them."

"Then let us get out of their way, for if they see me with you after the way I rushed off, they will conclude that our meeting was premeditated."

"You are quite right. Let us ride down here."

As soon as we had got out of sight of anyone on the road, I drew alongside my fair companion and slipped my arm round her slender waist, then drawing her quickly to me I kissed her lips ardently.

"Enough, enough!" she exclaimed, trying to release herself. "Here comes the rain!"

"I don't mind the rain as long as I have you!" And I renewed my amorous assault, clasping her passionately against me as I kissed her furiously, darting my tongue into her mouth, squeezing her waist with one hand while the other attacked her bosom, her knees, and her thighs, which I felt and pressed through the cloth of her habit. So impetuous was my attack that I nearly caused her to fall off her horse.

"Oh, oh, what are you doing? Is it the storm that has made you so mad?"

"Yes! A storm of love and desire. I am full of love's electricity, like the clouds."

"And so you want me to be your lightning conductor! But I thought I had become incapable of electrifying you to such an extent."

"You know well that you are to me what no other woman can be. And if you would like a proof of your power over me . . ."

"As a matter of fact, people who have known of our old liaison suspect me now to be with anyone but you."

"But you haven't answered my question! Do let us take advantage of our security. Let me prove to you that you have electrified me to the uttermost of my capacity. Will you? May I?"

"Well, yes! But you're not allowing for the storm!"

As a matter of fact the rain now had begun to come down heavily, rain that clears the air but which is a horrible nuisance to an out-of-doors rendezvous without any curtains beyond the kindly trees.

We went off at a gallop down the path. Was it never coming to an end? Soon I noticed that we were going away from our proper course, the fault of our hasty flight. I was somewhat upset by this, but said nothing. We continued to gallop. Presently a signpost came in sight; I rode up to it and found that the Chateau was a good three miles from where we were.

"Where are we?" she asked.

"Oh, not far off."

"Then which is the road? This way?"

Just then I caught sight of a hut hidden in the forest. It was a sort of hunting shelter with a lean-to for the horses. The sight put a droll idea into my mind. Here was a nest for an amorous pair.

At all events it would be only prudent to avail ourselves of this unexpected shelter. We tied the horses under the lean-to, and forcing open the locked door we went inside. We found ourselves in a fair-sized room, quite bare except for one or two straw-seated chairs and a fireplace. In the ceiling there was a trap door that evidently communicated with a hayloft.

Hardly had we entered when the rain began to come down in torrents. What we had experienced was nothing to what was now falling, a veritable deluge. I kindled a fine fire in the hearth with the debris and straw I found lying about. Then I took off my coat and hung it across the back of a chair in front of the fire. Mme. de Schoenfutz slipped out of her riding habit and did the same.

She looked deliciously piquant as she stood thus, décolleté, her pretty arms bare, with her riding breeches, her dainty riding boots, and a man's little silk hat.

I gently caught hold of her and drew her against me, then slipped my hand under her chemisette and getting hold of one of her round full breasts, I drew it out of its hiding place and kissed it passionately. "Suppose someone should come!" she whispered.

"Wait a moment," I replied, and went out. I brought the horses inside, then barricaded the door. Now no one could possibly suspect our presence, for even the fire (now reduced to a glowing mass) did not throw off any smoke to call attention to human habitation.

"Now we're at home."

Seated on a chair with Mme. de Schoenfutz on my knee, I surrendered myself to my desires. On her part she abandoned herself entirely to me, returning me kiss for kiss, laughing delightedly at the originality of our situation. She simply adored such situations. By now I had pulled both of her sweet little breasts out of her corset and was kissing them fiercely. Under my burning lips, the pretty little nipples began to swell up and get hard.

"I really believe they recognize you," she said laughingly.

"Then what about my third little friend, the sweetest, the sauciest, the wickedest of them all!" and my fingers unbuttoned the front of her riding breeches and slipped inside.

"It's an odd sensation," I remarked maliciously, "to find a cunt inside a man's breeches." And my happy hand set to work to caress and play with the sweet feminine hairs it found, then stole between a pair of soft plump satin-like thighs that it felt and handled. And then my finger made its way into a certain opening already warm and moist and commenced to play on her little quivering clitoris.

As her pleasure crept over her, my pretty companion began to become sweetly agitated. Her hand stole towards me; I delightedly guided it. Quickly unbuttoning my trousers I helped her to drag out what she was seeking and what she now had got hold of.

"Just suppose that you had found something like this when you put your hand inside my riding breeches," she remarked.

"What an idea!"

"He recognizes me, I'm sure. He wants to see his old friend."

The way in which we had placed ourselves was not propitious or convenient for the prosecution of our adventures. True pleasure demands horizontal position, and I, at all events, consider that one only cheats Venus if one sacrifices to her in the odd positions that are only allowable when there is absolutely no help for it. So instead of making her sit astride on my knees (as she seemed to expect) I suggested that I should climb into the hayloft to see whether we could not build for ourselves a more comfortable nest up there.

The ladder was rather rickety, however I got up all right. The loft was full of sweet-smelling hay. I quickly persuaded Mme. de Schoenfutz to join me, but as the ladder was a little short for her I had some little difficulty in raising her off it while she laughed and reveled in the adventure.

"Now, where?" she asked, looking about her.

Oh what a delicious question, as much as to say, "Where shall I place myself so as to let you have me, to yield myself to you, to let you do whatever you like to me."

I collected some bundles of hay and soon improvised an excellent couch on which I gently placed her head.

"The mice will see us," she exclaimed playfully. Then, "Oh, this hay is pricking me awfully!"

This I soon remedied by means of my horse rug, and then we were comfortably installed.

Outside the tempest continued to rage unabated, with loud claps of thunder and torrential rain. My pretty companion however had no alarm, and abandoned herself afresh to me. In the midst of our toyings and handlings of each other's persons, I whispered, "Do take this off, it's only a nuisance." And I pointed first to her stays, then to her riding breeches.

"You'll do the same?"

"Yes, of course. And at once."

Gracefully she consented to satisfy my prayer, and set

to work to take off her breeches, or rather her cloth
knickers buttoning at the knee. When she had let them
fall I helped her to draw her legs out of them and to pass
them over her little patent-leather riding boots, a task I
took care not to accomplish without availing myself of
the opportunity to effect sundry little ticklings and indiscreet touchings that provoked from her little screams of
laughter.

"I'm going to keep on my hat," she said, "for my hair
is damp and I would never be able to get it into order
again."

Oh, how bewitching she looked then, and what a
piquant costume! She stood in her chemise with her silk
riding hat on, and her patent-leather riding boots
halfway up her calf, the rest of her leg being covered with
a grey silk stocking fastened above the knee with a rose-
colored garter.

I dropped on my knees in front of her and pressed my
lips upon a forest of golden hairs through which I tried
to insert my tongue.

"No, no," she exclaimed, drawing herself back a little, "not standing upright!" Then she lay herself down,
and pleasure invaded the pair of us.

Her chemise I had turned back and the whole of her
lovely body was now exposed. I showered kisses all over
it, but especially all about her thighs, between which I
then recommenced my sweet occupation in a less unfa-
vorable posture than before. My skillful tongue soon sent
her out of herself, her stomach heaved agitatedly, then
jogged itself spasmodically upwards as if loath to lose a
single touch of my tongue.

Pleasure communicated demands reciprocity. This
was always our rule and practice in the days when she

was taking lessons from me in the Art and Practice of Love. Without arresting my ministrations, I placed myself in a position that I knew would recall to her our old conventions. Her soft hand showed me that she understood, as it gently seized the object I had placed at her disposal. I then brought myself still nearer, so that her mouth had even less distance than before to travel in order to carry out its sweet duty.

"No, no! That won't do!" she softly exclaimed, "you will disarrange my hair. Let me come on top of you!" and she gently freed herself in order to do so.

She took my place, put herself on top of me, turned without hesitation her lovely bottom towards my face, and then lowered herself till her delicious slit rested on my mouth. And immediately I felt my member kissed, caressed, and handled, then sucked in the most delightful fashion. I responded by furiously thrusting my tongue as deeply as I could into her throbbing quivering cunt.

The storm, the hunt, all were completely forgotten. What ecstasies we were reveling in, what delirious transports! What zest she was putting in her suction of me. My lessons had borne wonderful fruit. And I, with what fury I thrust my tongue into the grotto of love that was palpitating on my lips, how I licked, sucked, nibbled. But I began to feel I was . . .

"Diana, Diana, stop! . . . stop! . . . I'm coming! . . . coming! . . ."

Alas!—too late. A suction more subtle and overpowering than anything that had preceded it deprived me of the power of moving, and my boiling discharge shot into the sweet mouth of my companion.

Shocked by such a catastrophe, I feared a legitimate punishment. But nothing happened. To cover my fault, I continued to pass my tongue into and over Mme. de Schoenfutz's cunt till she lay motionless. Perhaps my now somewhat calmed ardor was expressed by my tongue. Perhaps my lovely companion herself had spent deliciously. Presently I began to make my apologies.

"My sweet Diana, really I beg pardon . . ."

She made no reply, but raised herself off me, rosy red, and approached me as if to kiss me, put her lips on mine, and spat into my mouth the liqueur she had been storing so carefully in hers. Then shaking with laughter she remarked wickedly, "There, you've got it all back."

Delighted by so happy a solution, I caught hold of her, captured her bottom, raised her chemise, and set to work to slap her playfully, but not for long, for I bent down and covered her charming hemispheres with numberless kisses.

Before long, thanks to a thousand erotic follies, the standard bearer of my desires, the "Leader of the shocking party" (as a witty English girl once called it) became again rampant and erect. This time we gave the preference to a sacrifice to Venus in the ordinary method, for however delicious may be other postures and the other ways of performing the act of fucking, they are more or less hors d'oeuvres, tidbits, rather than a substantial meal. But owing to her hat my partner took the upper place, and very soon, clasped in each other's arms, lips against lips, my prick penetrated into the sweet opening already lubricated by my kisses and tonguings.

Just then the rain came down with an intensity hitherto unequaled, as so often happens towards the end of a storm. Mme. de Schoenfutz began to squirm and wriggle in a most extraordinary way. It was with the greatest difficulty that I managed to keep her impaled on my prick in spite of my hands being firmly pressed on the two charming rotundities that women so love to exaggerate in their toilettes.

"The rain is coming through," she said. "I can feel some drops just in the small of my back. Oh, there's one!"

"Shall we change places?"

"No, no. Oh, there's another, just between the cheeks of my bottom. Oh, how it tickles!" And again she squirmed and wriggled in the most voluptuous way as she lay on me.

The rain was really coming through the roof. But what did we care? The blissful ecstatic crisis was approaching, our breath mixed on our humid lips. I began to feel that I could not hold back my boiling discharge for long. Among our mutual understandings it was decreed that I was not to deposit my tribute of love inside the shrine (whichever it might be) into which I had been permitted to perform my worship. My recent infraction was one that would carry no grave after consequences. It was only perhaps an offense to shame, but if I now should repeat it the result might be most serious and in fact might damage Mme. de Schoenfutz's reputation. So I murmured in her ear softly that I was getting to the end of my powers of self-control, that I must soon . . . spend . . . that something was just . . . coming! . . . and that I must withdraw my prick while I was sufficiently master of myself to do so!

"Wait, wait! One moment! . . . I'm finishing . . . also! . . ." she gasped brokenly as her movements on me accelerated, accompanied by convulsions of pleasure. A few ecstatic thrills, and then the sudden relaxing of her body announced that her blissful crisis had come and gone, and that she had spent! Then promptly I withdrew my prick out of its sweet nook and . . . discharged . . . not wasting my ammunition however, as I slipped my rampant prick between the quivering globes of her bottom and inundated the charming valley that lay between them with a deluge of another sort to what had come from the roof.

"Oh, oh! . . ." she ejaculated, "it reached right up to my back! It's much warmer than the rain!"

♋

After we had crept down again, we found our garments quite dry. I helped my companion to dress.

"Is my hair much tumbled? I expect you've rumpled it horribly!"

"No, not at all. It's all right." And I kissed her tenderly.

She drew out of her pocket a little powder box and passed the puff lightly over her face.

"You Viennese ladies are very fond of rice powder!" I said.

"Oh yes. I use it all over me."

"Don't I know it?" I replied maliciously.

"Oh, you wretch!"

We remounted our horses. The rain had ceased; the forest was full of the delightful fragrance that leaves give out after a shower.

Our road back took us close to a keeper's house where we made inquiries about the hunting and were told that it had not been recommenced. Just then a group of horsemen came up from T—— where they had taken shelter; among them was Monsieur de Z——. We joined them.

"So you took refuge here?" he inquired of me.

"No, not I. Mme. de Schoenfutz did. I came by just as she was remounting. I stopped with the keeper, Jean."

♋

In the drawing room the same evening, the conversation turned on the storm and the interrupted hunt, and everyone told how he or she had fared while sheltering.

"In the house I was in," said Mme. de Schoenfutz, "they made me taste a sort of white sauce . . . You know it," she added, looking at me.

"Yes, that was so, and I made you try it. But you did not seem to fancy it."

Her coolness simply dumbfounded me.

Then they all began to discuss what it could have been; everyone expressed some opinion, but an old maid insisted that she knew it.

"Of course, it was only milk thickened with maize powder! When it is warm and not too thick, it is very nice!"

The Diary of a Chambermaid

by Octave Mirbeau

———

My dear friend:

For two reasons, very strong and very precise, I wish to write your name at the head of these pages. First, that you may know how dear your name is to me. Second,—and I say it with a deep pride,—because I know you will like this book. Yes, you will like it, in spite of all its faults, because it is a book free from hypocrisy, and because it portrays life, life as you and I understand it. I have always in my mind's eye, my dear Huret, many of the faces, so strangely human, which you have arrayed in procession in a long series of social and literary studies. They haunt me. Perhaps it is because no one more subtly than you, and more profoundly than you, has felt, when surveying these human masqueraders, how sad and how comical a thing it is to be a man. May you find again in these pages that sadness which makes lofty souls laugh, that comicality which makes them weep.

OCTAVE MIRBEAU.

May, 1900.

The book that I publish under this title, "A Chambermaid's Diary," was really written by Mlle. Célestine R———, chambermaid. When I was asked to revise the manuscript, to correct it, and rewrite some parts of it, I refused at first, thinking, not without reason, that, just as it was, in all its disorder, this diary had a certain originality, a special savor, and that I could only render it commonplace by putting into it anything of myself. But Mlle. Célestine R——— was very pretty. She insisted. I finally yielded, for, after all, I am a man.

I confess that I was wrong. In doing this work which she asked of me,—that is, in adding here and there some accents to this book,—I am very much afraid that I have impaired its somewhat corrosive grace, diminished its sad power, and, above all, substituted simple literature for the emotion and life which these pages contained.

I say this to answer in advance the objections which certain grave and learned, and how noble, critics will not fail to raise.

O. M.

I.

TODAY, September 14, at three o'clock in the afternoon, in mild, gray, and rainy weather, I have entered upon my new place, the twelfth in two years. What is there to say of the places which I held in previous years? It would be impossible for me to count them. Ah! I can boast of having seen interiors and faces, and filthy souls. And it is not yet the end. Judging from the really extraordinary and dizzy way in which I have drifted, here and there, successively, from houses to employment-bureaus, and from employment bureaus to houses, from Bois de Boulogne to the Bastille, from the Observatory to Montmartre, from the Ternes to the Gobelins, everywhere, without ever succeeding in establishing myself anywhere, the masters in these days are, to say the least, hard to please. It is incredible.

The affair was arranged through an advertisement in the "*Figaro*," and without any interview with Madame. We wrote letters to each other, that is all; a risky method, often resulting in surprises on both sides. Madame's letters are well written, it is true. But they reveal a meddlesome and fastidious character. Ah! the explanations and the commentaries that she insisted upon, the whys and the becauses. I do not know whether Madame is stingy; at any rate she is hardly ruining herself with her letter-paper. It is bought at the Louvre. I

7

am not rich, but I have more elegance than that. I write on paper perfumed *à la peau d'Espagne,* beautiful paper, some of it pink, some light blue, which I have collected from my former mistresses. Some of it even bears a countess's coronet engraved upon it. That must have been a crusher for her.

Well, at last, here I am in Normandy, at Mesnil-Roy. Madame's estate, which is not far from the country, is called the Priory. This is almost all that I know of the spot where henceforth I am to live.

I am not without anxiety, or without regret, at having come, in consequence of a moment's rashness, to bury myself in the depths of the country. What I have seen of it frightens me a little, and I ask myself what further is going to happen to me here. Doubtless nothing good, and the usual worries. To worry is the clearest of our privileges. For every one who succeeds,—that is, for every one who marries a worthy young fellow or forms an alliance with an old man,—how many of us are destined to ill-luck, swept away in the great whirlwind of poverty? After all, I had no choice, and this is better than nothing.

This is not the first time that I have had a job in the country. Four years ago I had one. Oh! not for long, and in really exceptional circumstances. I remember this adventure as if it had happened yesterday. Although the details are a bit indecorous, and even horrible, I wish to tell it. Moreover, I charitably warn you that I intend, in writing this diary, to keep nothing back, in relation either to myself or to others. On the contrary, I intend to put into it all the frankness that is in life. It is not my fault if the souls from which we tear the veils, and which then appear in all their nakedness, exhale so strong an odor of rottenness.

Well, here it is.

I was taken on in an employment-bureau, by a sort of fat

governess, to be a chambermaid in the house of a certain M. Rabour, in Touraine. The conditions agreed on, it was decided that I should take the train on such a day, at such an hour, for such a station; which was done, according to the programme.

As soon as I had given up my ticket at the exit, I found, outside, a sort of coachman with a rubicund and churlish face, who asked me:

"Are you M. Rabour's new chambermaid?"

"Yes."

"Have you a trunk?"

"Give me your baggage ticket, and wait for me here."

He made his way to the platform. The employees hastened about him. They called him "Monsieur Louis" in a tone of friendly respect. Louis looked for my trunk in the pile of baggage, and had it placed in an English cart that stood near the exit.

"Well, will you get in?"

I took my seat beside him, and we started. The coachman peered at me out of the corner of his eye, and I examined him similarly. I saw at once that I had to do with a countryman, an unpolished peasant, an untrained domestic who had never served in grand establishments. That annoyed me. For my part, I like handsome liveries. I dote on nothing so much as on white leather knee-breeches tightly fitting nervous thighs. And how wanting in elegance he was, this Louis, without driving-gloves, with a full suit of grayish-blue drugget that was too big for him, and a flat cap of glazed leather, ornamented with a double row of gold lace. No, indeed, they are slow in this region. And, with all, a scowling, brutal air, but not a bad fellow at bottom. I know these types. At first they assume a knowing air with the new people, and later a more friendly footing is arrived at. Often more friendly than one would like.

We sat a long time without saying a word. He assumed the manners of a grand coachman, holding the reins high and

9

swinging his whip with rounded gestures. Oh! how ridiculous he was! For my part, with much dignity I surveyed the landscape, which had no special feature; simply fields, trees, and houses, just as everywhere else. He brought his horse down to a walk in order to ascend a hill, and then, suddenly, with a quizzing smile, he asked:

"I suppose that at least you have brought a good supply of shoes?"

"Undoubtedly," said I, astonished at this question, which rhymed with nothing, and still more at the singular tone in which he put it to me. "Why do you ask me that? It is a rather stupid question, don't you know, my old man?"

He nudged me slightly with his elbow, and, gliding over me a strange look whose two-fold expression of keen irony and, indeed, of jovial obscenity was unintelligible to me, he said, with a chuckle:

"Oh! yes, pretend that you know nothing. You are a good one, you are,—a jolly good one!"

Then he clacked his tongue, and the horse resumed its rapid gait.

I was puzzled. What could be the meaning of this. Perhaps nothing at all. I concluded that the good man was a little silly, that he did not know how to talk with women, and that he had been able to think of no other way to start a conversation which, however, I did not see fit to continue.

M. Rabour's estate was sufficiently large and beautiful. A pretty house, painted light green, and surrounded by broad lawns adorned with flowers and by a pine forest which gave forth an odor of turpentine. I adore the country, but, oddly enough, it makes me sad and sleepy. It was utterly stupid when I entered the vestibule where the governess was awaiting me,—she who had engaged me at the Paris employment-bureau, God knows after how many indiscreet questions as to my private habits and tastes, which ought to have made me distrustful. But in vain does one see and endure things stronger and stronger; they never teach you anything. The governess had not pleased me at the employment-bureau; here she instantly disgusted me. She seemed to me to have the air of an old procuress. She was a fat woman, and short, with puffed-up yellowish flesh, hair brushed flat and turning gray, huge and rolling breasts, and soft, damp hands as transparent as gelatine. Her grey eyes indicated wickedness, a cold calculating, vicious wickedness. The tranquil and cruel way in which she looked at you, searching soul and flesh, was almost enough to make you blush.

She escorted me into a little reception-room, and at once left me, saying that she was going to notify Monsieur, that Monsieur wished to see me before I should begin my service.

"For Monsieur has not seen you," she added. "I have taken you, it is true, but then it is necessary that you please Monsieur."

I inspected the room. It was extremely clean and orderly. The brasses, the furniture, the floor, the doors, thoroughly polished, waxed, varnished, shone like mirrors. No clap-trap, no heavy hangings, no embroidered stuffs, such as are seen in certain Paris houses; but serious comfort, an air of rich decency, of substantial country life, regular and calm. But my! how tiresome it must be to live here!

Monsieur entered. Oh! the queer man and how he amused me! Fancy a little old man, looking as if he had just stepped out of a band-box, freshly shaven, and as pink as a doll. Very erect, very sprightly, very inviting, in fact, he hopped about, in walking, like a little grasshopper in the fields. He saluted me, and then asked, with infinite politeness:

"What is your name, my child?"

"Célestine, Monsieur."

"Célestine!" he exclaimed. "Célestine? The devil! It is a pretty name,—that I do not deny,—but too long, my child, much too long. I will call you Marie, if you are willing. That is a very nice name, too, and it is short. And besides, I have

11

called all my chambermaids Marie. It is a habit which it would distress me to abandon. I would rather abandon the person."

They all have this queer mania of never calling you by your real name. I was not too much astonished, having already borne all the names of all the saints in the calendar. He persisted:

"So it will not displease you if I call you Marie? That is agreed, is it?"

"Why, certainly, Monsieur."

"A pretty girl; good character; very well, very well."

He had said all this to me in a sprightly and extremely respectful way, and without staring at me, without seeming to undress me with his eyes, after the fashion of men generally. Scarcely had he looked at me. From the moment that he entered the room, his eyes had remained obstinately fixed upon my shoes.

"You have others?" he asked, after a short silence, during which it seemed to me that his eyes became strangely brilliant.

"Other names, Monsieur?"

"No, my child, other shoes."

And with a slender tongue he licked his lips, after the manner of cats.

I did not answer at once. This word shoes, reminding me of the coachman's salacious joke, had astounded me. Then that had a meaning? On a more pressing interrogation I finally answered, but in a voice somewhat hoarse and thick, as if I were confessing a sin of gallantry:

"Yes, Monsieur, I have others."

"Glazed?"

"Yes, Monsieur."

"Highly, highly glazed?"

"Why, yes, Monsieur."

"Good, good. And of yellow leather?"

"I have none of that kind, Monsieur."

"You will have to have some; I will give you some."

"Thank you, Monsieur."

"Good, good! Be still!"

I was frightened, for dull gleams had just passed over his eyes, and drops of sweat were rolling down his forehead. Thinking that he was about to faint, I was on the point of shouting, of calling for help. But the crisis quieted down, and, after a few minutes, he continued in a calmer voice, though a little saliva still foamed at the corner of his lips.

"It is nothing. It is over. Understand me, my child. I am a little of a maniac. At my age that is allowed, is it not? For instance, I do not think it proper that a woman should black her own shoes, much less mine. I have a great respect for women, Marie, and cannot endure that. So I will black your shoes, your little shoes, your dear little shoes. I will take care of them. Listen to me. Every evening, before going to bed, you will carry your shoes into my room; you will place them near the bed, on a little table, and every morning, on coming to open my windows, you will take them away again."

And, as I manifested a prodigious astonishment, he added:

"Oh! now, it is nothing enormous that I ask of you; it is a very natural thing, after all. And if you are very nice" . . .

Quickly he took from his pocket two louis, which he handed to me.

"If you are very nice, very obedient, I will often make you little presents. The governess will pay you your wages every month. But between ourselves, Marie, I shall often make you little presents. And what is it that I ask of you? Come, now, it is not extraordinary. Is it, then, indeed, so extraordinary?"

Monsieur was getting excited again. As he spoke his eyelids rapidly rose and fell, like leaves in a tempest.

"Why do you say nothing, Marie? Say something. Why do you not walk? Walk a little, that I may see them move, that I may see them live,—your little shoes."

13

He knelt down, kissed my shoes, kneaded them with his feverish and caressing fingers, unlaced them. And, while kissing, kneading, and caressing them, he said, in a supplicating voice, in the voice of a weeping child.

"Oh! Marie, Marie, your little shoes; give them to me directly, directly, directly. I want them directly. Give them to me."

I was powerless. Astonishment had paralyzed me. I did not know whether I was really living or dreaming. On Monsieur's eyes I saw nothing but two little white globes streaked with red. And his mouth was all daubed with a sort of soapy foam.

At last he took my shoes away and shut himself up with them in his room for two hours.

"Monsieur is much pleased with you," said the governess to me, in showing me over the house. "Try to continue to please him. The place is a good one."

Four days later, in the morning, on going at the usual hour. to open the windows, I came near fainting with horror in the chamber. Monsieur was dead. Stretched on his back in the middle of the bed, he lay with all the rigidity of a corpse. He had not struggled. The bed-clothing was not disarranged. There was not the slightest trace of shock, of agony, of clinched hands striving to strangle Death. And I should have thought him asleep, if his face had not been violet, frightfully violet, the sinister violet of the egg-plant. And,— terrifying spectacle, which, still more than this face, caused me to quake with fear,—Monsieur held, pressed between his teeth, one of my shoes, so firmly pressing between his teeth that, after useless and horrible efforts, I was obliged to cut the leather with a razor, in order to tear it from him.

I am no saint; I have known many men, and I know, by experience, all the madness, all the vileness, of which they are capable. But a man like Monsieur? Oh! indeed, is it not

14

ridiculous all the same that such types exist? And where do they go in search of all their conceits, when it is so simple and so good to love each other prettily, as other people do?

I do not think that anything of that kind will happen to me here. Here, evidently, they are of another sort. But is it better? Is it worse? As to that, I know nothing.

There is one thing that torments me. I ought, perhaps, to have finished, once for all, with all these dirty places, and squarely taken the step from domesticity into gallantry, like so many others that I have known, and who—I say it without pride—had fewer "advantages" than I. Though I am not what is called pretty, I am better; without conceit I may say that I have an atmosphere, a style, which many society women and many women of the *demi-monde* have often envied me. A little tall, perhaps, but supple, slender, and well-formed, with very beautiful blonde hair, very beautiful deep-blue eyes, an audacious mouth, and, finally, an original manner and a turn of mind, very lively and languishing at once, that pleases men. I might have succeeded. But, in addition to the fact that, by my own fault, I have missed some astonishing opportunities, which probably will never come to me again, I have been afraid. I have been afraid, for one never knows where that will lead you. I have rubbed against so many miseries in that sphere of life; I have received so many distressing confidences. And those tragic calvaries from the Depot to the Hospital, which one does not always escape! And, for a background to the picture, the hell of Saint-Lazare! Such things cause one to reflect and shudder. Who knows, too, whether I should have had, as woman, the same success that I have had as chambermaid? The particular charm which we exercise over men does not lie solely in ourselves, however pretty we may be. It depends largely, as I have had occasion to know, on our environment, on the luxury and vice of our surroundings, on our mistresses themselves and on the desire which they excite. In loving us, it is a little of them and much of their mystery that men love in us.

But there is something else. In spite of my disolute life, I have luckily preserved, in the depths of my being, a very sincere religious feeling, which saves me from definitive falls and holds me back at the edge of the worst abysses. Ah! if there were no religion; if, on evenings of gloom and moral distress, there were no prayer in the churches; if it were not for the Holy Virgin, and Saint Anthony of Padua, and all the rest of the outfit,—we should be much more unhappy, that is sure. And what would become of us, and how far we should go, the devil only knows!

Finally,—and this is more serious,—I have not the least defence against men. I should be the constant victim of my disinterestedness and their pleasure. I am too amourous,—yes, I am too much in love with love, to draw any profit whatever out of love. It is stronger than I; I cannot ask money of one who gives me happiness and sets ajar for me the radiant gates of Ecstasy.

So here I am, then, at the Priory, awaiting what? Indeed, I do not know. The wisest way would be not to think about it, and trust everything to luck. Perhaps it is thus that things go best. Provided that to-morrow, and pursued even here by that pitiless mischance which never leaves me, I am not forced once more to quit my place. That would annoy me. For some time I have had pains in my loins, a feeling of weariness in my whole body; my stomach is becoming impaired, my memory is weakening; I am growing more irritable and nervous. Just now, when looking in the glass, I discovered that my face had a really tired look, and that my complexion—that amber complexion of which I was so proud—had taken on an almost ashen hue. Can I be growing old already? I do not wish to grow old yet. In Paris it is difficult to take care of one's self. There is no time for anything. Life there is too feverish, too tumultuous; one comes continually in contact with too many people, too many things, too many pleasures, too much of the unexpected. But you have to go on, just the same. Here it is calm. And what silence! The air that one breathes must be healthy and good. Ah! if, at the risk of being bored, I could but rest a little.

In the first place, I have no confidence. Certainly Madame is nice enough with me. She has seen fit to pay me compliments on my appearance, and to congratulate herself on the reports that she has received concerning me. Oh! her head, if she knew that these reports are false, or at least that they were given simply to oblige! What especially astonishes her is my elegance. And then, as a rule, they are nice the first day, these camels. While all is new, all is beautiful. That is a well-known song. Yes, and the next day the air changes into another one equally well known. Especially as Madame has very cold hard eyes, which do not please me,—the eyes of a miser, full of keen suspicion and spying inquiry. Nor do I like her dry and too thin lips, which seem to be covered with a whitish crust, or her curt, cutting speech, which turns an amiable word almost into an insult or a humiliation. When, in questioning me concerning this or that, concerning my aptitudes and my past, she looked at me with that tranquil and sly impudence of an old customs official which they all have, I said to myself:

"There is no mistake about it. Here is another one who is bound to put everything under lock and key, to count every evening her grapes and her lumps of sugar, and to put marks on the bottles. Oh! yes, indeed, we change and change, but we find always the same thing."

Nevertheless, it will be necessary to see, and not rely on this first impression. Among so many mouths that have spoken to me, among so many looks that have searched my soul, I shall find perhaps, some day, — who knows? — a friendly mouth, a sympathetic look. It costs me nothing to hope.

As soon as I had arrived, still under the deadening in-

fluence of four hours in a third-class railway carriage, and before any one in the kitchen had even thought of offering me a
slice of bread, Madame took me over the house, from cellar to
garret, in order to immediately familiarize me with my duties.
Oh! she does not waste her time, or mine. How big this house
is! And how many things and corners it contains! Oh! no,
thank you, to keep it in order as it should be, four servants
would not suffice. Besides the ground floor, which in itself is
very important,—for there are two little pavilions, in the form
of a terrace, which constitute additions and continuations,—it
has two stories, in which I shall have to be forever going up
and down, since Madame, who stays in a little room near the
dining-room, has had the ingenious idea of placing the linen-
room, where I am to work, at the top of the house, by the side
of our chambers. And cupboards, and bureaus, and drawers,
and store-rooms, and litters of all sorts,—if you like these things,
there are plenty of them. Never shall I find myself in all this.

At every minute, in showing me something, Madame said to
me:

"You will have to be careful about this, my girl. This is
very pretty, my girl. This is very rare, my girl. This is very
expensive, my girl."

She could not, then, call me by my name, instead of saying
all the time, "My girl," this "My girl," that, in that tone of
wounding domination which discourages the best wills and
straightway puts such a distance, so much hatred, between our
mistresses and us? Do I call her "little mother"? And then
Madame has always on her lips the words "very expensive."
It is provoking. Everything that belongs to her, even paltry
articles that cost four sous, are "very expensive." One has
no idea where the vanity of the mistress of a house can hide
itself. It is really pitiful. In explaining to me the working of
an oil lamp, which in no way differed from all other lamps,
she said to me:

"My girl, you know that this lamp is very expensive, and

that it can be repaired only in England. Take care of it, as if it were the apple of your eye.''

Oh! the cheek that they have, and the fuss that they make about nothing! And when I think that it is all done just to humiliate you, to astonish you!

And the house is not so much after all. There is really no reason to be so proud of it. The exterior, to be sure, with the great clusters of trees that sumptuously frame it and the gardens that descend to the river in gentle slopes, ornamented with broad rectangular lawns, gives an impression of some importance. But within it is sad, old, rickety, and has a musty smell. I do not understand how they can live in it. Nothing but rats' nests, break-neck wooden stairways, whose warped steps tremble and creak beneath your feet; low and dark passage-ways, whose floors, instead of being covered with soft carpets, consist of badly-laid tiles, of a faded red color, and glazed, glazed, slippery, slippery. The too thin partitions, made of too dry planks, make the chambers as sonorous as the inside of a violin. Oh! it is all hollow and provincial. It surely is not furnished in the Paris fashion. In all the rooms old mahogany, old worm-eaten stuffs, old worn-out faded rugs, and arm-chairs and sofas, ridiculously stiff, without springs, worm-eaten, and rickety. How they must grind one's shoulders! Really, I, who am so fond of light-colored hangings, broad elastic divans, where one can stretch voluptuously on heaps of cushions, and all these pretty modern furnishings, so luxurious, so rich, and so gay,—I feel utterly saddened by the gloomy sadness of these. And I am afraid that I shall never get accustomed to such an absence of comfort, to such a lack of elegance, to so much old dust and so many dead forms.

Nor is Madame dressed in Parisian fashion. She is lacking in style, and is unacquainted with the great dressmakers. She is somewhat of a fright, as they say. Although she shows a certain pretension in her costumes, she is at least ten years behind

19

CELESTINE

the fashion. And what a fashion! Still, she would not be bad-
looking, if she chose not to be; at least, she would not be too
bad-looking. Her worst fault is that she awakens in you no
sympathy,—that she is a woman in nothing. But she has regular features, pretty hair naturally blonde, and a beautiful skin;
in fact, she has too much color, as if she were suffering from
some internal malady. I know this type of woman, and I
am not to be deceived by the brilliancy of their complexion.
They are pink on the surface, yes, but within they are rotten.
They cannot stand up straight, they cannot walk, they cannot
live, except by the aid of girdles, trusses, pessaries, and a whole
collection of secret horrors and complex mechanisms. Which
does not prevent them from making a show in society. Yes.
indeed, they are coquettish, if you please; they flirt in the corners, they exhibit their painted flesh, they ogle, they wiggle;
and yet they are fit for nothing but preservation in alcohol.
Oh! misfortune! One has but little satisfaction with them, I
assure you, and it is not always agreeable to be in their service.

I do not know whether it is from temperament or from or-
ganic indisposition, but, judging from the expression of
Madame's face, her severe gestures, and the stiff bending of
her body, she cares nothing at all for love. She has the sharp-
ness and sourness of an old maid, and her whole person seems
dried up and mummified,—a rare thing with blondes. Not
such women as Madame does beautiful music, like that of
"Faust",—oh! that "Faust"!—cause to fall with languor and
swoon voluptuously in the arms of a handsome man. Oh, no
indeed! She does not belong to that class of very ugly women
into whose faces the ardor of sex sometimes puts so much of
radiant life, so much of seductive beauty. After all, though,
one cannot trust too securely in airs like those of Madame. I
have known women of the most severe and crabbed type, who
drove away all thought of desire and love, and who yet were
famous rovers.

Although Madame forces herself to be amiable, she surely

20

is not up to date, like some that I have seen. I believe her to be very wicked, very spying, very fault-finding,—a dirty character and a wicked heart. She must be continually at people's heels, pestering them in all ways. "Do you know how to do this?" and "Do you know how to do that?" or again: "Are you in the habit of breaking things? Are you careful? Have you a good memory? Are you orderly?" There is no end to it. And also: "Are you clean? I am very particular about cleanliness; I pass over many things, but I insist upon cleanliness." Does she take me for a farm girl, a peasant, a country servant? Cleanliness? Oh! I know that chestnut. They all say that. And often, when one goes to the bottom of things, when one turns up their skirts and examines their linen, how filthy they are! Sometimes it is disgusting enough to turn one's stomach.

Consequently I distrust Madame's cleanliness. When she showed me her dressing-room, I did not notice any bath, or any of the things that are necessary to a woman who takes proper care of herself. And what a scant supply she has of *bibelots*, bottles, and all those private and perfumed articles with which I am so fond of messing! I long, for the sake of amusement, to see Madame naked. She must be a pretty sight.

In the evening, as I was setting the table, Monsieur entered the dining-room. He had just returned from a hunt. He is a very tall man, with broad shoulders, a heavy black moustache, and a dull complexion. His manners are a little heavy and awkward, but he seems good-natured. Evidently he is not a man of genius, like M. Jules Lemaître, whom I have so often served in the Rue Christophe-Colomb, or a man of elegance, like M. de Janzé. Ah, M. Janzé! There was a man for you! Yet he is sympathetic. His thick and curly hair, his bull neck, his calves that look like a wrestler's, his thick, intensely red, and smiling lips, testify to his strength and good humor. He is not indifferent. That I saw directly from his mobile, sniffing, sensual nose, and from his extremely brilliant eyes, which are at once gentle and fun-loving. Never, I think, have I met a human being with such eyebrows, thick to the point of obscenity, and with so hairy hands. Like most men of little intelligence and great muscular development, he is very timid.

He surveyed me with a very queer air, an air in which there was kindness, surprise, and satisfaction,—something also of salaciousness, but without impudence, something of an undressing look, but without brutality. It is evident that Monsieur is not accustomed to such chambermaids as I, that I astonish him, and that I have made a great impression on him at the start. He said to me, with a little embarrassment:

"Ah, Ah! So you are the new chambermaid?"

I bent forward, slightly lowered my eyes, and then, modest and mutinous at once, I answered simply, in my gentlest voice:

"Why, yes, Monsieur."

Then he stammered:

"So you have come? That's very good, that's very good."

He would have liked to say something further,—was trying, indeed, to think of something to say,—but, being neither eloquent or at his ease, he did not find anything. I was greatly amused at his embarrassment. But, after a short silence, he asked:

"You come from Paris, like that?"

"Yes, Monsieur."

"That's very good, that's very good."

And growing bolder:

"What is your name?"

"Célestine, Monsieur."

He rubbed his hands,—a mannerism of his,—and went on:

"Célestine. Ah! Ah! that's very good. Not a common name; in fact, a pretty name. Provided Madame does not oblige you to change it. She has that mania."

I answered, in a tone of dignified submission:

"I am at Madame's disposition."

"Undoubtedly, undoubtedly. But it is a pretty name."

I almost burst out laughing. Monsieur began to walk up and down the room; then, suddenly, he sat down in a chair, stretched out his legs, and, putting into his look something like an apology, and into his voice something like a prayer, he asked:

"Well, Célestine,—for my part, I shall always call you Célestine,—will you help me to take off my boots? That does not annoy you, I hope."

"Certainly not, Monsieur."

"Because, you see, these confounded boots are very difficult to manage; they come off very hard."

With a movement that I tried to make harmonious and supple, and even provocative, I knelt before him, and, while I was helping him to take off his boots, which were damp and covered with mud, I was perfectly conscious that the perfumes of my neck were exciting his nose, and that his eyes were following with increasing interest the outlines of my form as seen through my gown. Suddenly he murmured:

"Great heavens! Célestine, but you smell good."

Without raising my eyes, I assumed an air of innocence:

"I, Monsieur?"

"Surely, you; it can hardly be my feet."

"Oh, Monsieur?"

And this "Oh! Monsieur!" at the same time that it was a protest in favor of his feet, was also a sort of friendly reprimand, — friendly to the point of encouragement, — for his familiarity. Did he understand? I think so, for again, with more force, and even with a sort of amorous trembling, he repeated:

"Célestine, you smell awfully good,—awfully good."

Ah! but the old gentleman is making free. I appeared as if slightly scandalized by his insistence, and kept silence. Timid as he is, and knowing nothing of the tricks of women, Monsieur was disturbed. He feared undoubtedly that he had gone too far, and suddenly changing his idea, he asked:

"Are you getting accustomed to the place, Célestine?"

That question? Was I getting accustomed to the place? And I had been there but three hours. I had to bite my lips to keep from laughing. The old gentleman has queer ways; and, really, he is a little stupid.

But that makes no difference. He does not displease me. In his very vulgarity he reveals a certain power and masculinity which are not disagreeable to me.

When his boots had been taken off, and to leave him with a good impression of me, I asked him, in my turn:

"I see Monsieur is a hunter. Has Monsieur had a good hunt today?"

"I never have good hunts, Célestine," he answered, shaking his head. "I hunt for the sake of walking,—for the sake of riding,—that I may not be here, where I find it tiresome."

"Ah! Monsieur finds it tiresome here?"

After a pause, he gallantly corrected himself.

"That is to say, I did find it tiresome. For now, you see, it is different."

Then, with a stupid and moving smile:

"Célestine?"

"Monsieur."

"Will you get me my slippers? I ask your pardon."

"But, Monsieur, it is my business."

"Yes, to be sure; they are under the stairs, in a little dark closet, at the left."

I believe that I shall get all that I want of this type. He is not shrewd; he surrenders at the start. Ah! one could lead him far.

The dinner, not very luxurious, consisting of the leavings from the day before, passed off without incident, almost silently. Monsieur devours, and Madame picks fastidiously at the dishes with sullen gestures and disdainful mouthings. But she absorbs powders, syrups, drops, pills, an entire pharmacy which you have to be very careful to place on the table, at every meal, beside her plate. They talked very little, and what they did say concerned local matters and people of little or no interest to me. But I gathered that they have very little company. Moreover, it was plain that their thoughts were not on what they were saying. They were watching me, each according to the ideas that prompted him or her, each moved by a different curiosity; Madame, severe and stiff, contemptuous even, more and more hostile, and dreaming already of all the dirty tricks that she would play me; Monsieur, slyly, with very significant winks, and, although he tried to conceal them, with strange looks at my hands. Really, I don't know what there is about my hands that so excites men. For my part, I seemed to be taking no notice of their game. I went and came with dignity, reserved, adroit, and distant. Ah! if they could have seen my soul, if they could have heard my soul, as I saw and heard theirs!

I adore waiting on table. It is there that one surprises one's masters in all the filthiness, in all the baseness of their inner natures. Prudent at first, and watchful of each other, little by little they reveal themselves, exhibit themselves as they are, without paint and without veils, forgetting that some one is hovering around them, listening and noting their defects, their moral humps, the secret sores of their existence, and all the infamies and ignoble dreams that can be contained in the respectable brains of respectable people. To collect these confessions, to classify them, to label them in our memory, for use as a terrible weapon on the day of settlement, is one of the great and intense joys of our calling, and the most precious revenge for our humiliations.

From this first contact with my new masters I have obtained no precise and formal indications. But I feel that things do not go well here, that Monsieur is nothing in the house, that Madame is everything, that Monsieur trembles before Madame like a little child. Oh! he hasn't a merry time of it, the poor man! Surely he sees, hears, and suffers all sorts of things. I fancy that I shall get some amusement out of it, at times. At dessert, Madame, who, during the meal, had been continually sniffing at my hands, my arms, and my waist, said, in a clear and cutting tone:

"I do not like the use of perfumes."

As I did not answer, pretending to ignore the fact that the remark was addressed to me, she added:

"Do you hear, Célestine?"

"Very well, Madame."

Then I looked stealthily at poor Monsieur, who likes perfumes, or who at least likes my perfume. With his elbows on the table, apparently indifferent, but really humiliated and distressed, he was following the flight of a wasp which had been lingering over a plate of fruit. And there was now a dismal silence in this dining-room, which the twilight had just invaded, and something inexpressibly sad, something unspeakably heavy, fell from the ceiling on these two beings, concerning whom I really asked myself of what use they are and what they are doing on earth.

"The lamp, Célestine."

It was Madame's voice, sharper than ever in the silence and the shade. It made me start.

"Do you not see that it is dark? I should not have to ask you for the lamp. Let it be the last time."

While lighting the lamp,—this lamp which can be repaired only in England,—I had a strong desire to cry out to poor Monsieur:

"Just wait a little, my old man, and fear nothing, and don't distress yourself. You shall eat and drink the perfumes that you so love, and of which you are so deprived. You shall breathe them, I promise you; you shall breathe them in my hair, my lips, on my neck. And the two of us will lead this blockhead a merry dance, I answer for it."

And, to emphasize this silent invocation, I took care, as I

placed the lamp upon the table, to slightly brush against Monsieur's arm, and I went out.

The servants' hall is not gay. Besides myself, there are only two domestics,—a cook, who is always scolding, and a gardener-coachman, who never says a word. The cook's name is Marianne; that of the gardener-coachman, Joseph. Stupid peasants. And what heads they have! She, fat, soft, flabby, sprawling, a neck emerging in a triple cushion from a dirty neckerchief which looks as if she wiped her kettles with it, two enormous and shapeless breasts rolling beneath a sort of blue cotton camisole covered with grease, her too short dress disclosing thick ankles and big feet encased in grey woolen; he, in shirt-sleeves, work-apron, and wooden shoes, shaven, dry, nervous, with an evil grimace on his lips which stretch from ear to ear, and a devious gait, the sly movements of a sacristan. Such are my two companions.

No dining-room for the servants. We take our meals in the kitchen, at the same table where, during the day, the cook does her dirty work, carves her meats, cleans her fish, and cuts up her vegetables, with fingers fat and round as sausages. Really, that is scarcely proper. The fire in the stove renders the atmosphere of the room stifling; odors of old grease, of rancid sauces, of continual fryings, circulate in the air. While we eat, a kettle in which the dogs' soup is boiling exhales a fetid vapor that attacks your throat and makes you cough. One almost vomits. More respect is shown for prisoners in their cells and dogs in their kennels.

We had bacon and cabbage, and stinking cheese; for drink, sour cider. Nothing else. Earthen plates, with cracked enamel, and which smell of burnt grease, and tin forks, complete this pretty service.

Being too new in the house, I did not wish to complain. But neither did I wish to eat. Do further damage to my stomach, no, thank you!

27

"Why don't you eat?" asked the cook.

"I am not hungry."

I uttered this in a very dignified tone; then Marianne grunted:

"Perhaps Mademoiselle must have truffles?"

Without showing anger, but with a stiff and haughty air, I replied:

"Why, you know, I have eaten truffles. Not everybody here can say as much."

That shut her up.

Meantime the gardener-coachman was filling his mouth with big pieces of bacon and examining me stealthily. I cannot say why, but this man has an embarrassing look, and his silence troubles me. Although he is no longer young, I am astonished at the suppleness and elasticity of his movements; the undulations of his loins are reptilian. Let me describe him in greater detail. His stiff, grizzled hair, his low forehead, his oblique eyes, his prominent cheek-bones, his broad, strong jaw, and his long, fleshy, turned-up chin, give him a strange character that I cannot define. Is he a simpleton? Is he a rascal? I cannot tell. Yet it is curious that this man holds my attention as he does. After a time this obsession lessens and disappears. And I realize that this is simply another of the thousands and thousands of tricks of my excessive, magnifying, and romantic imagination, which causes me to see things and people as too beautiful or as too ugly, and which compels me to make of this miserable Joseph a being superior to the stupid country-man, to the heavy peasant that he really is.

Towards the end of the dinner, Joseph, still without saying a word, took from his apron-pocket the "Libre Parole," and began to read it attentively, and Marianne, softened by having drunk two full decanters of cider, became more amiable. Sprawling on her chair, her sleeves rolled up and revealing bare arms, her cap set a little awry upon her uncombed hair, she asked me where I came from, where I had been, if I had had good places, and if I was against the Jews. And we talked for some time, in an almost friendly way. In my turn I asked her for information concerning the house, whether many people came and what sort of people, whether Monsieur was attentive to the chambermaids, whether Madame had a lover.

Oh! but you should have seen her head, and that of Joseph, too, whose reading was suddenly interrupted, now and then, by my questions. How scandalized and ridiculous they were! You have no idea how far behind the times they are in the country. They know nothing, they see nothing, they understand nothing; the most natural thing abashes them. And yet, he with his awkward respectability, she with her virtuous disorder, — nothing will get it out of my mind that they are intimate. Oh! indeed, one must really be in a bad way to be satisfied with a type like that.

"It is easy to see that you come from Paris, from I know not where," remarked the cook, in a tone of bitter reproach.

Whereupon Joseph, with a toss of his head, curtly added: "Sure."

And he began to read the "Libre Parole" again. Marianne rose heavily, and took the kettle from the fire. We talked no more.

Then I thought of my last place, of Monsieur Jean, the valet, so distinguished with his black side-whiskers and his white skin, for which he cared as if he were a woman. Ah! he was such a handsome fellow, Monsieur Jean, so gay, so nice, so delicate, so artful, when at night he read aloud to us from the "Fin de Siècle" or told us salacious and touching stories, or familiarized us with the contents of Monsieur's letters. Things have changed to-day. How did I ever come to get stranded here, among such people, and far from everything that I like?

I almost want to cry.

And I am writing these lines in my chamber, a dirty little chamber, at the top of the house, open to all winds, to the winter's cold, to the summer's burning heat. No other furniture than a paltry iron bed and a paltry white-wood wardrobe which does not close and where I have not room enough to arrange my things. No other light than a tallow candle that smokes and runs down into a brass candlestick. It is pitiful. If I wish to continue to write this diary, or even to read the novels that I have brought, or to tell my fortune with the cards, I shall have to buy wax candles with my own money, for, as for Madame's candles,—nit! as Monsieur Jean would say,—they are under lock and key.

To-morrow I will try to get a little settled. Over my bed I will nail my little gilt crucifix, and on the mantel I will place my painted porcelain virgin, together with my little boxes, my bric-à-brac, and the photographs of Monsieur Jean, so as to penetrate this hole with a ray of privacy and joy.

Marianne's room is next to mine. A thin partition separates us, and you can hear everything that goes on. I thought that Joseph, who sleeps in the outbuildings, might visit Marianne to-night. But no. For a long time Marianne turned about in her room, coughing, hawking, dragging chairs, moving a heap of things. Now she is snoring. It is doubtless in the day-time that they have their clandestine meetings.

A dog barks, far away, in the country. It is nearly two o'clock, and my light is going out. I, too, am obliged to go to bed. But I feel that I shall not sleep.

Ah! how old I shall grow in this hovel! Yes, indeed!

II.

I have not yet written a single time the name of my masters. It is a ridiculous and comical name: Lanlaire; Monsieur and Madame Lanlaire. You see at once the plays that can be made on such a name, and the pokes to which it is bound to give rise. As for their Christian names, they are, perhaps, more ridiculous than their surname, and, if I may say so, they complete it. That of Monsieur is Isidore; that of Madame, Euphrasie. Euphrasie! Think of it!

I have just been to the haberdasher's to match some silk. And the woman who keeps the shop has given me some information as to the house. It is not delightful. But, to be just, I must say that I have never met such a chattering jade. If the dealers of whom my masters buy speak in this way of them, what must be said of them by those whom they do not patronize? My! but they have good tongues in the country.

Monsieur's father was a manufacturer of cloths, and a banker, at Louviers. He went into a fraudulent bankruptcy that emptied all the little purses of the region, and was condemned to ten years' imprisonment, which, in view of the forgeries, abuses of confidence, thefts, and crimes of all sorts, that he had committed, was deemed a very light sentence. While he was serving his time at Gaillon, he died. But he had taken care to put aside, and in a safe place, it seems, four hundred and fifty thousand francs which, artfully withheld from the ruined creditors, constitute Monsieur's entire personal fortune. Ah! you see, it is no trick at all to be rich.

Madame's father was much worse, although he was never sentenced to imprisonment, and departed this life respected by all the respectable people. He was a dealer in men. The haberdasher explained to me that, under Napoleon III, when everybody was not obliged to serve in the army, as is the case today, the rich young men who were drawn by lot for service had the right to send a substitute. They applied to an agency or to a Monsieur who, in consideration of a premium varying from one to two thousand francs, according to the risks at the time, found them a poor devil, who consented to take their place in the regiment for seven years, and in case of war, to die for them. Thus was carried on in France the trade in whites, as in Africa the trade in blacks. There were men-markets, like cattle-markets, but for a more horrible butchery. That does not greatly astonish me. Are there, then, none to-day? What, I should like to know, are the employment-bureaus and the public houses, if not slave-fairs, butcher-shops for the sale of human meat?

According to the haberdasher, it was a very lucrative business, and Madame's father, who had a monopoly of it for the entire department, showed great skill in it,—that is to say, he kept for himself and put in his pocket the larger part of the premium. Ten years ago he died, mayor of Mesnil-Roy, substitute justice of the peace, councillor-general, president of the board of vestrymen, treasurer of the charity bureau, decorated, and leaving, in addition to the Priory, which he had bought for nothing, twelve hundred thousand francs, of which six hundred thousand went to Madame,—for Madame has a brother who has gone to the bad, and they do not know what has become of him. Well, say what you will, that is money that can hardly be called clean, if, indeed, there be any clean money. For my part, it is very simple; I have seen nothing but dirty money and wicked wealth.

The Lanlaires—is it not enough to disgust you?—have, then, more than a million. They do nothing but economize, and they spend hardly a third of their income. Curtailing everything, depriving others and themselves, haggling bitterly over bills, denying their words, recognizing no agreements save those that are written and signed, one must keep an eye on them, and in business affairs never open the door for any dispute whatever. They immediately take advantage of it, to avoid payment, especially with the little dealers who cannot afford the costs of a lawsuit, and the poor devils who are defenceless. Naturally, they never give anything, except from time to time to the church, for they are very pious. As for the poor, they may die of hunger before the door of the Priory, imploring and wailing. The door remains always closed.

"I even believe," said the haberdasher, "that, if they could take something from the beggar's sack, they would do it remorselessly, with a savage joy."

And she added, by way of a monstrous example:

"All of us here who earn our living with difficulty, when giving hallowed bread, buy cake for the purpose. It is a point of propriety and pride. They, the dirty misers, they distribute,—what? Bread, my dear young woman. And not first-class bread at that, not even white bread. No, workman's bread. Why, one day the wife of Paumier, the cooper, heard Madame Lanlaire say to the priest, who was mildly reproaching her for this avarice: 'Monsieur le curé, that is always good enough for these people.'"

One must be just, even with his masters. Though there is only one voice in regard to Madame, they have nothing against Monsieur. They do not detest Monsieur. All agree in declaring that Monsieur is not proud, that he would be generous to people, and would do much good, if he could. The trouble is that he cannot. Monsieur is nothing in his own house,—less than the servants, badly treated as they are, less than the cat, to whom everything is allowed. Little by little, and for the sake of tranquillity, he has abrogated all his authority as master of the house, all his dignity as a man, into the hands of his wife. Madame directs, regulates, organizes, administers everything. Madame attends to the stable, to the yard, to the garden, to the cellar, and to the woodhouse, and is sure to find something amiss everywhere. Never do things go to her liking, and she continually pretends that they are being robbed. What an eye she has! It is inconceivable. They play her no tricks, be sure, for she knows them all. She pays the bills, collects the dividends and rents, and makes the bargains. She has the devices of an old bookkeeper, the indelicacies of a corrupt process-server, the ingenious strategy of a usurer. It is incredible. Of course, she holds the purse, and ferociously; and she never loosens the strings, except to let in more money. She leaves Monsieur without a sou; the poor man has hardly enough to buy his tobacco. In the midst of his wealth, he is even more destitute than the rest of us here. However, he does not balk; he never balks. He obeys like the comrades. Oh! how queer he is at times, with his air of a tired and submissive dog! When, Madame being out, there comes a dealer with a bill, a poor man with his poverty, a messenger who wants a tip, you ought to see Monsieur. Monsieur is really a comical sight. He fumbles in his pockets, gropes about, blushes, apologizes, and says, with a sorrowful face:

"Why, I have no change about me. I have only thousand-franc bills. Have you change for a thousand francs? No? Then you will have to call again."

Thousand-franc bills, he, who never has a hundred sous about him. Even his letter-paper Madame keeps locked in a closet, of which she holds the key, and she gives it out to him sheet by sheet, grumbling:

"Thank you, but you use a tremendous amount of paper. To whom, then, can you be writing that you use so much?"

The only thing that they reproach him with, the only thing that they do not understand, is the undignified weakness in consequence of which he allows himself to be led in this way by such a shrew. For no one is ignorant of the fact—indeed, Madame shouts it from the house-top — that Monsieur and Madame are no longer anything to each other. Madame, who has some internal disease and can have no children, will not allow him to approach her.

"Then," asked the haberdasher, in finishing her conversation, "why is Monsieur so good and so cowardly toward a woman who denies him not only money, but pleasure? I would bring him to his senses, and rudely, too."

And this is what happens. When Monsieur, who is a vigorous man, and who is also a kindly man, wishes to enjoy himself away from home, or to bestow a little charity upon a poor man, he is reduced to ridiculous expedients, to clumsy excuses, to not very dignified loans, the discovery of which by Madame brings on terrible scenes,—quarrels that often last for months. Then Monsieur is seen going off through the fields, walking, walking, like a madman, making furious and threatening gestures, crushing the turf beneath his feet, talking to himself, in the wind, in the rain, in the snow; and then coming back at night more timid, more bowed, more trembling, more conquered than ever.

The curious, and also the melancholy, part of the matter is that, amid the worst recriminations of the haberdasher, among these unveiled infamies, this shameful vileness, which is hawked from mouth to mouth, from shop to shop, from house to house, it is evident that the jealousy of the town's-people toward the Lanlaires is even greater than their contempt for them. In spite of their criminal uselessness, of their social wrong-doing, in spite of all that they crush under the weight of their hideous million, this million none the less surrounds them with a halo of respectability, and almost of glory. The people bow lower to them than to others, and receive them more warmly than others. They call — with what fawning civility!—the dirty hovel in which they live in the filth of their soul, the château. To strangers coming to inquire concerning the curiosities of the region I am sure that the haberdasher herself, hateful though she is, would answer:

"We have a beautiful church, a beautiful fountain, and,

above all, we have something else very beautiful,—the Lanlaires, who posses a million and live in a château. They are frightful people, and we are very proud of them."

The worship of the million! It is a low sentiment, common not only to the *bourgois,* but to most of us also,—the little, the humble, the penniless of this world. And I myself, with my frank ways and my threats to break everything, even I am not free from this. I, whom wealth oppresses; I, who owe to it my sorrows, my vices, my hatreds, the bitterest of my humiliations, and my impossible dreams, and the perpetual torment of my life,—well, as soon as I find myself in presence of a rich man, I cannot help looking upon him as an exceptional and beautiful being, as a sort of marvellous divinity, and, in spite of myself, surmounting my will and my reason, I feel rising, from the depths of my being, toward this rich man, who is very often an imbecile, and sometimes a murderer, something like an incense of admiration. Is it not stupid? And why? Why?

On leaving this dirty haberdasher, and this strange shop, where, by the way, it was impossible for me to match my silk, I reflected with discouragement upon all that this woman had told me about my masters. It was drizzling. The sky was as dirty as the soul of this dealer in pinchbeck. I slipped along the slimy pavement of the street, and, furious against the haberdasher and against my masters, and against myself, furious against this country sky, against this mud, in which my heart and my feet were splashing, against the incurable sadness of the little town, I kept on repeating to myself:

"Well, here is a clean place for you! I had seen everything but this. A nice hole I have fallen into!"

Ah! yes, a nice hole indeed! And here is something more.

Madame dresses herself all alone, and does her own hair. She locks herself securely in her dressing-room, and it is with difficulty that I can obtain an entrance. God knows what she does in there for hours and hours! This evening, unable to restrain myself, I knocked at the door squarely. And here is the little conversation that ensued between Madame and myself:

"Tac, tac!"

"Who is there?"

Ah! that sharp, shrill voice, which one would like to force back into her throat with one's fist!

"It is I, Madame."

"What do you want?"

"I come to do the dressing-room."

"It is done. Go away. And come only when I ring for you."

That is to say that I am not even the chambermaid here. I do not know what I am here, and what my duties are. And yet, to dress and undress my mistresses and to do their hair is the only part of my work that I like. I like to play with night-gowns, with dresses and ribbons, to dabble among the linens, the hats, the laces, the furs, to rub my mistresses after the bath, to powder them, to rub their feet with pumice-stone, to perfume their breasts, to oxygenize their hair, to know them, in short, from the tips of their slippers to the peak of their chignon, to see them all naked. In this way they become for you something else than a mistress, almost a friend or an accomplice, often a slave. One inevitably becomes the confidant of a heap of things, of their pains, of their vices, of their disappointments in love, of the inner secrets of the household, of their diseases. To say nothing of the fact that, when one is adroit, one holds them by a multitude of details which they do not even suspect. One gets much more out of them. It is at once profitable and amusing. That is how I understand the work of a chambermaid.

You cannot imagine how many there are—how shall I say that?—how many there are who are indecent and lewd in their privacy, even among those who, in society, pass for the most reserved and the most strict, and whose virtue is supposed to be unassailable. Ah! in the dressing-rooms how the masks fall! How the proudest fronts crack and crumble!

Well, what am I going to do here? In this country hole, with an impertinent minx like my new mistress, I have no favors to dream of, no distractions to hope for. I shall do stupid housework, wearisome sewing, and nothing else. Ah! when I remember the places where I have served, that makes my situation still sadder, more intolerably sad. And I have a great desire to go away,—to make by bow once for all of this country of savages.

Just now I met Monsieur on the stairs. He was starting for a hunt. Monsieur looked at me with a salacious air. Again he asked me:

"Well, Célestine, are you getting accustomed to the place?"

Decidedly, it is a mania with him. I answered:

"I do not know yet, Monsieur."

Then, with effrontery:

"And Monsieur, is he getting accustomed here?"

Monsieur burst out laughing. Monsieur takes a joke well. Monsieur is really good-natured.

"You must get accustomed, Célestine. You must be accustomed. *Sapristi!*"

I was in a humor for boldness. Again I answered:

"I will try, Monsieur,—with Monsieur's aid."

I think that Monsieur was going to say something very stiff to me. His eyes shone like two coals. But Madame appeared at the top of the stairs. Monsieur was off in his direction, I in mine. It was a pity.

This evening, through the door of the *salon*, I heard Madame saying to Monsieur, in the amiable tone that you can imagine:

"I wish no familiarity with my servants."

Her servants? Are not Madame's servants Monsieur's servants. Well, indeed!

38

III.

September 18.

This morning (Sunday) I went to mass.

I have already declared that, without being pious, I have religion all the same. Say and do what you like, religion is always religion. The rich, perhaps, can get along without it, but it is necessary for people like us. I know very well that there are individuals who make use of it in a rather queer fashion,—that many priests and good sisters scarcely do it honor. But never mind. When one is unhappy,—and, in our calling, we get more than our share of unhappiness,—it is the only thing that will soothe you. Only that, and love. Yes, but love, that is another sort of consolation. Consequently, even in impious houses, I never missed mass. In the first place, mass is an excursion, a distraction, time gained from the daily ennui of the household. And, above all, we meet comrades, hear stories, and form acquaintances. Ah! if, on going out of the chapel of the Assumptionists, I had wished to listen to the good-looking old gentleman who whispered psalms of a curious sort in my ears, perhaps I should not be here today.

To-day the weather is improved. There is a beautiful sun, —one of those misty suns that make walking agreeable and sadness less burdensome. I know not why, but, under the influence of this blue and gold morning, I have something like gaiety in my heart.

We are about a mile from the church. The way leading to it is a pleasant one,—a little path winding between hedges. In spring it must be full of flowers, wild cherry trees, and the hawthorns that smell so good. I love the hawthorns. They remind me of things when I was a little girl. Otherwise the country is like the country everywhere else; there is nothing

39

astonishing about it. It is a very wide valley, and then, yonder, at the end of the valley, there are hills. In the valley there is a river, on the hills is a forest; all covered with a veil of fog, transparent and gilded, which hides the landscape too much to suit me.

Oddly enough, I keep my fidelity to nature as it is in Brittany. I have it in my blood. Nowhere else does it seem to me as beautiful; nowhere else does it speak better to my soul. Even among the richest and most fertile fields of Normandy I am homesick for the moors, and for that tragic and splendid sea where I was born. And this recollection, suddenly called up, casts a cloud of melancholy into the gaiety of this delightful morning.

On the way I meet women and women. With prayer-books under their arms, they, too, are going to mass,—cooks, chambermaids, and barn-yard scullions, thick-set and clumsy, and with the slow and swaying gait of animals. How queerly they are rigged out, in their holiday garb,—perfect mops. They smell powerfully of the country, and it is easy to see that they have not served in Paris. They look at me with curiosity,—a curiosity at once distrustful and sympathetic. They note enviously, in detail, my hat, my closely-fitting gown, my little baize jacket, and my umbrella rolled in its green silk cover. My costume— that of a lady—astonishes them, and especially, I think, my coquettish and smart way of wearing it. They nudge each other with their elbows, make enormous eyes, and open their mouths immoderately, to show each other my luxury and my style. And I go tripping along, nimbly and lightly, with my pointed shoes, and boldly lifting up my dress, which makes a sound of rustling silk against the skirts beneath. What can you expect? For my part, I am glad to be admired.

As they pass by me, I hear them say to each other, in a whisper:

"That is the new chambermaid at the Priory."

One of them, short, fat, red-faced, asthmatic, and who

seems to have great difficulty in carrying an immense paunch
on legs widely spread apart, undoubtedly to the better steady
it, approaches me with a smile, a thick, glutunous smile on her
glutonous lips:

"You are the new chambermaid at the Priory? Your
name is Célestine? You arrived from Paris four days ago?"

She knows everything already. She is familiar with everything, and with me. And there is nothing about this paunchy
body, about this walking goatskin, that so amuses me as the
musketeer hat,—a large, black, felt hat, whose plumes sway
in the breeze.

She continues:

"My name is Rose, Mam'zelle Rose; I am at M. Mauger's,
the next place to yours; he is a former captain. Perhaps you
have already seen him?"

"No, Mademoiselle."

"You might have seen him over the hedge that separates
the two estates. He is always working in the garden. He is
still a fine man, you know."

We walk more slowly, for Mam'zelle Rose is almost stifling.
She wheezes like a foundered mare. With every breath her
chest expands and contracts, then to expand again. She says,
chopping her words:

"I have one of my attacks. Oh! how people suffer these
days! It is incredible."

Then, between wheezes and hiccoughs, she encourages me:

"You must come and see me, my little one. If you need
anything, good advice, no matter what, do not hesitate. I am
fond of young people. We will drink a little glass of peach
brandy as we talk. Many of these young women come to our
house."

She stops a moment, takes breath, and then, in a lower
voice and a confidential tone, continues:

"And, say, Mademoiselle Célestine, if you wish to have
your letters addressed in our care, it would be more prudent.

41

A bit of good advice that I give you. Madame Lanlaire reads the letters, all the letters. Once she came very near being sentenced for it by the justice of the peace. I repeat, do not hesitate.''

I thank her, and we continue to walk. Although her body pitches and rolls like an old vessel in a heavy sea, Mademoiselle Rose seems now to breathe more easily. And we go on, gossiping:

"Oh! it will be a change for you here, surely. In the first place, my little one, at the Priory they never keep a chambermaid for any length of time. That is a settled manner. When Madame does not discharge them, Monsieur gets them into trouble. A terrible man, Monsieur Lanlaire. The pretty, the ugly, the young, the old,—all are alike to him. Oh! the house is well known. And everybody will tell you what I tell you. You are ill-fed there; you have no liberty; you are crushed with work. And chiding and scolding all the time. A real hell! One needs only to see you, pretty and well brought up as you are, to know, beyond a doubt, that you are not made to stay with such curmudgeons.''

All that the haberdasher told me, Mademoiselle Rose tells me again, with more disagreeable variations. So violent is this woman's passion for chattering that she finally forgets her suffering. Her malice gets the better of her asthma. And the scandal of the house goes its course, mingled with the private affairs of the neighborhood. Although already I know them all, Rose's stories are so black, and her words are so discouraging, that again I am thoroughly saddened. I ask myself if I had not better go at once. Why try an experiment in which I am conquered in advance?

Other women have overtaken us, curious, nosy, accompanying with an energetic ''For sure'' each of the revelations of Rose, who, less and less winded, continues to jabber:

"M. Mauger is a very good man, and all alone, my little one. As much as to say that I am the mistress. Why! a former captain; it is natural, isn't it? He is no manager; he knows nothing of household affairs; he likes to be taken care of and coddled, have his linen well kept, his caprices respected, nice dishes prepared for him. If he had not beside him a person in whom he had confidence, he would be plundered right and left. My God, there is no lack of thieves here!''

The intonation of her spasmodic utterances, and her winks, clearly revealed to me her exact situation in Captain Mauger's house.

''Why, you know, a man all alone, and who still has ideas. And besides, there is work to do all the same. And we are going to hire a boy to assist.''

This Rose is lucky. I, too, have often dreamed of entering an old man's service. It is disgusting. But at least one is tranquil, and has a future.

We traverse the entire district. Oh! indeed, it is not pretty. It in no way resembles the Boulevard Malesherbes. Dirty, narrow, winding streets, and houses that stand neither square or straight,—dark houses, of old, rotten wood, with high, tottering gables, and bulging stories that project one past the other, in the olden fashion. The people who pass are ugly, ugly, and I have not seen a single handsome fellow. The industry of the neighborhood is the manufacture of list-shoes. Most of the shoemakers, having been unable to deliver a week's product at the factory, are still at work. And behind the window-panes I see poor sickly faces, bent backs, and black hands hammering leather soles.

That adds still further to the dismal sadness of the place. It seems like a prison.

But here is the haberdasher, who, standing at her threshold, smiles at us and bows.

''You are going to eight o'clock mass? I went to seven o'clock mass. You have plenty of time. Will you not come in, a moment?''

Rose thanks her. She warns me against the haberdasher,

who is a malicious woman and speaks ill of anybody, a real
pest! Then she begins again to boast of her master's virtues
and of her easy place. I ask her:

"Then the captain has no family?"

"No family?" she cries, scandalized. "Well, my little one,
you are not on. Oh! yes, there is a family, and a nice one,
indeed! Heaps of nieces and cousins, — penniless people,
hangers-on, all of whom were plundering him and robbing him.
You should have seen that. It was an abomination. So you can
imagine whether I set that right,—whether I cleared the house
of all this vermin. Why, my dear young woman, but for me,
the captain now would be on his uppers. Ah! the poor man!
He is well satisfied with the way things are now."

I insist with an ironical intention, which, however, she does
not understand:

"And, undoubtedly, Mademoiselle Rose, he will remember
you in his will?"

Prudently, she replies:

"Monsieur will do as he likes. He is free. Surely I do
not influence him. I ask nothing of him. I do not ask him even
to pay me wages. I stay with him out of devotion. But he
knows life. He knows those who love him, who care for him
with disinterestedness, who coddle him. No one need think
that he is stupid as certain persons pretend,—Madame Lanlaire
at the head, who says things about us. It is she, on the contrary, who is evil-minded, Mademoiselle Célestine, and who has
a will of her own. Depend upon it!"

Upon this eloquent apology for the captain, we arrive at
the church.

The fat Rose does not leave me. She obliges me to take
a chair near hers, and begins to mumble prayers, to make genu-
flections and signs of the cross. Oh! this church! With its
rough timbers that cross it and sustain the staggering vault, it
resembles a barn; with the people in it, coughing, hawking,
running against benches, and dragging chairs around, it seems

also like a village wineshop. I see nothing but faces stupefied by ignorance, bitter mouths contracted by hatred. There are none here but wretched creatures who come to ask God to do something against somebody. It is impossible for me to concentrate my thoughts, and I feel a sort of cold penetrating me and surrounding me. Perhaps it is because there is not even an organ in this church. Queer, isn't it? but I cannot pray without an organ. An anthem on the organ fills my chest, and then my stomach; it completely restores me, like love. If I could always hear the strains of an organ, I really believe that I should never sin. Here, instead of an organ, there is an old woman, in the choir, with blue spectacles, and a poor little black shawl over her shoulders, who painfully drums on a sort of piano, wheezy and out of tune. And the people are always coughing and hawking, the droning of the priest and the responses of the choristers being drowned by a sound of catarrh. And how bad it all smells,—mingled odors of the muck-heap, of the stable, of the soil, of sour straw, of wet leather, of damaged incense. Really, they are very ill-bred in the country.

The mass drags along, and I grow weary. I am especially vexed at finding myself among people so ordinary and so ugly, and who pay so little attention to me. Not a pretty spectacle, not a pretty costume with which to rest my thought or cheer my eyes. Never did I better understand that I am made for the joy of elegance and style. Instead of being lifted up, as at mass in Paris, all my senses take offence, and rebel at once. For distraction, I follow attentively the movements of the officiating priest. Oh! thank you! he is a sort of tall, jovial fellow, very young, with an ordinary face, and a brick-red complexion. With his dishevelled hair, his greedy jaw, his gluttonous lips, his obscene little eyes, and his eyelids circled with black, I have sized him up at once. How he must enjoy himself at the table! And at the confessional, too,—the dirty things that he must say! Rose, perceiving that I am watching him, bends toward me, and says, in a very low voice:

"That is the new vicar. I recommend him to you. There is no one like him to confess the women. The curate is a holy man, certainly, but he is looked upon as too strict. Whereas the new vicar" . . .

She clacks her tongue, and goes back to her prayer, her head bent over the prie-Dieu.

Well, he would not please me, the new vicar; he has a dirty and brutal air; he looks more like a ploughman than a priest. For my part, I require delicacy, poetry, the beyond, and white hands. I like men to be gentle and *chic*, as Monsieur Jean was.

After mass Rose drags me to the grocery store. With a few mysterious words she explained to me that it is necessary to be on good terms with the woman who keeps it, and that all the domestics pay her assiduous court.

Another little dump,—decidedly, this is the country of fat women. Her face is covered with freckles, and, through her thin, light, flaxen hair, which is lacking in gloss, can be seen portions of her skull, on top of which a chignon stands up in a ridiculous fashion, like a little broom. At the slightest movement her breast, beneath her brown cloth waist, shakes like a liquid in a bottle. Her eyes, bordered with red circles, are bloodshot, and her ignoble mouth makes of her every smile a grimace. Rose introduces me:

"Madame Gouin, I bring you the new chambermaid at the Priory."

The grocer observes me attentively, and I notice that her eyes fasten themselves upon my waist with an embarrassing obstinacy. She says in a meaningless voice:

"Mademoiselle is at home here. Mademoiselle is a pretty girl. Mademoiselle is a Parisienne, undoubtedly?"

"It is true, Madame Gouin, I come from Paris."

"That is to be seen; that is to be seen directly. One need not look at you twice. I am very fond of the Parisiennes; they know what it is to live. I too served in Paris, when I was

46

young. I served in the house of a midwife in the Rue Guéné-gaud,—Madame Tripier. Perhaps you know her?"

"No."

"That makes no difference. Oh! it was a long time ago. But come in, Mademoiselle Célestine."

She escorts us, with ceremony, into the back shop, where four other domestics are already gathered about a round table.

"Oh! you will have an anxious time of it, my poor young woman," groaned the grocer, as she offered me a chair. "It is not because they do not patronize me at the château; but I can truly say that it is an infernal house, infernal! Is it not so, Mesdemoiselles?"

"For sure!" answer in chorus, with like gestures and like grimaces, the four domestics thus appealed to.

Madame Gouin continues:

"Oh! thank you, I would not like to sell to people who are continually haggling, and crying out, like polecats, that they are being robbed, that they are being injured. They may go where they like."

The chorus of servants responds:

"Surely they may go where they like."

To which Madame Gouin, addressing Rose more particularly, adds, in a firm tone:

"They do not run after them, do they, Mam'zelle Rose? Thank God! we have no need of them, do we?"

Rose contents herself with a shrug of her shoulders, putting into this gesture all the concentrated gall, spite, and contempt at her command. And the huge musketeer hat emphasizes the energy of these violent sentiments by the disorderly swaying of its black plumes.

Then, after a silence:

"Oh! well, let us talk no more about these people. Every time that I speak of them it turns my stomach."

Thereupon the stories and gossip begin again. An un-interrupted flow of filth is vomited from these sad mouths, as from a sewer. The back-shop seems infected with it. The impression is the more disagreeable because the room is rather dark and the faces take on fantastic deformities. It is lighted only by a narrow window opening on a damp and filthy court, —a sort of shaft formed by moss-eaten walls. An odor of pickle, of rotting vegetables, of red herring, persists around us, impregnating our garments. It is intolerable. Then each of these creatures, heaped up on their chairs like bundles of dirty linen, plunges into the narration of some dirty action, some scandal, some crime. Coward that I am, I try to smile with them, to applaud with them; but I feel something insurmoutable, something like frightful disgust. A nausea turns my stomach, forces its way to my throat, leaves a bad taste in my mouth, and presses my temples. I should like to go away. I cannot, and I remain there, like an idiot, heaped up like them on my chair, making the same gestures that they make,—I remain there, stupidly listening to these shrill voices that sound to me like dish-water gurgling and dripping through sinks and pipes.

I know very well that we have to defend ourselves against our masters, and I am not the last to do it, I assure you. But no; here, all the same, that passes imagination. These women are odious to me. I detest them, and I say to myself, in a low voice, that I have nothing in common with them. Education, contact with stylish people, the habit of seeing beautiful things, the reading of Paul Bourget's novels, have saved me from these turpitudes. Ah! the pretty and amusing monkey-tricks of the servants' halls in Paris,—they are far away!

As we are leaving, the grocer says to me, with an amiable smile:

"Pay no attention to the fact that your masters do not patronize me; you must come and see me again."

I go back with Rose, who finishes familiarizing me with the daily doings of the neighborhood. I had supposed that her stock of infamies was exhausted. Not at all. She discovers and invents new and more frightful ones. In the matter of calumny her resources are infinite. And her tongue goes on forever, without stopping. It does not forget anybody or anything. It is astonishing how, in a few minutes, one can dishonor people, in the country. Thus she escorts me back to the Priory gate. Even there she cannot make up her mind to leave me; talks on, talks incessantly, tries to envelop and stun me with her friendship and devotion. As for me, my head is broken by all that I have heard, and the sight of the Priory fills me with a feeling of discouragement. Ah! these broad, flowerless lawns! And this immense building, that has the air of a barrack or a prison, and where, from behind each window, a pair of eyes seems to be spying you.

The sun is warmer, the fog has disappeared, and the view of the landscape has become clearer. Beyond the plain, on the hills, I perceive little villages, gilded by the light, and enlivened by red roofs. The river running through the plain, yellow and green, shines here and there in silvery curves. And a few clouds decorate the sky with their light and charming frescoes. But I take no pleasure in the contemplation of all this. I have now but one desire, one will, one obsession,—to flee from this sun, from this plain, from these hills, from this house, and from this fat woman, whose malicious voice hurts and tortures me.

At last she gets ready to leave me, takes my hand, and presses it affectionately in her fat fingers gloved with mittens. She says to me:

"And then, my little one, Madame Gouin, you know, is a very amiable and very clever woman. You must go to see her often."

She lingers longer, and adds more mysteriously:

"She has relieved many young girls. As soon as they are in any trouble, they go to her. Neither seen or known. One can trust her, take my word for it. She is a very, very expert woman."

49

With eyes more brilliant, and fastening her gaze on me with a strange tenacity, she repeats:

"Very expert, and clever, and discreet. She is the Providence of the neighborhood. Now, my little one, do not forget to come to see us when you can. And go often to Madame Gouin's. You will not regret it. We will see each other soon again."

She has gone. I see her, with her rolling gait, moving away, skirting first the wall and then the hedge with her enormous person, and suddenly burying herself in a road, where she disappears.

I pass by Joseph, the gardener-coachman, who is raking the paths. I think that he is going to speak to me; he does not' speak to me. He simply looks at me obliquely, with a singular expression that almost frightens me.

"Fine weather this morning, Monsieur Joseph."

Joseph grunts I know not what between his teeth. He is furious that I have allowed myself to walk in the path that he is raking.

What a queer man he is, and how ill-bred! And why does he never say a word to me? And why does he never answer when I speak to him?

In the house I find Madame by no means contented. She gives me a very disagreeable reception, treats me very roughly.

"I beg you not to stay out so long in the future."

I desire to reply, for I am vexed, irritated, unnerved. But fortunately I restrain myself. I confine myself to muttering a little.

"What's that you say?"

"I say nothing."

"It is lucky. And furthermore, I forbid you to walk with M. Mauger's servant. She is very bad company for you. See, everything is late this morning, because of you."

I say to myself:

"*Zut! zut!* and *zut!* You make me tired. I will speak to whom I like. I will see anyone that it pleases me to see. You shall lay down no law for me, camel!"

I need only to see once more her wicked eyes, and hear her shrill voice and her tyrannical orders, in order to lose at once the bad impression, the impression of disgust, that I brought back from the mass, from the grocer, and from Rose. Rose and the grocer are right; the haberdasher also is right; all of them are right. And I promise myself that I will see Rose; that I will see her often; that I will return to the grocer's; that I will make this dirty haberdasher my best friend,—since Madame forbids me to do so. And I repeat internally, with savage energy:

"Camel! Camel! Camel!"

But I would have been much more relieved if I had had the courage to hurl and shout this insult full in her face.

During the day, after lunch, Monsieur and Madame went out driving. The dressing-room, the chambers, Monseiur's desk, all the closets, all the cupboards, all the sideboards, were locked. What did I tell you? Ah, well, thank you! no means of reading a letter, or of making up any little packages.

So I have remained in my room. I have written to my mother and to Monsieur Jean, and I have read "En Famille." What a delightful book! And how well written! It is queer, all the same; I am very fond of hearing dirty things, but I do not like to read them. I like only the books that make me cry.

For dinner they had boiled beef and broth. It seemed to me that Monsieur and Madame were very cool towards each other. Monsieur read the "Petit Journal" with provoking ostentation. He crumpled the paper, rolling all the time his kind, comical, gentle eyes. Even when he is in anger, Monsieur's eyes remain gentle and timid. At last, doubtless to start the

51

conversation, Monsieur, with his nose still buried in his paper, exclaimed:

"Hello! another woman cut to pieces!"

Madame made no answer. Very stiff, very straight, austere in her black silk dress, her forehead wrinkled, her look stern, she did not cease her dreaming. About what?

It is, perhaps, because of me that Madame is sulky with Monsieur.

IV.

For a week I have been unable to write a single line in my diary. When it comes night, I am tired, exhausted, at the end of my strength. I think of nothing but going to bed and to sleep. To sleep! If I could always sleep!

Oh! what a shabby place, My God! You can have no idea of it!

For a yes, for a no, Madame makes you run up and down the two cursed flights of stairs. One has not even time to sit down in the linen-room and breathe a little, when . . . drinn! . . . drinn! . . . drinn! . . . one has to get up and start again. It makes no difference if one is not feeling well, drinn! . . . drinn! . . . drinn! In these days I have pains in my loins that bend me in two, and gripe my stomach, and almost make me cry out. That cuts no figure; drinn! . . . drinn! . . . drinn! . . . One has no time to be sick; one has not the right to suffer. Suffering is a master's luxury. We, we must walk, and fast, and forever; walk at the risk of falling. Drinn! . . . drinn! . . . drinn! . . . And if one is a little slow in coming at the sound of the bell, then there are reproaches and angry scenes.

"Well, what are you about? You do not hear, then? Are you deaf? I have been ringing for three hours. It is getting to be very provoking."

And this is what generally happens.

"Drinn! . . . drinn! . . . drinn! . . ."

That throws you from your chair, as if impelled by a spring.

"Bring me a needle."

I go for a needle.

53

"All right! Bring me some thread."
I go for the thread.
"Very good! Bring me a button."
I go for the button.
"What is this button? I did not ask for this button. You never understand anything. A white button, number four. And be quick about it."

And I go for the white button, number four. You can imagine how I storm, and rage, and abuse Madame, within myself. During these goings and comings, these ascents and descents, Madame has changed her mind. She wants something else, or she wants nothing at all.

"No, take away the needle and the button. I have no time."

My back is broken, my knees absolutely stiff, I can do no more. That suffices for Madame; she is satisfied. And to think that there is a society for the protection of animals!

In the evening, when making her examination of the linen-room, she storms:

"What! you have done nothing? What do you do all day long, then? I will not pay you to be idle from morning till night."

I reply rather curtly, for this injustice fills me with rebellion:

"Why, Madame has been interrupting me all day."

"I have been interrupting you, I? In the first place, I forbid you to answer me. I want no remarks, do you understand? I know what I am talking about."

And she goes away, slamming the door, and grumbling as if she would never stop. In the corridors, in the kitchen, in the garden, her shrill voice can be heard for hours. Oh! how tiresome she is!

Really one knows not how to take her. What can she have in her body that keeps her always in such a state of irritation?

And how quickly I would drop her, if I were sure of finding a place directly!

Just now I was suffering even more than usual. I felt so sharp a pain that it seemed as if a beast were tearing the interior of my body with its teeth and claws. Already, in the morning, on rising, I had fainted because of loss of blood. How have I had the courage to keep up, and drag myself about, and do my work? I do not know. Occasionally, on the stairs, I was obliged to stop, and cling to the banister, in order to get my breath and keep from falling. I was green, with cold sweats that wet my hair. It was enough to make one scream, but I am good at bearing pain, and it is a matter of pride with me never to complain in presence of my masters. Madame surprised me at a moment when I thought that I was about to faint. Everything was revolving about me,—the banister, the stairs, and the walls.

"What is the matter with you?" she said to me, rudely.

"Nothing."

And I tried to straighten up.

"If there is nothing the matter with you," rejoined Madame, "why these manners? I do not like to see funereal faces. You have a very disagreeable way of doing your work."

In spite of my pain, I could have boxed her ears.

Amid these trials, I am always thinking of my former places. To-day it is my place in the Rue Lincoln that I most regret. There I was second chambermaid, and had, so to speak, nothing to do. We passed the day in the linen-room, a magnificent linen-room, with a red felt carpet, and lined from ceiling to floor with great mahogany cupboards, with gilded locks. And we laughed, and we amused ourselves in talking nonsense, in reading, in mimicing Madame's receptions, all under the eye of an English governess, who made tea for us,—the good tea that Madame bought in England for her little morning breakfasts. Sometimes, from the servants' hall, the butler—

one who was up to date—brought us cakes, caviare on toast, slices of ham, and a heap of good things.

I remember that one afternoon they obliged me to put on a very swell costume belonging to Monsieur,—to Coco, as we called him among ourselves. Naturally we played at all sorts of *risqués* games; we even went very far in our fun-making.

Ah! that was a place!

I am beginning to know Monsieur well. They were right in saying that he is an excellent and generous man, for, if he were not, there would not be in the world a worse rascal, a more perfect sharper. The need, the passion that he feels for being charitable, impell him to do things that are not very admirable. His intention is praiseworthy, but the result upon others is often disastrous, all the same. It must be confessed that his kindness has been the cause of dirty little tricks, like the following:

Last Tuesday a very simple old man, father Pantois, brought some sweet-briers that Monsieur had ordered,—of course without Madame's knowledge. It was toward the end of the day. I had come down for some hot water for a belated bath. Madame, who had gone to town, had not yet returned. And I was chattering in the kitchen with Marianne, when Monsieur, cordial, joyous, unreserved, and noisy, brought in father Pantois. He immediately had him served with bread, cheese, and cider. And then he began to talk with him.

The good man excited my pity, so worn, thin, and dirtily clad was he. His pantaloons were in rags; his cap was a mass of filth. And his open shirt revealed a part of his bare breast, chapped, crimped, seasoned like old leather. He ate greedily.

"Well, father Pantois," cried Monsieur, rubbing his hands, "that goes better, eh?"

The old man, with his mouth full, thanked him.

"You are very good Monsieur Lanlaire. Because, you see,

since this morning, at four o'clock, when I left home, I have put nothing in my stomach,—nothing at all."

"Well, eat away, Father Pantois. Regale yourself, while you are about it."

"You are very good, Monsieur Lanlaire. Pray excuse me."

The old man cut off enormous pieces of bread, which he was a long time in chewing, for he had no teeth left. When he was partially satisfied, Monsieur asked him:

"And the sweet-briers, father Pantois? They are fine this year, eh?"

"There are some that are fine; there are some that are not so fine; there are almost all sorts, Monsieur Lanlaire. Indeed, one can scarcely choose. And they are hard to pull up, you can believe. And besides, Monsieur Porcellet will not let us take them from his woods any more. We have to go a long way now to find them, a very long way. If I were to tell you that I come from the forest of Raillon,—more than three leagues from here? Yes, indeed, Monsieur Lanlaire."

While the good man was talking, Monsieur had taken a seat at the table beside him. Gay, almost uproarious, he slapped him on the shoulder, and exclaimed:

"Five leagues! you are a jolly good one, father Pantois. Always strong, always strong."

"Not as much as that, Monsieur Lanlaire; not so much as that."

"Nonsense!" inisited Monsieur, "strong as an old Turk,—and good-humored, yes, indeed! They don't make any more like you these days, father Pantois. You are of the old school, you are."

The old man shook his head, his gaunt head, of the color of old wood, and repeated:

"Not so much as that. My legs are weakening, Monsieur Lanlaire; my arms are getting soft. And then my back. Oh! my confounded back! My strength is almost gone. And then the wife, who is sick, and who never leaves her bed,—what a bill for medicines! One has little luck, one has little luck. If at least one did not grow old? That, you see, Monsieur Lanlaire, that is the worst of the matter.''

Monsieur sighed, made a vague gesture, and then, summing up the question philosophically, said:

"Oh! yes, but what do you expect, father Pantois? Such is life. One cannot be and have been. That's the way it is.''

"To be sure; one must be reasonable.''

"That's it.''

"We live while we can, isn't it so, Monsieur Lanlaire?''

"Indeed it is.''

And, after a pause, he added in a voice that had become melancholy:

"Besides, everybody has his sorrows, father Pantois.''

"No doubt of it.''

There was a silence. Marianne was cutting up herbs. It was growing dark in the garden. The two big sunflowers, which could be seen in the perspective of the open door, were losing their color and disappearing in the shade. And father Pantois kept on eating. His glass had remained empty. Monsieur filled it, and then, suddenly abandoning his metaphysical heights, he asked:

"And what are the sweet-briers worth this year?''

"Sweet-briers, Monsieur Lanlaire? Well, this year, taking them as they come, sweet-briers are worth twenty-two francs a hundred. It is a little dear, I know; but I cannot get them for less; really I cannot.''

Like a generous man, who despises considerations of money, Monsieur interrupted the old man, who was getting ready to justify himself by explanations.

"It is all right, father Pantois. It is agreed. Do I ever haggle with you? In fact, instead of twenty-two francs, I will pay you twenty-five for your sweet-briers.''

"Ah! Monsieur Lanlaire, you are too good!''

"No, no; I am just. I am for the people, I am; for labor, don't you know?"

And, with a blow on the table, he went higher still.

"No, not twenty-five,—thirty, father Pantois. I will pay you thirty francs, do you hear that?"

The good man lifted his poor eyes to Monsieur, in astonishment and gratitude, and stammered:

"I hear very well. It is a pleasure to work for you, Monsieur Lanlaire. You know what work is, you do."

Monsieur put an end to these effusions.

"And I will go to pay you,—let us see; to-day is Tuesday, —I will go to pay you on Sunday. Does that suit you? And at the same time I will take my gun. Is it agreed?"

The gleam of gratitude which had been shining in the eyes of father Pantois faded out. He was embarrassed, troubled; he stopped eating.

"You see," said he, timidly,— "well, in short, if you could pay it to-night, that would oblige me greatly, Monsieur Lanlaire. Twenty-two francs, that's all; pray excuse me."

"You are joking, father Pantois," replied Monsieur, with superb assurance; "certainly; I will pay you that directly. I proposed that only for the purpose of making a little trip and paying you a little visit."

He fumbled in the pockets of his pantaloons, then in those of his vest and waistcoat, and, assuming an air of surprise, he cried:

"Well, there! here I am again without change! I have nothing but confounded thousand-franc bills."

With a forced and really sinister laugh, he asked:

"I will bet that you have not change for a thousand francs, father Pantois?"

Seeing Monsieur laugh, father Pantois thought that it was proper for him to laugh too, and he answered, jovially:

"Ha! ha! ha! I have never even seen these confounded bills."

"Well, on Sunday then," concluded Monsieur.

Monsieur had poured out a glass of cider for himself, and was drinking with father Pantois, when Madame, whom they had not heard coming, suddenly entered the kitchen, like a gust of wind. Ah! her eye, when she saw that! when she saw Monsieur sitting at table beside the poor old man, and drinking with him!

"What's this?" she exclaimed, her lips all white.

Monsieur stammered, and hemmed and hawed.

"It is some sweet-briers; you know very well, my pet; some sweet-briers. Father Pantois has brought me some sweet-briers. All the rose-bushes were frozen this winter."

"I have ordered no sweet-briers. We need no sweet-briers here."

This was said in a cutting tone. Then she made a half-circuit of the room, and went out, slamming the door and showering insults. In her anger she had not noticed me.

Monsieur and the poor puller of sweet-briers had risen. Embarrassed, they looked at the door through which Madame had just disappeared. Then they looked at each other, without daring to say a word. Monsieur was the first to break this painful silence.

"Well, then, on Sunday, father Pantois."

"On Sunday, Monsieur Lanlaire."

"And take good care of yourself, father Pantois."

"You also, Monsieur Lanlaire."

"And thirty francs, mind you. I do not take back what I said."

"You are very good."

And the old man, trembling on his legs, and with back bent, went away, and disappeared in the darkness.

Poor Monsieur! he must have received his lecture! And, as for father Pantois, if ever he gets his thirty francs,—well, he will be lucky.

I do not wish to justify Madame, but I think that Monsieur is wrong in talking familiarly with people that are too far beneath him. It is not dignified.

I know very well that he doesn't lead a gay life, to be sure, and that he takes such opportunities as offer. That is not always convenient. When he comes back late from a hunt, dirty and wet, and singing to keep up his courage, Madame gives him a warm reception.

"Ah! it is very nice of you to leave me alone all day!"

"But you know very well, my pet" . . .

"Be still."

She sulks for hours and hours, her forehead stern, her mouth ugly. He follows her about everywhere, trembling and stammering excuses.

"But, my pet, you know very well" . . .

"Let me alone; you make me tired."

The next day, naturally, Monsieur does not go out, and Madame exclaims:

"Why do you wander about thus in the house, like a soul in torment?"

"But, my pet" . . .

"You would do much better to go out, to go hunting, the devil knows where? You annoy me; you unnerve me. Go away."

So that he never knows what to do, whether to go or stay, to be here or elsewhere. A difficult problem. But, as in either case Madame scolds, Monsieur has taken the course of going away as often as possible. In that way he does not hear her scold.

Ah! it is really pitiful.

The other morning, as I was going to spread a little linen on the hedge, I saw him in the garden. Monsieur was gardening. The wind having blown down some dahlias during the night, he was refastening them to their props.

61

Very often, when he does not go out before lunch, Monsieur works in the garden; at least, he pretends to be occupying himself with something or other in his platbands. It is always time gained from the ennui of the household. During these moments there are no scenes. Away from Madame, he is no longer the same man. His face lightens up, his eyes shine. Naturally gay, his gaiety comes to the surface. Really, he is not disagreeable to me now, and, though still bent on his idea, seems to pay no attention to me. But outside he never fails to address me a pleasant little word, after making sure, however, that Madame cannot be spying him. When he does not dare to speak to me, he looks at me, and his look is more eloquent than his words. Moreover, I amuse myself in exciting him in all ways, although I have taken no resolution concerning him.

In passing by him, in the path where he was working, bent over his dahlias, with bits of string between his teeth, I said to him, without slackening my pace:

"Oh! how hard Monsieur is working this morning!"

"Yes, indeed," he answered; "these confounded dahlias! You see" . . .

He invited me to stop a minute.

"Well, Célestine, I hope you are getting accustomed to the place, now?"

Always his mania! Always the same difficulty in engaging in conversation! To please him, I replied with a smile:

"Why, yes, Monsieur, certainly; I am getting accustomed here."

"I am glad to hear it. It is not bad here; really, it is not bad."

He quite straightened up, gave me a very tender look, and repeated: "It is not bad," thus giving himself time to think of something ingenious to say to me.

He took from his teeth the bits of string, tied them at the top of the prop, and, with legs spread apart, and his two palms resting on his hips, with a knowing look, and frankly obscene eyes, he cried:

"I'll bet, Célestine, that you led a gay life in Paris? Say, now, didn't you?"

I was not expecting this. And I had a great desire to laugh. But I lowered my eyes modestly, with an offended air, and, trying to blush, as was proper under the circumstances, I exclaimed, in a tone of reproach:

"Oh! Monsieur!"

"Well, what?" he insisted; "a pretty girl like you,—with such eyes! Oh! yes, you must have had a gay time. And so much the better. For my part, I am for amusement; yes, I am for love."

Monsieur was becoming strangely animated. And, on his robust, muscular person I recognized the most evident signs of amorous exaltation. He was on fire; desire was flaming in his eyes. I deemed it my duty to pour a good shower of cold water on this fire. In a very dry tone, and at the same time very loftily, I said:

"Monsieur is mistaken. Monsieur thinks that he is speaking to his other chambermaids. Monsieur must know, however, that I am a good girl."

And with great dignity, to show exactly to what extent this outrage had offended me, I added:

"It will serve Monsieur right, if I go to complain to Madame directly."

And I made a pretence of starting. Monsieur quickly grasped me by the arm.

"No, no," he stammered.

How did I ever say all that without bursting? How did I ever succeed in burying in my throat the laugh that was ringing there? Really, I don't know.

Monsieur was prodigiously ridiculous. Livid now, with mouth wide open, his whole person bearing a twofold expression of annoyance and fear, he remained silent, digging into his neck with his nails.

Near us an old pear tree twisted its pyramid of branches, eaten by lichens and mosses. A few pears hung within reach of his hand. A magpie was chattering ironically at the top of a neighboring chestnut tree. Crouching behind the border of box, the cat was pawing at a bumble-bee. The silence was becoming more and more painful for Monsieur. At last, after efforts that were almost sorrowful,—efforts that brought grotesque grimaces to his lips,—Monsieur asked:

"Do you like pears, Célestine?"

"Yes, Monsieur."

I did not disarm; I answered in a tone of lofty indifference.

In the fear of being surprised by his wife, he hesitated a few seconds. And suddenly, like a thieving child, he took a pear from the tree, and gave it to me,—oh! how piteously! His knees bent, his hand trembled.

"There, Célestine, hide that in your apron. You never have any in the kitchen, do you?"

"No, Monsieur."

"Well, I will give you some occasionally, because . . . because . . . I wish you to be happy."

The sincerity and ardor of his desire, his awkwardness, his clumsy gestures, his bewildered words, and also his masculine power, all had a softening effect upon me. I relaxed my face a little, veiled the severity of my look with a sort of smile, and, half ironically, half coaxingly, I said to him:

"Oh! Monsieur, if Madame were to see you?"

Again he became troubled, but, as we were separated from the house by a thick curtain of chestnut trees, he quickly recovered himself, and, growing more defiant as I became less severe, he exclaimed, with easy gestures:

"Well, what? Madame? And what of her? I care nothing for Madame. I do not intend that she shall annoy me. I have enough of her. I am over my head in Madame."

I declared gravely:

"Monsieur is wrong. Monsieur is not just. Madame is a very amiable woman."

He gave a start.

"Very amiable? She? Ah! Great God! But you do not know, then, what she has done? She has spoiled my life. I am no longer a man; I am nothing at all. I am the laughing-stock of the neighborhood. And all on account of my wife. My wife? She . . . she . . . she is a hussy,—yes, Célestine, a hussy . . . a hussy . . . a hussy."

I gave him a moral lecture. I talked to him gently, hypo-critically boasting of Madame's energy and order and all her domestic virtues. At each of my phrases he became more exasperated.

"No, no. A hussy! A hussy!"

However, I succeeded in calming him a little. Poor Monsieur! I played with him with marvelous ease. With a simple look I made him pass from anger to emotion. Then he stammered:

"Oh! you are so gentle, you are! You are so pretty! You must be so good! Whereas that hussy" . . .

"Oh! come, Monsieur! come, come!"

He continued:

"You are so gentle! And yet, what? . . . you are only a chambermaid."

For a moment he drew nearer to me, and in a low voice said:

"If you would, Célestine?"

"If I would what?"

"If you would . . . you know very well; yes, you know very well."

"Monsieur wishes me perhaps to betray Madame with Monsieur?"

He misunderstood the expression of my face; and, with

65

eyes standing out of his head, the veins in his neck swollen, his lips moist and frothy, he answered, in a smothered voice:

"Yes; yes, indeed."

"Monsieur doesn't think of such a thing?"

"I think of nothing else, Célestine."

He was very red, his face congested.

"Ah! Monsieur is going to begin again?"

He tried to grasp my hand, to draw me to him.

"Well, yes," he stammered, "I am going to begin again; I am going to begin again, because . . . because . . . I am mad over you, Célestine; because I think of nothing else; because I cannot sleep; because I feel really sick. And don't be afraid of me; have no fears! I am not a brute. No, indeed; I swear it. I . . . I" . . .

"Another word, Monsieur, and this time I tell everything to Madame. Suppose some one were to see you in the garden in this condition?"

He stopped short. Distressed, ashamed, thoroughly stupid, he knew not what to do with his hands, with his eyes, with his whole person. And he looked, without seeing them, at the ground beneath his feet, at the old pear tree, at the garden. Conquered at last, he untied the bits of string at the top of the prop, bent again over the fallen dahlias, and sad, infinitely so, and supplicating, he groaned:

"Just now, Célestine, I said to you . . . I said to you . . . as I would have said anything else to you,—as I would have said no matter what. I am an old fool. You must not be angry with me. And, above all, you must not say anything to Madame. You are right, though; suppose some one had seen us in the garden?"

I ran away, to keep from laughing.

Yes, I wanted to laugh. And, nevertheless, there was an emotion singing in my heart, something—what shall I call it? —something material. And, besides, it would have been amusing, because of Madame. We shall see, later.

Monsieur did not go away all day. He straightened his dahlias, and during the afternoon he did not leave the wood-house, where he split wood furiously for more than four hours. From the linen-room I listened, with a sort of pride, to the blows of the axe.

Yesterday Monsieur and Madame spent the entire afternoon at Louviers. Monsieur had an appointment with his lawyer, Madame with her dressmaker. Her dressmaker!

I took advantage of this moment of rest to pay a visit to Rose, whom I had not seen since that famous Sunday. And I was not adverse to making the acquaintance of Captain Mauger.

A true type of an old sea-dog, this man, and such as you seldom see, I assure you. Fancy a carp's head, with a moustache and a long gray tuft of beard. Very dry, very nervous, very restless, he cannot stay in one place for any length of time, and is always at work, either in his garden, or in a little room where he does carpentering, humming military airs or imitating the bugle of the regiment.

The garden is very pretty,—an old garden divided into square beds in which old-fashioned flowers are cultivated,—those very old flowers that are found now only in very old fields and in the gardens of very old priests.

When I arrived, Rose, comfortably seated in the shade of an acacia, beside a rustic table, on which lay her work-basket, was mending stockings, and the captain, squatting on the grass, and wearing an old foraging-cap on his head, was stopping the leaks in a garden-hose which had burst the night before.

They welcomed me enthusiastically, and Rose ordered the little servant, who was weeding a bed of marguerites, to go for the bottle of peach brandy and some glasses.

The first courtesies exchanged, the captain asked:

"Well, he has not croaked, then, your Lanlaire? Oh! you can boast of serving in a famous den! I really pity you, my dear young woman."

67

He explained to me that formerly Monsieur and he had lived as good neighbors, as inseparable friends. A discussion apropos of Rose had brought on a deadly quarrel. Monsieur, it seems, reproached the captain with not maintaining his dignity with his servant,—with admitting her to his table.

Interrupting his story, the captain forced my testimony:

"To my table! Well, have I not the right? Is it any of his business?"

"Certainly not, captain."

Rose, in a modest voice, sighed:

"A man living all alone; it is very natural isn't it?"

Since this famous discussion, which had come near ending in blows, the two old friends had passed their time in lawsuits and tricks. They hated each other savagely.

"As for me," declared the captain, "when I find any stones in my garden, I throw them over the hedge into Lanlaire's. So much the worse if they fall on his bell-glasses and on his garden-frames? Or, rather, so much the better! Oh! the pig! Wait now, let me show you."

Having noticed a stone in the path, he rushed to pick it up, approached the hedge cautiously, creeping like a trapper, and threw the stone into our garden with all his might. We heard a noise of breaking glass. Then, returning to us triumphantly, shaking, stifled, twisted with laughter, he exclaimed:

"Another square broken! The glazier will have to come again."

Rose looked at him with a sort of maternal admiration, and said: "Is he not droll? What a child! And how young, for his age!"

After we had sipped a little glass of brandy, Captain Mauger desired to do me the honors of the garden. Rose excused herself for her inability to accompany us, because of her asthma, and counselled us not to stay too long.

"Besides," said she, jokingly, "I am watching you."

The captain took me through the paths, among the beds

bordered with box and filled with flowers. He told me the names of the prettiest ones, remarking each time that there were no such to be seen in the garden of that pig of a Lanlaire. Suddenly he plucked a little orange-colored flower, odd and charming, twirled the stem gently in his fingers, and asked me:

"Did you ever eat any of these?"

I was so surprised by this preposterous question that I stood with mouth closed. The captain declared:

"Well, I have eaten them. They are perfect to the taste. I have eaten all the flowers that are here. Some are good; some are not so good; and some don't amount to much. But, as for me, I eat everything."

He winked, clacked his tongue, tapped his belly, and repeated in a louder voice, in which an accent of defiance was uppermost:

"I eat everything, I do."

The way in which the captain had just proclaimed this strange confession of faith revealed to me that his vanity in life was to eat anything. I amused myself in humoring his mania.

"And you are right, Captain."

"Surely," he answered, not without pride. "And it is not only plants that I eat; I eat animals also,—animals that nobody else has eaten,—animals that are not known. I eat everything, I do."

We continued our walk among the flower-beds, through the narrow paths where pretty corollas, blue, yellow, and red, were swaying in the breeze. And, as he looked at the flowers, it seemed to me that the captain's belly gave little starts of joy. His tongue passed over his chapped lips with a slight smack.

He said to me further:

"And I am going to confess to you. There are no insects, no birds, no earth-worms that I have not eaten. I have eaten skunks and snakes, rats and crickets and caterpillars. I have eaten everything. It is well known in the neighborhood. When they find a beast, dead or alive, a beast unknown to anybody, they say to themselves: 'I must take it to Captain Mauger.' They bring it to me, and I eat it. In winter especially, when it is very cold, unknown birds pass this way, coming from America, or from a greater distance perhaps. They bring them to me, and I eat them. I will bet that there is not a man in the world who has eaten as many things as I have. I eat everything."

The walk over, we returned to sit down under the acacia. And I was getting ready to leave, when the captain cried:

"Oh! I must show you something curious,—something that you have never seen, I am sure."

And he called in a loud voice:

"Kléber! Kléber!"

Between two calls he explained to me:

"Kléber is my ferret. A phenomenon!"

And he called again:

"Kléber! Kléber!"

Then, on a branch above us, between green and golden leaves, there appeared a pink snout and two little black, sharp, bright eyes.

"Oh! I knew well that he was not far away. Come, come here, Kléber. Psstt!"

The animal crept along the branch, ventured upon the trunk, and descended carefully, burying its claws in the bark. His body, covered with white fur and marked with pale yellow spots, had the supple movements, the graceful undulations, of a serpent. He touched ground, and in two bounds was on the knees of the captain, who began to caress him joyfully.

"Oh! the good Kléber! Oh, the charming little Kléber!"

He turned to me:

"Did you ever see a ferret as tame as that? He follows me about the garden everywhere, like a little dog. I have only to call him, and he is there directly, his tail frisking, his head lifted. He eats with us, sleeps with us. Indeed, I love the little beast as if he were a person. Why, Mademoiselle Célestine,

I have refused three hundred francs for him. I would not sell him for a thousand francs,—no, not for two thousand francs. Here, Kléber.''

The animal lifted its head toward its master; then it climbed upon him, mounted his shoulders, and, after a thousand caresses and a thousand pretty tricks, rolled itself around the captain's neck, like a handkerchief. Rose said nothing. She seemed vexed.

Then an infernal idea flashed into my mind.

"I will bet you," I said, suddenly,— "I will bet you, Captain, that you would not eat your ferret."

The captain looked at me with profound astonishment, and then with infinite sadness. His eyes became round, his lips quivered.

"Kléber?" he stammered; "eat Kléber?"

Evidently this question had never occurred to him, who had eaten everything. A sort of new world, strangely comestible, appeared before him.

"I will bet," I repeated, ferociously, "that you would not eat your ferret."

Bewildered, distressed, moved by a mysterious and invincible shock, the old captain had risen from his bench. He was extraordinarily agitated.

"Just say that again, and see!" he stammered.

For the third time, violently, separating each word, I said:

"I will bet that you would not eat your ferret."

"I would not eat my ferret? What's that you say? You say that I would not eat it? Yes, you say that? Well, you shall see. I tell you that I eat everything."

He seized the ferret. As one breaks a loaf of bread, he broke the little beast's back with a snap, and threw it, dead without a shock, without a spasm, on the sandy path, shouting to Rose:

"Make me a stew out of that for dinner!"

71

And, madly gesticulating, he ran to shut himself up in the house.

For some minutes I felt a real and unspeakable horror. Still completely dazed by the abominable action that I had just committed, I rose to go. I was very pale. Rose accompanied me. With a smile she confided to me:

"I am not sorry for what has just happened. He was too fond of his ferret. I do not wish him to love anything. He loves his flowers already too much to suit me."

After a short silence, she added:

"But he will never forgive you for that. He is not a man to be defied. An old soldier, you know!"

Then, a few steps farther on:

"Pay attention, my little one. They are beginning to gossip about you in the neighborhood. It seems that you were seen the other day, in the garden, with Monsieur Lanlaire. It is very imprudent, believe me. He will get you into trouble, if he hasn't already done so. You want to look out for yourself."

And, as she closed the gate behind me:

"Well, *au revoir!* Now I must go to make my stew."

All day long I saw before my eyes the body of the poor ferret, lying there on the sandy path.

This evening, at dinner, when dessert was being served, Madame said to me, very severely:

"If you like prunes, you have only to ask me for them; I will see if I can give you any; but I forbid you to take them."

I answered:

"I am not a thief, Madame, and I do not like prunes."

Madame insisted:

"I tell you that you have taken some prunes."

I replied:

"If Madame thinks me a thief, Madame has only to pay me and let me go."

Madame snatched the plate of prunes from my hand.

"Monsieur ate five this morning; there were thirty-two; now there are but twenty-five; then you have taken two. Don't let that happen again."

It was true. I had eaten two of them. She had counted them!

Did you ever in your life?

V.

My mother is dead. I received the news this morning, in
a letter from home. Although I have never had anything but
blows from her, the news has given me pain, and I have cried,
and cried, and cried. Seeing me crying, Madame said:

"Again these manners?"

I answered:

"My mother, my poor mother, is dead!"

Then Madame, in her ordinary voice:

"It is a pity, but I can do nothing about it. At any rate,
the work must not suffer."

And that was all. Oh! indeed, Madame's kindness will
never kill her.

What has made me most unhappy is the fact that I have
seen a coincidence between my mother's death and the murder
of the little ferret. It seems to me like a punishment from
heaven, and that perhaps my mother would not be dead if I
had not obliged the captain to kill poor Kléber. In vain have
I repeated to myself that my mother died before the ferret.
That had no effect; the idea has pursued me all day long, like
a remorse.

I should have liked to go home. But Audierne is so far
away,—at the end of the world, it seems. And I have no money.
When I shall receive my first month's wages, I shall have to
pay the employment-bureau. I shall not have enough to even
pay the few little debts contracted during the days when I
was on the pavement.

And then, of what use would it be to go? My brother is
in the naval service, and his vessel is in China, I believe, for
it is a very long time since we had any news from him. And

74

my sister Louise? Where is she now? I do not know. Since she left us to follow Jean de Duff to Concarneau, nothing has been heard from her. She must have rolled hither and thither, the devil knows where! Perhaps she is in a public house; perhaps she, too, is dead. And perhaps, also, my brother is dead.

Yes, why should I go there? In what way would it help me? There is no one there now who interests me, and surely my mother has left nothing. Her rags and the little furniture that she had certainly will not pay her brandy bill.

It is queer, all the same; as long as she was living, I almost never thought of her! I felt no desire to see her again. I wrote to her only when I changed my place, and then simply to give her my address. She has beaten me so much! I was so unhappy with her, she being always drunk. And yet, on learning suddenly that she is dead, my soul is plunged in mourning, and I feel more alone than ever.

And I remember my childhood with singular clearness. I see again all the things and beings among whom I began the stern apprenticeship of life. There is really too much sorrow on one side, too much happiness on the other. The world is not just.

One night, I remember,—I was very small, moreover,—I remember that we were awakened with a start by the whistle of the life-saving boat. Oh! those calls in the tempest and in the darkness,—how lugubrious they are! Since the night before, the wind had been blowing a gale. The harbor bar was white and furious. Only a few sloops had been able to get back. The others, the poor others, were surely in danger.

Knowing that my father was fishing in the vicinity of the Ile de Sein, my mother was not too anxious. She hoped that he had put into the island harbor, as he had done so often before. Nevertheless, on hearing the whistle of the life-saving boat, she arose, trembling and very pale, wrapped me hurriedly in a thick woolen shawl, and started for the breakwater. My sister Louise, who was already grown, and my younger brother, followed her, crying:

"Oh! Holy Virgin! Oh! Our Jesus!"

And she, too, cried:

"Oh! Holy Virgin! Oh! Our Jesus!"

The narrow streets were full of people,—women, old men, children. A crowd of frightened shadows were hastening to the pier, where the groaning of the boats could be heard. But they could not stay on the breakwater because of the strong wind, and especially because of the waves, which, beating against the stone embankment, swept it from end to end, with the noise of a cannonade. My mother took the path . . . "Oh! Holy Virgin! Oh! Our Jesus!" . . . took the path that winds around the estuary to the lighthouse. Everything was black on land, and on the sea, which was black also, could be seen, from time to time, in the distance, by the rays from the light-house, the white breaking of enormous waves. In spite of the shocks . . . "Oh! Holy Virgin! Oh! Our Jesus!" . . . in spite of the shocks and in a way lulled by them, in spite of the wind and in a way stunned by it, I went to sleep in my mother's arms. I awoke in a low room, and I saw, among sombre backs, gloomy faces, and waving arms,— I saw, on a camp bed, lighted by two tallow candles, a great corpse . . . "Oh! Holy Virgin! Oh! Our Jesus!" . . . a frightful corpse, long and naked, perfectly rigid, the face crushed, the limbs streaked with bleeding gashes and covered with black and blue spots. It was my father.

I see him still. His hair was glued to his skull, and filled with a mass of sea-weed that made a sort of crown. Men were bending over him, rubbing his skin with warm flannels and forcing air into his mouth. There was the mayor; there was the rector; there was the captain of customs; there was the marine policeman. I was frightened; I freed myself from my shawl, and, running between the legs of these men, over the wet stone floor, I began to cry,—to call papa,—to call mamma. A neighbor took me away.

From that moment my mother took to drinking furiously. At first she really tried to work in the sardine-packing establishments, but, as she was always drunk, none of her employers would keep her. Then she stayed at home to intoxicate herself, quarrelsome and gloomy; and, when she was full of brandy, she beat us. How does it happen that she did not kill me?

I avoided the house as much as I could. I spent my days in playing on the pier, in thieving in the gardens, and in paddling in the puddles when the tide was low. Or else, on the Plogoff road, at the bottom of a grassy decline, sheltered from the sea wind and covered with thick bushes, I misbehaved with the little boys, among the hawthorns. On returning at night, I generally found my mother stretched on the tile floor across the threshold, inert, her mouth covered with vomit, and a broken bottle in her hands. Often I had to step over her body. Her awakenings were terrible. She was seized with a passion for destruction. Without listening to my prayers or my cries, she tore me from the bed, pursued me, kicked me, and knocked me against the furniture, crying:

"I'll have your hide! I'll have your hide!"

Many times I thought I should die.

And then she debauched herself, to get money with which to buy liquor. At night, every night, low knocks were heard at the door of our house. A sailor entered, filling the room with a strong odor of sea-salt and fish. He lay down, remained an hour, and went away. And another came, after him, lay down also, remained another hour, and went away. There were struggles and terrifying uproars in the darkness of these abominable nights, and several times the police interfered.

Thus years rolled by. I was not wanted anywhere; nor was my sister, or my brother. They avoided us in the streets.

The respectable people drove us with stones from their houses, to which we went, sometimes to steal, sometimes to beg. One day my sister Louise, who also had got into bad ways with the sailors, ran away. And then my brother enlisted as a cabin-boy. I was left alone with my mother.

At the age of ten I was no longer chaste. Made familiar with love by the sad example of mamma, perverted by the little boys with whom I associated, my physical development had been very rapid. In spite of deprivations and blows, living continually in the open sea air, free and strong, I had grown so fast that at the age of eleven I experienced the first awakenings of womanhood. Beneath my girlish exterior, I was almost a woman.

At the age of twelve I was a woman quite, and no longer a virgin. Violated? No, not exactly. Consenting? Yes, almost, —at least in the degree in which the artlessness of my vice and the candor of my depravity were consistent with consent. The thing occurred one Sunday, after high mass, near the beach, on the Saint Jean side, in a recess in the cliff, in a dark hole among the rocks where the sea-gulls came to build their nests, and where the sailors sometimes hid the wreckage which they found at sea. The man was the foreman of a sardine-packing establishment,—an old, hairy, ill-smelling man, whose face was nothing but a dirty mass of beard and hair. He gave me an orange. He had a funny name,—M. Cléophas Biscouille.

And here is an incomprehensible thing, of which I have found no explanation in any novel. Ugly, brutal, and repulsive though M. Biscouille was, when I think of him now,—and I often do,—how happens it that it is never with a feeling of detestation for him, never with a disposition to curse him? At this recollection, which I call up with satisfaction, I feel a sort of great gratitude, a sort of great tenderness, and also a sort of real regret at having to say to myself that never shall I see this disgusting personage again.

In this connection may I be permitted to offer here, humble though I am, my personal contribution to the biography of great men.

M. Paul Bourget was the intimate friend and spiritual guide of the Countess Fardin, in whose house last year I served as chambermaid. I had always heard it said that he alone knew, even to its subsoil, the complex soul of woman. And many times I had had the idea of writing to him, in order to submit to him this case of passional psychology. I had not dared. Do not be too much astonished at the gravity of such preoccupations. They are not usual among domestics, I admit. But in the *salons* of the countess they never talked of anything but psychology. It is an admitted fact that our mind is modeled on that of our masters, and that what is said in the *salon* is said also in the servants' hall. Unhappily we had not in the servants' hall a Paul Bourget, capable of elucidating and solving the cases of feminism that we discussed there. The explanations of Monsieur Jean himself were not satisfactory to me.

One day my mistress sent me to carry an "urgent" letter to the illustrious master. He handed me the reply himself. Then I made bold to put to him the question that tormented me, pretending, however, that the heroine of this ticklish and obscure story was a friend of mine. M. Paul Bourget asked:

"What is your friend? A woman of the people? A poor woman, undoubtedly?"

"A chambermaid, like myself, illustrious master."

A superior grimace, a look of disdain, appeared on M. Bourget's face. Ah! *sapristi!* he does not like the poor.

"I do not occupy myself with these souls," said he. "These are too little souls. They are not even souls. They are outside the province of my psychology."

I understood that, in this province, one begins to be a soul only with an income of a hundred thousand francs.

Not so M. Jules Lemaitre, also a familiar of the house.

When I asked him the same question, he answered, prettily. catching me about the waist:

"Well, charming Célestine, your friend is a good girl, that is all. And, if she resembles you, I would say a couple of words to her, you know,—hey! hey! hey!"

He, at least, with his face of a little hump-backed and merry-making faun, put on no airs; and he was good-natured. What a pity that he has fallen among the priests!

With all that, I know not what would have become of me in that hell of an Audierne, if the Little Sisters of Pont-Croix, finding me intelligent and pretty, had not taken me in, out of pity. They did not take advantage of my age, of my ignorance, of my trying and despised situation, to make use of me, to secrete me for their benefit, as often happens in such establishments, which carry human exploitation to the point of crime. They were poor, candid, timid, charitable little beings, who were not rich, and who did not even dare to extend their hands to passers-by or to beg at the doors of houses. There was sometimes much poverty among them, but they got along as best they could. And, amid all the difficulties of living, they continued none the less to be gay, and to sing continually like larks. Their ignorance of life had something touching about it, something which brings the tears to my eyes to-day, now that I can better understand their infinite and pure kindness.

They taught me to read, to write, to sew, to do housework; and, when I had become almost expert in these necessary things, they got me a place as a little housemaid in the house of a retired colonel, who came every summer, with his wife and his two daughters, to occupy a sort of dilapidated little château near Comfort. Worthy people, certainly, but so sad, so sad! And maniacs, too! Never a smile on their faces, never a sign of joy in their garments, which were always black. The colonel had had a lathe put in at the top of the house, and there, all day long, he turned egg cups out of box-wood, or else those oval balls, called "eggs," which housewives use in mending stockings. Madame drew up petition after petition, in order to obtain a tobacco-shop. And the two daughters, saying nothing, doing nothing, one with a duck's beak, the other with a rabbit's face, yellow and thin, angular and faded, dried up on the spot, like two plants lacking everything,—soil, water, sunshine. They bored me enormously. At the end of eight months I left them, in a moment of rashness which I have regretted.

But then! I heard Paris breathing and living around me. Its breath filled my heart with new desires. Although I did not go out often, I had admired with a prodigious astonishment the streets, the shop-windows, the crowds, the palaces, the brilliant equipage, the jeweled women. And, when, at night, I went to bed in the sixth story, I envied the other domestics of the house, and their pranks which I found charming, and their stories which left me in a state of marvelous surprise. Though I remained in the house but a short time, I saw there, at night, in the sixth story, all sort of debaucheries, and took my part in them with the enthusiasm and emulation of a novice. Oh! the vague hopes and the uncertain ambitions that I cherished there, in that fallacious ideal of pleasure and vice!

Alas! yes, one is young, one knows nothing of life, one entertains imaginations and dreams. Oh! the dreams! Stupidities! I have supped on them, in the words of M. Xavier, a prettily perverted boy, of whom I shall have something to say later.

And I have rolled. Oh! how I have rolled! It is frightful when I think of it.

Yet I am not old, but I have had a very close view of things; I have seen people naked. And I have sniffed the odor of their linen, of their skin, of their soul. In spite of perfumes, they do not smell good. All that a respected interior, all that a respectable family, can hide in the way of filth, shameful vice, and base crimes, beneath the appearance of virtue,—ah! I know it well. It makes no difference if they are rich, if they have rags of silk and velvet and gilded furniture; it makes no

difference if they wash in silver tubs and make a great show,—
I know them. They are not clean. And their heart is more
disgusting than was my mother's bed.

Oh! how a poor domestic is to be pitied, and how lonely
she is! She may live in houses full of joyous and noisy people,
but how lonely she is always! Solitude does not consist in living
alone; it consists in living with others, with people who take
no interest in you, with whom you count for less than a dog
gorged with goodies, or than a flower cared for as tenderly as
a rich man's child,—people of whom you have nothing but their
cast-off garments or the spoiled remains of their table.

"You may eat this pear; it is rotten. Finish this chicken
in the kitchen; it smells bad."

Every word is contemptuous of you, every gesture dis-
paraging of you, placing you on a level lower than that of the
beasts. And you must say nothing; you smile and give thanks;
unless you would pass for an ingrate or a wicked heart. Sometimes, when doing my mistresses' hair, I have had a mad desire
to tear their neck, to scratch their bosom with my nails.

Fortunately one is not always under the influence of these
gloomy ideas. One shakes them off, and arranges matters to
get all the fun one can, by himself.

This evening, after dinner, Marianne, seeing that I was
utterly sad, was moved to pity, and tried to console me. She
went to get a bottle of brandy from the depths of the sideboard, where it stood among a heap of old papers and dirty
rags.

"You must not grieve like that," she said to me; "you
must shake yourself a little, my poor little one; you must console yourself."

And, having poured me out a drink, she sat for an hour,
with elbows on the table, and, in a drawling and lamenting
voice, told me gloomy stories of sickness, of child-birth, of the
death of her mother, of her father, and of her siste'r. With

every minute her voice became thicker; her eyes moistened; and she repeated, as she licked her glass:

"You must not grieve like that. The death of your mamma,—oh! it is a great misfortune! But what do you expect? We are all mortal. Oh! my God! Oh! my poor little one!"

Then she suddenly began to weep and weep, and while she wept and wept, she did not cease to wail:

"You must not grieve; you must not grieve."

At first it was a plaint; but soon it became a sort of frightful bray, which grew louder and louder. And her big belly, and her big breasts, and her triple chin, shaken by her sobs, heaved in enormous surges.

"Be still, then, Marianne," I said to her; "Madame might hear you, and come."

But she did not listen to me, and, crying louder than ever, exclaimed:

"Ah! what a misfortune! what a great misfortune!"

So that I too, my stomach turned by drink, and my heart moved by Marianne's tears, began to sob like a Madeleine. All the same, she is not a bad girl.

But I am getting tired here; I am getting tired! I am getting tired. I should like to get a place in the house of some member of the *demi-monde,* or else in America.

VI.

October 1.

Poor Monsieur! I believe that I was too harsh with him the other day, in the garden. Perhaps I went further than I should. He is such a simpleton that he imagines that he has given me serious offence, and that my virtue is impregnable. Oh! those humiliated, imploring looks, which never cease to ask my pardon!

Although I have become more teasing and agreeable, he says no more to me about the matter, and cannot make up his mind to try a new direct attack,—not even the classic device of a button to be sewed on a pair of pantaloons. A clumsy device, but one that does not often fail of its effect. My God! how many such buttons have I sewed on!

And yet it is plain that he desires me,—that he is dying of desire and more. The least of his words betrays a confession, an indirect confession of his desire; and what a confession! But he is also more and more timid; he is afraid to come to a decision. He fears that it might bring about a definite rupture, and no longer trusts in my encouraging looks.

On one occasion, approaching me with a strange expression, with a sort of haggard look in his eyes, he said to me:

"Célestine . . . you . . . you . . . black . . . my shoes . . . very well . . . very . . . very . . . well . . . Never . . . have . . . my . . . shoes . . . been blacked . . . like that."

Then I expected the button trick. But no! Monsieur gasped and slobbered as if he had eaten a pear that was too big and juicy.

Then he whistled for his dog, and started off.

But here is something stronger.

84

Yesterday Madame had gone to market,—for she does her own marketing. Monsieur had been out since dawn, with his gun and his dog. He came back early, having killed three thrushes, and immediately went up to his dressing-room to take a tub and dress, as usual. Oh, for that matter, Monsieur is very clean, and he is not afraid of water. I thought it a favorable opportunity to try something that might at least put him at his ease with me. Leaving my work, I started for the dressing-room, and for a few seconds I stood there listening, with my ear glued to the door. Monsieur was walking back and forth in his room. He was whistling and singing:

Et allez donc, Mam'zelle Suzon! . . .

Et ron, ronron . . . petit patapon . . .

A habit that he has of mingling a number of refrains when singing.

I heard chairs moving about, cupboards opening and closing, and then the water stream into the tub, and the "Ahs" and "Ohs" and "Fuuiis" and "Brrs" which the shock of the cold water wrung from Monsieur. Then, suddenly, I opened the door.

Monsieur stood facing me, shivering, with wet skin, and the sponge in his hands running like fountain. Oh! his head, his eyes! he seemed to stand transfixed. I think I never saw a man so astounded. Having nothing with which to cover his body, with a gesture instinctively modest and comical he used the sponge as a fig-leaf. It required great strength of will on my part to suppress the laugh which this spectacle loosened within me. I noticed that Monsieur has thick tufts of hair on his shoulders, and that his chest was like a bear's. But my! he is a fine man, all the same.

Naturally, I uttered a cry of alarmed modesty, as was proper, and closed the door again violently. But, once outside the door, I said to myself: "Surely he will call me back; and what is going to happen then?" I waited some minutes. Not a sound,—except the crystalline sound of a drop of water falling,

85

from time to time, into the tub. "He is reflecting," thought I; "he does not dare to come to a decision; but he will call me back." In vain. Soon the water streamed again. Then I heard Monsieur wiping and rubbing himself, and clearing his throat; old slippers dragged over the floor; chairs moved about, and cupboards opened and closed. Finally Monsieur began again to sing:

Et allez donc, Mam'zelle Suzon! . . .
Et ron, ronron . . . petit patapon . . .

"No, really, he is too stupid!" I murmured, in a low voice, furiously spiteful.

And I went back to the linen-room, firmly resolved to take no further pity on him.

In the afternoon Monsieur kept revolving around me, in an absent-minded way. He joined me in the yard, whither I had gone to throw some refuse on the muck-heap. And as I, for the sake of laughing a little at his embarrassment, apologized for what had happened in the morning, he whispered:

"That is nothing, that is nothing; on the contrary."

He tried to detain me, stammering I know not what. But I dropped him then and there, in the middle of the phrase in which he was floundering; and, in a cutting voice, I said these words:

"I ask Monsieur's pardon. I have no time to talk to Monsieur. Madame is waiting for me."

"*Sapristi!* Célestine, listen to me a moment."

"No, Monsieur."

When I turned the corner of the path leading to the house, I could see Monsieur. He had not stirred from the spot. With head lowered, and irresolute legs, he was still looking at the muck-heap, scratching his neck.

After dinner, in the *salon,* Monsieur and Madame had a hot quarrel.

Madame said:

"I tell you that you are paying attention to this girl."

Monsieur answered:

"I? Well, indeed, that's an idea! Come, my pet; such a loose creature,—a dirty thing, and possibly diseased. Oh! really, that is too much."

Madame resumed:

"Do you think, then, that I don't know your conduct and your tastes?"

"Permit me; oh! permit me."

"And all the dirty creatures whom you meet in the fields!"

I heard the floor creak under Monsieur's feet, as he walked back and forth in the *salon,* with feverish animation.

"I? Well, indeed, such ideas as you have! Where did you find them all, my pet?"

Madame was obstinate:

"And the little Jézureau? And only fifteen years old, you wretch! And on whose account I had to pay five hundred francs! But for which, to-day you perhaps would be in prison, like your thief of a father."

Monsieur stopped walking. He sank into a chair. He became silent.

The discussion ended with these words from Madame:

"However, it is all one to me. I am not jealous. You can behave as you like with this Célestine. But it must not cost me money."

Oh, no! Now I have them both.

This evening we remained longer than usual in the kitchen. I helped Marianne to make up her accounts. She did not succeed in getting them straight. I have noticed that, like all trusted persons, she pinches here, and steals there, all that she can. She even has tricks that astonish me; but she has to make her accounts square with them. Sometimes she gets lost in her figures, which embarrasses her greatly with Madame, who is very quick to find out anything wrong in them. Joseph is becoming a little more human with us. Now, from time to

CELESTINE

time, he condescends to speak to me. This evening, for instance, he did not go as usual to see the sacristan, his intimate
friend. And, while Marianne and I were working, he read
the "Libre Parole." That is his newspaper. He does not admit that any other is fit to read. I have noticed that several
times, while reading, he looked at me with a new expression
in his eyes.

The reading finished, Joseph saw fit to tell me what his
political opinions are. He is weary of the republic, which is
ruining and disgracing him. He wants a sword.

"As long as we do not have a sword, and a very red one,
there will be nothing done," said he.

He is for religion . . . because . . . in short . . . well
. . . he is for religion.

"Until religion shall have been restored in France, as we
used to have it; until everybody is obliged to go to mass and
to confession,—there will be nothing done, my God!"

He has hung up in his harness-room portraits of the pope
and of Drumont; in his chamber, that of Déroulède; in the
little seed-room those of Guérin and General Mercier,—terrible
fellows, patriots, real Frenchmen! He preciously collects all
the anti-Jewish songs, all the colored portraits of the generals,
all the caricatures of the circumcised. For Joseph is violently
anti-Semitic. He belongs to all the religious, military, and
patriotic societies of the department. He is a member of the
"Anti-Semitic Youth" of Rouen, a member of the "Anti-Jewish
Old Age," of Louviers, and a member also of an infinite number of groups and sub-groups, such as the "National Cudgel,"
the "Norman Alarm-Bell," the "Bayados du Vexin," etc.
When he speaks of the Jews, there are sinister gleams in his
eyes, and his gestures show blood-thirsty ferocity. And he
never goes to town without a club.

"As long as there is a Jew left in France, there is nothing
done."

88

And he adds:

"Ah! my God! if I were in Paris, I would kill and burn and gut these cursed sheenies. There is no danger that the traitors will come to live at Mesnil-Roy. They know very well what they are about, these mercenaries!"

He joins in one and the same hatred Protestants, Free Masons, freethinkers, all the brigands who never set foot in the churches, and who are, moreover, nothing but Jews in disguise. But he does not belong to the Clerical party; he is for religion, that's all!

As for the ignoble Dreyfus, he had better not think of coming back to France from Devil's Island. Oh, no! And Joseph strongly advises the unclean Zola not to come to Louviers to give a lecture, as it is reported that he intends to do. His hash would be settled, and Joseph himself would settle it. This miserable traitor of a Zola, who, for six hundred thousand francs, has delivered the entire French army, and also the entire Russian army, to the Germans and the English? And this is no humbug, no gossip, no lightly-spoken word; no, Joseph is sure of it. Joseph has it from the sacristan, who has it from the priest, who has it from the bishop, who has it from the pope, who has it from Drumont. Ah! the Jews may visit the Priory. They will find, written by Joseph, in the cellar, in the attic, in the stable, in the coachhouse, under the lining of the harnesses, and even on the broom-handles, and everywhere, these words: "Long Live the Army! Death to the Jews!"

From time to time Marianne approves these violent remarks with nods of her head and silent gestures. She, too, undoubtedly is being ruined and disgraced by the republic. She, too, is for the sword, for the priests, and against the Jews, —about whom she knows nothing, by the way, except that they are lacking something somewhere.

And certainly I, too, am for the army, for the country, for religion, and against the Jews. Who, then, among us house-servants, from the lowest to the highest, does not profess these nickel-plated doctrines? Say what you will of the domestics,—it is possible that they have many faults,—but it cannot be denied that they are patriots. Take myself, for instance; politics is not in my line, and it bores me. But, a week before I started for this place, I squarely refused to serve as chambermaid in the house of Labori; and all the comrades who were at the employment-bureau that day refused also.

"Work for that dirty creature? Oh, no, indeed! Never!"

Yet, when I seriously question myself, I do not know why I am against the Jews, for I used to serve in their houses in the days when one could still do so with dignity. I find that at bottom the Jews and the Catholics are very much alike. They are equally vicious, have equally vile characters, equally ugly souls. They all belong to the same world, you see, and the difference in religion counts for nothing. Perhaps the Jews make more show, more noise; perhaps they make a greater display of the money that they spend. But, in spite of what you hear about their management and their avarice, I maintain that it is not bad to be in their houses, where there is even more leakage than in Catholic houses.

But Joseph will hear nothing of all this. He reproaches me with being a bogus patriot and a bad Frenchwoman, and, with prophecies of massacre on his lips, and with bloody visions of broken heads and gashed bellies before his eyes, he went off to bed.

Straightway Marianne took the bottle of brandy from the sideboard. We needed to recover ourselves, and we talked of something else. Marianne, who every day becomes more confiding, told me of her childhood, of the hard time that she had in her youth, and how, when in the employ, as a servant of a woman who kept a tobacco-shop at Caen, she was seduced by a hospital-surgeon,—a delicate, slender, blonde young fellow, who had blue eyes and a pointed, short, and silky beard,—oh! how silky! She became pregnant, and the tobacco merchant, who herself was intimate with any number of people, including all the sub-officers of the garrison, turned her out. So young, on the pavements of a great city, and carrying a child! Ah! the poverty that she experienced, her friend having no money. And surely she would have died of hunger, if the surgeon had not found her a queer place in the medical school.

"My God! yes," she said, "at the Boratory I killed rabbits and guinea-pigs. It was very nice."

And the recollection brought to Marianne's thick lips a smile that seemed to me strangely melancholy.

After a silence, I asked her:

"And the kid! What became of it?"

Marianne made a vague and far-away gesture,—a gesture that seemed to pull aside the heavy veils from the limbos where her child was sleeping. She answered in that harsh voice which alcohol produces:

"Oh! well, you can imagine. What should I have done with it, my God!"

"Like the little guinea-pigs, then?"

And she poured herself out a drink.

We went up to our rooms somewhat intoxicated.

VII.

Decidedly, autumn is here. Frosts which were not expected so soon have browned the last flowers of the garden.
The dahlias, the poor dahlias, witnesses of Monsieur's amorous
timidity, are dried up; dried up also are the big sunflowers
that mounted guard at the kitchen-door. There is nothing left
in the devastated flower-beds,—nothing but a few sorry-looking
geraniums here and there, and five or six clusters of asters,
whose blue flowers—the dull blue of rottenness—are bending
toward the ground in anticipation of death. The garden-plots
of Captain Mauger, whom I saw just now over the hedge,
present a scene of veritable disaster, and everything is of the
color of tobacco.

The trees, through the fields, are beginning to turn yellow
and to lose their foliage, and the sky is funereal. For four days
we have been living in a thick fog, a brown fog that smelt of
soot and that did not dissipate even in the afternoon. Now it
is raining, an icy, beating rain, which a fierce wind, blowing
in squalls from the northwest, occasionally intensifies.

Ah! I am not comfortably situated here. In my room it
is bitter cold. The wind blows into it, and the water penetrates
the cracks in the roof, principally around the two windows
which stingily illuminate this dark hole. And the noise of
lifting slates, of shocks that shake the roof, of creeking timbers
and of squeaking hinges, is deafening. In spite of the urgent
need of repairs, I have had all the difficulty in the world in
getting Madame to order the plumber to come to-morrow morning. And I do not dare yet to ask for a stove, although, being
very chilly, I feel that I shall not be able to live in this mortal
room through the winter. This evening, to stop the wind and

the rain, I have had to stuff old skirts into the cracks. And this weather-vane above my head, never ceasing to turn on its rusty pivot, at times shrieks out so sharply in the night that one would take it for Madame's voice in the corridors, after a scene.

My first feelings of revolt having quieted down a little, my life proceeds here monotonously and stupidly; and I am gradually getting accustomed to it, without too great moral suffering. No one ever comes here; one would take it for a cursed house. And, outside of the petty domestic incidents that I have related, never does anything happen. All the days are alike, and all the tasks, and all the faces. It is ennui and death. But I am beginning to be so stupid that I am accommodating myself to this ennui, as if it were a natural thing. Even the deprivation of love does not cause me too much embarrasment, and I endure without too painful struggles this chastity to which I am condemned, or to which, rather, I have condemned myself, —for I have abandoned Monsieur, I have dropped Monsieur finally. Monsieur bores me, and I am angry with him for having, out of cowardice, disparaged me so grossly in talking with Madame. Not that he is becoming resigned, or ceasing to pay attention to me. On the contrary, he persists in revolving about me, with eyes that grow rounder and rounder, and a mouth that grows more and more frothy. According to an expression that I have read in I have forgotten what book, it is always toward my trough that he drives the pigs of his desire to drink.

Now that the days are shortening, Monsieur spends the afternoon at his desk, where he does the devil knows what, occupying his time in moving about old papers without reason, in checking off seed-catalogues and medical advertisements, and in distractedly turning the leaves of old hunting-books. You should see him when I go in at night to close the blinds or attend to his fire. Then he rises, coughs, sneezes, clears his throat, runs against the furniture, upsets objects, and tries in all sorts of stupid ways to attract my attention. It is enough to make one twist with laughter. I make a pretence of hearing nothing, of not understanding his puerile tricks; and I go away, silent and haughty, without looking at him any more than if he were not there.

Last evening, however, we exchanged the following brief remarks:

"Célestine!"

"Monsieur desires something?"

"Célestine, you are unkind to me; why are you unkind to me?"

"Why, Monsieur knows very well that I am a loose creature!" . . .

"Oh! come!"

"A dirty thing!" . . .

"Oh! come, come!"

"And possibly diseased."

"Oh! heavens! Célestine! Come, Célestine, listen to me!"

"Bah!"

Oh! I have enough of him. It no longer amuses me to upset his head and his heart by my coquetries.

In fact, nothing amuses me here. And the worst of it is that nothing bores me, either. Is it the air of this dirty country, the silence of the fields, the heavy, coarse food that I eat? A feeling of torpor is taking possession of me,—a feeling, moreover, which is not without charm. At any rate, it dulls my sensibility, deadens my dreams, and helps me to endure Madame's insolence and scolding. Thanks to it also, I feel a certain content in chattering, at night, for hours, with Marianne and Joseph,—this strange Joseph who does not go out any more, and seems to find pleasure in remaining with us. The idea that Joseph perhaps is in love with me,—well, that flatters me. Yes, indeed, I have got to that point. And then I read, and read,—novels, novels, and more novels. I have reread Paul

Bourget. His books do not excite my enthusiasm as they used to. In fact they tire me, and I consider them false and superficial. They are conceived in that state of soul which I know well from having experienced it when, dazzled and fascinated, I came in contact with wealth and luxury. I am all over it to-day, and these things no longer astonish me. They still astonish Paul Bourget. Oh! I would not be so silly now as to go to him for psychological explanations, for I know better than he what there is behind a parlor portière and under a lace dress.

A thing to which I cannot get accustomed is the receiving of no letters from Paris. Every morning, when the carrier comes, I feel a sort of laceration in my heart at realizing that I am so abandoned by everybody; and it is in this way that I can best measure the extent of my solitude. In vain have I written to my old comrades, and especially to Monsieur Jean, urgent and disconsolate letters; in vain have I implored them to pay some attention to me, to take me out of my hell, to find me a place in Paris, however humble it may be. Not one of them answers me. I would never have believed in so much indifference, in so much ingratitude.

And this forces me to cling more tightly to what I have left,—my memories and the past. Memories in which, in spite of everything, joy dominates suffering; a past which renews my hope that all is not over with me, and that it is not true that an accidental fall means irreparable ruin. That is why, alone in my room, while, on the other side of my partition, Marianne's snoring represents to me the distressing present, I try to drown this ridiculous sound in the sound of my old-time joys, and I passionately scrutinize this past, in order to reconstruct from its scattered bits the illusion of a future.

This very day, October 6, is a date full of recollections. During the five years that have elapsed since the tragedy which I now desire to relate, all the details have remained deep-rooted within me. There is a dead boy in this tragedy, a poor little dead boy, sweet and pretty, whom I killed by giving him too many caresses and too many joys, by giving him too much of life. And during the five years since he died,—died of me,— this will be the first time that I have not gone, on the sixth of October, to cover his grave with the usual flowers. But of these flowers, which I shall not carry to his grave, I will make a more durable bouquet, which will adorn and perfume his beloved memory better than the graveyard flowers adorn and perfume the bit of earth in which he sleeps. For the flowers of which the bouquet that I shall make will be composed I will gather, one by one, in the garden of my heart,—in the garden of my heart, where not only grow the mortal flowers of debauchery, but where bloom also the great white lilies of love.

I remember that it was on a Saturday. At the employment-bureau in the Rue du Colisée, which I had visited regularly every morning for a week in search of a place, I was introduced to an old lady in mourning. Never had I met a face more engaging, a look more gentle, manners more simple; never had I heard more winning words. She received me with a great politeness that warmed my heart.

"My child," she said to me, "Mme. Paulhat-Durand (that was the name of the woman who kept the employment-bureau) has spoken to me of you in terms of the highest praise. I believe that you deserve it, for you have an intelligent face, frank and gay, which pleases me greatly. I am in need of a person worthy of trust and capable of devotion. Devotion! Ah! I know that I am asking a thing that is not easy to give; for, after all, you do not know me, and you have no reason to be devoted to me. Let me explain to you my situation. But do not remain standing, my child; come and sit down beside me."

The moment I am spoken to gently, the moment that I am not looked upon as a being outside of others and on the fringe

of life, as something between a dog and a parrot, in that moment
I am touched, and at once I feel the soul of my childhood reborn within me. All my spite, all my hatred, all my spirit of
rebellion, I forget as by a miracle, and toward the people who
speak to me in a human fashion I feel no sentiments save those
of sacrifice and love. I know also, from experience, that it is
only the unfortunate who place the suffering of the humble on
a footing with their own. There is always insolence and distance in the kindness of the fortunate.

When I had taken my seat beside this venerable lady in
mourning, I already loved her; I really loved her.

She sighed:

"It is not a very gay place that I offer you, my child."

With a sincerity of enthusiasm that did not escape her,
I earnestly protested:

"That does not matter, Madame. Anything that Madame
may ask of me I will do."

And it was true. I was ready for anything.

She thanked me with a kind and tender look, and continued:

"Well, this is it. I have had many trials in my life. I
have lost all of my family, with the exception of a grandson,
who now, he also, is threatened with death from the terrible
disease of which the others have died."

Fearing to pronounce the name of this terrible disease, she
indicated it to me by placing upon her chest her old hand,
gloved in black, and then, with a more painful expression, continued:

"Poor little fellow! He is a charming child, an adorable
being, in whom I have placed my last hopes. For, when he is
gone, I shall be all alone. And, my God! what shall I do upon
earth?"

Her eyes filled with tears. She wiped them away with her
handkerchief, and went on:

97

"The doctors assure me that they can save him,—that the disease is not yet deep-seated. They have prescribed a *régime* from which they expect very good results. Every afternoon Georges must take a sea-bath, or, rather he must dip himself for a second in the sea. Then his whole body must be rubbed vigorously with a hair-glove, to stimulate the circulation; then he must be obliged to drink a glass of old port; and then he must lie stretched for at least an hour in a very warm bed. That is what I want of you in the first place, my child. But understand me well; what I specially want is youth, grace, gaiety, life. In my house it is these things that are most lacking. I have two very devoted servants, but they are old and sad, and possessed of manias. Georges cannot endure them. And I myself, with my old white head and my perpetual wearing of mourning,—I feel that I am an affliction to him. And, what is worse still, I feel also that I often am unable to hide from him my apprehensions. Oh! I know that this, perhaps, is not exactly the *role* for a young girl like you, beside so young a boy as Georges; for he is only nineteen! The world undoubtedly will find something to say about it. But I care not for the world; I care only for my sick grandchild, and I have confidence in you. You are a good woman, I suppose?"

"Oh! yes, Madame," I cried, certain in advance of being the sort of saint of whom this disconsolate grandmother was in search, for the salvation of her child.

"And he, the poor little one, my God! In his condition! In his condition, you see, he needs, more than sea-baths perhaps, the continual companionship of a pretty face, a fresh young laugh, something to drive from his mind the idea of death, some one to give him confidence in life. Will you undertake it?

"I accept, Madame," I answered, moved to the depths of my being. "And Madame may be sure that I will take good care of M. Georges."

It was agreed that I should enter upon my duties that

very evening, and that we should start on the next day but one for Houlgate, where the lady in mourning had rented a beautiful villa near the beach.

The grandmother had not lied. M. Georges was a charming, an adorable child. His beardless face had the loveliness of that of a beautiful woman; womanly also were his indolent movements, and his long, white, supple hands, through which could be seen the network of his veins. But what ardent eyes! Pupils consumed by a dull fire, beneath eyelids ringed with blue, and seemingly burned by the flaming gaze! What an intense focus of thought, of passion, of sensibility, of intelligence, of inner life! And to what an extent already had the red flowers of death invaded his cheeks! It seemed as if it were not of disease, as if it were not of death, that he was dying, but of an excess of life, of the fever of life that was in him, gnawing at his organs and withering his flesh! When his grandmother took me to him, he was stretched on a long chair, and holding in his long white hands an odorless rose. He received me, not as servant, but almost as a friend whom he expected. And from the first moment I became attached to him with all the strength of my soul.

Our establishment at Houlgate was effected without incident, as our journey had been also. Everything was ready, when we arrived. We had only to take possession of the villa, —a roomy, elegant villa, full of life and gaiety, and separated from the beach by a broad terrace covered with wicker-chairs and tents of many colors. A stone stairway, cut in the embankment, led to the sea, and against its lower steps sounded the music of the waves when the tide was coming in. M. George's room, on the ground floor, commanded an admirable view of the sea from large bay-windows. My own room—not the room of a servant, but that of a master—was opposite M. George's, across a passage-way, and was hung with light cretonne. From its windows one looked out into a little garden, where were growing some sorry-looking spindle-trees and some sorrier-looking rose-bushes. To express in words my joy, my pride, my emotion, and the pure and new elevation of mind that I felt at being thus treated and petted, admitted, like a lady, to comfort, to luxury, and to a share in that thing so vainly coveted which is called the family; to explain how, by a simple wave of the wand of that miraculous fairy, kindness, there came instantly an end to the recollection of my past humiliations and a conception of all the duties laid upon me by the dignity that belongs to a human being, and at last vouchsafed to me,—is quite beyond me. But I can say at least that I really perceived the magic of the transfiguration. Not only did the mirror testify that I had suddenly become more beautiful, but my heart assured me that I was really better. I discovered within me sources, sources, sources,—inexhaustible sources, ever-flowing sources, of devotion, of sacrifice, of hero-ism; and I had but one thought,—to save, by intelligent care, by watchful fidelity, and by marvelous skill, — to save M. Georges from death.

With a robust faith in my power of cure, I said in positive tones to the poor grandmother, who was in a state of perpetual despair, and often spent her days in weeping in the adjoining room:

"Do not weep, Madame. We will save him. I swear to you that we will save him."

And, in fact, at the end of a fortnight's time, M. Georges was much improved. A great change in his condition had taken place. The fits of coughing had diminished in number and intensity; his sleep and appetite were becoming more regular. He no longer had, in the night, those copious and terrible sweats that left him gasping and exhausted in the morning. His strength was so far recovered that we could take long drives and short walks, without serious fatigue. It was a sort of resurrection. As the weather was very fine, and the air very warm, but tempered by the sea-breeze, on days when we did not leave the premises we spent most of the time on the terrace, in the shelter of the tents, awaiting the bathing hour,—the hour of "the little dip in the sea," as M. Georges gaily called it. For he was gay, always gay; never did he speak of his illness, never of death. I really believe that in all those days he never once uttered the terrible word death. On the other hand, he was much amused by my chatter, provoking it if necessary; and I, confiding in his eyes, reassured by his heart, won by his indulgence and his grace, told him everything that came into my mind,— farces, follies and songs. My little childhood, my little desires, my little misfortunes, and my dreams, and my rebellions, and my various experiences with ludicrous or infamous masters,—I told him all, without much masking of the truth, for, young though he was, and separated from the world, and shut up as he had always been, he nevertheless, by a sort of prescience, by a marvelous divination which the sick possess, understood life thoroughly. A real friendship, that his nature surely facilitated, and that his solitude caused him to desire, and, above all, that the intimate and constant care with which I delighted his poor moribund flesh brought about, so to speak, automatically, sprang up between us. I was happy to a degree that I cannot picture, and my mind gained in refinement by incessant contact with his.

M. Georges adored poetry. For entire hours, on the terrace, to the music of the waves, or else at night in his room, he asked me to read him the poems of Victor Hugo, of Baudelaire, of Verlaine, of Mæterlinck. Often he closed his eyes, and lay motionless, with his hands folded on his breast, and I, thinking that he was asleep, stopped reading; but he smiled, and said:

"Go on, little one; I am not asleep. I can listen better so. I hear your voice better. And your voice is charming."

Sometimes it was he who interrupted me. After concentrating his thoughts, he slowly recited, with a prolongation of the rhythms, the lines that had excited in him the greatest enthusiasm, and he tried—oh! how I loved him for that!—to make me understand them, to make me feel their beauty. One day he said to me,—and I have kept these words as a relic:

"The sublimity of poetry, you see, lies in the fact that it does not take an educated person to understand it and to love it. On the contrary. The educated do not understand it, and generally they despise it, because they have too much pride. To love poetry it is enough to have a soul,—a little soul, naked, like a flower. Poets speak of the souls of the simple, of the sad, of the sick. And that is why they are eternal. Do you know that, when one has sensibility, one is always something of a poet? And you yourself, little Célestine, have often said to me things that are as beautiful as poetry."

"Oh! Monsieur Georges, you are making fun of me."

"Not in the least. And you are unaware that you have said these beautiful things. And that is the delightful part of it."

For me those were unique hours; whatever destiny may bring me, they will sing in my heart as long as I may live. I felt that indescribably sweet sensation of becoming a new being, of witnessing, so to speak, from minute to minute, the revelation of something unknown in me, and which yet was I. And to-day, in spite of worse falls, thoroughly reconquered as I am by all that is bad and embittered in me, if I have kept this passionate fondness for reading, and sometimes that impulse toward things superior to my social environment and to myself; if, trying to regain confidence in the spontaneity of my nature, I have dared—I who am so ignorant—to write this diary,—it is to M. Georges that I owe it.

Oh! yes, I was happy,— happy especially at seeing the pretty patient gradually reborn, his flesh swelling out and his face blooming again, through the flow of a new sap; happy at the joy, and the hopes, and the certainties, that the rapidity of this resurrection gave to the entire house, of which I was now the queen and the fairy. They attributed to me, they attributed to the intelligence of my care, to the vigilance of my devotion, and, more still perhaps, to my constant gaiety, to my youth so full of charm, to my surprising influence over Georges, this incomparable miracle. And the poor grandmother thanked me, overwhelmed me with gratitude and blessings, and also with presents, like a nurse to whom has been confided a baby almost dead, and who, with her pure and healthy milk, reconstructs his organs, brings back his smile, and restores him to life.

Sometimes, forgetful of her station, she took my hands, caressed them, kissed them, and, with tears of joy, said to me:

"I knew very well . . . I . . . when I saw you . . . I knew very well!"

And already projects were being formed,—journeys to the land of sunshine, fields full of roses!

"You shall never leave us; never more, my child."

Her enthusiasm often embarrassed me, but I finally came to believe that I deserved it. If, as many others would have done in my place, I had chosen to abuse her generosity. . . Oh, misfortune!

And what was to happen happened.

On the day of which I speak, the weather had been very warm, very heavy, and very threatening. Across the sky, above the leaden and perfectly flat sea, rolled stifling clouds, thick red clouds, through which the storm could not break. M. Georges had not gone out, even to the terrace, and we had remained in his room. More nervous than usual, a nervousness due undoubtedly to the electricity in the atmosphere, he had even refused to let me read poetry to him.

"That would tire me," he said. "And, besides, I feel that you would read very badly to-day."

He had gone into the *salon*, where he had tried to play a little on the piano. The piano having plagued him, he had at once come back into the room, where he had sought to divert himself for a moment by drawing, as it seemed to me, some feminine profiles. But he had not been slow in abandoning paper and pencil, fuming with some impatience:

"I cannot; I am not in the mood. My hand trembles. I don't know what is the matter with me. And you,—there is something the matter with you, too. You are restless."

Finally he had stretched himself on his long chair, near the large bay-window, through which one could see a vast expanse of water. Fishing-boats in the distance, fleeing from the ever-threatening storm, were re-entering the port of Trouville. With a distracted look he followed their manœuvres and their grey sails.

As M. Georges had said, I was restless; I could not keep still; I was continually moving about, to find something with which to occupy his mind. Of course I found nothing, and my agitation did not have a quieting influence on his.

"Why do you move about so? Why do you enervate yourself? Stay beside me."

I had asked him:

"Would you not like to be on one of those little boats yonder? I would."

"Oh! do not talk for the sake of talking. Why say useless things? Stay beside me."

Scarcely had I taken my seat beside him, when, the sight of the sea becoming utterly unendurable to him, he asked me to lower the blind.

"This bad light exasperates me; this sea is horrible. I do not wish to look at it. Everything is horrible to-day. I do not wish to see anything; I wish to see you only."

I had gently chided him.

"Oh! Monsieur Georges, you are not good. You are not behaving well. If your grandmother were to come in and see you in this condition, you would make her cry again."

Having raised himself a little on the cushions:

"In the first place, why do you call me 'Monsieur Georges'? You know that I do not like it."

"But I cannot call you 'Monsieur Gaston'!"

"Call me 'Georges' for short naughty girl."

"Oh! I could not; I could never do that!"

Then he had sighed:

"Is it not curious? Are you, then, still a poor little slave?"

Then he had lapsed into silence. And the rest of the day passed off, half in enervation, half in silence, which was also an enervation, and more painful.

In the evening, after dinner, the storm at last broke out. The wind began to blow violently, the waves to beat against the embankment with a heavy sullen sound. M. Georges would not go to bed. He felt that it would be impossible for him to sleep, and in a bed sleepless nights are so long! He on his long chair, I sitting near a little table on which, veiled by a shade, was burning a lamp that shed a soft, pink light about us, we said nothing. Although his eyes were more brilliant than usual, M. Georges seemed calmer, and the pink reflection from the lamp heightened his color, and outlined more clearly in the light the features of his delicate and charming face. I was engaged in sewing.

Suddenly he said to me:

"Leave your work for a little while, Célestine, and sit beside me."

I always obeyed his desires, his caprices. At times he manifested an effusive and enthusiastic friendship, which I attributed to gratitude. This time I obeyed as usual.

"Nearer, still nearer," he exclaimed.

Then:

"Now give me your hand."

Without the slightest mistrust I allowed him to take my hand, which he caressed.

"How pretty your hand is! And how pretty your eyes are! And how pretty you are, altogether, altogether, altogether!"

105

He had often spoken to me of my kindness, but never had he told me that I was pretty; at least, he had never told me so with such an air. Surprised and, in reality, charmed by these words, which he uttered in a grave and somewhat gasping voice, I instinctively drew back.

"No, no, do not go away; stay near me, close to me. You cannot know how much good it does me to have you near me, how it warms me. See, I am no longer nervous, agitated; I am no longer sick; I am content, happy, very happy."

And, having chastely placed his arm about my waist, he obliged me to sit down beside him on the long chair. And he asked:

"Are you uncomfortable so?"

I was not reassured. In his eyes burned a fire more ardent than ever. His voice trembled more—with that trembling which I know,—oh! yes, how I know it!—that trembling which is given to the voice of all men by the violent desire of love. I was very much moved, and I was very cowardly; my head was whirling a little. But, firmly resolved to defend myself against him, and especially to energetically defend him against himself, I answered in a childish way:

"Yes, Monsieur Georges, I am very uncomfortable; let me get up."

His arm did not leave my waist.

"No, no, I beg of you, be nice."

And in a tone the coaxing gentleness which I cannot describe, he added:

"You are very timid. What are you afraid of, then?"

At the same time he approached his face to mine, and I felt his warm breath with its insipid odor,—something like an incense of death.

My heart seized with an inexpressible anguish, I cried:

"Monsieur Georges! Oh! Monsieur Georges, let me go. You will make yourself sick. I beg of you! Let me go."

I did not dare to struggle, because of his weakness, out

of respect for the fragility of his members. I simply tried—and how carefully!—to put away his hand, which, awkward, timid, trembling, was trying to unhook my waist. And I repeated:

"Let me go! You are behaving very badly, Monsieur Georges. Let me go!"

His effort to hold me against him had tired him. His embrace soon weakened. For a few seconds he breathed with greater difficulty and then a dry cough shook his chest.

"You see, Monsieur Georges," I said to him, with all the gentleness of a maternal reproach, "you are wilfully making yourself sick. You will listen to nothing. And all will have to be begun over again. Great progress we shall make in this way! Be good, I beg of you! And, if you were very nice, do you know what you would do? You would go to bed directly."

He withdrew his hand, stretched out on the long chair, and, as I replaced beneath his head the cushions that had slipped down, he sadly sighed:

"After all, you are right; I ask your pardon."

"You have not to ask my pardon, Monsieur Georges; you have to be quiet."

"Yes, yes," he exclaimed, his eyes fixed on the spot in the ceiling where the lamp made a circle of moving light. "I was a little mad . . . to have dreamed for a moment that you could love me,—me who have never had love,—me who have never had anything but suffering. Why should you love me? It would cure me to love you. Since you have been here beside me, and since the beginning of my desire for you; since you have been here with your youth, and your freshness, and your eyes, and your hands,—your little silky hands, whose attentions are the gentlest of caresses; since the time I began to dream of you alone,—I have felt boiling within me, in my soul and in my body, new vigor, a wholly unknown life. That is to say, I

107

did feel that,—for now . . . In short, what do you expect!
I was mad! And you, you are right.''

I was greatly embarrassed. I knew not what to say; I
knew not what to do. Powerful and opposite feeling pulled
me in all directions. An impulse rushed me toward him, a
sacred duty held me back. And in a silly fashion, because I
was not sincere, because I could not be sincere in a struggle
where these desires and this duty combatted with equal force,
I stammered:

''Monsieur Georges, be good. Do not think of these ugly
things. It makes me sick. Come, Monsieur Georges, be very
nice.''

But he repeated:

''Why should you love me? Truly, you are right in not
loving me. You think me ill. You fear to poison your mouth
with the poisons of mine; you are fraid of contracting my disease—the disease of which I am dying, am I not?—from one of
my kisses. You are right.''

The cruel injustice of these words struck me to the heart.

''Do not say that, Monsieur Georges,'' I cried, wildly;
''what you say is horrible and wicked. And you really give
me too much pain, too much pain.''

I seized his hands; they were moist and burning. I bent
over him; his breath had the raucous ardor of a forge.

''It is horrible, horrible!''

He continued:

''A kiss from you,—why! that meant my resurrection, my
complete restoration to life. Oh! you have believed seriously
in your baths, in your port wine, in your hair-glove. Poor
little one! It is in your love that I have bathed, it is the wine
of your love that I have drunk, it is the revulsion of your life
that has set a new blood flowing beneath my skin. It is because I have so hoped and longed and waited for your kiss
that I have begun to live again to be strong,— for I am strong
now. But I am not angry with you for refusing me; you are

108

right in refusing. I understand; I understand. You are a timid little soul, without courage; a little bird that sings on one branch, and then on another, and flies away at the slightest noise . . . frroutt!''

''These are frightful things which you are saying, Monsieur Georges.''

He still went on, while I wrung my hands:

''Why are they frightful? No, indeed, they are not frightful; they are true. You think me sick. You think that one is sick when one has love. You do not know that love is life,—eternal life. Yes, yes, I understand, since your kiss, which is life for me, might, you fancy, be death for you. Let us say no more about it.''

I could not listen further. Was it pity? Was it the bleeding reproach and bitter challenge that these atrocious and sacrilegious words conveyed? Was it simply the impulsive and savage love that suddenly took possession of me? I do not know. Perhaps it was all of these together. What I know is that I allowed myself to fall, like a mass, on the long chair, and that, lifting in my hands the child's adorable head, I wildly cried:

''There, naughty boy, see how afraid I am of you! See, then, how afraid I am of you!''

I glued my lips to his lips, I pressed my teeth against his, with such quivering fury that my tongue seemed to penetrate the deepest sores of his chest, to lick them, to drink from them, to draw out of them all the poisoned blood and all the mortal pus. His arms opened, and closed again about me, in an embrace.

And what was to happen happened.

Well, no. The more I think about it, the surer I am that what threw me into Georges's arms, what fastened my lips to his, was, first and only, an imperative, spontaneous movement of protest against the base sentiments that Georges—through strategy, perhaps—attributed to my refusal. It was, above all, an act of fervent, disinterested, and very pure piety, which meant to say:

"No, I do not think that you are sick; no, you are not sick. And the proof is that I do not hesitate to mingle my breath with yours, to breathe it, to drink it, to impregnate my lungs with it, to saturate with it all my flesh. And, even though you were really sick, even though your disease were contagious and fatal to any one approaching it, I do not wish you to entertain concerning me this monstrous idea that I am afraid of contracting it, of suffering from it, and of dying from it."

Nor had I foreseen and calculated the inevitable result of this kiss, and that I would not have the strength, once in my friend's arms, once my lips on his, to tear myself from this embrace and put away this kiss. But there it is, you see! When a man holds me in his arms, my skin at once begins to burn, and my head to turn and turn. I become drunk; I become mad; I become savage. I have no other will than that of my desire. I see only him; I think only of him; and I suffer myself to be led by him, docile and terrible, even to crime!

Oh! that first kiss of M. Georges, his awkward and delicious caresses, the passionate artlessness of all his movements, and the wondering expression of his eyes in presence of the mystery, at last unveiled, of woman and of love! But, the intoxication passed, when I saw the poor and fragile child, panting, almost swooning in my arms, I felt a frightful remorse,—at least the terrifying sensation that I had just committed a murder.

"Monsieur Georges! Monsieur Georges! I have made you ill. Oh! poor little one!"

But he,—with what feline, tender, and trusting grace, with what dazzled gratitude, he rolled against me, as if in search of protection. And he said to me, his eyes filed with ecstasy:

"I am happy. Now I can die."

And, as I cursed my weakness in my despair, he repeated: "I am happy. Oh! stay with me; do no leave me. It seems to me, you see, that, if I were left alone, I could not endure the violence of my happiness, although it is so sweet."

While I was helping him to go to bed, he had a fit of coughing. Fortunately it was short. But, short though it was, it lacerated my soul. After having relieved and cured him, was I going to kill him now? I thought that I should be unable to keep the tears back. And I detested myself.

"It is nothing; it is nothing," he exclaimed, with a smile; "you must not grieve, since I am so happy. And besides, I am not sick, I am not sick. You will see how soundly I shall sleep against you. For I wish to sleep upon your breast, as if I were your little child,—my head upon your breast."

"And if your grandmother should ring for me to-night, Monsieur Georges?"

"Oh no! Oh no! Grandmother will not ring. I wish to sleep against you."

During the fortnight that followed that memorable night, that delicious and tragic night, a sort of fury took possession of us, mingling our kisses, our bodies, our souls, in an embrace, in an endless possession. We were in haste to enjoy, in compensation for the lost past; we desired to live, almost without rest, the love of which we felt that death, now near at hand, was to be the climax.

A sudden change had taken place in me. In my kiss there was something sinister and madly criminal. Knowing that I was killing Georges, I was furiously bent upon killing myself also, of the same joy and of the same disease. Deliberately I sacrificed his life and mine. With a wild and bitter exaltation I breathed and drank in death, all the death, from his mouth; and I besmeared my lips with his poison. Once, when he was coughing, seized, in my arms, with a more violent attack than usual, I saw, foaming on his lips, a huge and unclean clot of blood-streaked phlegm.

"Give! give! give!"

111

And I swallowed the phlegm with murderous avidity, as I would have swallowed a life-giving cordial.

Monsieur Georges was not slow in wasting away. His crises became more and more frequent, more painful. He spat blood, and had long periods of swooning, during which he was thought to be dead. His body grew thin, hollow, and emaciated, until it really resembled an anatomical specimen. And the joy that had regained possession of the house changed very speedily into dismal sorrow. The grandmother began again to pass her days in the *salon*, crying, praying, on the alert for sounds, and, with her ear glued to the door that separated her from her child, undergoing a frightful and continual anguish of hearing a cry,—a rattle,—a sigh, the last,—the end of everything dear and still living that was left to her here below. When I went out of the room, she followed me, step by step, about the house, wailing:

"Why, my God, why? And what then has happened?"

She said to me also:

"You are killing yourself, my poor little one. But you cannot pass all your nights by Georges's side. I am going to send for a sister to take your place."

But I refused. And she cherished me all the more for this refusal, seeming to think that, having already worked one miracle, I could now work another. Is it not frightful? I was her last hope.

As for the doctors, summoned from Paris, they were astonished at the progress of the disease, and that it had worked such ravages in so short a time. Not for a moment did they or anyone suspect the terrible truth. Their intervention was confined to the prescribing of quieting potions.

Monsieur Georges alone remained gay, happy,—steadily gay, unalterably happy. Not only did he never complain, but his soul continually poured itself out in effusions of gratitude. He spoke only to express his joy. Sometimes, at night, in his room, after terrible crises, he said to me:

112

"I am happy. Why grieve and weep? Your tears do something to spoil my joy, the ardent joy with which I am filled. Oh! I assure you that death is not a high price to pay for the superhuman happiness which you have given me. I was lost; death was in me; nothing could prevent it from being in me. You have rendered it radiant and pleasant. Then do not weep, dear little one. I adore you, and I thank you."

My fever of destruction had entirely vanished now. I lived in a condition of frightful disgust with myself, in an unspeakable horror of my crime, of my murder. There was nothing left me but the hope, the consolation, or the excuse that I had contracted my friend's disease, and would die with him, and at the same time.

And what was to happen happened.

We were then in the month of October, precisely the sixth of October, The autumn having remained mild and warm that year, the doctors had counselled a prolongation of the patient's stay at the seaside, pending the time when he could be taken to the south. All day long, on that sixth of October, Monsieur Georges had been quieter. I had opened wide the large bay-window in his room, and there, lying on his long chair, beside the window, protected from the air by warm coverings, he had breathed for at least four hours, and deliciously, the iodic emanations from the offing. The life-giving sun, the good sea odors, the deserted beach, now occupied again by the shell-fishermen, delighted him. Never had I seen him gayer. And this gaiety on his emaciated face, where the skin, growing thinner from week to week, covered the bones like a transparent film, had something funereal about it, and so painful to witness that several times I had to leave the room in order to weep freely. He refused to let me read poetry to him. When I opened the book, he said:

"No; you are my poem; you are all my poems, and far the most beautiful of all."

He was forbidden to talk. The slightest conversation fatigued him, and often brought on a fit of coughing. Moreover, he had hardly strength enough to talk. What was left to him of life, of thought, of will to express, of sensibility, was concentrated in his gaze, which had become a glowing fireplace, in which the soul continually kindled a flame of surprising and supernatural beauty. That evening, the evening of the sixth of October, he seemed no longer to be suffering. Oh! I see him still, stretched upon his bed, his head high upon his pillow, his long thin hands playing tranquilly with the blue fringe of the curtain, his lips smiling at me, and his eyes, which, in the shade of the bed, shone and burned like a lamp, following all my goings and comings.

They had placed a couch in the room for me, a nurse's couch and—oh! irony, in order doubtless to spare his modesty and mine—a screen behind which I could undress. But often I did not lie upon the couch; Monsieur Georges wanted me always by his side. He was really comfortable, really happy, only when I was near him.

After having slept two hours, almost peacefully, he awoke toward midnight. He was a little feverish; the spots at the points of his cheek-bones were a little redder. Seeing me sitting at the head of his bed, my cheeks damp with tears, he said to me, in a tone of gentle reproach:

"What, weeping again? You wish, then, to make me sad, and to give me pain? Why do you not lie down? Come and lie down beside me."

I cried, shaken by sobs:

"Ah! Monsieur Georges, do you wish me, then, to kill you? Do you wish me to suffer all my life from remorse at having killed you?"

All my life! I had already forgotten that I wanted to die with him, to die of him, to die as he died.

"Monsieur Georges! Monsieur Georges! Have pity on me, I implore you!"

But his lips were on my lips. Death was on my lips.

"Be still!" he exclaimed, gasping. "I have never loved you so much as to-night."

Suddenly his arms relaxed and fell back, inert, upon the bed; his lips abandoned mine. And from his mouth, turned upward, there came a cry of distress, and then a flow of hot blood that spattered my face. With a bound I was out of bed. A mirror opposite revealed my image, red and bloody. I was mad, and, running about the room in bewilderment, it was my impulse to call for aid. But the instinct of self-preservation, the fear of responsibilities, of the revelation of my crime, and I know not what else that was cowardly and calculating, closed my mouth, and held me back at the edge of the abyss over which my reason was tottering. Very clearly and very speedily I realized that it would not do for any one to enter the room in its present condition.

O human misery! There was something more spontaneous than my grief, more powerful than my fear; it was my ignoble prudence and my base calculations. In my terror I had the presence of mind to open the door of the *salon,* and then the door of the ante-room, and listen. Not a sound. Everybody in the house was asleep. Then I returned to the bedside. I raised George's body, as light as a feather, in my arms. I lifted up his head, maintaining it in an upright position in my hands. The blood continued to flow from his mouth in pitchy filaments; I heard his chest discharging itself through his throat, with the sound of an empty bottle. His eyes, turned up, showed nothing but their reddish globes between the swollen eyelids.

"Georges! Georges! Georges!"

I let go his body; his body sank upon the bed. I let go his head; his head fell back heavily upon the pillow. I placed my hand upon his heart; his heart had ceased to beat.

"Georges! Georges! Georges!"

The horror of this silence, of these mute lips, of this corpse red and motionless, and of myself, was too much for me. And, crushed with grief, crushed with the frightful necessity of restraining my grief, I fell to the floor in a swoon.

How many minutes did this swoon last, or how many centuries? I do not know. On recovering consciousness, one torturing thought dominated all others, — that of removing every accusing sign. I washed my face, I redressed myself, and —yes, I had the frightful courage,—I put the bed and the room to rights. And, when that was done, I awoke the house; I cried the terrible news through the house.

Oh! that night! That night I suffered all the tortures that hell contains.

And this night here at the Priory reminds me of it. The storm is raging, as it raged there the night when I began my work of destruction on that poor flesh. And the roaring of the wind through the trees in the garden sounds to me like the roaring of the sea against the embankment of the forever-cursed Houlgate villa.

Upon our return to Paris, after M. Georges's funeral, I did not wish to remain in the poor grandmother's service, in spite of her repeated entreaties. I was in a hurry to go away, that I might see no more of that tearful face,—that I might no longer hear the sobs that lacerated my heart. And, above all, I was in a hurry to get away from her gratitude, from the necessity which she felt, in her doting distress, of continually thanking me for my devotion, for my heroism, of calling me her "daughter, her dear little daughter," and of embracing me with madly effusive tenderness. Many times during the fortnight in which I consented to call upon her, in obedience to her request, I had an intense desire to confess, to accuse myself, to tell her everything that was lying so heavily on my soul and often stifling me. But what would have been the use? Would it have given her any relief whatever? It would simply have added a more bitter affliction to her other afflictions, and the horrible thought and the inexpiable remorse that, but for

116

me, her dear child perhaps would not be dead. And then, I must confess that I had not the courage. I left her house with my secret, worshipped by her as if I were a saint, overwhelmed with rich presents and with love.

Now, on the very day of my departure, as I was coming back from Mme. Paulhat-Durand's employment-bureau, I met in the Champs-Elysées a former comrade, a valet, with whom I had served for six months in the same house. It was fully two years since I had seen him. After our first greetings, I learned that he, as well as I, was looking for a place. Only, having for the moment some nickel-plated extra jobs, he was in no hurry to find one.

"This jolly Célestine!" he exclaimed, happy at seeing me again; "as astonishing as ever!"

He was a good fellow, gay, full of fun, and fond of a good time. He proposed:

"Suppose we dine together, eh?"

I needed to divert myself, to drive far away from me a multitude of sad images, a multitude of obsessing thoughts. I accepted.

"Good!" he exclaimed.

He took my arm, and led me to a wine-shop in the Rue Cambon. His heavy gaiety, his coarse jokes, his vulgar obscenity, I keenly appreciated. They did not shock me. On the contrary, I felt a certain rascally joy, a sort of crapulous security, as if I were resuming a lost habit. To tell the truth, I recognized myself, I recognized my own life and my own soul in those dissipated eyelids, in that smooth face, in those shaven lips, which betray the same servile grimace, the same furrow of falsehood, the same taste for passional filth, in the actor, the judge, and the valet.

After dinner we strolled for a time on the boulevards; then he took me to see a cinematograph exhibition. My will was a little weak from having drunk too much Saumur wine. In the darkness of the hall, as the French army was marching across the illuminated screen amid the applause of the spectators, he caught me about the waist, and imprinted a kiss upon the back of my neck which came near loosening my hair.

"You are astonishing!" he whispered. "Oh! how good you smell!"

He accompanied me to my hotel, and we stood for a few minutes on the sidewalk, silent and a little stupid. He was tapping his shoes with the end of his cane; I, with head lowered, my elbows pressed closely against my body, and my hands in my muff, was crushing a bit of orange-peel beneath my feet.

"Well, *au revoir!*" I said to him.

"Oh, no," he exclaimed, "let me go up with you. Come, Célestine."

I defended myself, in an uncertain fashion, for the sake of form. He insisted.

"Come, what is the matter with you? Heart troubles? Now is the very time" . . .

He followed me. In this hotel they did not look too closely at the guests who returned at night. With its dark and narrow staircase, its slimy banister, its vile atmosphere, its fetid odors, it seemed like a house for the accommodation of transients and cut-throats. My companion coughed, to give himself assurance. And I, with my soul full of disgust, reflected:

"Oh! indeed! this is not equal to the Houlgate villas or to the warm and richly-adorned mansions in the Rue Lincoln."

What a hussy one is sometimes! Oh, misery me!

And my life began again, with its ups and downs, its changes of front, its *liasons* as quickly ended as begun, and its sudden leaps from opulent interiors into the street, just as of old.

Singular thing! I, who in my amorous exaltation, my ardent thirst for sacrifice, had sincerely and passionately wished to die, was haunted for long months by the fear of having contracted Monsieur Georges's disease from his kisses. The slightest indisposition, the most fleeting pain, filled me with real terror. Often at night I awoke with mad frights and icy sweats. I felt of my chest, where, by suggestion, I suffered from pains and lacerations; I examined the discharges from my throat, in which I saw red streaks; and I gave myself a fever, by frequent counting of my pulse. It seemed to me, as I looked in the glass, that my eyes were growing hollow, and that my cheeks were growing pinker, with that mortal pink that colored Monsieur Georges's face. One night, as I was leaving a public ball, I took cold, and I coughed for a week. I thought that it was all over with me. I covered my back with plasters, and swallowed all sorts of queer medicines; I even sent a pious offering to Saint Anthony of Padua. Then, as, in spite of my fear, my health remained good, showing that I had equal power to endure the fatigues of toil and of pleasure, it all passed away.

Last year, on the sixth of October, I went to lay flowers on M. Georges's grave, as I had done every year when that sad date came round. He was buried in the Montmartre cemetery. In the main path I saw, a few steps ahead of me, the poor grandmother. Oh! how old she was, and how old also were the two old servants who accompanied her! Arched, bent, tottering, she walked heavily, sustained at the arm-pits by her two old servants, as arched, as bent, as tottering, as their mistress. A porter followed them, carrying a large bunch of red and white roses. I slackened my pace, not wishing to pass them and be recognized. Hidden behind the wall of a high monument, I waited until the poor and sorrowful old woman had placed her flowers, told her beads, and dropped her tears upon her grandson's grave. They came back with the same feeble steps, through the smaller path, brushing against the wall of the vault on the other side of which I was hiding. I concealed myself still more, that I might not see them, for it seemed to me that it was my remorse, the phantoms of my remorse, that were filing by me. Would she have recognized me? Ah! I do

119

not think so. They walked without looking at anything, without seeing even the ground about them. Their eyes had the fixity of the eyes of the blind; their lips moved and moved, and not a word came from them. One would have said that they were three old dead souls, lost in the labyrinth of the cemetery, and looking for their graves. I saw again that tragic night, and my red face, and the blood flowing from Georges' mouth. It sent a shiver to my heart. At last they disappeared.

Where are they to-day, those three lamentable shades? Perhaps they are a little more dead; perhaps they are dead quite. After having wandered on for days and nights, perhaps they have found the hole of silence and of rest of which they were in search.

All the same, it is a queer idea that the unfortunate grandmother had, in choosing me as a nurse for a young and pretty boy like Monsieur Georges. And really, when I think of the matter again, and realize that she never suspected anything, that she never saw anything, that she never understood anything, this seems to me the most astonishing feature of the matter. Ah! one can say it now; they were not very sharp, the three of them. They had an abundance of confidence.

I have seen Captain Mauger again, over the hedge. Crouching before a freshly-dug bed, he was transplanting pansies and gilly-flowers. As soon as he saw me, he left his work, and came to the hedge to talk. He is no longer angry with me for the murder of his ferret. He even seems very gay. Bursting with laughter, he confides to me that this morning he has wrung the neck of the Lanlaires' white cat. Probably the cat avenges the ferret.

"It is the tenth that I have gently killed for them," he cries, with ferocious joy, slapping his thigh, and then rubbing his grimy hands. "Ah! the dirty thing will scratch no more compost from my garden-frames; it will no longer ravage my seed-plots, the camel! And, if I could also wring the necks of your Lanlaire and his female! Oh! the pigs! Oh! oh! oh! that's an idea.''

This idea makes him twist with laughter for a moment. And suddenly, his eyes sparkling with a stealthy malice, he asks:

"Why don't you put some smart-weed in their bed? The dirty creatures! Oh! I would give you a package of it for the purpose. That's an idea!"

Then:

"By the way, you know?   Kléber? my little ferret?"

"Yes.   Well?"

"Well, I ate him.   Alas! alas!"

"He was not very good, was he?"

"Alas! he tasted like bad rabbit."

And that was all the funeral sermon that the poor animal got.

The captain tells me also that a week or two ago he caught a hedge-hog under a wood-pile. He is engaged in taming him. He calls him Bourbaki. Ah! That's an idea! An intelligent, comical, extraordinary beast that eats everything!

"Yes, indeed!" he exclaims. "In the same day this confounded hedge-hog has eaten beefsteak, mutton stew, salt bacon, gruyère cheese, and preserves. He is astonishing. It is impossible to satisfy him. He is like me; he eats everything!"

Just then the little domestic passes the path, with a wheelbarrow full of stones, old sardine-boxes, and a heap of *débris,* which he is carrying to the refuse-heap.

"Come here!" calls the captain.

And, as, in answer to his question, I tell him that Monsieur has gone hunting, that Madame has gone to town, and that Joseph has gone on an errand, he takes from the wheelbarrow each of the stones, each bit of the *débris,* and, one after another, throws them into the garden, crying in a loud voice:

"There, pig!   Take that, you wretch!"

The stones fly, the bits of *débris* fall upon a freshly-worked bed, where Joseph the day before had planted peas.

"Take that! And this, too! And here is another, in the bargain!"

The bed, soon covered with *débris*, becomes a confused heap. The captain's joy finds expression in a sort of hooting and disorderly gestures. Then, turning up his old grey moustache, he says to me, with a triumphant and rakish air:

"Mademoiselle Célestine, you are a fine girl, for sure! You must come and see me, when Rose is no longer here, eh? Ah! that's an idea!"

Well, indeed! He has no cheek!

VIII.

At last I have received a letter from Monsieur Jean. It is very dry, this letter. From reading it, one would think that there never had been any intimacy between us. Not a word of friendship, not a particle of tenderness, not a recollection! He tells me only of himself. If he is to be believed, it seems that Jean has become an important personage. That is to be seen and felt from the patronizing and somewhat contemptuous air which he assumes toward me at the beginning of his letter. In short, he writes to me only to astonish me. I always knew that he was vain,—indeed, he was such a handsome fellow!— but I never realized it so much as to-day. Men cannot stand success or glory.

Jean is still first *valet de chambre* in the house of the Countess Fardin, and at this moment the countess is perhaps the most-talked-of woman in France. To his capacity of *valet de chambre* Jean adds the *role* of a participant in political manifestations and of royalist conspirator. He manifests with Coppée, Lemaitre, Quesnay de Beaurepaire; he conspires with General Mercier,—and all to overturn the republic. The other evening he accompanied Coppée to a meeting of the "Patrie Française." He strutted on the platform, behind the great patriot, and held his overcoat all the evening. For that matter, he can say that he has held all the overcoats of all the great patriots of this time. That will count for something in his life. Another evening, at the exit of a Dreyfusard meeting, to which the countess had sent him to "smash the jaws of the cosmopolitans," he was arrested and taken to the station-house for having spat upon these people without country, and shouted at the top of his voice: "Death to the Jews! Long Live the

King! Long Live the Army!'' The countess threatened the government with an interpellation in the chamber and Monsieur Jean was at once released. His mistress even added twenty francs a month to his wages, in compensation for this lofty feat of arms. M. Arthur Meyer printed his name in the ''Gaulois.'' His name figures also opposite the sum of a hundred francs in the ''Libre Parole,'' among the subscribers to the fund for a monument for Colonel Henry. Coppée inscribed it there officially. Coppée also made him an honorary member of the ''Patrie Française,''—an astonishment society. All the servants in the great houses belong to it. There are also counts, marquises, and dukes. On coming to breakfast yesterday, General Mercier said to Jean: ''Well, my brave Jean?'' My brave Jean! Jules Guérin, in the ''Anti-Juif,'' has written, under the heading, ''Another Victim of the Sheenies!'' an article beginning: ''Our valiant anti-Semitic comrade, M. Jean,'' etc. And finally, M. Forain, who now is always at the house, has had Jean pose for a design, which is to symbolize the soul of the country. M. Forain thinks that Jean has ''just the mug for that.'' He receives at this moment an astonishing number of illustrious decorations, of serious tips, and of honorary and extremely flattering distinctions. And if, as there is every reason to believe, General Mercier decides to summon Jean for the coming Zola trial, to give false testimony, —the nature of which the staff will decide upon soon,—nothing will be lacking to complete his glory. This year, in high society, there is nothing so fashionable and effective as false testimony. To be selected for a perjurer, besides bringing certain and swift glory, is as good as winning the capital prize in a lottery. M. Jean clearly perceives that he is making a greater and greater sensation in the neighborhood of the Champs-Elysées. When, in the evening, he goes to the café in the Rue Francois I. to play pool for a turkey, or when he takes the countess's dog out for an airing, he is the object of universal curiosity and respect; so are the dogs, for that matter. That is why, in view of a celebrity which cannot fail to spread from the neighborhood over Paris, and from Paris over France, he has become a subscriber to a clipping-bureau, just as the countess has done. He will send me the smartest things that are written about him. This is all that he can do for me, for I must understand that he has no time to attend to my affairs. He will see, later,—"when we shall be in power," he writes me, carelessly. Everything that happens to me is my fault; I have never known how to conduct myself; there has never been any sequence in my ideas; I have wasted the best places, without profit. If I had not been such a hot-head, I, too, perhaps would be on the best terms with General Mercier, Coppée, Déroulède; and perhaps, although I am only a woman, I should see my name sparkling in the columns of the "Gaulois," which is so encouraging for all sorts of domesticity. Etc., etc.

To read this letter almost made me cry, for I felt that Monsieur Jean is quite gone from me, and that I can no longer count on him, on him or on anybody! He does not tell me a word of my successor. Ah! I see her from here, I see them from here, both of them, in the chamber that I know so well, kissing and caressing each other, and making the round of the public balls and the theatres together, as we used to do so prettily. I see him in his putty-colored overcoat, returning from the races, after having lost his money, and saying to her, as so many times he has said to me: "Lend me your jewels and your watch, that I may hang them up." Unless his new *role* of participant in political manifestations and of royalist conspirator has filled him with new ambitions, and he has abandoned the loves of the servants' hall for the loves of the *salon*. He will come back to them.

Is all that happens to me really my fault? Perhaps. And yet it seems to me that a fatality of which I have never been the mistress has weighed upon my entire existence, and has prevented me from ever staying more than six months in the same place. When they did not discharge me, I left, disgusted beyond endurance. It is funny, and it is sad,—I have always been in a hurry to be "elsewhere," I have always entertained a mad hope of "those chimerical elsewheres," which I invest with the vain poesy, the illusory mirage of far-away distances, especially since my stay at Houlgate with poor M. Georges. That stay has left me with a certain anxiety, a certain unattainable ideas and forms. I really believe that this too short and sudden glimpse of a world which I had better never have known at all, being unable to know it better, has been very harmful to me. Oh! how disappointing are these ways leading to the unknown! One goes on and on, and it is always the same thing. See that sparkling horizon yonder. It is blue, it is pink, it is fresh, it is as light and luminous as a dream. It must be fine to live there. You approach, you arrive. There is nothing. Sand, pebbles, hills as dismal as walls. There is nothing else. And above this sand, these pebbles, these hills, there is a gray, opaque, heavy sky,—a sky which kills the day, and whose light weeps dirty tears. There is nothing,—nothing of that which one is looking for. Moreover, I do not know what I am looking for; and neither do I know who I am.

A domestic is not a normal being, a social being. He is an incongruous personage, made up of pieces and bits that cannot fit into one another, that can only lie next one another. He is something worse,—a monstrous human hybrid. He is no longer of the people, whence he came; neither is he of the *bourgeoisie,* among whom he lives and toward whom he tends. He has lost the generous blood and the artless strength of the people that he has denied, and has gained the shameful vices of the *bourgeoisie,* without having succeeded in acquiring the means of satisfying them,—the vile sentiments, the cowardly fears, the criminal appetites, without the setting, and consequently without the excuse, of wealth. With a soiled soul, he traverses this respectable *bourgeois* world, and, simply from having breathed the mortal odor that rises from these putrid sinks, he loses forever the security of his mind, and even the

126

very form of his personality. At the bottom of all these recollections, amid this host of figures among whom he wanders, a phantom of himself, he finds nothing to work upon but filth,—that is, suffering. He laughs often, but his laugh is forced. This laugh does not come from joy found or from hope realized, and it shows the bitter grimace of rebellion, the hard and contracted curve of sarcasm. Nothing is more sorrowful and ugly than this laugh; it burns and withers. It would have been better, perhaps, if I had wept. And then, I do not know. And then, *zut!* Come what will.

But nothing comes at all,—never anything. And I cannot accustom myself to that. It is this monotony, this absolute fixity in life, that is the hardest thing for me to endure. I should like to go away from here. Go away? But where and how? I do not know, and I stay.

Madame is always the same; distrustful, methodical, severe, rapacious, without an impulse, without a caprice, without a particle of spontaneity, without a ray of joy upon her marble face. Monsieur has resumed his habits, and I imagine, from certain sullen airs, that he has a spite against me because of my severity; but his spites are not dangerous. After breakfast, armed and gaitered, he starts off on a hunting expedition, returns at night, asks me only to help him in taking off his boots, and goes to bed at nine o'clock. He is still awkward, comical, and irresolute. He is growing fat. How can people as rich as they are be resigned to so dismal an existence? Sometimes I question myself regarding Monsieur. What should I have done with him? He has no money, and would have given me no pleasure. And especially as Madame is not jealous!

The terrible thing about this house is its silence. I cannot get used to it. Yet, in spite of myself, I am beginning to glide, to "walk in the air," as Joseph says. Often in these dark passage-ways, alongside these cold walls, I seem to myself like a spectre, like a ghost. And I am stifling in it all. And I stay.

My sole diversion is to go on Sunday, after mass, to call on Mme. Gouin, the grocer. Disgust holds me back, but ennui, stronger than disgust, takes me there. There at least we are ourselves again,—all of us together. We gossip, we laugh, we tell stories as we sip our little black-currant cocktails. There we find a little of the illusion of life. The time passes. A few Sundays ago I missed a little woman, with running eyes and a rat-like nose, whom I had seen there previously. I inquire about her.

"It is nothing; it is nothing," said the grocer, in a tone to which she tried to impart a certain mystery.

"She is sick, then?"

"Yes, but it is nothing. In two days it will be all gone."

And Mam'zelle Rose looks at me with confirmatory eyes, which seem to say:

"Ah, you see, this is a very skilful woman."

To-day I have learned at the grocer's that a party of hunters found yesterday, in the forest of Raillon, among the briers and dead leaves, the body of a little girl, horribly outraged. It seems that she was the daughter of a road-laborer. She was known in the neighborhood as the little Claire. She was a little bit simple, but sweet and pretty, and she was not twelve years old! A rich windfall, as you can imagine, for a place like the grocer's shop, where they had to content themselves with telling the same stories week after week. Consequently the tongues rattled famously.

According to Rose, always better informed than the others, the little Claire had been cut open with a knife, and her intestines were protruding through the wound. Her neck and throat still bore visible marks of strangling fingers. There was still to be seen in the short heather the trampled and trodden spot where the crime had been committed. It must have happened at least a week ago, for the body was almost entirely decomposed.

128

The assembled domestics relate a heap of things; they remember that the little Claire was always in the woods. In the spring she gathered there jonquils and lilies of the valley and anemones, of which she made pretty bouquets for the ladies of the town; she also went there to look for morels, which she sold on Sunday at the market. In summer there were mushrooms of all sorts, and other flowers. But at this time of year why did she go to the woods, where there was nothing left to pick?

One says, discreetly:

"Why had the father shown no anxiety regarding the child's disappearance? Perhaps he did it himself?"

To which another no less discreetly replies:

"But, if he had wanted to do it himself, he had no need to take his daughter to the woods; come now."

Mlle. Rose intervenes:

"It all looks very suspicious to me."

With knowing airs, the airs of one who is in possession of terrible secrets, she goes on in a lower voice, a voice of dangerous confidence:

"Oh! I know nothing about it; I make no assertions. But" . . .

And she leaves our curiosity hanging on this "but."

"What then? what then?" they cry from all sides, with outstretched necks and open mouths.

"But . . . I should not be astonished . . . if it were" . . .

We are breathless.

"Monsieur Lanlaire. There, that is what I think, if you want to know," she concludes, with an expression of base and atrocious ferocity.

Several protested; others reserve judgment. I declare that Monsieur Lanlaire is incapable of such a crime, and I cry:

"He, Lord Jesus? Oh, the poor man! He would be too much afraid."

"Incapable? Ta, ta, ta! And the little Jézureau? And Valentin's little girl? And the little Dougère? Do you remember them? Incapable?"

"It is not the same thing; it is not the same thing."

In their hatred of Monsieur they do not, like Rose, go so far as to make a formal charge of murder. That he outrages little girls who consent to be outraged,—yes, that is possible. That he kills them,—that is scarcely credible. But Rose stormily insists. She froths at the mouth; she pounds the table with her soft, fat hands; she cries, with excited gestures:

"Do I not tell you yes? I am sure of it."

Mme. Gouin, who has been listening in a dreamy fashion, finally declares, in her meaningless voice:

"Oh! indeed, young women, in these matters one can never tell. As for the little Jézureau, it was a famous bit of luck, I assure you, that he did not kill her."

In spite of the authority of the grocer, in spite of the obstinacy of Rose, who will not consent to change the subject, they pass in review, one after another, all the people in the neighborhood who could have done the deed. They find heaps of them,—all those whom they detest, all those of whom they have any jealousy, against whom they have any spite. Finally the pale little woman with the rat-like nose remarks:

"You know that last week there were two capuchins begging around here, who did not present a very inviting appearance, with their dirty beards. May it not have been they?"

A cry of indignation arises:

"Worthy and pious monks? The good God's holy souls! It is abominable!"

And, as we take our departure, after laying everybody under suspicion, Rose, bent on establishing her theory, repeats:

"Do I not tell you that it is he? It is he, be sure!"

Before re-entering the house, I stop a moment in the harness-room, where Joseph is polishing his harnesses. Above a dresser, on which bottles of varnish and boxes of blacking are symmetrically arranged, I see flaming on the pine wainscoting the portrait of Drumont. To give him greater majesty, undoubtedly, Joseph has recently adorned him with a crown of laurel. Opposite, the portrait of the pope is almost entirely hidden by a horse-blanket hung upon a nail. Anti-Jewish pamphlets and patriotic songs are piled up on a shelf, and in a corner Joseph's club stands lonely among the brooms.

Suddenly I say to Joseph, solely from a motive of curiosity:

"Do you know, Joseph, that the little Claire has been found in the woods, murdered and outraged?"

At first Joseph cannot suppress a movement of surprise,—is it really surprise? Rapid and furtive as this movement was, it seems to me that, at the sound of the little Claire's name, a sort of strange shock, something like a shudder, passed through him. He recovers very quickly.

"Yes," he says, in a firm voice, "I know it. I was told so in the neighborhood this morning."

Now he is indifferent and placid. He rubs his harnesses methodically with a thick, black cloth. I admire the muscular development of his bare arms, the harmonious and powerful suppleness of his biceps, the whiteness of his skin. I cannot see his eyes under the lowered lids,—his eyes so obstinately fixed upon his work. But I see his mouth, his large mouth, his enormous jaw, the jaw of a cruel and sensual beast. And I feel a sort of light tremor at my heart. I ask him further:

"Do they know who did it?"

Joseph shrugs his shoulders. Half jesting, half serious, he answers:

"Some vagabonds, undoubtedly; some dirty sheenies."

Then, after a short silence:

"Puuutt! you will see that they will not pinch them. The magistrates are all sold."

He hangs up the finished harness, and, pointing to Drumont's portrait, in its laurel halo, he adds:

131

"If we only had him? Oh, misfortune!"

I know not why I left him with a singular feeling of uneasiness in my soul.

At any rate, this story is going to give us something to talk about, something to divert us a little.

Sometimes, when Madame is out, and I cannot stand the ennui, I go to the iron fence by the roadside, where Mlle. Rose comes to meet me. Always on the watch, nothing that goes on in our place escapes her. She sees all who come in and go out. She is redder, fatter, flabbier than ever. Her lips hang more than they did, and she is more and more haunted by obscene ideas. Every time that we meet, her first look is at my person, and her first words, uttered in her thick voice, are:

"Remember my advice. As soon as you notice anything, go straight to Mme. Gouin; straight."

It is a veritable obsession, a mania. A little annoyed, I reply:

"But why do you expect me to notice anything? I know nobody here."

"Ah!" she exclaims, "a misfortune comes so quickly! A moment of forgetfulness,—it is very natural,—and there you are! Sometimes one does not know how it happens. I have seen some who were as sure as you are, and then it happened all the same. But with Mme. Gouin one can rest easy. So expert a woman is a real blessing to a town. Why, formerly, my dear little one, you saw nothing but children around here. The town was poisoned with children. An abomination! They swarmed in the streets, like chickens in a hen-yard. They bawled on the door-steps, and made a terrible hullaballoo. One saw nothing else. Well, I don't know whether you have noticed it, but to-day there are no more to be seen, almost none at all."

With a more slimy smile, she continues:

"Not that the girls amuse themselves any less. Oh! heavens, no! On the contrary. You never go out in the evening; but, if you were to take a walk at nine o'clock under the chestnut trees, you would see. Everywhere couples on the benches, kissing and caressing. It is a very pretty spectacle. Oh! to me, you know, love is so pretty. I perfectly understand that one cannot live without love. Yes, but it is very annoying also to have a lot of children tagging at one's heels. Well, they have none now; they have no more. And it is to Mme. Gouin that they owe that. Just a disagreeable moment to pass through; after all, it is not like having to swallow the sea. In your place I would not hesitate. A pretty girl like you, so distinguished, and who must have so good a figure,—a child would be a murder.''

"Reassure yourself. I have no desire to have one."

"Yes, I know; nobody has any desire to have one. Only . . . But, tell me, has Monsieur never made advances to you?"

"Why, no."

"That is astonishing, for he has a great reputation for that. Not even that morning in the garden?"

"I assure you."

Mam'zelle Rose shakes her head.

"You are unwilling to say anything. You distrust me. Well, that is your business. Only, we know what we know."

Peasants pass in the road, and salute Mam'zelle Rose, with respect.

"How do you do, Mam'zelle Rose? And the captain,— is he well?"

"Very well, thank you. He is drawing some wine just now."

Bourgeois pass in the road, and salute Mam'zelle Rose with respect.

"How do you do, Mam'zelle Rose? And the captain?"

"Always vigorous, thank you; you are very good."

The priest passes in the road, with a slow step, wagging his head. At the sight of Rose, he bows, smiles, closes his breviary, and stops.

133

"Ah! it is you, my dear child? And the captain?"

"Thank you, Father, things are going very nicely. The captain is busy in the cellar."

"So much the better, so much the better! I hope that he has planted some beautiful flowers, and that next year, on Corpus Christi day, we shall have again a superb street altar."

"You may be sure of it, Father."

"All my friendships to the captain, my child."

"And the same to you, Father."

And, as he goes away, his breviary again open:

"*Au revoir! au revoir!* All that a parish needs is parishioners like you."

And I go back, a little sad, a little discouraged, a little hateful, leaving this abominable Rose to enjoy her triumph, saluted by all, respected by all, fat, happy, hideously happy. Soon, I am sure, the priest will place her in a niche in his church, between two candles, with a nimbus of gold about her, like a saint.

IX.

Joseph puzzles me. His ways are really mysterious, and I do not know what goes on in this silent and furious soul. But surely something extraordinary. His look sometimes is difficult to endure,—so difficult that mine avoids its intimidating fixity. He has a slow and gliding gait, that frightens me. One would say that he was dragging a ball riveted to his ankle, or, rather, the recollection of a ball. Is this a relic of a prison or of a convent? Both, perhaps. His back, too, frightens me, and also his large, powerful neck, tanned by the sun till it looks like old leather, and stiffened with sinews that stretch and strain like ropes. I have noticed on the back of his neck a collection of hard muscles that stand out in an exaggerated fashion, like those of wolves and wild beasts which have to carry heavy prey in their jaws.

Apart from his anti-Semitic craze, which indicates in Joseph a great violence and a thirst for blood, he is rather reserved concerning all matters. It is even impossible to know what he thinks. He has none of the swagger, and none of the professional humility, by which true domestics are to be recognized. Never a word of complaint, never the slightest disparagement of his masters. He respects his masters, without servility, and seems to be devoted to them, without ostentation. He does not sulk at his work, even when it is most repulsive. He is ingenious; he knows how to do everything, even the most difficult and different things, not a part of his regular work. He treats the Priory as if it were his own, watches it, guards it jealously, defends it. He drives away the poor, the vagrant, and the unfortunate, sniffing and threatening like a bull-dog. He is a type of the old-time servant, of the domestic of the

135

days before the revolution. Of Joseph they say in the neighborhood: "There is nobody like him. A pearl!" I know that
they try to get him away from the Lanlaires. From Louviers,
from Elbeuf, from Rouen, he receives the most flattering offers.
He refuses them, and does not boast of having refused them.
Oh, no, indeed! He has been here for fifteen years, and he con-
siders this house as his own. As long as they want him, he
will stay. Madame, suspicious as she is, and seeing evil everywhere, places a blind confidence in him. She, who believes in
nobody, believes in Joseph, in Joseph's honesty, in Joseph's
devotion.

"A pearl! He would throw himself into the fire for us,"
she says.

And, in spite of her avarice, she overwhelms him with
petty generosities and little gifts.

Nevertheless, I distrust this man. He disturbs me, and at
the same time he interests me prodigiously. Often I have seen
frightful things passing in the troubled water, in the dead
water of his eyes. Since I have been observing him, I have
changed the opinion that I formed of him when I first entered
this house,—the opinion that he is a gross, stupid, and clumsy
peasant. I ought to have examined him more attentively. Now
I think him singularly shrewd and crafty, and even better
than shrewd, worse than clever; I know not how to express
myself concerning him. And then—is it because I am in the
habit of seeing him every day?—I no longer find him so ugly
or so old. Habit, like a fog, tends to palliate things and beings.
Little by little it obscures the features of a face and rubs down
deformities; if you live with a humpback day in and day out,
after a time he loses his hump. But there is something else;
I am discovering something new and profound in Joseph,
which upsets me. It is not harmony of features or purity of
lines that make a man beautiful to a woman. It is something
less apparent, less defined, a sort of affinity, and, if I dare say
so, a sort of sexual atmosphere, pungent, terrible, or intoxicat-

ing, to the haunting influence of which certain women are susceptible, even in spite of themselves. Well, such an atmosphere emanates from Joseph. The other day I admired him as he was lifting a cask of wine. He played with it like a child with its rubber ball. His exceptional strength, his supple skill, the terrible leverage of his loins, the atletic push of his shoulders, all combined to make me dreamy. The strange and unhealthy curiosity, prompted by fear as much as by attraction, which is excited in me by the riddle of these suspicious manners, of this closed mouth, of this impressing look, is doubled by this muscular power, this bull's back. Without being able to explain it to myself further, I feel that there is a secret correspondence between Joseph and me,—a physical and moral tie that is becoming a little more binding every day.

From the window of the linen-room where I work, I sometimes follow him with my eyes in the garden. There he is, bending over his work, his face almost touching the ground, or else kneeling against the wall where the espaliers stand in line. And suddenly he disappears, he vanishes. Lower your head, and, before you can raise it again, he is gone. Does he bury himself in the ground? Does he pass through the walls? From time to time I have occasion to go to the garden to give him an order from Madame. I do not see him anywhere, and I call him:

"Joseph! Joseph! where are you?"

Suddenly, without a sound, Joseph arises before me, from behind a tree, from behind a vegetable-bed. He rises before me in the sunlight, with his severe and impenetrable mask, his hair glued to his skull, and his open shirt revealing his hairy chest. Where does he come from? From what hole does he spring? From what height has he fallen?

"Oh! Joseph, how you frightened me!"

And over Joseph's lips, and in his eyes, there plays a terrific smile, which really has the swift, short flashes of a knife. I believe that this man is the devil.

137

CELESTINE

The murder of the little Claire continues to be the all-absorbing topic, and to excite the curiosity of the town. They fight for the local and Paris newspapers that give the news. The "Libre Parole" accuses the Jews squarely and by wholesale, and declares that it was a "ritual murder." The magistrates have visited the spot, made inquiries and examinations, and questioned many people. Nobody knows a thing. Rose's charge, which has been circulating, has been met everywhere with an incredulous shrug of the shoulders. Yesterday the police arrested a poor peddler, who had no trouble in proving that he was not in the vicinity at the time of the crime. The father, to whom public rumor pointed, has been exonerated. Moreover, he bears an excellent reputation. So nowhere is there any clue to put justice on the track of the guilty. It seems that this crime excites the admiration of the magistrates, and was committed with a surprising skill,—undoubtedly by professionals, by Parisians. It seems also that the prosecuting attorney is pushing the affair in a very tame fashion and for the sake of form. The murder of a poor girl is not a very interesting matter. So there is every reason to believe that no clue will ever be found, and that the case will soon be pigeonholed, like so many others that have not told their secret.

I should not wonder if Madame believed her husband guilty. That is really comical, and she ought to know him better. She has behaved very queerly ever since the news. She has ways of looking at Monsieur that are not natural. I have noticed that during meals, whenever the bell rings, she gives a little start.

After breakfast to-day, as Monsieur manifested an intention of going out, she prevented him.

"Really, you may as well remain here. Why do you need to be always going out?"

She even walked with Monsieur for a full hour in the garden. Naturally Monsieur perceives nothing; he does not lose

138

a mouthful of food or a puff of tobacco-smoke. What a stupid blockhead!

I had a great desire to know what they could be saying to each other when they were alone,—the two of them. Last night, for more than twenty minutes, I listened at the door of the *salon*. I heard Monsieur crumpling a newspaper. Madame, seated at her little desk, was casting up her accounts.

"What did I give you yesterday?" Madame asked.

"Two francs," answered Monsieur.

"You are sure?"

"Why, yes, my pet."

"Well, I am short thirty-eight sous."

"It was not I who took them."

"No, it was the cat."

Of the other matter they said not a word.

In the kitchen Joseph does not like to have us talk about the little Claire. When Marianne or I broach the subject, he immediately changes it, or else takes no part in the conversation. It annoys him. I do not know why, but the idea has come to me—and it is burying itself deeper and deeper in my mind —that it was Joseph who did it. I have no proofs, no clues to warrant my suspicion,—no other clues than his eyes, no other proofs than the slight movement of surprise that escaped him when, on my return from the grocer's, I suddenly, in the harness-room, threw in his face for the first time the name of the little Claire murdered and outraged. And yet this purely intuitive suspicion has grown, first into a possibility, and then into a certainty. Undoubtedly I am mistaken. I try to convince myself that Joseph is a "pearl." I say to myself over and over again that my imagination takes mad flights, obedient to the influence of the romantic perversity that is in me. But all in vain; the impression remains, in spite of myself, never leaves me for a moment, and is assuming the tormenting and grimacing form of a fixed idea. And I have an irresistible desire to ask Joseph:

"Say, Joseph, was it you who outraged the little Claire in the woods? Was it you, old pig?"

The crime was committed on a Saturday. I remember that Joseph, at about that date, went to the forest of Raillon to get some heath mould. He was absent all day, and did not return to the Priory with his load till late in the evening. Of that I am sure. And—an extraordinary coincidence—I remember certain restless movements, certain troubled looks, that he had that evening, when he came back. I took no notice of them then. Why should I have done so? But to-day these facial details come back to me forcibly. But was it on the Saturday of the crime that Joseph went to the forest of Raillon? I seek in vain to fix the date of his absence. And then, had he really the restless movements, the accusing looks, that I attribute to him, and which denounce him to me? Is it not I who am bent upon suggesting to myself the unusual strangeness of those movements and those looks? Am I not determined, without reason and against all probability, that it shall be Joseph— a pearl—who did it? It irritates me, and at the same time confirms me in my apprehensions, that I cannot reconstruct before my eyes the tragedy of the forest. If only the judicial examination had revealed fresh tracks of a cart on the dead leaves and on the heather in the neighborhood? But no; the examination revealed nothing of the kind; it revealed the outrage and murder of a little girl, and that is all. Well, it is precisely that which so excites me. This cleverness of the assassin in leaving not the slightest trace of his crime behind him, this diabolical invisibility,—I feel in it and see in it the presence of Joseph. Enervated, I make bold suddenly, after a silence, to ask him this question:

"Joseph, what day was it that you went to the forest of Raillon to get heath mould? Do you remember?"

Without haste, without a start, Joseph puts down the

newspaper that he is reading. Now his soul is steeled against surprises.

"Why do you ask?" he says.

"Because I want to know."

Joseph looks at me with his heavy, searching gaze. Then, without affectation, he seems to be ransacking his memory in search of recollections that are already old. And he answers:

"Indeed, I do not remember exactly; I think, though, that it was on a Saturday."

"The Saturday when the body of the little Claire was found in the woods?" I go on, giving to this inquiry, too quickly uttered, an aggressive tone.

Joseph does not take his eyes from mine. His look has become so sharp and so terrible that, in spite of my customary effrontery, I am obliged to turn away my head.

"Possibly," he says again; "indeed, I really think that it was that Saturday."

And he adds:

"Oh! these confounded women! You would do much better to think of something else. If you read the newspaper, you would see that they have been killing Jews again in Algeria. That at least is something worth while."

Apart from his look, he is calm, natural, almost good-natured. His gestures are easy; his voice no longer trembles. I become silent, and Joseph, picking up the newspaper that he had laid on the table, begins to read again, in the most tranquil fashion in the world.

For my part, I have begun to dream again. Now that I am about it, I should like to find in Joseph's life some act of real ferocity. His hatred of the Jews, his continual threats to torture, kill, and burn them,—all this, perhaps, is nothing but swagger, and political swagger at that. I am looking for something more precise and formal, some unmistakable evidence of Joseph's criminal temperament. And I find nothing but vague and moral impressions, hypotheses to which my desire or

141

my fear that they may be undeniable realities gives an importance and a significance which undoubtedly they do not possess. My desire or my fear? I do not know which of these two sentiments it is that moves me.

But yes. Here is a fact, a real fact, a horrible fact, a revealing fact. I do not invent it; I do not exaggerate it; I did not dream it; it is exactly as I state it. It is one of Joseph's duties to kill the chickens, rabbits, and ducks. He kills the ducks by the old Norman method of burying a pin in their head. He could kill them with a blow, without giving them pain. But he loves to prolong their suffering by skilful refinements of torture. He loves to feel their flesh quiver and their heart beat in his hands; he loves to follow, to count, to hold in his hands, their suffering, their convulsions, their death. Once I saw Joseph kill a duck. He held it between his knees. With one hand he grasped it by the neck, with the other he buried a pin in its head; and then he turned and turned the pin in the head, with a slow and regular movement. One would have thought he was grinding coffee. And, as he turned the pin, Joseph said, with savage joy:

"It is necessary to make it suffer. The more it suffers, the better its blood will taste."

The animal had freed its wings from Joseph's knees; they were beating, beating. Its neck, in spite of Joseph's grasp, twisted into a frightful spiral, and beneath its feathers its flesh heaved. Then Joseph threw the animal upon the stone floor of the kitchen, and, with elbows on his knees and chin in his joined palms, he began to follow, with a look of hideous satisfaction, its bounds, its convulsions, the mad scratching of its yellow claws upon the floor.

"Stop then, Joseph," I cried. "Kill it at once; it is horrible to make animals suffer."

And Joseph answered:

"That amuses me. I like to see that."

I recall this memory; I evoke all its sinister details; I

heard all the words that were spoken. And I have a desire, a still more violent desire, to cry to Joseph:

"It was you who outraged the little Claire in the woods. Yes, yes; I am sure of it now; it was you, you, you, old pig."

There is no longer any doubt of it; Joseph must be a tremendous scoundrel. And this opinion that I have of his moral personality, instead of driving me from him, far from placing a wall of horror between us, causes me, not to love him perhaps, but to take an enormous interest in him. It is queer, but I have always had a weakness for scoundrels. There is something unexpected about them that lashes the blood,—a special odor that intoxicates you,—something strong and bitter that attracts you sexually. However infamous scoundrels may be, they are never as infamous as the respectable people. What annoys me about Joseph is that he has the reputation, and, to one who does not know his eyes, the manners, of an honest man. I should like him better if he were a frank and impudent scoundrel. It is true that he would love that halo of mystery, that prestige of the unknown, which moves and troubles and attracts me—yes, really, attracts me—toward this old monster.

Now I am calmer, because I am certain, and because nothing henceforth can remove the certainty from my mind, that it was he who outraged the little Claire in the woods.

For some time I have noticed that I have made a considerable impression upon Joseph's heart. His bad reception of me is at an end; his silence toward me is no longer hostile or contemptuous, and there is something approaching tenderness in his nudges. His looks have no more hatred in them,—did they ever have any, however?—and, if they are still so terrible at times, it is because he is seeking to know me better, always better, and wishes to try me. Like most peasants, he is extremely distrustful, and avoids trusting himself to others, for he thinks that they are planning to "take him in." He must be in possession of numerous secrets, but he hides them jealously, under a severe, scowling, and brutal mask, as one locks treasures in a strong-box equipped with solid bars and mysterious bolts. However, his distrust of me is lessening. He is charming toward me, in his way. He does all that he can to show his friendship for me, and to please me. He relieves me of my most painful duties; takes upon himself the heavy work that is given me to do; and all without roguishness, without any underlying gallantry, without seeking to provoke my gratitude, without trying to get any profit from it whatsoever. On my side, I keep his affairs in order, mend his stockings and his pantaloons, patch his shirts, and arrange his closet with much more care and coquetry than I do Madame's. And he says to me, with a look of satisfaction:

"That is very well, Célestine. You are a good woman,—an orderly woman. Order, you see, means fortune. And, when one is pretty besides,—when one is a beautiful woman, there is nothing better."

Hitherto we have talked together only for brief moments. At night, in the kitchen, with Marianne, the conversation has to be general. No intimacy is permissible between us two. And, when I see him alone, nothing is more difficult than to make him talk. He refuses all long conversations, fearing, undoubtedly, to compromise himself. A word here, a word there, amiable or crusty, and that is all. But his eyes speak, though his lips are silent. And they prowl around me, and they envelop me, and they descend into me, into my very depths, in order to turn my soul inside out and see what is in it.

For the first time we had a long talk yesterday. It was at night. The masters had gone to bed; Marianne had gone to her room earlier than usual. Not feeling disposed to read or write, it was tiresome for me to remain alone. Still obsessed by the image of the little Claire, I went to find Joseph in the harness-room, where, seated at a little whitewood table, he was sorting seeds by the light of a dark lantern. His friend, the sacristan, was there, standing near him, holding under his two arms packages of little pamphlets, red, green, blue, tri-color. With big round eyes surpassing the arch of the eye-brows, flattened skull, and wrinkled, yellow, and cross-grained skin, he looked like a toad. He had also the bounding heaviness of a toad. Under the table the two dogs, rolled into a ball, were sleeping, with their heads buried in their shaggy skins.

"Ah! it is you, Célestine?" exclaimed Joseph.

The sacristan tried to hide his pamphlets, but Joseph reassured him.

"We can talk before Mademoiselle. She is an orderly woman."

And he gave him directions.

"So, old man, it is understood, isn't it? At Bazoches, at Courtain, at Fleur-sur-Tille. And let them be distributed tomorrow, in the day time. And try to get subscriptions. And let me tell you again; go everywhere, into all the houses,—even the houses of republicans. Perhaps they will show you the door, but that makes no difference. Keep right on. If you win one of these dirty pigs, it is always so much gained. And then, remember that you get five francs for every republican."

The sacristan nodded his head approvingly. Having tucked the pamphlets under his arms, he started off, Joseph accompanying him as far as the iron fence. When the latter returned, he noticed my curious face, my inquisitive eyes.

"Yes," he said, carelessly, "some songs, and some pictures, and some pamphlets against the Jews, which are being distributed for propagandism. I have made an arrangement with the priests: I work for them. It is in the line of my own ideas, surely; but I must say also that I am well paid."

He sat down again at the little table where he was sorting his seeds. The two dogs, awakened, took a turn about the room, and went to lie down again farther off.

"Yes, yes," he repeated, "I get good pay. Oh! the priests have money enough."

And, as if fearing that he had said too much, he added:

"I tell you this, Célestine, because you are a good woman and an orderly woman, and because I have confidence in you. It is between ourselves, you know."

After a silence:

"What a good idea it was of yours to come out here to-night!" he thanked me; "it is very nice of you; it flatters me."

Never had I seen him so amiable, so talkative. I bent over the little table very near him, and, stirring the sorted seeds in the plate, I answered coquettishly:

"It is true, too; you went away directly after dinner; we had no time to gossip. Shall I help you sort your seeds?"

"Thank you, Célestine, I have finished."

He scratched his head.

"*Sacristi!*" he exclaimed, with annoyance, " I ought to go and see to my garden-frames. The field-mice do not leave me a salad, the vermin! But then, no, indeed, I must talk with you, Célestine."

Joseph rose, closed the door, which had been left half open, and led me to the back of the harness-room. For a minute I was frightened. The little Claire, whom I had forgotten, appeared before my eyes on the forest heath, frightfully pale and bleeding. But there was nothing wicked in Joseph's looks; they were timid, rather. We could scarcely see each other in this dark room, lighted by the dull and hazy gleams of the lantern. Up to this point Joseph's voice had trembled. Now it suddenly took on assurance, almost gravity.

"For some days I have been wanting to confide this to you, Célestine," he began; "well, here it is. I have a feeling of friendship for you. You are a good woman, an orderly woman. Now I know you very well."

I thought it my duty to assume an archly mischievous smile, and I replied:

"You must admit that it has taken you some time. And why were you so disagreeable with me? You never spoke to me; you were always rough with me. You remember the scenes that you made me when I went through the paths that you had just raked? Oh! how crusty you were!"

Joseph began to laugh, and shrugged his shoulders:

"Oh! yes; why, you know, one cannot get acquainted with people at the very start. And women especially,—it takes the devil to know them. And you came from Paris! Now I know you very well."

"Since you know me so well, Joseph, tell me, then, what I am."

With set lips and serious eyes, he said:

"What you are, Célestine? You are like me."

"I am like you, I?"

"Oh! not in your features, of course. But you and I, in the very depths of the soul, are the same thing. Yes, yes, I know what I say."

Again there was a moment of silence. Then he resumed, in a voice that was less stern:

"I have a feeling of friendship for you, Célestine. And then" . . .

"And then?" . . .

"I have some money, too,—a little money."

"Ah?"

"Yes, a little money. Why, one does not serve forty years in good houses without saving something. Is it not so?"

"Surely," I answered, more and more astonished by Joseph's words and manner. "And you have much money?"

"Oh! only a little."

"How much? Let me see."

Joseph gave a slight chuckle.

"You may know well that it is not here. It is in a place where it is making little ones."

"Yes, but how much?"

Then in a low voice, almost a whisper:

"Perhaps fifteen thousand francs; perhaps more."

"My! but you are well fixed, you are!"

"Oh! perhaps less, too. One cannot tell."

Suddenly the two dogs lifted their heads simultaneously, bounded to the door, and began to bark. I made a movement of fright.

"That's nothing," said Joseph, reassuringly, giving each of them a kick in the side; "simply people passing in the road. Why, it is Rose, going home. I know her step."

And, in fact, a few seconds later I heard a sound of dragging steps in the road, and then a more distant sound of a closing gate. The dogs became silent again.

I had sat down on a stool in a corner of the harness-room. Joseph, with his hands in his pockets, walked back and forth in the narrow room, his elbows hitting against the pine wainscoting from which leather straps were hanging. We did not speak, I being horribly embarrassed and regretting that I had come, and Joseph being plainly tormented by what he had still to say to me. After some minutes he made up his mind.

"There is another thing that I must confide to you, Célestine. I am from Cherbourg. And Cherbourg is a tough town, full of sailors and soldiers, of jolly lascars who do not deny themselves pleasure; business is good there. Well, I know a fine opportunity just now at Cherbourg. It is a matter of a little café near the water. A little café in a first-rate location. The army is drinking a great deal these days; all the patriots are in the street; they shout and bawl and get thirsty. Now is the time to get it. One could make hundreds and thousands, I promise you. Only, you see, there must be a woman there,— an orderly woman, a pretty woman, well equipped, and not afraid of slang and smut. The sailors and soldiers are good-natured and gay and full of fun. They get drunk on the slightest provocation, and they are fond of women, and spend much for them. What do you think about it, Célestine?"

"I?" I exclaimed, stupefied.

"Yes; just suppose the case. Would you like it?"

"I?"

I did not know what he was coming at. I trembled from surprise to surprise. Utterly upset, I could think of no answer to make. He insisted:

"You, of course. And who, then, do you expect to come to the little café? You are a good woman; you are orderly; you are not one of those affected creatures who do not know even how to take a joke; and you are patriotic! And then you are pretty, very nice to look at; you have eyes to drive the whole Cherbourg garrison crazy. Just the cheese! Now that I know you well, now that I know all that you can do, this idea keeps continually running through my head."

"Well? And you?"

"I, too, of course. We would marry, like good friends."

"Then," cried I, with sudden indignation, "you want me to prostitute myself to make money for you?"

Joseph shrugged his shoulders, and said tranquilly:

"All depends on the intention, Célestine. That is understood, is it not?"

Then he came to me, took my hands, pressed them so tightly that I screamed with pain, and stammered:

"I dream of you, Célestine; I dream of you in the little café. I am crazy over you."

And, as I stood in amazement, a little frightened by this confession, and without a gesture or a word, he continued:

"And then, perhaps there are more than fifteen thousand francs. Perhaps more than eighteen thousand francs. One never knows how many little ones this money makes. And then, things . . . things . . . jewels . . . you would be tremendously happy in the little café."

He held my waist clasped in the powerful vise of his arms. And I felt his whole body against me, trembling with desire. If he had wished, he could have taken me and stifled me without the slightest resistance on my part. And he continued to unfold his dream:

"A little café, very pretty, very clean, very shining. And

149

then, at the bar, before a large mirror, a beautiful woman, dressed in the costume of Alsace-Lorraine, with a beautiful silk waist and broad velvet ribbons. Hey, Célestine? Think of that! I will talk with you about it again one of these days; I will talk with you about it again.''

I found nothing to say,—nothing, nothing, nothing. I was stupefied by this thing, of which I had never dreamed; but I was also without hatred, without horror, of this man's cynicism. Clasping me with the same hands that had clasped, stifled, strangled, murdered the little Claire in the woods, Joseph repeated:

''I will talk with you about it again. I am old; I am ugly. Possibly. But to fix a woman, Célestine,—mark this well,— there is nobody like me. I will talk with you about it again.''

To fix a woman! How he fills one with forebodings! Is it a threat? Is it a promise?

To-day Joseph has resumed his customary silence. One would think nothing had happened last night between us. He goes, he comes, he works, he eats, he reads his paper, just as usual. I looked at him, and I should like to detest him. I wish that his ugliness would fill me with such immense disgust as to separate me from him forever. Well, no. Ah! how queer it is! This man sends shivers through me, and I feel no disgust, since it was he who killed and outraged the little Claire in the woods.

X.

Nothing gives me so much pleasure as to find in the newspapers the name of a person in whose house I have served. This pleasure I felt this morning more keenly than ever before, in learning from the "Petit Journal" that Victor Charrigaud has just published a new book, which has met with much approval and of which everybody speaks in admiration. This book is entitled, "From Five to Seven," and is a howling success. It is, says the article, a series of brilliant and cutting society studies, which, beneath their light exterior, hide a profound philosophy. Yes, rely upon it! At the same time that they praise Victor Charrigaud for his talent, they also compliment him highly on his elegance, on his distinguished social position, on his *salon*. Ah! let us say a word of his *salon*. For eight months I was the Charrigauds' chambermaid, and I really believe that I have never met such boors. God knows, however!

Everybody is familiar with the name Victor Charrigaud. He has already published a series of books that have made a sensation. "Their Little Garters," "How They Sleep," "The Sentimental Bigoudis," "Humming-Birds and Parrots," are among the most celebrated. He is a man of infinite wit, a writer of infinte talent; unhappily, success and wealth have come to him too quickly. His beginnings aroused the greatest hopes. Everybody was struck with his great faculty of observation, with his powerful gift of satire, with his implacable and just irony that penetrated so deeply humanity's ridiculous side. A well-informed and free mind, to which social conventions were nothing but falsehood and servility, a generous and clear-sighted soul, which, instead of bending under the humiliating level of prejudice, bravely directed its impulses to-

151

ward a pure and elevated social ideal. At least so Victor Charrigaud was described to me by one of his friends, a painter, who was stuck on me, and whom I used sometimes to go to see, and from whom I got the opinions just expressed and the details that are to follow regarding the literature and the life of this illustrious man.

Among the ridiculous things that Charrigaud had lashed so severely, there was none that he had treated so harshly as snobbishness. In his lively conversation, well supported by facts, even more than in his books, he branded its moral coward-ice and its intellectual barrenness with a bitter precision in the picturesque, a comprehensive and merciless philosophy, and sharp, profound, terrible words, which, taken up by some and passed on by others, were repeated at the four corners of Paris, and at once became classics, in a way. A complete and aston-ishing psychology of snobbishness is contained in the impres-sions, the traits, the concise profiles, the strangely-outlined and life-like silhouettes, of which this prodigal and never-wearying originality was an ever-flowing source. It seems, then, that, if any one should have escaped that sort of moral influenza which rages so violently in the *salons*, it was Victor Charrigaud, bet-ter protected than anybody else against contagion by that ad-mirable antiseptic—irony. But man is nothing but surprise, contradiction, incoherence, and folly.

Scarcely had he felt the first caresses of success, when the snob that was in him—and that was the reason why he was able to paint the snob with such force of expression—revealed it-self, exploded, one might say, like an engine that has received an electric shock. He began by dropping those friends that had become embarrasing or compromising, keeping only those who, some by their recognized talent, others by their position in the press, could be useful to him, and bolster his young fame by their persistent puffery. At the same time he made dress and fashion a subject of most careful consideration. He was seen in frock coats of an audacious Philippism, wearing collars and cravats of the style of 1830 much exaggerated, velvet waistcoats of irresistible cut, and showy jewels; and he took from metal cases, inlaid with too precious stones, cigarettes sumptuously rolled in gilt paper. But, heavy of limb and awkward of movement, he retained, in spite of everything, the unwieldy gait of the Auvergne peasants, his compatriots. Too new in a too sudden elegance in which he did not feel at home, in vain did he study himself and the most perfect models of Parisian style; he could not acquire that ease, that supple, delicate, and upright line which he saw in the young swells at the clubs, at the race-courses, at the theatres, and at the restaurants, and which he envied them with a most violent hatred. It astonished him, for, after all, he patronized only the most select furnishing houses, the most famous tailors, memorable shirt-makers, and what shoemakers! what shoemakers! Examining himself in the glass, he threw insults at himself, in his despair.

"In vain do I cover myself with velvets, silks, and satin; I always look like a boor. There is always something that is not natural."

As for Madame Charrigaud, who previously had dressed very simply and with discreet taste, she, too, sported showy and stunning costumes, with hair too red, jewels too big, silks too rich, giving her the air of a laundry queen, the majesty of a Mardi-Gras empress. They made a great deal of sport of her, sometimes cruelly. Old comrades, at once humiliated and delighted by so much luxury and so much bad taste, avenged themselves by saying jestingly of this poor Victor Charrigaud:

"Really, for an ironist, he has no luck."

Thanks to fortunate manœuvres, incessant diplomacy, and more incessant platitudes, they were received into what they called—they too—real society, in the houses of Jewish bankers, Venezuelan dukes, and vagrant arch-dukes, and in the houses of very old ladies, crazed over literature, panderism, and the Academy. They thought of nothing but cultivating and developing these new relations, and of acquiring others more desirable and more difficult of attainment,—others, others, and always others.

One day, to free himself from an obligation which he had stupidly assumed by accepting an invitation to the house of a friend who was not a conspicuous personage, but whom he was not yet ready to drop, Charrigaud wrote him the following letter:

> *My Dear Old Friend*:
>   We are disconsolate. Excuse us for not keeping our promise for Monday. But we have just received, for that very day, an invitation to dine at the Rothschilds. It is the first. You understand that we cannot refuse. It would be disastrous. Fortunately, I know your heart. Far from being angry with us, I am sure that you will share our joy and our pride.

Another day he was telling of the purchase that he had just made of a villa at Deauville:

"I really don't know for whom these people took us. They undoubtedly took us for journalists, for Bohemians. But I quickly let them see that I had a notary."

Gradually he eliminated all that remained of the friends of his youth, — those friends whose simple presence in his house was a constant and disagreeable reminder of the past, and a confession of that stain, of that social inferiority, — literature and labor. And he contrived also to extinguish the flames that sometimes kindled in his brain, and to finally stifle that cursed wit whose sudden revival on certain occasions it frightened him to feel, supposing it to be dead forever. Then, it was no longer enough for him to be received in the houses of others; he desired, in turn, to receive others in his own house. His occupancy of a residence of some pretension, which he had just bought in Auteuil, was made the pretext for a dinner.

154

I entered their service at the time when the Charrigauds had at last resolved to give this dinner. Not one of those private dinners, gay and without pose, such as they had been in the habit of giving, and which for some years had made their house so charming, but a really elegant, really solemn dinner, a stiff and chilly dinner, a select dinner, to which should be ceremoniously invited, together with some correct celebrities of literature and art, some society personalities, not too difficult to reach, not too regularly established, but sufficiently decorative to shed a little of their brilliancy upon their hosts.

"For the difficult thing," said Victor Charrigaud, "is not to dine in the city, but to give a dinner at home."

After thinking over the plan for a long time, Victor Charrigaud made this proposition:

"Well, I have it. I think that at first we can have only divorced women—with their lovers. We must begin somewhere. There are some who are very suitable, and whom the most Catholic newspapers speak of with admiration. Later, when our connections shall have become more extensive, and at the same time more select,—why, we can let the divorced people slide."

"You are right," approved Mme. Charrigaud. "For the moment, the important thing is to get the best people among those who are divorced. Say what you will, the time has come when a divorce gives a person a certain position."

"It has at least the merit of abolishing adultery," chuckled Charrigaud. "Adultery is now very old-fashioned. Nobody but friend Bourget now believes in adultery,—Christian adultery,—and in English furniture."

To which Mme. Charrigaud replied, in a tone of nervous vexation:

"How you tire me, with your maliciously wicked remarks! You will see, you will see that, because of them, we shall never be able to establish a desirable *salon*."

And she added:

155

"If you really wish to become a man of society, you must learn first either to be an imbecile or to hold your tongue."

They made, unmade, and remade a list of guests, which, after laborious combinations, was finally settled upon as follows:

The Countess Fergus, divorced, and her friend, the economist and deputy, Joseph Brigard.

The Baroness Henri Gogsthein, divorced, and her friend, the poet, Théo. Crampp.

The Baroness Otto Butzinghen, and her friend, the Viscount Lahyrais, clubman, sportsman, gambler, and trickster.

Mme. de Rambure, divorced, and her friend, Mme. Tiercelet, suing for divorce.

Sir Harry Kimberly, symbolist musician, and his young friend, Lucien Sartorys, as beautiful as a woman, as supple as a *peau de Suède* glove, as slender and blonde as a cigar.

The two academicians, Joseph Dupont de la Brie, collector of obscene coins, and Isidore Durand de la Marne, author of gallant memoirs in private and severe student of Chinese at the Institute.

The portrait-painter, Jasques Regaud.

The psychological novelist, Maurice Fernancourt.

The society reporter, Poult d'Essoy.

The invitations were sent out, and, thanks to the mediation of influential persons, all were accepted.

The Countess Fergus alone hesitated:

"The Charrigauds?" said she. "Is theirs really a proper house? Has he not been engaged in all sorts of pursuits on Montmartre, in the past? Do they not say that he sold obscene photographs, for which he had posed, with an artificial bust? And are there not some disagreeable stories afloat regarding her? Did she not have some rather vulgar experiences before her marriage? Is it not said that she has been a model,—that she has posed for the altogether? What a horror! A woman who stripped before men who are not even her lovers?"

Finally she accepted the invitation, on being assured that Mme. Charrigaud had posed only for the head, that Charrigaud, who was very vindictive, would be quite capable of disgracing her in one of his books, and that Kimberly would come to this dinner. Oh! if Kimberly had promised to come! Kimberly, such a perfect gentleman, and so delicate and so charming, really charming!

The Charrigauds were informed of these negotiations and these scruples. Far from taking offence, they congratulated themselves that they had successfully conducted the former and overcome the latter. It was now a matter of time only of watching themselves, and, as Mme. Charrigaud said, of behaving themselves like real society people. This dinner, so marvelously prepared and planned, so skilfully negotiated, was really their first manifestation in the new avatar of their eloquent destiny, of their social ambitions. It must, then, be an astonishing affair.

For a week beforehand everything was topsy-turvy in the house. It was necessary that the apartments should be made to look like new, and that there should be no hitch. They tried various lighting arrangements and table decorations, that they might not be embarrassed at the last moment. Over these matters, M. and Mme. Charrigaud quarreled like porters, for they had not the same ideas, and their æsthetic views differed on all points, she inclining to sentimental arrangements, he preferred the severe and "artistic."

"It is idiotic," cried Charrigaud. "They will think that they are in a grisette's apartments. Ah! what a laughing-stock we shall be!"

"You had better not talk," replied Mme. Charrigaud, her nervousness reaching the point of paroxysm. "You are still what you used to be, a dirty tavern bum. And besides, I have enough of it; my back is broken with it."

"Well, that's it; let us have a divorce, my little wolf, let us have a divorce. By that means we at least shall complete the series, and cast no reflection on our guests."

They perceived also that there would not be enough silverware, glassware, and plates. They must rent some, and also rent some chairs, for they had only fifteen, and even these were not perfect. Finally, the menu was ordered of one of the grand caterers of the Boulevard.

"Let everything be ultra-stylish," ordered Mme. Charrigaud, "and let no one be able to recognize the dishes that are served. Shrimp hash, goose-liver cutlets, game that looks like ham, ham that looks like cake, truffles in whipped cream, and mashed potatoes in branches,—cherries in squares and peaches twisted into spirals. In short, have everything as stylish as possible."

"Rest easy," declared the caterer. "I know so well how to disguise things that I defy anybody to know what he is eating. It is a specialty of the house."

At last the great day arrived.

Monsieur rose early,—anxious, nervous, agitated. Madame, who had been unable to sleep all night, and weary from the errands of the day before and the preparations of all sorts, could not keep still. Five or six times, with wrinkled brow, out of breath, trembling and so weary that, as she said, she felt her belly in her heels, she made a final examination of the house, upset and rearranged bric-à-brac and furniture without reason, and went from one room to another without knowing why and as if she were mad. She trembled lest the cooks might not come, lest the florist might fail them, and lest the guests might not be placed at table in accordance with strict etiquette. Monsieur followed her everywhere, clad only in pink silk drawers, approving here, criticising there.

"Now that I think about it again," said he, "what a queer idea that was of yours to order centauries for the table decoration! I assure you that blue becomes black in the light. And then, after all, centauries are nothing but simple corn-flowers. It will look as if we had been to the fields to gather corn-flowers."

"Oh! corn-flowers! how provoking you are!"

"Yes, indeed, corn-flowers. And the corn-flower, as Kimberly said very truly the other evening at the Rothschilds, is not a society flower. Why not also corn poppies?"

"Let me alone," answered Madame. "You drive me crazy with all your stupid observations. A nice time to offer them, indeed!"

But Monsieur was obstinate:

"All right, all right; you will see, you will see. Provided, my God, that everything goes off tolerably well, without too many accidents, without too many delays. I did not know that to be society people was so difficult, so fatiguing, and so complicated a matter. Perhaps we ought to have remained simple boors."

And Madame growled:

"Oh for that matter, I see clearly that nothing will change you. You scarcely do honor to a woman."

As they thought me pretty, and very elegant to look at, my masters had allotted to me also an important *role* in this comedy. First I was to preside over the cloak-room, and then to aid, or rather superintend, the four butlers, four tall lascars, with immense side-whiskers, selected from several employment-bureaus to serve this extraordinary dinner.

At first all went well. Nevertheless, there was a moment of alarm. At quarter before nine the Countess Fergus had not yet arrived. Suppose she had changed her mind, and resolved at the last moment not to come? What a humiliation! What a disaster! The Charrigauds were in a state of consternation. Joseph Brigard reassured them. It was the day when the countess had to preside over her admirable "Society for the Collection of Cigar-Stumps for the Army and Navy." The sessions sometimes did not end till very late.

"What a charming woman!" said Mme. Charrigaud, ecstatically, as if this eulogy had the magic power to hasten the coming of "this dirty countess," whom, at the bottom of her soul, she cursed.

159

"And what a brain!" said Charrigaud, going her one better, though really entertaining the same feeling. "The other day at the Rothschilds I felt that it would be necessary to go back to the last century to find such perfect grace and such superiority."

"And even then!" said Joseph Brigard, capping the climax. "You see, my dear Monsieur Charrigaud, in democratic societies based upon equality" . . .

He was about to deliver one of those semi-gallant, semi-sociological discourses which he was fond of retailing in the *salons,* when the Countess Fergus entered, imposing and majestic, in a black gown embroidered with jet and steel that showed off the fat whiteness and soft beauty of her shoulders. And it was amid murmurs and whispers of admiration that they made their way ceremoniously to the dining-room.

The beginning of the dinner was rather cold. In spite of her success, perhaps even because of her success, the Countess Fergus was a little haughty, or, at least, too reserved. She seemed to wear an air of condescension at having honored with her presence the humble house of "these little people." Charrigaud thought he noticed that she examined with a discreetly but visibly contemptuous pout the rented silverware, the table decoration, Mme. Charrigaud's green costume, and the four butlers whose too long side-whiskers dipped into the dishes. He was filled with vague terrors and agonizing doubts as to the proper appearance of his table and his wife. It was a horrible minute!

After some commonplace and laborious replies, exchanged apropos of trivial topics then current, the conversation gradually became general, and finally settled down upon the subject of correctness in society life.

All these poor devils, all these poor wretches, male and female, forgetting their own social irregularities, showed a strangely implacable severity toward persons whom it was allowable to suspect, not even of stains or blemishes, but simply

160

of some formal lack of respect for society laws,—the only ones that ought to be obeyed. Living, in a certain sense, outside of their social ideal, thrown back, so to speak, to the margin of that existence whose disgraced correctness and regularity they honored as a religion, they undoubtedly hoped to get into it again by driving out others. The comicality of this was really intense and savory. They divided the universe into two great parts: on the one side, that which is regular; on the other, that which is not; here the people that one may receive; there the people that one may not receive. And these two great parts soon became pieces, and the pieces became thin slices, the subdivision going on *ad infinitum*. There were those in whose houses one may go only for the evening. Those in whose houses one may not dine, but to which one may go for the evening. Those whom one may receive at his table, and those to whom one may accord only admission to his *salon*,—and even then only under certain circumstances, clearly defined. There were also those in whose houses one may not dine and whom one should not receive at one's house, and those whom one may receive at one's house and in whose houses one may not dine; those whom one may receive at breakfast, and never at dinner; and those in whose country houses one may dine, but never in their Paris residences, etc. The whole being supported with demonstrative and peremptory examples, well-known names being cited by way of illustration.

"Shades," said the Viscount Lahyrais, sportsman, clubman, gambler, and trickster. "The whole thing lies there. It is by the strict observance of shades that a man is really in society, or is not."

I believe that I never heard such dreary things. As I listened to them, I really felt a pity for these unfortunates.

Charrigaud neither ate or drank, and said nothing. Although he was scarcely in the conversation, he nevertheless felt its enormous and forbidding stupidity like a weight upon his skull. Impatient, feverish, very pale, he watched the service, tried to catch favorable or ironical impressions of the faces of his guests, and mechanically, with movements more and more accelerated, and in spite of the warnings of his wife, rolled big pellets of bread-crumb between his fingers. When a question was put to him, he answered in a bewildered distracted, far-away voice:

"Certainly . . . certainly . . . certainly."

Opposite him, very stiff in her green gown, upon which spangles of green steel glittered with a phosphorescent brilliancy, and wearing an aigrette of red feathers in her hair, Mme. Charrigaud bent to right and to left, and smiled, without ever a word,—a smile so eternally motionless that it seemed painted on her lips.

"What a goose!" said Charrigaud to himself; "what a stupid and ridiculous woman! And what a carnival costume! To-morrow, because of her, we shall be the laughing-stock of Parisian society."

And on her side Mme. Charrigaud, beneath the fixity of her smile, was thinking:

"What an idiot this Victor is! And what a bad appearance he makes! To-morrow we shall catch it on account of his pellets."

The topics of correctness in society being exhausted, there followed an embarrassing lull in the conversation, which Kimberly broke by telling of his last trip to London.

"Yes," said he, "I spent in London an intoxicating week; and, ladies, I witnessed a unique thing. I attended a ritual dinner which the great poet, John-Giotto Farfadetti, gave to some friends to celebrate his betrothal to the wife of his dear Frederic-Ossian Pinggleton."

"How exquisite that must have been!" minced the Countess Fergus.

"You cannot imagine," answered Kimberly, whose look and gestures, and even the orchid that adorned the button-hole of his coat, expressed the most ardent ecstasy.

And he continued:

"Fancy, my dear friends, in a large hall, whose blue walls, though scarcely blue, are decorated with white peacocks and gold peacocks,—fancy a table of jade, inconceivably and delightfully oval. On the table some cups, in which mauve and yellow bonbons harmonized, and in the centre a basin of pink crystal, filled with kanaka preserves . . . and nothing more. Draped in long white robes, we slowly passed in turn before the table, and we took, upon the points of our golden knives, a little of these mysterious preserves, which then we carried to our lips . . . and nothing more."

"Oh! I find that moving," sighed the countess, "so moving!"

"You cannot imagine. But the most moving thing — a thing that really transformed this emotion into a painful laceration of our souls—was when Frederic-Ossian Pinggleton sang the poem of the betrothal of his wife and his friend. I know nothing more tragically, more superhumanly beautiful."

"Oh! I beg of you," implored the Countess Fergus, "repeat this prodigious poem for our benefit, Kimberly."

"The poem, alas! I cannot. I can give you only its essence."

"That's it, that's it! The essence."

In spite of his morals, in which they cut no figure, Kimberly filled women with mad enthusiasm, for his specialty was subtle stories of transgression and of extraordinary sensations. Suddenly a thrill ran round the table, and the flowers themselves, and the jewels on their beds of flesh, and the glasses on the table-cloth, took attitudes in harmony with the state of souls. Carrigaud felt his reason departing. He thought that he had suddenly fallen into a mad-house. Yet by force of will, he was still able to smile, and say:

"Why, certainly . . . certainly."

The butlers finished passing something that resembled a ham, from which, in a flood of yellow cream, cherries poured like red larvæ. As for the Countess Fergus, half swooning, she had already started for extra-terrestrial regions.

Kimberly began:

"Frederic-Ossian Pinggleton and his friend, John-Giotto Farfadetti, were finishing their daily tasks in the studio which they occupied in common. One was the great painter, the other the great poet; the former short and stout, the latter tall and thin; both alike clad in drugget robes, their heads alike adorned with Florentine BONNETS, both alike neurasthenics, for they had, in different bodies, like souls and lily-twin spirits. John Giotto Farfadetti sang in his verses the marvelous symbols that his friend, Frederic-Ossian Pinggleton, painted on his canvases, so that the glory of the poet was inseparable from that of the painter, and that their works and their immortal geniuses had come to be confounded in one and the same adoration."

Kimberly stopped for a moment. The silence was religious. Something sacred hovered over the table. He continued:

"The day was nearing its end. A very soft twilight was enveloping the studio in a pallor of fluid and lunar shade. Scarcely could one still distinguish on the mauve walls the long, supple, waving, golden algæ that seemed to move in obedience to the vibration of some deep and magic water. John-Giotto Farfadetti closed the sort of antiphonary on the vellum of which, with a Persian reed, he wrote, or rather engraved, his eternal poems; Frederic-Ossian Pinggleton turned his lyre-shaped easel against a piece of drapery, placed his heart-shaped palette upon a fragile piece of furniture, and the two, facing one another, stretched themselves, with august poses of fatigue, upon a triple row of cushions, of the color of sea-weed."

"Hum!" said Mme. Tiercelet, with a slightly warning cough.

"No, not at all," said Kimberly, reassuringly; "it is not what you think."

And he continued:

"In the centre of the studio, from a marble basin in which the petals of roses were bathing, a voilent perfume was rising. And on a little table long-stemmed narcissusses were dying, like souls, in a narrow vase whose neck opened into the calyx of a lily, strangely green and distorted."

"Impossible to forget!" said the countess, in a quivering voice, so low that it could scarcely be heard.

And Kimberly, without stopping, went on with his naration:

"Outside, the street became more silent, because deserted. From the Thames came, muffled by the distance, the distracted voices of sirens, the gasping voices of marine boilers. It was the hour when the two friends, giving themselves over to dreaming, preserved an ineffable silence."

"Oh! I see them so clearly!" said Madame Tierselet, in a tone of admiration.

"And that 'ineffable,' how evocative it is!" applauded the Countess Fergus, "and so pure!"

Kimberly profited by these flattering interruptions to take a swallow of champagne. Then, feeling that he was listened to with more passionate attention than before, he repeated:

"Preserved an ineffable silence. But on this special evening John-Giotto Farfadetti murmured: 'I have a poisoned flower in my heart.' To which Frederic-Ossian Pinggleton answered: 'This evening a sorrowful bird has been singing in my heart.' The studio seemed moved by this unusual colloquy. On the mauve wall, which was gradually losing its color, the gold algæ seemed to spread and contract, and to spread and contract again, in harmony with the new rhythms of an unusual undulation, for it is certain that the soul of man communicates to the soul of things its troubles, its passions, its fervors, its transgressions, its life."

"How true that is!"

This cry, coming from several mouths at once, did not

prevent Kimberly from going on with the recital, which henceforth was to unfold itself amid the silent emotion of his hearers. His voice became even more mysterious.

"This minute of silence was poignant and tragic. 'Oh! my friend!' implored John-Giotto Farfadetti, 'you who have given me everything, you whose soul is so marvelously twin with mine, you must give me something of yourself that I have not yet had, and from the lack of which I am dying.' 'Is it, then, my life that you ask?' said the painter; 'it is yours; you can take it.' 'No, it is not your life; it is more than life; it is your wife!' 'Botticellina!' cried the poet. 'Yes, Botticellina; Botticellinetta; flesh of your flesh, the soul of your soul, the dream of your dream, the magic sleep of your sorrows!' 'Botticellina! Alas! Alas! It was to be. You have drowned yourself in her, she has drowned herself in you, as in a bottomless lake, beneath the light of the moon. Alas! Alas! It was to be.' Two tears, phosphorescent in the penumbra, rolled from the eyes of the painter. The poet answered: "Listen to me, oh! my friend! I love Botticellina, and Botticellina loves me, and we shall both die of loving one another, and of not daring to tell one another, and of not daring to unite. She and I are two fragments, long ago separated, of one and the same living being, which for perhaps two thousand years have been seeking and calling one another, and which meet at last to-day. Oh! my dear Pinggleton, unknown life has these strange, terrible, and delicious fatalities. Was there ever a more splendid poem than that which we are living to-night?' But the painter kept on repeating, in a voice more and more sorrowful, this cry: 'Botticellina! Botticellina!' He rose from the triple row of cushions upon which he was lying, and walked back and forth in the studio, feverishly. After some minutes of anxious agitation, he said: 'Botticellina was Mine. Henceforth must she be Thine?' 'She shall be Ours!' replied the poet, imperiously; 'for God has chosen you to be the point of suture for this severed soul which is She and which is I! If not, Botticellina possesses the magic pearl that dissipates dreams, I the dagger that delivers from corporeal chains. If you refuse, we shall love each other in death.' And he added, in a deep tone that resounded through the studio like a voice from the abyss: 'Perhaps it would be better so.' 'No,' cried the painter, 'you shall live. Botticellina shall be Thine, as she has been Mine. I will tear my flesh to shreads, I will tear my heart from my breast, I will break my head against the wall, but my friend shall be happy. I can suffer. Suffering, too, is voluptuousness, in another form!' 'And a voluptuousness more powerful, more bitter, more fierce than any other!' exclaimed John-Giotto Farfadetti, ecstatically; 'I envy your fate, do you know? As for me, I really believe that I shall die either of the joy of my love or of the sorrow of my friend. The hour has come. Adieu!' He rose, like an archangel. At that moment the drapery moved, opening and closing again on an illuminating apparition. It was Botticellina, draped in a flowing robe, of the color of the moonlight. Her floating hair shone around her like artificial fire. In her hand she held a golden key. An ecstasy was on her lips, and the night-sky in her eyes. John-Giotto rushed forward, and disappeared behind the drapery. Then Frederic-Ossian Pinggleton lay down again on the triple row of cushions, of the color of sea-weed. And, while he buried his nails in his flesh, and while the blood streamed from him as from a fountain, the golden algæ, now scarcely visible, gently quivered upon the wall, which was gradually taking on a coating of darkness. And the heart-shaped palette and the lyre-shaped easel resounded long and long, in nuptial songs."

For some moments Kimberly was silent; then, while the emotion that prevailed around the table was choking throats and compressing hearts, he concluded:

"And this is why I have dipped the point of my golden knife in the preserves prepared by kanaka virgins in honor of a betrothal more magnificent than any that our century, in its ignorance of beauty, has ever known."

167

The dinner was over. They rose from the table in religious silence, but thrilled through and through. In the *salon* Kimberly was closely surrounded and warmly congratulated. The looks of all the women converged radiantly upon his painted face, surrounding it with a halo of ecstasies.

"Ah! I should so like to have my portrait painted by Frederic-Ossian Pinggleton," cried Mme. de Rambure; "I would give anything to enjoy such happiness."

"Alas! Madame," answered Kimberly, "since the sorrowful and sublime event which I have related, Frederic-Ossian Pinggleton has been unwilling to paint human faces, however charming they may be; he paints only souls."

"And he is right! I should so like to be painted as a soul!"

"Of what sex?" asked Maurice Fernancourt, in a slightly sarcastic tone, visibly jealous of Kimberly's success.

The latter said, simply:

"Souls have no sex, my dear Maurice. They have" . . .

"Hair on their paws," said Victor Charrigaud, in a very low voice, so as to be heard only by the psychological novelist, to whom he was just then offering a cigar.

And, dragging him into the smoking-room, he whispered:

"Ah! old man! I wish I could shout the most filthy things, at the top of my voice, in the faces of all these people. I have enough of their souls, of their green and perverse loves, of their magic preserves. Yes, yes, to say the coarsest things, to besmear one's self with good black fetid mud for a quarter of an hour, —oh! how exquisite that would be, and how restful! And how it would relieve me of all these nauseating lilies that they have put into my heart! And you?"

But the shock had been too great, and the impression of Kimberly's recital remained. They could no longer interest themselves in the vulgar things of earth,—in topics of society, art, and passion. The Viscount Lahyrais himself, clubman, sportsman, gambler, and trickster, felt wings sprouting all over him. Each one felt the need of collecting his thoughts, of being alone, of prolonging the dream, of realizing it. In spite of the efforts of Kimberly, who went from one to another, asking: "Did you ever drink sable's milk? Ah! then, drink sable's milk; it is ravishing!" the conversation could not be resumed; so that, one after another, the guests excused themselves, and slipped away. At eleven o'clock all had gone.

When they found themselves face to face, alone, Monsieur and Madame looked at each other for a long time, steadily and with hostility, before exchanging their impressions.

"For a pretty fizzle, you know, it is a pretty fizzle," declared Monsieur.

"It is your fault," said Madame, in a tone of bitter reproach.

"Well, that's a good one!"

"Yes, your fault. You paid no attention to anything; you did nothing but roll dirty pellets of bread in your fat fingers. Nobody could get a word out of you. How ridiculous you were! It is shameful."

"Well, you needn't talk," rejoined Monsieur. "And your green gown, and your smiles, and your blunders. It was I perhaps, it was I undoubtedly, who told of Pinggleton's sorrow, who ate kanaka preserves, who painted souls,—I doubtless am the lily-worshipper."

"You are not even capable of being," cried Madame, at the height of her exasperation.

For a long time they hurled insults at one another. And Madame, after having arranged the silverware and the opened bottles in the sideboard, took herself off to her room, and shut herself up.

Monsieur continued to roam about the house in a state of agitation. Suddenly noticing me in the dining-room, where I was putting things a little to rights, he came to me, and, taking me about the waist, he said:

"Ah, Célestine, you do not know the immense delight that

169

you give me. To see a woman who is not a soul! To touch a woman who is not a lily! Kiss me.''

You may judge whether I was expecting that.

But the next day, when they read in the ''Figaro'' an article in which their dinner, their elegance, their taste, their wit, and their social connections were pompously celebrated, they forgot everything, and talked of nothing but their great success. And their soul set sail for more illustrious conquests and more sumptuous snobberies.

''What a charming woman is the Countess Fergus!'' said Madame, at lunch, as they were finishing the leavings of the dinner.

''And what a soul!'' said Monsieur, in confirmation.

''And Kimberly, would you believe it? There's an astonishing talker for you! And so exquisite in his manners!''

''It is a mistake to make sport of him. After all, his vice concerns no one but himself; it is none of our business.''

''Certainly not.''

And she added, indulgently:

''Ah! if it were necessary to pick everybody to pieces!''

All day long, in the linen-room, I have amused myself in calling up the queer things that happened in that house,—the passion for notoriety with which, from that time, Madame was so filled that she would prostitute herself to all the dirty journalists who would promise her an article on her husband's books or a word about her costumes and her *salon,* and Monsieur's complacency in letting this vile conduct go on, though perfectly aware of it. With admirable cynicism he said: ''At any rate it is less expensive than paying by the line at the newspaper offices.'' Monsieur, on his side, fell to the lowest depths of baseness and unscrupulousness. He called that the politics of the *salon,* and society diplomacy.

I am going to write to Paris to have them send me my old master's new book. But how rotten it must be at bottom!

XI.

Now all talk of the little Claire has ceased. As was expected, the case has been abandoned. So Joseph and the forest of Raillon will keep their secret forever. Of that poor little human creature no more will be said henceforth than of the body of a blackbird that dies in the woods, in a thicket. The father continues to break stone on the highway, as if nothing had happened, and the town, stirred and roused for a moment by this crime, resumes its usual aspect,—an aspect still more dismal because of the winter. The very bitter cold keeps people shut up in their houses. One can scarcely get a glimpse of their pale and sleepy faces behind the frosty windows, and in the streets one seldom meets anybody except ragged vagabonds and shivering dogs.

To-day Madame sent me on an errand to the butcher's shop, and I took the dogs with me. While I was there, an old woman timidly entered the shop, and asked for meat,—"a little meat to make a little soup for my sick boy." The butcher selected, from the *débris* piled up in a large copper pan, a dirty bit, half bone, half fat, and, after carefully weighing it, announced:

"Fifteen sous."

"Fifteen sous!" exclaimed the old woman; "but that is impossible! And how do you expect me to make soup out of that?"

"As you like," said the butcher, throwing the piece back into the pan. "Only, you know, I am going to send you your bill to-day. If it is not paid by to-morrow, then the process-server!"

"Give it to me," said the old woman, then, with resignation.

171

When she had gone, the butcher explained to me:

"Nevertheless, if we did not have the poor to buy the inferior parts, we really should not make enough out of an animal. But these wretches are getting to be very exacting nowadays."

And, cutting off two long slices of good red meat, he threw them to the dogs.

The dogs of the rich,—indeed! they are not poor.

At the Priory events succeed one another. From the tragic they pass to the comical, for one cannot always shudder. Tired of the captain's mischief-making, and acting on Madame's advice, Monsieur has at last brought suit before a justice of the peace. He claims damages and interest for the breaking of his bell-glasses and his frames, and for the devastation of the garden. It seems that the meeting of the two enemies in the office of the justice was really something epic. They blackguarded one another like rag-pickers. Of course, the captain denies, with many oaths, that he has ever thrown stones or anything else into Lanlaire's garden; it is Lanlaire who throws stones into his.

"Have you witnesses? Where are your witnesses? Dare to produce witnesses," screams the captain.

"Witnesses?" rejoins Monsieur; "there are the stones, and all the dirty things with which you have been continually covering my land. There are the old hats, and the old slippers, that I pick up every day, and that everybody recognizes as having belonged to you."

"You lie."

"You are a scoundrel, a drunken rake."

But, it being impossible for Monsieur to bring admissible and conclusive testimony, the justice of the peace, who, moreover, is the captain's friend, invites Monsieur to withdraw his complaint.

"And for that matter, permit me to say to you," concluded

172

the magistrate, "it is highly improbable, it is quite inadmissible, that a valiant soldier, an intrepid officer, who has won all his stripes on fields of battle, amuses himself in throwing stones and old hats upon your land, like a small boy."

"Egad!" vociferates the captain, "this man is an infamous Dreyfusard. He insults the army."

"I?"

"Yes, you! What you are trying to do, you dirty Jew, is to disgrace the army. Long live the army!"

They came near taking each other by the hair, and the justice had much difficulty in separating them. Since then Monsieur has stationed permanently in the garden two invisible witnesses, behind a sort of board shelter, in which are pierced, at the height of a man, four round holes, for the eyes. But the captain, being warned, is lying low, and Monsieur is out the cost of his watchers.

I have seen the captain two or three times, over the hedge. In spite of the frost, he stays in his garden all day long, working furiously at all sorts of things. For the moment he is putting oil-paper caps on his rose-bushes. He tells me of his misfortunes. Rose is suffering from an attack of influenza, and then—with her asthma! . . . Bourbaki is dead. He died of a congestion of the lungs, from drinking too much cognac. Really, the captain has no luck. And surely that bandit of a Lanlaire has cast a spell over him. He wishes to get the upper hand of him, to rid the country of him, and he submits to me an astonishing plan of campaign.

"Here is what you ought to do, Mademoiselle Célestine. You ought to lodge with the prosecuting attorney at Louviers a complaint against Lanlaire for outrages on morals and an assault on modesty. Ah! that's an idea!"

"But, captain, Monsieur has never outraged my morals or assaulted my modesty."

"Well, what difference does that make?"

"I cannot."

"What! you cannot? But there is nothing simpler. Lodge your complaint, and summon Rose and me. We will come to declare, to certify in a court of justice, that we have seen everything, everything, everything. A soldier's word amounts to something, especially just now, thunder of God! And remember that, after that, it will be easy to rake up the case of little Claire, and involve Lanlaire in it. Ah! that's an idea! Think it over, Mademoiselle Célestine; think it over."

Ah! I have many things, much too many things, to think over just now. Joseph is pressing me for a decision; the matter cannot be postponed. He has heard from Cherbourg that the little café is to be sold next week. But I am anxious, troubled. I want to, and I don't want to. One day the idea pleases me, and the next it doesn't. I really believe that I am afraid that Joseph wants to drag me into terrible things. I cannot come to a decision. He is not brutal in his method of persuasion; he advances arguments, and tempts me with promises of liberty, of handsome costumes, of secure, happy, triumphant life.

"But I must buy the little café," he says to me. "I cannot let such an opportunity go by. And if the Revolution comes? Think of it, Célestine; that means fortune right away. And who knows? The Revolution—ah! bear that in mind—is the best thing possible for the cafés."

"Buy it, at any rate. If it is not I, it will be somebody else."

"No, no, it must be you. Nobody else will do. I am crazy over you. But you distrust me."

"No, Joseph, I assure you."

"Yes, yes; you have had ideas about me."

I do not know, no, really, I do not know, where, at that moment, I found the courage to ask him:

"Well, Joseph, tell me that it was you who outraged the little Claire in the woods."

Joseph received the shock with extraordinary tranquillity. He simply shrugged his shoulders, swayed back and forth a few seconds, and then, giving a hitch to his pantaloons, which had slipped a little, he answered, simply:

"You see? Did I not tell you so? I know your thoughts; I know everything that goes on in your mind."

His voice was softer, but his look had become so terrifying that it was impossible for me to articulate a word.

"It is not a question of the little Claire; it is a question of you."

He took me in his arms, as he did the other evening.

"Will you come with me to the little café?"

Shuddering and trembling, I found strength to answer:

"I am afraid; I am afraid of you, Joseph. Why am I afraid of you?"

He held me cradled in his arms. And, disdaining to justify himself, happy perhaps at increasing my terrors, he said to me, in a paternal tone:

"Well, well, since that is the case, I will talk with you again about it to-morrow."

A Rouen newspaper is circulating in town, in which there is an article that is creating a scandal among the pious. It is a true story, very droll, and somewhat *risqué,* which happened lately at Port Lançon, a pretty place situated three leagues from here. And it gains in piquancy from the fact that everybody knows the personages. Here again is something for people to talk about, for a few days. The newspaper was brought to Marianne yesterday, and at night, after dinner, I read the famous article aloud. At the first phrases Joseph rose, with much dignity, very severe and even a little angry. He declared that he does not like dirty stories, and that he cannot sit and listen to attacks on religion. "You are not behaving well in reading that, Célestine; you are not behaving well.''

And he went off to bed.

To-day, November 10, it took us all day to clean the silver service. That is an event in the house,—a traditional epoch, like the preserve-canning season. The Lanlaires possess a magnificent silver service, containing old pieces, rare and very beautiful. It comes from Madame's father, who took it, some say on deposit, others say as security for money lent to a neighboring member of the nobility. Young people for military service were not all that this blusterer bought. Everything was fish that came to his net, and one swindle more or less made no difference to him. If the grocer is to be believed, the story of this silver service is one of the most doubtful, or one of the clearest, as you choose to look at it. It is said that Madame's father got his money back, and then, thanks to some circumstance the nature of which I do not know, succeeded in keeping the silver service in the bargain. An astonishing piece of sharp practice!

Of course, the Lanlaires never use it. It remains locked up at the back of a closet in the servants' hall, in three great boxes lined with red velvet and fastened to the wall by solid iron clamps. Every year, on the tenth of November, it is taken from the boxes, and cleaned under Madame's supervision. And it is never seen again until the following year. Oh! Madame's eyes in presence of her silver service,—her silver service in our hands! Never have I seen in a woman's eyes such aggressive cupidity.

Are they not curious,—these people who hide everything, who bury their silver, their jewels, all their wealth, all their happiness, and who, being able to live in luxury and joy, persist in living a life of ennui bordering on deprivation?

The work done, the silver service locked up for a year in its boxes, and Madame having gone away after satisfying herself that none of it has stuck to our fingers, Joseph said to me, with a queer air:

"That is a very beautiful silver service, you know, Célestine. Especially 'the cruet of Louis XVI.' Ah! *sacristi!* and how heavy it is! The whole business is worth perhaps twenty-five thousand francs, Célestine; perhaps more. One does not know what it is worth."

And, looking at me steadily and heavily, piercing the very depths of my soul, he asked:

"Will you come with me to the little café?"

What relation can there be between Madame's silver service and the little café at Cherbourg? Really, I don't know why, but Joseph's slightest words make me tremble.

XII.

I have said that I would speak of M. Xavier. The memory of this boy pursues me, runs continually through my head. Among so many faces his is one of those that come back most frequently to my mind. Sometimes with regret, sometimes with anger. All the same, he was prettily droll and prettily vicious, M. Xavier, with his irregular features and his blonde and brazen face. Ah! the little rascal! Really one may say of him that he belonged to his epoch.

One day I was engaged as chambermaid by Mme. de Tarves, in the Rue de Varennes. A nickel-plated establishment, an elegant retinue, and handsome wages. A hundred francs a month, with washing, and wine, and everything, included. The morning that I arrived at the house, in a highly satisfied state of mind, Madame had me shown into her dressing-room. An astonishing room, hung with cream silk, and Madame, a tall woman, extremely made up, her skin too white, her lips too red, her hair too blonde, but nevertheless pretty, rustling,— with an imposing presence, and style! So much was not to be gainsaid.

I already possessed a very keen eye. Even from rapidly passing through a Parisian interior, I was able to judge of its habits and morals, and, although furniture lies as well as faces, I was rarely mistaken. In spite of the sumptuous and decent appearance of this establishment, I felt at once the disorganization that prevailed there, the broken ties, the intrigue, the haste, the feverish life, the private and hidden filth,—not sufficiently hidden, however, to prevent me from detecting the odor, always the same! Moreover, in the first looks exchanged between new and old servants there is a sort of masonic sign, generally

178

spontaneous and involuntary, which immediately informs you regarding the general spirit of the establishment. As in all other professions, servants are very jealous of each other, and they defend themselves ferociously against new-comers. Even I, who am so easy in my ways, have suffered from these jealousies and hatreds, especially on the part of women who were enraged at my beauty. But, for the contrary reason, men—I must do them this justice—have always welcomed me cordially.

In the look of the *valet de chambre* who had opened the door for me at the house of Mme. de Tarves I had clearly read these words: "This is a queer box . . . with ups and downs . . . nothing like security . . . but plenty of fun, all the same. You can come in, my little one." So, in making my way to the dressing-room, I was prepared, to the extent of these uncertain and summary impressions, for something peculiar. But I must confess that I had no idea of that which really awaited me.

Madame was writing letters at a little jewel of a desk. A large skin of white astrachan served as a carpet for the room. On the cream silk walls I was astonished to see engravings of the eighteenth century, more than licentious, almost obscene, not very far from the very old enamels representing religious scenes. In a glass cabinet a quantity of old jewels, ivories, miniature snuff-boxes, and gallant little Saxon porcelains, very rich, of gold and silver. A little yellow dog, a ball of silky and shiny hair, was asleep on a long chair, between two mauve silk cushions.

Madame said to me:

"Célestine, is it not? Ah! I do not like that name at all. I will call you Mary, in English. Mary, you remember? Mary, yes; that is more suitable."

That is in the order of things. We servants have not a right even to a name of our own, because in all the houses there are daughters, cousins, dogs, and parrots that have the same name that we have.

"Very well, Madame," I answered.

"Do you know English, Mary?"

"No, Madame. I have already told Madame so."

"Ah! to be sure. I regret it. Turn a little, Mary, that I may look at you."

She examined me from every point of view, front, back, and profile, murmuring from time to time:

"Well, she is not bad; she is rather good-looking."

And suddenly:

"Tell me, Mary, have you a good figure . . . a very good figure?"

This question surprised and disturbed me. I did not grasp the connection between my service in the house and the shape of my body. But, without waiting for my reply, Madame said, talking to herself, and surveying my entire person from head to foot, through her *face-à-main:*

"Yes, she seems to have a good figure enough."

Then, addressing me directly, she exclaimed, with a satisfied smile:

"You see, Mary, I like to have about me only women with good figures. It is more suitable."

I was not at the end of my surprises. Continuing to examine me minutely, she cried, suddenly:

"Oh! your hair! I desire you to do your hair otherwise. Your hair is not done with elegance. You have beautiful hair; you should make the most of it. A fine head of hair is a very important matter. See, like that; something in that style."

She dishevelled a little the hair on my forehead, repeating:

"Something in that style. She is charming. See, Mary, you are charming. It is more suitable."

And, while she was patting my hair, I asked myself if Madame was not a little off.

When she had finished, being satisfied with my hair, she asked:

"Is that your prettiest gown?"

"Yes, Madame."

"It is not much, your prettiest gown. I will give you some of mine which you can make over. And your underwear?"

She raised my skirt, and turned it up slightly.

"Yes, I see," said she; "that will not do at all. And your linen, is it suitable?"

Vexed by this invasive inspection, I answered, in a dry voice:

"I do not know what Madame means by suitable."

"Show me your linen; go and get me your linen. And walk a little . . . again . . . come back . . . turn around . . . she walks well, she has style."

As soon as she saw my linen, she made a face:

"Oh, this cotton cloth, these stockings, these chemises, — horrible! And this corset! I do not wish to see that in my house. I do not wish you to wear that in my house. Wait, Mary; help me."

She opened a pink lacker wardrobe, pulled out a large drawer full of fragrant garments, and emptied its contents, pell-mell, on the carpet.

"Take that, Mary; take it all. You will see there are some stitches to be taken, some repairs to be made, some little places to be mended. You will attend to that. Take it all; there is a little of everything; there is enough there to fit you out with a pretty wardrobe, a suitable *trousseau*. Take it all."

Indeed, there was everything,—silk corsets, silk stockings, silk and fine linen chemises, loads of drawers, delicious ruffs, and ornamented petticoats. A strong odor, an odor of *peau d'Espagne*, of jasmine, of well-groomed woman, in short, an odor of love, rose from these piled-up garments whose soft, faded, or violent colors glistened on the carpet like a basket of flowers in a garden. I could not get over it; I stood thoroughly stupefied, contented and embarrassed at once, before this pile of pink, mauve, yellow, and red stuffs, in which there still were ribbons of brighter shades and delicate bits of lace. And Madame stirred up these old things that were still so pretty, these undergarments that were scarcely worn, showed them to me, selected for me, and advised me, indicating her preferences.

"I like the women in my service to be coquettish, elegant; I like to have them smell good. You are a brunette; here is a red skirt that will become you marvelously. Moreover, all these things will become you very well. Take them all."

I was in a state of profound stupefaction. I knew not what to do; I knew not what to say. Mechanically, I repeated:

"Thank you, Madame. How good Madame is! Thank you, Madame."

But Madame did not leave me time to get a clear idea of my own thoughts. She talked and talked, by turns familiar, shameless, maternal, pandering, and so strange!

"It is like cleanliness, Mary, care of the body, private toilets. Oh! I insist upon that, above all things. On this point I am exacting,—exacting to the point of mania."

She entered into intimate details, insisting always on this word "suitable," that came back continually to her lips apropos of things that were scarcely so,—at least, to my thinking. As we finished our sorting of the garments, she said to me:

"A woman, no matter what woman, should always be well kept. For the rest, Mary, you will do as I do; this is a point of capital importance. You will take a bath to-morrow. I will show you."

Then Madame took me to her room, showed me her closets, her hangings, the place for everything, familiarized me with the service, all the time making remarks that seemed to me queer and not natural.

"Now," said she, "let us go to M. Xavier's room. That, too, will be in your charge. M. Xavier is my son, Mary."

M. Xavier's room was situated at the other end of the vast apartment. A coquettish room, hung in blue cloth with yellow trimmings. On the walls colored English engravings representing hunting and racing scenes, teams, châteaux. A cane-holder stood in front of a panel,—a real panoply of canes, with a hunting-horn in the middle, flanked by two mail-coach trumpets crossed. One the mantel, among many bibelots, cigarboxes, and pipes, a photograph of a pretty boy, very young and still beardless, with the insolent face of a precocious dude and the uncertain grace of a girl,—the whole producing an effect that pleased me.

"That is M. Xavier," said Madame.

I could not help exclaiming, undoubtedly with too much warmth:

"Oh! what a handsome boy!"

"Well, well, Mary!" exclaimed Madame.

I saw that my exclamation had not offended her, for she had smiled.

"M. Xavier is like all young people," she said to me. "He is not very orderly. You must be orderly for him; and his room must be perfectly kept. You will enter the room every morning at nine o'clock; you will bring him his tea; at nine o'clock, you understand, Mary? Sometimes M. Xavier comes home late. Perhaps he will not receive you well in the morning, but that makes no difference. A young man should be awakened at nine o'clock."

She showed me where M. Xavier kept his linen, his cravats, his shoes, accompanying each detail with some remark like this:

"My son is a little sharp, but he is a charming child."

Or else:

"Do you know how to fold pantaloons? Oh! M. Xavier is especially particular about his pantaloons."

As for the hats, it was agreed that I need pay no attention to them, the glory of their daily ironing belonging to the *valet de chambre.*

I found it extremely odd that, in a house where there was a *valet de chambre,* Madame should select me to serve M. Xavier.

"It is funny, but perhaps it is not very suitable," I said

to myself, parodying the word which my mistress was constantly repeating apropos of no matter what.

It is true that everything seemed odd to me in this odd house.

In the evening, in the servants' hall, I learned many things. "An extraordinary box," they explained to me. "It is very astonishing at first, and then you get used to it. Sometimes there isn't a sou in the whole house. Then Madame goes, comes, runs, goes away and comes back again, nervous, tired, her mouth filled with high words. As for Monsieur, he never leaves the telephone. He shouts, threatens, begs, and raises the devil through the instrument. And the process-servers! It has often happened that the butler had to give something out of his own pocket, on account, to furious tradesmen who were unwilling to supply anything more. On one reception day the electricity and gas were cut off. And then, suddenly, there comes a rain of gold. The house is overflowing with wealth. Where does it come from? That nobody knows exactly. As for the servants, they wait months and months for their wages. But they are always paid at last; only after what scenes, after what insults, after what squabbles! It is incredible."

Well, indeed, a nice place I had tumbled into! And such was my luck, for the one time in my life when I had good wages.

"M. Xavier has not yet come in to-night," said the *valet de chambre*.

"Oh!" exclaimed the cook, looking at me persistently, "perhaps he will return now."

And the *valet de chambre* related that that very morning a creditor of M. Xavier had come again to raise a row. It must have been a very dirty matter, for Monsieur had sung small, and had been obliged to pay a heavy sum,—at least four thousand francs.

"Monsieur was in a pretty rage," he added; "I heard him

184

say to Madame: 'This cannot last; he will disgrace us; he will disgrace us.' "

The cook, who seemed very philosophical, shrugged her shoulders.

"Disgrace them?" said she, with a chuckle; "little they care about that. It is the having to pay that bothers them."

This conversation made me ill at ease. I understood vaguely that there might be some relation between Madame's garments, Madame's words, and M. Xavier. But exactly what?

I did not sleep at all well that night, haunted by strange dreams and impatient to see M. Xavier.

The *valet de chambre* had not lied. A queer box, indeed!

Monsieur was in the pilgrimages,—I don't know exactly what, — president, director, or something of that sort. He picked up pilgrims where he could, among the Jews, the Protestants, the vagabonds, even among the Catholics; and once a year he took these people to Rome, to Lourdes, to Paray-le-Monial, not without gaining notoriety and profit, of course. The pope didn't see through it, and religion triumphed. Monsieur occupied himself also with charitable and political works: "The League against Secular Education," "The League against Obscene Publications," "The Society of Amusing and Christian Libraries," "The Society for the Collection of Congreganist Sucking-Bottles for the Nursing of Working People's Children." And any number of others. He presided over orphan asylums, alumnæ, convents, clubs, employment-bureaus. He presided over everything. Oh! the trades that he had! He was a plump little man, very lively, very neat, very clean-shaven, whose manners, at the same time sugary and cynical, were those of a shrewd priest full of the devil. Sometimes the newspapers contained references to him and his works. Naturally, some of them extolled his humanitarian virtues and his high apostolic sanctity; others treated him as an old rascal and a dirty scoundrel. In the servants' hall we were much amused over these quarrels, although it is rather *chic* and flattering to be in the service of masters who are talked about in the newspapers. Every week Monsieur gave a grand dinner, followed by a grand reception, which were attended by celebrities of all sorts, academicians, reactionary senators, Catholic deputies, recalcitrant priests, intriguing monks, and archbishops. There was one especially to whom they paid especial attention, a very old Assumptionist, Father something or other, a sanctimonious and venomous man, who was always saying spiteful things with a contrite and pious air. And everywhere, in every room, there were portraits of the pope. Ah! he must have seen some tall things in that house, the Holy Father.

For my part, Monsieur was not to my liking. He did too many things, he loved too many people. And yet nobody knew half the things that he did and half the people that he loved. Surely he was a sly old dog.

On the day after my arrival, as I was helping him to put on his overcoat in the ante-chamber, he asked me:

"Do you belong to my society,—Society of the Servants of Jesus?"

"No. Monsieur."

"You must join it. It is indispensable. I am going to enter your name."

"Thank you, Monsieur. May I ask Monsieur what this society is?"

"An admirable society, which takes in girl mothers and gives them a Christian education."

"But, Monsieur, I am not a girl mother."

"That makes no difference. There are also women just out of prison; there are repentant prostitutes; there is a little of everything. I am going to enter your name."

He took from his pocket some carefully-folded newspapers, and handed them to me.

"Hide these; read them when you are alone: They are very curious."

And he chucked me under the chin, saying with a slight clack of his tongue:

186

"Ah! she is a queer little one,—yes, indeed, a very queer little one!"

When Monsieur had gone, I looked at the newspapers that he had left with me. They were the "Fin de Siècle," the "Rigolo," the "Petites Femmes de Paris." Dirty sheets, indeed!

Oh! the *bourgeois!* What an eternal farce! I have seen many of them, and of the most different kinds. They are all alike. For instance, I was once a domestic in the house of a republican deputy. He spent his time in railing at the priests. A blower, indeed! you should have seen him. He would not hear a word about religion, or the pope, or the good sisters. If people had listened to him, they would have overturned all the churches and blown up all the convents. Well, on Sunday he went to mass, secretly, in far-away parishes. At the slightest ailment he sent for the priests, and all his children were brought up by Jesuits. He would never consent to meet his brother after the latter's refusal to marry in church. All hypocrites, all cowards, all disgusting, each in his own way.

Madame de Tarves was also in the charity line: she too presided over religious committees and benevolent societies, and organized charity sales. That is to say, she was never at home, and things in the house went on as they could. Very often Madame returned late, coming from the devil knows where. Oh! I know these returns; they directly acquainted me with the sort of works in which Madame was engaged, and with the queer capers that were cut in her committees. But she was nice with me. Never an abrupt word, never a reproach. On the contrary, she treated me familiarly, almost like a comrade; and so far did she carry this that sometimes, she forgetting her dignity and I my respect, we talked nonsense together and said *risqués* things. She gave me advice as to the arrangement of my little affairs, encouraging my coquettish tastes, deluged me with glycerine and *peau d'Espagne,* covered my arms with cold cream, sprinkled me with powder. And during these operations she was continually saying:

"You see, Mary, a woman must be well groomed. Her skin must be white and soft. You have a pretty face; you must learn how to set it off. You have a very fine bust; you must give it its full value. Your legs are superb; you must be able to show them. It is more suitable."

I was content. Yet within I still was not free from anxiety and obscure suspicions. I could not forget the surprising stories that they told me in the servants' hall. There, when I praised Madame and enumerated her kindnesses toward me, the cook said:

"Yes, yes, that's all right; but wait and see what follows. What she wants of you is to be intimate with her son, that he may be kept in the house more, and thus may cost these curmudgeons less money. She has already tried that with others. She has even induced friends of hers to come here,—married women,—young girls,—yes, young girls, the trollop! But M. Xavier does not fall in with this. He prefers to roam elsewhere. You will see; you will see."

And she added, with a sort of hateful regret:

"If I were in your place, how I would blackmail them! I would not hesitate, be sure."

These words made me slightly ashamed of my comrades in the servants' hall. But, to reassure myself, I preferred to believe that the cook was jealous of Madame's evident preference for me.

I went every morning at nine o'clock to open M. Xavier's curtains and carry him his tea. It is queer; I always entered his room with my heart beating and a strong feeling of apprehension. It was a long time before he paid any attention to me. I turned this way and that, prepared his things for him, arranged his garments, trying to look pretty and show myself off to advantage. He spoke to me only to complain, in the growling voice of one who is half awake, of being disturbed too early. I was put out by this indifference, and I redoubled the silent tricks of coquetry which I had carefully planned. I was expecting every day something that did not happen; and this silence on the part of M. Xavier, this disdain for my person, irritated me to the last degree. What should I have done, if that which I expected had happened? I did not ask myself. I simply wanted it to happen.

M. Xavier was really a very pretty boy, even prettier than his photograph. A light blonde moustache—two little arcs of gold—set off his lips better than in his portrait, their red and fleshy pulp inviting a kiss. His light blue eyes, dusted with yellow, were strangely fascinating, and his movements were characterized by the indolence, the weary and cruel grace, of a girl or young deer. He was tall, slender, very supple, ultra-modern in his elegance, and wonderfully seductive through his evident cynicism and corruption. In addition to the fact that he had pleased me from the first, his resistance, or, rather, his indifference, caused my desire to quickly ripen into love.

One morning I found M. Xavier awake, and sitting on the edge of the bed. I remember that he wore a white silk shirt with blue dots. I modestly started to withdraw, but he called me back:

"Oh! what is the matter? Come in. You are not afraid of me, are you?"

With his two hands clasped over his leg, and his body swaying to and fro, he surveyed me for a long time with the utmost effrontery, while I, with slow and graceful movements, and blushing a little, placed a tray on the little table near the mantel. And, as if he then really saw me for the first time, he said:

"Why, you are a very stylish girl. How long then, have you been here?"

"Three weeks, Monsieur."

"Well, that's astonishing!"

189

"What is astonishing, Monsieur?"

"That I have never noticed that you were so beautiful. Come here!" said he.

I approached, trembling a little. Without a word he took me by the waist, and forced me to sit down beside him.

"Oh! Monsieur Xavier," I sighed, struggling, but not very vigorously. "Stop, I beg of you. If your parents were to see you?"

But he began to laugh:

"My parents! Oh! my parents, you know,—I have supped on them."

This was a phrase that he was continually using. When one asked him anything, he answered: "I have supped on that." And he had supped on everything.

To gain a little time I asked him:

"There is one thing that puzzles me, Monsieur Xavier. How does it happen that one never sees you at Madame's dinners?"

"You certainly don't expect me, my dear . . . oh! no, you know, Madame's dinners tire me too much."

"And how is it," I insisted, "that your room is the only one in the house in which there is not a picture of the pope?"

This observation flattered him. He answered:

"Why, my little baby, I am an Anarchist, I am. Religion, the Jesuits, the priests,—oh, no, I have enough of them. I have supped on them. A society made up of people like papa and mamma? Oh! you know . . . none of that in mine, thank you!"

Now I felt at ease with M. Xavier, in whom I found, together with the same vices, the drawling accent of the Paris toughs. It seemed to me that I had known him for years and years. In his turn he asked me:

"Tell me, are you intimate with papa?"

"Your father!" I cried, pretending to be scandalized. "Oh, Monsieur Xavier! Such a holy man!"

His laugh redoubled, and rang out loudly:

"Papa! Oh! papa! Why, he is intimate with all the servants here. Then you are not yet intimate with papa? You astonish me."

"Oh! no," I replied, laughing also. "Only he brings me the 'Fin de Siècle,' the 'Rigolo,' the 'Petites Femmes de Paris'."

That set him off in a delirium of joy, and, shaking more than ever with laughter, he cried:

"Papa! Oh! he is astonishing!"

And, being now well started, he continued in a comical tone:

"He is like mamma. Yesterday she made me another scene. I am disgracing her,—her and papa. Would you believe it? And religion, and society, and everything! It is twisting. Then I declared to her: 'My dear little mother, it is agreed; I will settle down to a regular life on the day when you shall have given up your lovers.' That was a hot one, eh? That shut her up. Oh! no, you know, they make me very tired, these authors of my being. I have supped on their lectures. By the way, you know Fumeau, don't you?"

"No, Monsieur Xavier."

"Why, yes . . . why, yes . . . Anthime Fumeau?"

"I assure you that I do not."

"A fat fellow, very young, very red-faced, ultra-stylish, the finest teams in Paris. Fumeau . . . an income of three millions. Tartlet the Kid? Why, yes, you know him."

"But I tell you that I do not know him."

"You astonish me! Why, everybody knows him. Don't you know the Fumeau biscuit? The young fellow who had a judicial adviser appointed for him two months ago? Don't you remember?"

"Not at all, I swear to you, Monsieur Xavier."

"Never mind, little turkey. Well, I played a good one on Fumeau last year,—a very good one. Guess what? You do not guess?"

"How do you expect me to guess, since I do not know him?"

"Well, it was this, my little baby. I introduced Fumeau to my mother. Upon my word! What do you think of that for a discovery? And the funniest part of it is that in two months mamma succeeded in blackmailing Fumeau to the tune of three hundred thousand bones. What a godsend that, for papa's works! Oh! they know a thing or two; they are up to snuff! But for that, the house would have gone up. We were over head and ears in debt. The priests themselves were refusing to have anything to do with us. What do you say to that, eh?"

"I say, Monsieur Xavier, that you have a queer way of treating the family."

"What do you expect, my dear? I am an Anarchist, I am. I have supped on the family."

That morning Madame was even nicer than usual with me. "I am well satisfied with your service," she said to me. "Mary, I raise your wages ten francs."

"If she raises me ten francs every time," thought I to myself, "that will not be bad. It is more suitable."

Oh! when I think of all that! I, too, have supped on it.

M. Xavier's fancy did not last long; he had quickly "supped on me." Not for a moment, moreover, was I able to keep him in the house. Several times, on entering his room in the morning, I found the bed undisturbed and empty. M. Xavier had been out all night. The cook knew him well, and she had told the truth when she said: "He prefers to roam elsewhere." He pursued his old habits, and went in search of his customary pleasures, as before. On those mornings I felt a sudden pain in my heart, and all day long I was sad, sad!

The unfortunate part of it all is that M. Xavier had no feeling. He was not poetical, like M. Georges. He did not vouchsafe me the slightest attention. Never did he say to me a kind and touching word, as lovers do in books and plays. Moreover, he liked nothing that I liked; he did not like flowers, with the exception of the big carnations with which he adorned the buttonhole of his coat. Yet it is so good to whisper to each other things that caress the heart, to exchange disinterested kisses, to gaze for eternities into one another's eyes. But men are such coarse creatures; they do not feel these joys,—these joys so pure and blue. And it is a great pity. M. Xavier knew nothing but vice, found pleasure only in debauchery. In love all that was not vice and debauchery bored him.

"Oh! no, you know, that makes me very tired. I have supped on poetry. The little blue flower . . . we must leave that to papa."

To him I was always an impersonal creature, the domestic to whom he gave orders and whom he maltreated in the exercise of his authority as master, and with his boyish cynical jests. And he often said to me, with a laugh in the corner of his mouth,—a frightful laugh that wounded and humiliated me:

"And papa? Really, you are not yet intimate with papa? You astonish me."

Once I had not the power to keep back my tears; they were choking me. M. Xavier became angry at once:

"Oh! no, you know, that is the most tiresome thing of all. Tears, scenes? You must stop that, my dear; or else, good evening! I have supped on all that nonsense."

For my part I feel an immense and imperative need of that pure embrace, of that chaste kiss, which is no longer the savage bite of the flesh, but the ideal caress of the soul. I need to rise from the hell of love to the paradise of ecstasy, to the fullness, the delicious and candid silence, of ecstasy. But M. Xavier had supped on ecstasy.

Nothing pained me so much as to see that I had not left the slightest trace of affection, not the smallest tenderness, in his heart. Yet I believe that I could have loved the little scoundrel,—that I could have devoted myself to him, in spite

193

of everything, like a beast. Even to-day I think regretfully of his impudent, cruel, and pretty phiz, and of his perfumed skin. And I have often on my lips, from which, since then, so many lips ought to have effaced it, the acid taste, the burning sensation of his kiss. Oh! Monsieur Xavier! Monsieur Xavier!

One evening, before dinner, when he had returned to dress, —my! but how nice he looked in evening dress!—and as I was carefully arranging his affairs in the dressing-room, he asked me, without embarrassment or hesitation, and almost in a tone of command, precisely as he would have asked me for hot water:

"Have you five louis? I am in absolute need of five louis to-night. I will return them to you to-morrow."

That very morning Madame had paid me my wages. Did he know it?

"I have only ninety francs," I answered, a little ashamed, —ashamed of his question, perhaps, but more ashamed, I think, at not having the entire sum that he asked.

"That makes no difference," said he: "go and get me the ninety francs. I will return them to you to-morrow."

He took the money, and, by way of thanks, said in a dry, curt tone that froze my heart: "That's good!" Then, putting out his foot with a brutal movement, he commanded insolently:

"Tie my shoes. And be quick about it; I am in a hurry."

I looked at him sadly, imploringly:

"Then you are not to dine here this evening, Monsieur Xavier?"

"No, I dine in town. Make haste."

As I tied his shoes, I moaned:

"And you will not return to-night? I shall cry all night long. It is not nice of you, Monsieur Xavier."

His voice became hard and thoroughly wicked.

"If you lent me your ninety francs that you might say that, you can take them back. Here, take them!"

"No, no," I sighed. "You know very well that it was not for that."

"Well, then, don't bother me."

He had quickly finished dressing, and he started off without kissing me and without saying a word.

The next day nothing was said about returning the money, and I did not wish to claim it. It gave me pleasure to think that he had something of me. And now I understand the women who kill themselves with toil, the women who sell themselves to passers-by, at night, on the sidewalks, the women who steal, and the women who kill, in order to get a little money with which to procure indulgences for the little man whom they love. That is what has happened to me, in fact. Or has it really happened to me in the degree that I say? Alas! I do not know. There are moments when, in presence of a man, I feel so soft, so soft, without will, without courage, so yielding . . . yes, so yielding!

Madame was not slow in changing her manner toward me. Instead of treating me nicely, as she had done before, she became severe, exacting, fault-finding. I was only a blockhead; I never did anything right; I was awkward, unclean, ill-bred, forgetful, dishonest. And her voice, which at first had been so sweet, so much like the voice of a comrade, now became as sour as vinegar. She gave me orders in a blunt and humiliating tone. No more gifts of underwear, no more cold cream and powder, no more of the secret counsels and private confidences that had so embarrassed me at first. No more of that suspicious comradeship which at bottom I felt not to be kindness, and which caused me to lose my respect for this mistress who raised me to the level of her own vice. I snapped at her sharply, strong in my knowledge of all the open or hidden infamies of the house. We got to quarreling like fish-wives, hurling our week's notice at each other's heads, like dirty rags.

"What, then, do you take my house for?" she cried. "Do you think you are working for a fast woman?"

Think of her cheek! I answered:

195

"Oh! your house is a clean one, indeed! You can boast it. And you? Let us talk about it; yes, let us talk about it! You are clean, too! And what about Monsieur? Oh! la! la! And do you think they don't know you in the neighborhood, and in Paris? Why, you are notorious, everywhere. Your house? A brothel. And, in fact, there are brothels which are not as dirty as your house."

And so these quarrels went on; we exchanged the worst insults and the lowest threats; we descended to the vocabulary of the street-walkers and the prisons. And then, suddenly, everything quieted down. M. Xavier had only to show signs of a reviving interest in me,—fleeting, alas!—when straightway began again the suspicious familiarity, the shameful complicities, the gifts of garments, the promises of doubled wages, the washing with Simon cream,—it is more suitable,—and the initiations into the mysteries of refined perfumes. M. Xavier's conduct toward me was the thermometer by which Madame regulated her own. The latter's kindness immediately followed the former's caresses. Abandonment by the son was accompanied by insults from the mother. I was the victim, continually tossed back and forth, of the enervating fluctuations to which the intermittent love of this capricious and heartless boy was subject. One would have thought that Madame must have played the spy with us, must have listened at the door, must have kept tabs for herself on the different phases of our relations. But no. She simply had the instinct of vice, that's all. She scented it through walls and souls, as a dog inhales in the breeze the far-away odor of game.

As for Monsieur, he continued to dance about among all these events, among all the hidden dramas of this house, alert, busy, cynical, and comical. In the morning he disappeared, with his face of a little pink and shaven faun, with his documents, with his bag stuffed with pious pamphlets and obscene newspapers. In the evening he reappeared, cravated with respectability, armored with Christian Socialism, his gait a little slower, his gestures a little more oily, his back slightly bent, doubtless under the weight of the good work done during the day. Regularly every Friday he gave me the week's issues of indecent journals, awaiting just the right occasion for making his declaration, and contenting himself with smiling at me with the air of an accomplice, caressing my chin, and saying to me, as he passed his tongue over his lips:

"Ho, ho, she is a very queer little one, indeed!"

As it amused me to watch Monsieur's game, I did not discourage him, but I promised myself to seize the first exceptionally favorable opportunity to sharply put him where he belonged.

One afternoon I was greatly surprised to see him enter the linen-room, where I sat alone, musing sadly over my work. In the morning I had had a painful scene with M. Xavier, and was still under the influence of the impression it had left on me. Monsieur closed the door softly, placed his bag on the large table near a pile of cloth, and, coming to me, took my hands and patted them. Under his blinking eyelid his eye turned, like that of an old hen dazzled by the sunlight. It was enough to make one die of laughter.

"Célestine," said he, "for my part, I prefer to call you Célestine. That does not offend you, does it?"

I could hardly keep from bursting.

"Why, no, Monsieur," I answered, holding myself on the defensive.

"Well, Célestine, I think you charming! There!"

"Really, Monsieur?"

"Adorable, in fact; adorable, adorable!"

"Oh! Monsieur!"

His fingers had left my hand, and were caressing my neck and chin with fat and soft little touches.

"Adorable, adorable!" he whispered.

He tried to embrace me. I drew back a little, to avoid his kiss.

"Stay, Célestine, I beg of you. I do not annoy you, do I?"

"No, Monsieur; you astonish me."

"I astonish you, you little rogue. I astonish you? Oh! you don't know me."

His voice was no longer dry. A fine froth moistened his lips.

"Listen to me, Célestine. Next week I am going to Lourdes; yes, I conduct a pilgrimage to Lourdes. Do you wish to come to Lourdes? I have a way of taking you to Lourdes. Will you come? Nobody will notice anything. You will stay at the hotel; you will take walks, or do what you like. And I will meet you in the evening."

What stupefied me was not the proposition in itself,—for I had been expecting it a long time,—but the unforeseen form which Monsieur gave it. Yet I preserved all my self-possession. And, desirous of humiliating this old rake, of showing him that I had not been the dupe of Madame's dirty calculations and his own, I lashed him squarely in the face with these words:

"And M. Xavier? Say, it seems to me that you are forgetting M. Xavier? What is he to do while we are amusing ourselves in Lourdes, at the expense of Christianity?"

An indirect and troubled gleam, the look of a surprised deer, lighted in the darkness of his eyes. He stammered:

"M. Xavier?"

"Why, yes!"

"Why do you speak to me of M. Xavier? There is no question of M. Xavier? M. Xavier has nothing to do with this."

I redoubled my insolence.

"On your word? Oh! don't pretend to be ignorant. Am I hired, yes or no, to be company for M. Xavier? Yes, am I not? Well, I am company for him. But you? Oh! no, that is not in the bargain. And then, you know, my little father, you are not my style."

And I burst out laughing in his face.

He turned purple; his eyes flamed with anger. But he did not think it prudent to enter into a discussion, for which I was terribly armed. He hastily picked up his bag, and slunk away, pursued by my laughter.

The next day, apropos of nothing, Monsieur made some gross remarks to me. I flew into a passion. Madame happened along. I became mad with anger. The scene that ensued between us three was so frightful, so low, that I cannot undertake to describe it. In unspeakable terms I reproached them with all their filth and with all their infamy. I demanded the return of the money that I had lent M. Xavier. They foamed at the mouth. I seized a cushion, and hurled it violently at Monsieur's head.

"Go away! Get out of here, at once, at once!" screamed Madame, threatening to tear my face with her nails.

"I erase your name from the membership of my society; you no longer belong to my society, lost creature, prostitute!" vociferated Monsieur, stuffing his bag with thrusts of his fists.

Finally Madame withheld my week's wages, refused to pay the ninety francs that I had lent M. Xavier, and obliged me to return all the rags that she had given me.

"You are all thieves," I cried.

And I went away, threatening them with the commissary of police and the justice of the peace.

Alas! the commissary of police pretended that the affair did not concern him. The justice of the peace advised me to let it drop. He explained:

"In the first place, Mademoiselle, you will not be believed. And that is as it should be. What would become of society if a servant could be right against a master? There would be no more society, Mademoiselle. That would be anarchy."

I consulted a lawyer; he demanded two hundred francs. I wrote to M. Xavier; he did not answer me. Then I counted up my resources. I had three francs fifty left—and the street pavement.

XIII.

And I see myself again at Neuilly, with the sisters of Our Lady of Thirty-Six Sorrows, a sort of house of refuge, and also an employment-bureau for housemaids. My! but it is a fine establishment, with a white front, and at the rear of a large garden. In the garden, which is ornamented, at intervals of fifty steps, with statues of the Virgin, there is a little chapel, very new and sumptuous, built from the proceeds of the collections. Large trees surround it. And every hour one hears the tolling of the bells. It is so nice to hear the bells toll. It stirs in one's heart memories of things so old and long forgotten. When the bells toll, I close my eyes and listen, and I see again landscapes which perhaps I never saw before, and which I recognize all the same,—very peaceful landscapes, imbued with all the transformed recollections of childhood and youth, . . . and bagpipes, . . . and, on the moor bordering on the beaches, the slowly-moving panorama of holiday crowds. Ding . . . dinn . . . dong! It is not very gay; it is not the same thing as gaiety; it is even sad at bottom,—sad, like love. But I like it. In Paris one never hears anything but the fountaineer's horn, and the deafening trumpet of the tramway.

In the establishment of the sisters of Our Lady of Thirty-Six Sorrows, you sleep in attic dormitories; you are fed meagrely on scraps of meat and spoiled vegetables, and you pay twenty-five sous a day to the institution. That is to say, the sisters withhold twenty-five sous from your wages, when they have secured a place for you. They call that getting you a place for nothing. Further, you have to work from six o'clock in the morning until nine in the evening, like the inmates of prisons. You are not allowed to go out. Meals and religious exercises take the place of recreation. Ah! the good sisters do not bore themselves, as M. Xavier would say; and their charity is a famous trap. They rope you in finely! But there it is,—I shall be stupid all my life. The stern lessons of experience, the succession of misfortunes, never teach me anything, are of no use to me. I am always crying out and raising a row, but in the end I am always victimized by everybody.

Several times comrades had spoken to me of the sisters of Our Lady of Thirty-Six Sorrows.

"Yes, my dear, it seems that only very swell people come to the box, . . . countesses, . . . marchionesses. One may chance on astonishing places."

I believed it. And then, in my distress, I remembered with some feeling, booby that I am, the happy years that I spent with the little sisters of Pont-Croix. Moreover, I had to go somewhere. Beggars cannot be choosers.

When I arrived, there were forty housemaids there. Many came from a great distance,—from Brittany, from Alsace, from the south,—girls who had never yet had a place,—awkward, clumsy, with livid complexions, sly airs, and singular eyes that looked over the walls of the convent at the mirage of Paris lying beyond. Others, not as green, were just out of place, like myself.

The sisters asked me whence I came what I knew how to do, whether I had good references, and whether I had any money left. I told them all sorts of things, and without further inquiry they welcomed me, saying:

"This dear child! We will find her a good place."

We all were their "dear children." While waiting for the promised good place, each of these dear children was put at some work, according to her faculties. Some did cooking and housework; others worked in the garden, digging in the soil, like navvies. I was promptly put at sewing, having, said Sister Boniface, supple fingers and a distinguished air. I began by mending the chaplain's pantaloons and the drawers of a sort of monk who was just then preaching a retreat in the chapel. Oh! those pantaloons! Oh! those drawers! Surely they did not resemble M. Xavier's. Then they intrusted to me tasks less ecclesiastical,—quite profane, in fact,—the making of fine and delicate linen garments, among which I again found myself in my element. I participated in the making of elegant bridal *trousseaux*, of rich baby-linen, ordered of the good sisters by charitable and wealthy ladies who were interested in the establishment.

At first, after so many shocks, in spite of the bad food, the chaplain's pantaloons, the lack of liberty, in spite of all the fierce exploitation that I could plainly see, I felt a sense of real relief amid this calm and silence. I did not reason much; I felt rather a need of prayer. Remorse over my past conduct, or, rather, the weariness resulting from it, prompted me to fervent repentance. Several times in succession I confessed to the chaplain. He was a queer man, this chaplain, very round and red, a little rude in manner and in speech, and afflicted with a disagreeable body-smell. He asked me strange questions, and insisted on knowing my favorite authors.

"Armand Silvestre? Yes. To be sure, he is dirty. I would not give you his works instead of the 'Imitation.' No, not that; yet he is not dangerous. But you must not read impious books, books against religion,—Voltaire, for instance. No, never; never read Voltaire,—that is a mortal sin,—or Renan, or Anatole France. They are dangerous."

"And Paul Bourget, Father?"

"Paul Bourget! He is entering on the right path; that I do not deny. But his Catholicism is not sincere,—not yet; at least, it is much mixed. Your Paul Bourget makes upon me the impression of a wash-basin,—yes, that is it—of a wash-basin, in which no matter what has been washed, and in which olives from Calvary are swimming amid hair and soapsuds. You should wait a little before reading him! Huysmans! Well, he is a little stiff in his expressions,—yes, indeed, very stiff,—but he is orthodox."

And he said to me further:

"Yes . . . Ah! you do mad things with your body! That is not good. No, indeed, that is always bad. But, sin for sin, it is better to sin with your masters, when they are pious persons, than with people of your own condition. It is less serious, less irritating to the good God. And perhaps these people have dispensations. Many have dispensations."

As I named M. Xavier and his father, he cried:

"No names. I do not ask you for names. Never tell me names. I do not belong to the police. Besides, those are rich and respectable people whom you have just named,—extremely religious people. Consequently you are wrong; you are rebellious against morality and against society."

These ridiculous conversations considerably cooled my religious zeal, my ardor for repentance. The work, too, annoyed me. It made me homesick for my own calling. I felt impatient desires to escape from this prison, to return to the privacies of dressing-rooms. I sighed for the closets full of sweet-smelling linen, the wardrobes stuffed with silks, satins, and velvets, so smooth to the touch, and the bath-rooms where white flesh is lathered with oily soaps. And the stories of the servants' hall, and the unforeseen adventures, and the evenings on the stairs and in the chambers! It is really curious; when I have a place, these things disgust me, but, when I am out of place, I miss them. I was tired also, excessively tired, sickened in fact, from having eaten for a week nothing but preserves made out of spoiled currants, of which the good sisters had purchased a large quantity in the Levallois market. Anything that the holy women could rescue from the refuse-heap was good enough for us.

What completed my irritation was the evident, the persistent effrontery with which we were exploited. Their game was a very simple one, and they took little pains to conceal it. They found places only for those girls of whom they could make no use themselves. Those from whom they could reap any profit whatever they held as prisoners, taking advantage of their talents, of their strength, and of their simplicity. As the height of Christian charity, they had found a way of having servants who paid for the privilege of working, and whom they stripped, without remorse and with inconceivable cynicism, of their modest resources and their little savings, after making a profit out of their labor. And the costs kept running on.

I complained, at first feebly, and then more forcibly, that they had not once summoned me into the reception-room, but to all my complaints the hypocrites answered:

"A little patience, my dear child! We are planning to get you an excellent place, my dear child; for you we desire an exceptional place. We know what sort of a place you should have. As yet not one has offered itself such as we wish for you, and such as you deserve."

Days and weeks passed. The places were never good enough, never exceptional enough for me. And the costs kept running on.

Although there was a watcher in the dormitory the things that went on every night were enough to make one shudder. As soon as the watcher had finished her round, and every one seemed to be asleep, you could see white forms arise and glide about among the beds. The good sisters, holy women, closed their eyes that they might see nothing, stopped up their ears that they might hear nothing. Wishing to avoid scandal, they tolerated horrors of which they feigned ignorance. And the costs kept running on.

Fortunately, when I was at the very depth of my ennui, I was delighted by the entrance into the establishment of a little friend, Clémence, whom I called Cléclé, and whom I had known in a place where I had worked in the Rue de l'Université. Cléclé was a charming pink blonde, extremely gay and lively, and very fly. She laughed at everything, accepted everything, and was contented everywhere. Devoted and faithful, she knew but one pleasure,—that of being useful to others. Vicious to the marrow of her bones, her vice had nothing repugnant about it, it was so gay, artless, and natural. She bore vice as a plant bears flowers, as a cherry-tree bears cherries. Her pretty, bird-like chatter sometimes made me forget my feeling of weariness, and put to sleep my tendency to rebel. Our two beds were next to each other; and one night she told me, in a funny sort of whisper, that she had just had a place in the house of a magistrate at Versailles.

"Fancy, there was nothing but animals in the den,—cats, three parrots, a monkey, and two dogs. And they all had to be taken care of. Nothing was good enough for them. We were fed on old scraps, the same as in this box here. But they had what was left over of the poultry; they had cream, and cakes, and mineral water, my dear! Yes, the dirty beasts drank nothing but Evian water, because of an epidemic of typhoid fever that was raging at Versailles. In the winter Madame had the cheek to take the stove out of my chamber, and put it in the room where the monkey and the cats slept. Would you believe it? I detested them, especially one of the dogs, a horrible old pug, that was always sniffing at my skirts, in spite of the kicks that I gave it. The other morning Madame caught me whipping it. You can imagine the scene. She showed me the door in double-quick time."

Oh! this Cléclé! how agreeable and amusing she was!

People have no idea of all the annoyances to which domestics are subjected, or of the fierce and eternal exploitation under which they suffer. Now the masters, now the keepers of employment-bureaus, now the charitable institutions, to say nothing of the comrades, some of whom are capable of terrible meanness. And nobody takes any interest in anybody else. Each one lives, grows fat, and is entertained by the misery of some one poorer than himself. Scenes change, settings are shifted, you traverse social surroundings that are different and even hostile, but everywhere you find the same appetites and

205

passions. In the cramped apartments of the *bourgeois* and in
the elegant mansion of the banker you meet the same filth, and
come in contact with the inexorable. The result of it all, for
a girl like me, is that she is conquered in advance, wherever
she may go and whatever she may do. The poor are the human
manure in which grow the harvests of life, the harvests of
joy which the rich reap, and which they misuse so cruelly
against us. They pretend that there is no more slavery. Oh!
what nonsense? And what are domestics, then, if not slaves?
Slaves in fact, with all that slavery involves of moral vileness,
inevitable corruption, and hate-engendering rebellion. Servants
learn vice in the houses of their masters. Entering upon their
duties pure and innocent,—some of them,—they are quickly
made rotten by contact with habits of depravity. They see
nothing but vice, they breathe nothing but vice, they touch
nothing but vice. Consequently, from day to day, from minute
to minute, they get more and more used to it, being defenceless
against it, being obliged, on the contrary, to serve it, to care
for it, to respect it. And their revolt arises from the fact
that they are powerless to satisfy it, and to break down all the
obstacles in the way of its natural expansion. Oh! it is extraordinary. They demand of us all the virtues, complete resignation, all the sacrifices, all the heroisms, and only those vices
that flatter the vanity of the masters, and which yield them a
profit. And all this in return for contempt and wages ranging
from thirty-five to ninety francs a month. No, it is too much!
Add that we live in perpetual distress of mind, in a perpetual
struggle between the ephemeral semi-luxury of the places that
we fill, and the anguish which the loss of these places causes
us. Add that we are continually conscious of the wounding
suspicions that follow us everywhere,—bolting doors, padlock-
ing drawers, marking bottles, numbering cakes and prunes,
and continually putting us to shame by invasive examination
of our hands, our pockets, and our trunks. For there is not a
door, not a closet, not a drawer, not a bottle, not an article,

that does not cry out to us: "Thief! thief! thief!" And also the continuous vexation caused by that terrible inequality, that frightful disproportion in our destinies, which, in spite of familiarities, smiles, and presents, places between our mistresses and ourselves an impassable abyss, a whole world of sullen hatreds, suppressed desires, and future vengeances,—a disproportion which is rendered every minute more perceptible, more humiliating, more disgracing, by the caprices, and even by the kindnesses, of those beings that know no justice and feel no love,—the rich. Did you ever think for a moment of the mortal and legitimate hatred, of the murderous—yes, murderous—desires with which we must be filled when we hear of our masters, in trying to describe something base and ignoble, cry out in our presence, with a disgust that casts us so violently outside the pale of humanity: "He has the soul of a domestic; that is the sentiment of a domestic." Then what do you expect us to become in these hells? Do these mistresses really imagine that I should not like to wear fine dresses, ride in fine carriages, have a gay time with lovers, and have servants of my own? They talk to us of devotion, of honesty, of fidelity. Why, but it would choke you to death, my little chippies!

Once, in the Rue Cambon . . . how many of these places I have had! . . . the masters were marrying their daughter. They gave a grand reception in the evening, at which the wedding-presents were exhibited, — enough of them to fill a furniture-van. By way of jest I asked Baptiste, the *valet de chambre:*

"Well, Baptiste, and you? What is your present?"

"My present?" exclaimed Baptiste, with a shrug of his shoulders.

"Yes, tell me, what is it?"

"A can of petroleum lighted under their bed. That is my present."

It was a smart answer. Moreover, this Baptiste was an astonishing man in politics.

207

"And yours, Célestine?" he asked, in his turn.

"Mine?"

I contracted my two hands into the shape of talons, and, pretending to claw a face ferociously, I answered:

"My nails, in their eyes!"

The butler, without being asked, remarked quietly, while arranging flowers and fruits in a glass dish with his fastidious fingers:

"I would be satisfied to sprinkle their faces in church with a bottle of good vitriol."

And he stuck a rose between two pears.

Oh! yes, how we love them! The extraordinary thing is that these revenges are not taken more frequently. When I think that a cook, for instance, holds her masters' lives in her hands every day; a pinch of arsenic instead of salt, a little dash of strychnine instead of vinegar, and the thing is done. Well, no, it must be that we have servitude in our very blood!

I have no education, and I write what I think and what I have seen. Well, I say that all this is not beautiful. I say that from the moment when any one installs another under his roof, though he were the last of poor devils, or the lowest of disreputable girls, he owes them protection, he owes them happiness. I say also that, if the master does not give it to us, we have a right to take it, even from his strong-box, even from his blood.

But enough of this! I do wrong to think of things that make my head ache and turn my stomach. I come back to my little stories.

I had much difficulty in leaving the sisters of Our Lady of Thirty-Six Sorrows. In spite of Cléclé's companionship, I was growing old in the box, and beginning to be hungry for liberty. When they understood that I had made up my mind to go, then the worthy sisters offered me places and places. There were places only for me. But I am not always a fool, and I

208

have a keen eye for rascalities. All these places I refused. In all of them I found something that did not suit me. You should have seen the heads of these holy women. It was laughable. They had calculated on finding me a place in the house of some old bigot, where they could get back out of my wages the cost of my board with usury, and I enjoyed playing them a trick in my turn.

One day I notified Sister Boniface that it was my intention to go that very evening. She had the cheek to answer me, raising her arms to heaven:

"But, my dear child, it is impossible."

"How so? Why is it impossible?"

"Why, my dear child, you cannot leave the house like that. You owe us more than seventy francs. You will have to pay us first these seventy francs."

"And with what?" I replied. "I have not a sou; you can search me."

Sister Boniface gave me a hateful look, and then declared, with severe dignity: "But, Mademoiselle, do you know that this is a robbery? And to rob poor women like us is worse than robbery; it is a sacrilege, for which the good God will punish you. Reflect."

Then anger got the better of me, I cried:

"Say, then, who is it that steals here,—you or I? No, but you are astonishing, my little mothers."

"Mademoiselle, I forbid you to speak in this way."

"Oh! don't talk to me. What? One does your work, one toils like a beast for you from morning to night, one earns enormous money for you, you give us food which dogs would refuse, and then we must pay you into the bargain! Indeed, you have no cheek!"

Sister Boniface had turned very pale. I felt that coarse, filthy, furious words were on her lips, and ready to leave them; but, not daring to let them go, she stammered:

"Silence! You are a girl without shame, without religion.

CELESTINE

God will punish you. Go, if you will; but we keep your trunk.''

I planted myself squarely before her, in an attitude of defiance, and, looking her full in the face, I said:

"Well, I should like to see you try it. Just try to keep my trunk, and you will have a visit from the commissary of police in short order. And, if religion consists in patching the dirty pantaloons of your chaplains, in stealing bread from poor girls, in speculating on the horrors that go on every night in the dormitory'' . . .

The good sister was fairly white. She tried to cover my voice with her own.

"Mademoiselle, Mademoiselle!''

"Oh! don't pretend ignorance of the dirty things that go on every night in the dormitory! Do you dare to tell me, in my face, your eyes looking into mine, that you are ignorant of them? You encourage them because they are profitable to you,—yes, because they are profitable to you.

"If religion is all that; if it is religious to keep a prison and a brothel,—well, then, I have enough of religion. My trunk, do you hear? I wish my trunk. You will give me my trunk at once.''

Sister Boniface was frightened.

"I do not wish to discuss with a lost creature,'' said she, in a voice of dignity. "All right; you shall go.''

"With my trunk?''

"With your trunk.''

"Very well! but it takes tall talk to get one's rights here. It is worse than at the custom-house.''

I went, in fact, that very evening. Cléclé, who was very nice, and who had saved something, lent me twenty francs. I went to engage a room in a lodging-house in the Rue de la Sourdière, and I bought a seat among the gallery-gods at the Porte-Saint-Martin. The play was "The Two Orphans.'' How true it is! Almost my own story.

I passed there a delightful evening, weeping, weeping, weeping.

210

XIV.

Rose is dead. Decidedly, misfortune hangs over the captain's house. Poor captain! His ferret dead . . . Bourbaki dead . . . and now it is Rose's turn! After a sickness of some days, she was carried off day before yesterday, in the evening, by a sudden attack of congestion of the lungs. She was buried this morning. From the windows of the linen-room I saw the procession pass in the road. The heavy coffin, borne by six men, was covered with crowns and bunches of white flowers, like that of a young virgin. A considerable crowd, in long, dark, babbling files, — all Mesnil-Roy — followed Captain Mauger, who, wearing a tightly-fitting black frock-coat, and holding himself very stiffly, led the mourners, in thoroughly military fashion. And the church bells, tolling in the distance, responded to the sound of the rattle waved by the beadle. Madame had warned me that I was not to go to the funeral. However, I had no desire to go. I did not like this fat and wicked woman; her death leaves me very calm and indifferent. Yet perhaps I shall miss Rose; perhaps I shall miss my occasional conversations with her in the road. But what a source of gossip this event must be at the grocer's!

I was curious to know what impression this sudden death had made upon the captain. And, as my masters were visiting, I took a walk in the afternoon along the hedge. The captain's garden is sad and deserted. A spade stuck in the ground indicates abandoned work. "The captain will not come into the garden," said I to myself; "he is undoubtedly weeping in his chamber, among the souvenirs." And suddenly I perceive him. He has taken off his fine frock-coat, and put on his working-clothes again, and, with his old foraging-cap on his head, he is

211

engaged in manuring his lawns. I even hear him humming a march in a low voice. He leaves his wheelbarrow, and comes toward me, carrying his fork on his shoulder.

"I am glad to see you, Mademoiselle Célestine."

I should like to offer him consolation or pity. I search for words, for phrases. But how can one find a touching word in presence of such a droll face? I content myself with repeating:

"A great misfortune, captain, a great misfortune for you! Poor Rose!"

"Yes, yes," he says, tamely.

His face is devoid of expression. His movements are uncertain. He adds, jabbing his fork into a soft spot in the ground near the hedge:

"Especially as I cannot get along without anybody."

I insist upon Rose's domestic virtues.

"You will not easily replace her, Captain."

Decidedly, he is not touched at all. One would say even, from looking at his eyes that have suddenly become brighter and from watching his movements, now more alert, that he has been relieved from a great weight.

"Bah!" says he, after a short silence, "everything can be replaced."

This resignation astonishes me, and even scandalizes me a little. To amuse myself, I try to make him understand all he has lost in losing Rose.

"She knew so well your habits, your tastes, your manias! She was so devoted to you!"

"Well, if she had not been, that would have been the last straw," he growled.

And, making a gesture by which he seems to put aside all sorts of objections, he goes on:

"Besides, was she so devoted to me? Oh! I may as well tell you the truth. I had had enough of Rose. Yes, indeed! After we took a little boy to help us, she attended to nothing

in the house, and everything went badly, very badly. I could
not even have an egg boiled to my taste. And the scenes that
went on, from morning to night, apropos of nothing. If I
spent ten sous, there were cries and reproaches. And, when I
talked with you, as I am doing now,—well, there was a row,
indeed; for she was jealous, jealous. Oh! no. She went for
you; you should have heard her. In short, I was no longer
at home in my own house."

He breathes deeply, noisily, and, with the new and deep
joy that a traveler feels on returning from a long journey, he
contemplates the sky, the bare grass-plots in the garden, the
violet interlacings of the branches of the trees against the light,
and his little house.

This joy, so offensive to Rose's memory, now seems to me
very comical. I stimulate the captain to further confidences.
And I say to him, in a tone of reproach:

"Captain, I think you are not just to Rose."

"Egad!" he rejoins, quickly. "You do not know; you
don't know anything about it. She did not go to tell you of
all the scenes that she made, her tyranny, her jealousy, her
egoism. Nothing belonged to me here any longer. Everything
in my house was hers. For instance, you would not believe it,
my Voltaire arm-chair was never at my disposition. She had
it all the time. She had everything, for that matter. To think
that I could no longer eat asparagus with oil, because she did
not like it! Oh! she did well to die. It was the best thing
that could happen to her, for, in some way or other, I should
have gotten rid of her. Yes, yes, I should have gotten rid of
her. She was becoming too much for me. I had had enough.
And let me tell you; if I had died before her, Rose would have
been prettily trapped. I had a bitter pill in store for her.
My word for it!"

His lip curls in a smile that ends in an atrocious grimace.
He continues, chopping each of his words with moist little puffs
of laughter:

"You know that I made a will, in which I gave her everything,—house, money, dividends, everything. She must have told you; she told everybody. Yes, but what she did not tell you, because she did not know it, is that, two months later, I made a second will, cancelling the first, in which I did not leave her anything,—not a sou."

Unable to contain himself longer, he bursts out laughing, a strident laugh that scatters through the garden like a flight of scolding sparrows. And he cries:

"Ah! that's an idea, hey? Oh! her head,—you can see it from here,—on learning that I had left my fortune to the French Academy. For, my little Célestine, it is true; I had left my fortune to the French Academy. Ah! that's an idea!"

I allow his laughter to become quieter, and then I gravely ask him:

"And now, Captain, what are you going to do?"

The captain gives me a long, sly, amorous look, and says:

"Well, that depends on you."

"On me."

"Yes, on you; on you alone."

"And how is that?"

A moment of silence follows, during which, straightening up and twisting his pointed beard, he seeks to envelope me in a seductive fluid.

"Come," he says, suddenly, "let us go straight to the point. Let us speak squarely,—soldier-fashion. Do you wish to take Rose's place?"

I was expecting the attack. I had seen it coming from the depth of his eyes. It does not surprise me. I receive it with a serious and unmoved expression.

"And the wills, Captain?"

"Oh! I tear them up."

I object:

"But I do not know how to cook."

"Oh! I will do the cooking; I will make my bed; I will do everything."

214

He becomes gallant, sprightly; his eye sparkles. He leans towards the hedge, stretching out his neck. His eyes become bloodshot. And in a lower voice he says:

"If you came to me, Célestine,—well" . . .

"Well, what?"

"Well, the Lanlaires would die of rage. Ah! that's an idea!"

I lapse into silence, and pretend to be profoundly dreaming. The captain becomes impatient. He digs the heels of his shoes into the sandy path.

"See, Célestine, thirty-five francs a month; the master's table; the master's room; a will; does that suit you? Answer me."

"We will see later. But, while waiting, take another."

And I run away that I may not blow into his face the tempest of laughter that is roaring in my throat.

I have, then, only the embarrassment of choice. The captain or Joseph? To live as a servant-mistress, with all the contingencies that such a position involves,—that is, to remain still at the mercy of a stupid, coarse, changeable man, and dependent upon a thousand disagreeable circumstances and a thousand prejudices; or else to marry, and thus acquire a sort of regular and respected liberty, in a situation free from the control of others, and liberated from the caprice of events? Here at last a portion of my dream promises to be realized.

It is very evident that I should have liked a realization on a grander scale. But, when I think how few chances present themselves, in general, in the existence of a woman like me, I must congratulate myself that something is coming to me at last other than this eternal and monotonous tossing back and forth from one house to another, from one bed to another, from one face to another face.

Of course, I put aside at once the captain's plan. Moreover, I had no need of this last conversation with him to know the sort of grotesque and sinister mountebank, the type of odd humanity, that he represents. Beyond the fact that his physical ugliness is complete,—for there is nothing to relieve and correct it,—he gives one no hold on his soul. Rose believed firmly in her assured domination over this man, and this man tricked her. One cannot dominate nothing; one can have no influence over emptiness. I cannot, without choking with laughter, think of myself for an instant in the arms of this ridiculous personage and caressing him. Yet, in spite of this, I am content, and I feel something akin to pride. However low the source from which it comes, it is none the less an homage, and this homage strengthens my confidence in myself and in my beauty.

Quite different are my feelings toward Joseph. Joseph has taken possession of my mind. He retains it, he holds it captive, he obsesses it. He disturbs me, bewitches me, and frightens me, by turns. Certainly, he is ugly, brutally, horribly ugly; but, when you analyze this ugliness, you find something formidable in it, something that is almost beauty, that is more than beauty, that is above beauty,—something elemental. I do not conceal from myself the difficulty, the danger, of living, whether married or not, with such a man, of whom I am warranted in suspecting everything, and of whom, in reality, I know nothing. And it is this that draws me to him with a dizzy violence. At least he is capable of many things in crime, perhaps, and perhaps also in the direction of good. I do not know. What does he want of me? What will he do with me? Should I be the unscrupulous instrument of plans that I know nothing of, the plaything of his ferocious passions? Does he even love me? And why does he love me? For my beauty; for my vices; for my intelligence; for my hatred of prejudices,—he who makes parade of all the prejudices? I do not know. In addition to this attraction which the unknown and mysterious has for me, he exercises over me the bitter, powerful charm of force. And this charm, yes, this charm acts

more and more on my nerves, conquers my passive and submissive flesh. It is something which I cannot define exactly,
something that takes me wholly, by my mind and by my sex,
revealing in me instincts of which I was unaware, instincts
that slept within me without my knowledge, and that no love,
no thrill of voluptuousness had before awakened. And I
tremble from head to foot when I remember the words of Joseph, saying to me:

"You are like me, Célestine. Oh! not in features, of
course. But our two souls are alike; our two souls resemble
each other."

Our two souls! Is that possible?

These sensations that I feel are so new, so imperious, so
strongly tenacious, that they do not leave me a minute's rest,
and that I remain always under the influence of their stupefying fascination. In vain do I seek to occupy my mind with
other thoughts. I try to read and walk in the garden, when
my masters are away, and, when they are at home, to work
furiously at my mending in the linen-room. Impossible! Joseph has complete possession of my thought. And not only
does he possess it in the present, but he possesses it also in
the past. Joseph so interposes himself between my entire past
and myself that I see, so to speak, nothing but him, and that
this past, with all its ugly or charming faces, draws farther
and father from me, fades away, disappears. Cléophas Biscouille; M. Jean; M. Xavier; William, of whom I have not yet
spoken; M. Georges, himself, by whom I believed my soul to
have been branded forever, as the shoulder of the convict is
branded by the red iron; and all those to whom, voluntarily,
joyously, passionately, I have given a little or much of myself,
of my vibrant flesh and of my sorrowful heart,—all of them
shadows already! Uncertain and ludicrous shadows that fade
away until they are hardly recollections, and then become confused dreams . . . intangible, forgotten realities . . . vapors
. . . nothing. Sometimes, in the kitchen, after dinner, when

looking at Joseph and his criminal mouth, and his criminal eyes, and his heavy cheek-bones, and his low, knotty, humpy forehead, upon which the lamplight accumulates hard shadows, I say to myself:

"No, no, it is not possible. I am under the influence of a fit of madness; I will not, I cannot, love this man. No, no, it is not possible."

And yet it is possible, and it is true. And I must at last confess it to myself, cry out to myself: "I love Joseph!"

Ah! now I understand why one should never make sport of love; why there are women who rush, with all the consciousness of murder, with all the invincible force of nature, to the kisses of brutes and to the embraces of monsters, and who voluptuously sound the death-rattle in the sneering faces of demons and bucks.

Joseph has obtained from Madame six days' leave of absence, and to-morrow he is to start for Cherbourg, pretending to be called by family matters. It is decided; he will buy the little café. But for some months he will not run it himself. He has some one there, a trusted friend, who is to take charge of it.

"Do you understand?" he says to me. "It must first be repainted, and made to look like new; it must be very fine, with its new sign, in gilt letters: "To the French Army!' And besides, I cannot leave my place yet. That I cannot do."

"Why not, Joseph?"

"Because I cannot now."

"But when will you go, for good?"

Joseph scratches his neck, gives me a sly glance, and says:

"As to that I do not know. Perhaps not for six months yet; perhaps sooner; perhaps even later. I cannot tell. It depends."

I feel that he does not wish to speak. Nevertheless I insist:

"It depends on what?"

He hesitates to answer; then, in a mysterious and, at the same time, somewhat excited tone, he says:

"On a certain matter; on a very important matter."

"But what matter?"

"Oh! on a certain matter, that's all."

This is uttered in a brusque voice,—a voice not of anger exactly, but of impatience. He refuses to explain further.

He says nothing to me of myself. This astonishes me, and causes me a painful disappointment. Can he have changed his mind? Has my curiosity, my hesitation, wearied him? Yet it is very natural that I should be interested in an event in the success or failure of which I am to share. Can the suspicion that I have not been able to hide, my suspicion of the outrage committed by him upon the little Claire, have caused Joseph to reflect further, and brought about a rupture between us? But I feel from the tremor of my heart that my resolution, deferred out of coquetry, out of disposition to tease, was well taken. To be free, to be enthroned behind a bar, to command others, to know that one is looked at, desired, adored by so many men! And that is not to be? And this dream is to escape me, as all the others have? I do not wish to seem to be throwing myself at Joseph's head, but I wish to know what he has in his mind. I put on a sad face, and I sigh:

"When you have gone, Joseph, the house will no longer be endurable to me. I have become so accustomed to you now, to our conversations."

"Oh! indeed!"

"I too shall go away."

Joseph says nothing.

He walks up and down the harness-room, with anxious brow and preoccupied mind, his hands nervously twirling a pair of garden-shears in the pocket of his blue apron. The expression of his face is unpleasant. I repeat, as I watch him go back and forth:

219

"Yes, I shall go away; I shall return to Paris."

He utters not a word of protest, not a cry; not even an imploring glance does he turn upon me. He puts a stick of wood in the stove, as the fire is low, and then begins again his silent promenade up and down the room. Why is he like this? Does he, then, accept this separation? Does he want it? Has he, then, lost his confidence in me, the love that he had for me? Or does he simply fear my imprudence, my eternal questions?

Trembling a little, I ask him:

"Will it cause you no pain, Joseph, if we do not see each other again?"

Without halting in his walk, without even glancing at me out of the corner of his eye, in the manner so characteristic of him, he says:

"Of course. But what can you expect? One cannot oblige people to do what they refuse to do. A thing either pleases, or it does not please."

"What have I refused to do, Joseph?"

"And besides, you are always full of bad ideas about me," he continues, without answering my question.

"Why do you say that?"

"Because" . . .

"No, no, Joseph; you no longer love me; you have something else in mind now. I have refused nothing; I have reflected, that is all. It is natural enough, isn't it? One does not make a life-contract without reflection. My hesitation, on the contrary, ought to make you think well of me. It proves that I am not light-headed,—that I am a serious woman."

"You are a good woman, Célestine, an orderly woman."

"Well, then?"

At last Joseph stops walking, and, gazing at me with profound and still suspicious, but yet tenderer, eyes, he says, slowly:

"It is not that, Célestine. There is no question of that. I

do not prevent you from reflecting. Reflect all you like. There is plenty of time, and we will talk again on my return. But what I do not like, you see, is so much curiosity. There are things that do not concern women; there are things" . . .

And he finishes his phrase with a shake of his head.

After a moment's silence he resumes:

"I have nothing else in mind, Célestine. I dream of you; I am crazy over you. As true as the good God exists, what I have said once I say always. We will talk it over again. But you must not be curious. You do what you do; I do what I do. In that way there is no mistake, no surprise."

Approaching me, he grasps my hands.

"I have a hard head, Célestine; yes, indeed! But what is in it stays in it, and cannot be gotten out of it. I dream of you, Célestine, of you . . . in the little café."

XV.

Joseph started for Cherbourg yesterday morning, as had
been agreed. On coming down stairs, I find him already gone.
Marianne, half awake, with swollen eyes and hawking throat,
is pumping water. The plate from which Joseph has just
eaten his soup, and the empty cider-pitcher, are still on the
kitchen table. I am anxious, and at the same time I am content, for I feel that, starting from to-day, a new life is at last
preparing for me. The sun has scarcely risen; the air is cold.
Beyond the garden the country is still sleeping under a curtain of fog, and in the distance, coming from an invisible
valley, I hear the very feeble sound of a locomotive whistle.
It is the train that bears Joseph and my destiny. I can eat no
breakfast; it seems to me that something huge and heavy fills
my stomach. I no longer hear the whistle. The fog is thick-
ening; it has entered the garden.

And if Joseph were never to come back?
All day long I have been distracted, nervous, extremely
agitated. Never did the house weigh more heavily upon me;
never did the long corridors seem more dismal, more icily
silent; never have I so much detested the crabbed face and
shrill voice of Madame. Impossible to work. I have had with
Madame a very violent scene, in consequence of which I really
thought that I should be obliged to go. And I ask myself what
I am going to do during these six days, without Joseph. I
dread the ennui of being alone, at meals, with Marianne. I
really need somebody to talk to.

As a rule, as soon as it comes night, Marianne, under the
influence of drink, falls into a state of complete stupefaction.

222

Her brain becomes torpid; her tongue becomes thick; her lips hang and shine like the worn brink of an old well; and she is sad, sad to the point of weeping. I can get nothing out of her but little plaints, little cries, something like the puling of a child. Nevertheless, last night, less drunk than usual, she confided to me, amid never-ending groans, that she is afraid she is in trouble. Well, that caps the climax! My first impulse is to laugh. But soon I feel a keen sorrow,—something like the cutting of a lash in the pit of my stomach. Suppose it were through Joseph? I remember that, on the day of my arrival here, I at once suspected them. But since then nothing has happened to justify this stupid suspicion. On the contrary. No, no, it is impossible. It cannot be. I ask:

"You are sure, Marianne?"

"Sure? No," she says; "I am only afraid."

"And through whom?"

She hesitates to answer; then, suddenly, with a sort of pride, she declares:

"Through Monsieur."

This time I came near bursting with laughter. Marianne, mistaking my laugh for one of admiration, begins to laugh, too.

"Yes, yes, through Monsieur," she repeats. "I am going to see Madame Gouin to-morrow."

I feel a real pity for this poor woman whose brain is so dark and whose ideas are so obscure. Oh! how melancholy and lamentable she is! And what is going to happen to her now? An extraordinary thing,—love has given her no radiance, no grace. She has not that halo of light with which voluptuousness surrounds the ugliest faces. She has remained the same,—heavy, flabby, lumpy.

I left her with a somewhat heavy heart. Now I laugh no more; I will never laugh at Marianne again, and the pity that I feel for her turns into a real and almost painful emotion.

But I feel that my emotion especially concerns myself. On returning to my room, I am seized with a sort of shame and

223

great discouragement. One should never reflect upon love. How sad love is at bottom! And what does it leave behind? Ridicule, bitterness, or nothing at all. What remains to me now of Monsieur Jean, whose photograph is on parade on the mantel, in its red plush frame? Nothing, except my disappointment at having loved a vain and heartless imbecile. Can I really have loved this insipid beauty, with his white and unhealthy face, his regulation black mutton-chops, and his hair parted down the middle? This photograph irritates me. I can no longer have continually before me those two stupid eyes that look at me with the unchangeable look of an insolent and servile flunky. Oh! no, let it go to keep company with the others, at the bottom of my trunk, pending the time when I shall make of my more and more detested past a fire of joy and ashes.

And I think of Joseph. Where is he at the present moment? What is he doing? Is he even thinking of me? Undoubtedly he is in the little café. He is looking, discussing, measuring; he is picturing to himself the effect that I shall produce at the bar, before the mirror, amid the dazzling of the glasses and the multi-colored bottles. I wish that I knew Cherbourg, its streets, its squares, its harbor, that I might represent Joseph to myself going and coming, conquering the city as he has conquered me. I turn and turn again in my bed, a little feverish. My thought goes from the forest of Raillon to Cherbourg, from the body of Claire to the little café. And, after a painful period of insomnia, I finally go off to sleep with the stern and severe image of Joseph before my eyes, the motionless image of Joseph outlining itself in the distance against a dark and choppy background, traversed by white masts and red yards.

To-day, Sunday, I paid a visit in the afternoon to Joseph's room. The two dogs follow me eagerly. They seem to be asking me where Joseph is. A little iron bed, a large cupboard, a sort of low commode, a table, two chairs, all in white-wood, and a porte-manteau, which a green lustring curtain, running on a rod, protects from the dust,—these constitute the furnishings. Though the room is not luxurious, it is extremely orderly and clean. It has something of the rigidity and austerity of a monk's cell in a convent. On the white-washed walls, between the portraits of Déroulède and General Mercier, holy pictures unframed,—Virgins, an Adoration of the Magi, a Massacre of the Innocents, a view of Paradise. Above the bed a large crucifix of dark wood, serving as a holy-water basin, and barred with a branch of consecrated box.

It is not very delicate, to be sure, but I could not resist my violent desire to search everywhere, in the hope, vague though it were, of discovering some of Joseph's secrets. Nothing is mysterious in this room, nothing is hidden. It is the naked chamber of a man who has no secrets, whose life is pure, exempt from complications and events. The keys are in the furniture and in the cupboards; not a drawer is locked. On the table some packages of seeds and a book, "The Good Gardener." On the mantel a prayer-book, whose pages are yellow, and a little note-book, in which have been copied various recipes for preparing encaustic, Bordelaise stew, and mixtures of nicotine and sulphate of iron. Not a letter anywhere; not even an account-book. Nowhere the slightest trace of any correspondence, either on business, politics, family matters, or love. In the commode, beside worn-out shoes and old hose-nozzles, piles of pamphlets, numerous numbers of the "Libre Parole." Under the bed, mouse-traps and rat-traps. I have felt of everything, turned everything upside down, emptied everything, — coats, mattress, linen, and drawer. There is nothing else. In the cupboard nothing has been changed. It is just as I left it a week ago, when I put it in order in Joseph's presence. Is it possible that Joseph has nothing? Is is possible that he is so lacking in those thousand little intimate and familiar things whereby a man reveals his tastes, his passions, his thoughts, a little of that which dominates his life? Ah! yes, here! From the back of the table drawer, I take a cigar-box, wrapped in paper and strongly tied with string running four times around. With great difficulty I untie the knots, I open the box, and on a bed of wadding I see five consecrated medals, a little silver crucifix, and a rosary of red beads. Always religion!

My search concluded, I leave the room, filled with nervous irritation at having found nothing of what I was searching for, and having learned nothing of what I wanted to know. Decidedly, Joseph communicates his impenetrability to everything that he touches. The articles that he possesses are as silent as his lips, as unfathomable as his eyes and brow. The rest of the day I have had before me, really before me, Joseph's face, enigmatical, sneering, and crusty, by turns. And it has seemed to me that I could hear him saying to me:

"And much farther you have got, my awkward little one, in consequence of your curiosity. Ah! you can look again, you can search my linen, my trunks, my soul; you will never find anything out."

I do not wish to think of all this any more; I do not wish to think of Joseph any more. My head aches too hard, and I believe that I should go mad. Let us return to my memories.

Scarcely had I left the good sisters of Neuilly, when I fell again into the hell of the employment-bureaus. And yet I had firmly resolved never to apply to them again. But, when one is on the pavements, without money enough to buy even a bit of bread, what is one to do? Friends, old comrades? Bah! They do not even answer you. Advertisements in the newspapers? They cost a great deal, and involve interminable correspondence,—a great lot of trouble for nothing. And besides, they are very risky. At any rate, one must have something ahead, and Cléclé's twenty francs had quickly melted in my hands. Prostitution? Street-walking? To take men home with you who are often more destitute than yourself? Oh! no, indeed. For pleasure,—yes, as much as you like. But for money? I cannot; I do not know how; I am always victimized. I was even obliged to hang up some little jewels that I had, in order to pay for my board and lodging. Inevitably, hard luck brings you back to the agencies of usury and human exploitation.

Oh! the employment-bureaus, what dirty traps they are! In the first place, one must give ten sous to have her name entered; and then there is the risk of getting a bad place. In these frightful dens there is no lack of bad places; and, really, one has only the embarrassment of choice between one-eyed hussies and blind hussies. Nowadays, women with nothing at all, keepers of little four-penny grocery stores, pretend to have servants and to play the *role* of countess. What a pity! If, after discussions, and humiliating examinations, and still more humiliating haggling, you succeed in coming to terms with one of these rapacious *bourgeoises,* you owe to the keeper of the employment-bureau three per cent. of your first year's wages. So much the worse, if you remain but ten days in the place she has procured for you. That does not concern her; her account is good, and the entire commission is exacted. Oh! they know the trick; they know where they send you, and that you will come back to them soon. Once, for instance, I had seven places in four months and a half. A run on the black; impossible houses, worse than prisons. Well, I had to pay the employment-bureau three per cent. of seven years' wages,— that is, including the ten sous required for each fresh entrance of my name, more than ninety francs. And nothing had been accomplished, and all had to be begun over again. Is that just, I want to know? Is it not abominable robbery?

Robbery? In whatever direction one turns, one sees nothing but robbery anywhere. Of course it is always those who have nothing who are the most robbed, and robbed by those who have all. But what is one to do? One rages and rebels, and then ends by concluding that it is better to be robbed than to die like a dog in the street. Oh! the world is arranged on a fine plan, that's sure! What a pity it is that General Boulanger did not succeed! At least he, it seems, loved domestics.

The employment-bureau in which I was stupid enough to have my name entered is situated in the Rue du Colisée, at the back of a court-yard, on the third floor of a dark and very old house,—almost a house for working-people. At the very entrance the narrow and steep staircase, with its filthy steps that stick to your shoes and its damp banister that sticks to your hands, blows into your face an infected air, an odor of sinks and closets, and fills your heart with discouragement. I do not pretend to be fastidious, but the very sight of this staircase turns my stomach and cuts off my legs, and I am seized with a mad desire to run away. The hope which, on the way, has been singing in your head is at once silenced, stifled by this thick and sticky atmosphere, by these vile steps, and these sweating walls that seem to be frequented by glutinous larvæ and cold toads. Really, I do not understand how fine ladies dare to venture into this unhealthy hovel. Frankly, they are not disgusted. But what is there to-day that disgusts fine ladies? They would not go into such a house to help a poor person, but to worry a domestic they would go the devil knows where!

This bureau was run by Mme. Paulhat-Durand, a tall woman of almost forty-five years, who, underneath her very black and slightly wavy hair, and in spite of soft flesh crammed into a terrible corset, still preserved remnants of beauty, a majestic deportment, . . . and such an eye! My! but she must have had fun in her day! With her austere elegance, always wearing a black watered-silk dress, a long gold chain falling in loops over her prominent bosom, a brown velvet cravat around her neck, and with very pale hands, she seemed the perfection of dignity and even a little haughty. She lived, outside of marriage, with a city employee, M. Louis. We knew him only by his Christian name. He was a queer type, extremely near-sighted, with mincing movements, always silent, and presenting a very awkward appearance in a grey jacket that was too short for him. Sad, timid, bent, although young, he seemed, not happy, but resigned. He never dared to speak to us, or even to look at us, for the madame was very jealous. When he came in, with his bag of papers under his arm, he contented himself with slightly lifting his hat in our direction, without turning his head toward us, and, with a dragging step, glided into the hall, like a shadow. And how tired the poor fellow was! At night M. Louis attended to the correspondence, kept the books, . . . and did the rest.

Mme. Paulhat-Durand was named neither Paulhat or Durand; these two names, which go so well together, she acquired, it seems, from two gentlemen, dead to-day, which whom she had lived, and who had supplied her with funds to open her employment-bureau. Her real name was Josephine Carp. Like many keepers of employment-bureaus, she was an old chambermaid. That was to be seen, moreover, in her pretentious bearing, in her manners, modeled upon those of the great ladies in whose service she had been, and beneath which, in spite of her gold chain and black silk dress, one could see the filth of her inferior origin. She showed all the insolence of an old domestic, but she reserved this insolence for us exclusively, showing her customers, on the contrary, a servile obsequiousness, proportioned to their wealth and social rank.

"Oh! what a set of people, Madame, the Countess," said she, with an air of affectation. "Chambermaids *de luxe*,—that is, wenches who are unwilling to do anything, who do not work, and whose honesty and morality I do not guarantee,—as many of those as you want! But women who work, who sew, who know their trade,—there are no more of them; I have no more of them; nobody has any more of them. That's the way it is."

Yet her bureau was well patronized. She had the custom especially of the people in the Champs-Elysées quarter, consisting largely of foreigners and Jewesses. Ah! the scandals that I know about them!

The door opens into a hall leading to the *salon*, where Mme. Paulhat-Durand is enthroned in her perpetual black silk dress. At the left of the hall is a sort of dark hole, a vast ante-room with circular benches, and in the middle a table recovered with faded red serge. Nothing else. The ante-room is lighted only by a narrow strip of glass set in the upper part of the partition which separates the room from the employment-bureau, and running its entire length. A bad light, a light more gloomy than darkness, comes through the glass, coating objects and faces with something less than a twilighty glimmer.

We came there every morning and every afternoon, heaps of us,—cooks and chambermaids, gardeners and valets, coachmen and butlers,—and we spent our time in telling each other of our misfortunes, in running down the masters, and in wishing for extraordinary, fairy-like, liberating places. Some brought books and newspapers, which they read passionately; others wrote letters. Now gay, now sad, our buzzing conversations were often interrupted by the sudden erruption of Mme. Paulhat-Durand, like a gust of wind.

"Be silent, young women," she cried. "It is impossible to hear ourselves in the *salon*."

Or else she called in a curt, shrill voice:

"Mademoiselle Jeanne!"

Mlle. Jeanne rose, arranged her hair a little, followed the madame into the bureau, from which she returned a few moments later, with a grimace of disdain upon her lips. Her recommendations had not been found sufficient. What did they require then? The Monthyon prize? A maiden's diploma?

Or else they had been unable to agree upon wages.

"Oh! no, the mean things! A dirty dance hall . . . nothing to pinch. She does her own marketing. Oh! la! la! Four children in the house! Think of it!"

The whole punctuated by furious or obscene gestures.

We all passed into the bureau by turns, summoned by Mme. Paulhat-Durand, whose voice grew shriller and shriller, and whose shining flesh at last became green with anger. For my part, I saw directly with whom I had to deal, and that the place did not suit me. Then, to amuse myself, instead of submitting to their stupid questions, I questioned the fine ladies themselves.

"Madame is married?"

"Undoubtedly."

"Ah! And Madame has children?"

"Certainly."

"Dogs?"

"Yes."

"Madame makes the chambermaid sit up?"

"When I go out in the evening . . . evidently."

"And Madame often goes out in the evening?"

Pursing up her lips, she was about to answer, but I, casting a contemptuous glance at her hat, her costume, and her entire person, said, in a curt and disdainful voice:

"I regret it, but Madame's place does not please me. I do not go into houses like Madame's."

And I sailed out triumphantly.

One day a little woman, with hair outrageously dyed, with lips painted with minium, with enameled cheeks, as insolent as a guinea-hen, and perfumed like a bidet, after asking me thirty-six questions, put a thirty-seventh:

"Are you well behaved? Do you receive lovers?"

"And Madame?" I answered very quietly, showing no astonishment.

Some, less difficult to please, or more weary or more timid, accepted infected places. They were hooted.

"*Bon voyage!* We shall see you soon again."

At the sight of us thus piled up on our benches, with legs spread apart, dreamy, stupid, or chattering, and listening to

the successive calls of the madame: "Mademoiselle Victoire!
. . . Mademoiselle Irène! . . . Mademoiselle Zulma!" it
sometimes seemed to me as if we were in a public house,
awaiting the next caller. That seemed to me funny or sad, I
don't know which; and one day I remarked upon it aloud.
There was a general outburst of laughter. Each one immediately delivered herself of all the exact and marvelous information of which she was in possession concerning establishments of that character. A fat and puffy creature, who was
peeling an orange, said:

"Surely that would be better. They are sure of a living
in those places. And champagne, you know, young women;
and chemises with silver stars; and no corsets!"

I remember that that day I thought of my sister Louise,
undoubtedly shut up in one of those houses. I pictured to
myself her life, possibly happy, at least tranquil, in any case
exempt from the danger of poverty and hunger. And, more
than ever disgusted with my dismal and beaten youth, with my
wandering existence, with my dread of the morrow, I too
dreamed:

"Yes, perhaps that would be better."

And evening came, and then night,—a night hardly darker
than the day. We became silent, fatigued from having talked
too much, from having waited too long. A gas jet was lighted
in the hall, and regularly, at five o'clock, through the glass in
the door, we could see the slightly-bent outline of M. Louis
passing very quickly, and then vanishing. It was the signal
for our departure.

Often old women, runners for public houses, procurers with
a respectable air, and quite like the good sisters in their honeyed
sweetness, awaited us at the exit on the sidewalk. They followed us discreetly, and, in some darker corner of the street,
behind the groups of trees in the Champs-Elysées, out of sight
of the police, they approached us.

"Come, then, to my house, instead of dragging out your

poor life from anxiety to anxiety, and from poverty to poverty. In my house you will find pleasure, luxury, money; you will find liberty.''

Dazzled by the marvelous promises, several of my little comrades listened to these love-brokers. With sadness I saw them start. Where are they now?

One evening one of these prowlers, fat and flabby, whom I had already brutally dismissed, succeeded in getting me to go with her to a café in the Rond-Point, where she offered me a glass of chartreuse. I see her still, with her hair turning grey, her severe costume of a *bourgeoise* widow, her plump and sticky hands, loaded with rings. She reeled off her story with more spirit and conviction than usual, and, as I remained indifferent to all her humbug inducements, she cried:

''Oh! if you only would, my little one. I do not need to look at you twice to see how beautiful you are in all respects. And it is a real crime to let such beauty go to waste, and be squandered in the company of house-servants. With your beauty, you would quickly make a fortune! Oh! you would have a bag of money in a very little time. You see, I have a wonderful set of customers,—old gentlemen, very influential, and very, very generous. All that is best in Paris comes to my house,—famous generals, powerful magistrates, foreign ambassadors.''

She drew nearer to me, lowering her voice.

''And if I were to tell you that the president of the republic himself . . . why, yes, my little one! That gives you an idea of what my house is. There is not one like it in the world. Rabineau's is nothing side of my house. And stay! yesterday at five o'clock the president was so well pleased that he promised me the academic palms . . . for my son, who is chief auditor in a religious educational institution at Auteuil.''

She looked at me a long time, searching me body and soul, and repeated:

''Oh! if you would! What a success!''

I offered a heap of objections, my lack of fine linen, of costumes, of jewels. The old woman reassured me.

"Oh, if that's all," said she, "you need not worry, because in my house, you understand, natural beauty is the chief adornment."

"Yes, yes, I know, but still" . . .

"I assure you that you need not worry," she insisted, with benevolence. "Listen, sign a contract with me for three months, and I will give you an outfit of the best, such as no soubrette of the Théâtre-Français ever had. My word for it!"

I asked time to reflect.

"Well, all right! reflect," counseled this dealer in human flesh. "Let me give you my address, at any rate. When your heart speaks,—well, you will have only to come. Oh! I am perfectly confident. And to-morrow I am going to announce you to the president of the republic."

We had finished drinking. The old woman settled for the two glasses, and took from a little black pocket-book a card, which she slyly slipped into my hand. When she had gone, I looked at the card, and I read.

MADAME REBECCA RANVET
Millinery

At Mme. Paulhat-Durand's I witnessed some extaordinary scenes. As I cannot describe them all, unfortunately, I select one to serve as an example of what goes on daily in this house.

I have said that the upper part of the partition separating the ante-room from the bureau consists of a strip of glass covered with transparent curtains. In the middle of the strip is a casement-window, ordinarily closed. One day I noticed that, by some oversight, of which I resolved to take advantage, it had been left partly open. Putting a small stool upon the bench, I stood upon it, and thus succeeded in touching with my chin the frame of the casement-window, which I softly pushed. I was thus enabled to look into the room, and here is what I saw.

A lady was seated in an arm-chair; a chambermaid was standing in front of her; in the corner Mme. Paulhat-Durand was distributing some cards among the compartments of a drawer. The lady had come from Fontainebleau in search of a servant. She may have been fifty years old. In appearance a rich and rough *bourgeoise*, dressed soberly, provincial in her austerity. The maid, puny and sickly, with a complexion that had been made livid by poor food and lack of food, had nevertheless a sympathetic face, which, under more fortunate circumstances, would perhaps have been pretty. She was very clean and trim in a black skirt. A black jersey moulded her thin form, and on her head she wore a linen cap, prettily set back, revealing her brow and her curly brown hair.

After a detailed, sustained, offensive, aggressive examination, the lady at last made up her mind to speak.

"Then," said she, "you offer yourself as . . . what? As a chambermaid?"

"Yes, Madame."

"You do not look like one. What is your name?"

"Jeanne Le Godec."

"What did you say?"

"Jeanne Le Godec, Madame."

The lady shrugged her shoulders.

"Jeanne," she exclaimed. "That is not a servant's name; that is a name for a young girl. If you enter my service, you do not expect, I suppose, to keep this name Jeanne?"

"As Madame likes."

Jeanne had lowered her head, and was leaning with her two hands on the handle of her umbrella.

"Raise your head," ordered the lady; "stand up straight. Don't you see you are making a hole in the carpet with the point of your umbrella? Where do you come from?"

"From Saint-Brieuc."

"From Saint-Brieuc!"

235

CELESTINE

And she gave a pout of disdain that quickly turned into a frightful grimace. The corners of her mouth and eyes contracted, as if she had swallowed a glass of vinegar.

"From Saint-Brieuc!" she repeated. "Then you are a Breton? Oh! I do not like the Bretons. They are obstinate and dirty."

"I am very clean, Madame," protested the poor Jeanne.

"You say so. However, we haven't reached that yet. How old are you?"

"Twenty-six."

"Twenty-six? Not counting the nursing months, no doubt? You look much older. It is not worth while to deceive me."

"I am not deceiving Madame. I assure Madame I am only twenty-six. If I look older, it is because I have been sick a long time."

"Oh! you have been sick?" replied the *bourgeoise*, in a voice of sneering severity. "Oh! you have been sick a long time? I warn you, my girl, that the place, though not a very hard one, is of some importance, and that I must have a woman of very good health."

Jeanne tried to repair her imprudent words. She declared:

"Oh! I am cured, quite cured."

"That is your affair. Moreover, we haven't reached that yet. You are married or single, which? What are you?"

"I am a widow, Madame."

"Ah! You have no child, I suppose?"

And, as Jeanne did not answer directly, the lady insisted, more sharply:

"Say, have you children, yes or no?"

"I have a little girl," she confessed, timidly.

Then, making grimaces and gestures as if she were scattering a lot of flies, she cried:

"Oh! no child in the house; no child in the house; not under any consideration. Where is your little girl?"

"She is with my husband's aunt."

236

"And what is this aunt?"

"She keeps a wine-shop in Rouen."

"A deplorable calling. Drunkenness and debauchery,—that is a pretty example for a little girl! However, that concerns you, that is your affair. How old is your little girl?"

"Eighteen months, Madame."

Madame gave a start, and turned violently in her armchair. This was too much for her; she was scandalized. A sort of growl escaped from her lips.

"Children! Think of it! Children, when one cannot bring them up, or have them at home! These people are incorrigible; the devil is in their bodies!"

Becoming more and more aggressive, and even ferocious, she addressed herself to Jeanne again, who stood trembling before her gaze.

"I warn you," said she, enunciating each word separately, "I warn you that, if you enter my service, I will not allow you to bring your little girl to my house. No goings and comings in the house; I want no goings and comings in the house. No, no. No strangers, no vagabonds, no unknown people. One is exposed quite enough with the ordinary run of callers. Oh! no, thank you!"

In spite of this declaration, which was not very prepossessing, the little servant dared to ask, nevertheless:

"In that case, Madame surely will permit me to go and see my little girl, once a year,—just once a year!"

"No."

Such was the reply of the implacable *bourgeoise*. And she added:

"My servants never go out. It is the principle of the house,—a principle on which I am not willing to compromise. I do not pay domestics that they may make the round of doubtful resorts, under pretence of going to see their daughters. That would be really too convenient. No, no. You have recommendations?"

"Yes, Madame."

She drew from her pocket a paper in which were wrapped some recommendations, yellow, crumpled, and soiled; and she silently handed them to Madame, with a trembling hand. Madame, with the tips of her fingers, as if to avoid soiling them, and with grimaces of disgust, unfolded one, which she began to read aloud:

" 'I certify that the girl J' " . . .

Suddenly interrupting herself, she cast an atrocious look at Jeanne, who was growing more anxious and troubled.

" 'The girl'? It plainly says 'girl.' Then you are not married? You have a child, and you are not married? What does that mean?"

The servant explained.

"I ask Madame's pardon. I have been married for three years, and this recommendation was written six years ago. Madame can see the date for herself."

"Well, that is your affair."

And she resumed her reading of the recommendation.

" . . . 'that the girl Jeanne Le Godec has been in my service for thirteen months, and that I have no cause of complaint against her, on the score of work, behavior, and honesty." Yes, it is always the same thing. Recommendations that say nothing, that prove nothing. They give one no information. Where can one write to this lady?"

"She is dead."

"She is dead. To be sure, evidently she is dead. So you have a recommendation, and the very person who gave it to you is dead. You will confess that has a somewhat doubtful look."

All this was said with a very humiliating expression of suspicion, and in a tone of gross irony. She took another recommendation.

"And this person? She is dead, too, no doubt?"

"No, Madame. Mme. Robert is in Algeria with her husband, who is a colonel."

"In Algeria!" exclaimed the lady. "Naturally. How do you expect anybody to write to Algeria? Some are dead, others are in Algeria. The idea of seeking information in Algeria! This is all very extraordinary."

"But I have others, Madame," implored the unfortunate Jeanne Le Godec. "Madame can see for herself. Madame can inform herself."

"Yes, yes! I see you have many others. I see that you have been in many places,—much too many places. At your age, that is not very prepossessing! Well, leave me your recommendations, and I will see. Now something else. What can you do?"

"I can do housework, sew, wait on table."

"Are you good at mending?"

"Yes, Madame."

"Do you know how to fatten poultry?"

"No, Madame. That is not my business."

"Your business, my girl," declared the lady, severely, "is to do what your masters tell you to do. You must have a detestable character."

"Why, no, Madame. I am not at all inclined to talk back."

"Naturally. You say so; they all say so; and they are not to be touched with a pair of tongs. Well, let me see, I believe I have already told you that the place, while not particularly hard, is of some importance. The servants rise at five o'clock."

"In winter too?"

"In winter too. Yes, certainly. And why do you say: 'In winter too'? Is there less work to be done in winter? What a ridiculous question! The chambermaid does the stairs, the *salon,* Monsieur's study, the chamber of course, and attends to all the fires. The cook does the ante-chamber, the halls, and the dining-room. I am very particular on the score of cleanliness. I cannot bear to see a speck of dust in the house. The

239

door-knobs must be well polished, the furniture must shine, and the mirrors must be thoroughly cleaned. The chambermaid has charge of the poultry-yard."

"But, Madame, I know nothing about poultry-yards."

"Well, you will learn. The chambermaid soaps, washes, and irons, except Monsieur's shirts; she does the sewing,—I have no sewing done outside, except the making of my costumes; she waits on table, helps the cook to wipe the dishes, and does the polishing. There must be order, perfect order. I am a stickler for order and cleanliness, and especially for honesty. Moreover, everything is under lock and key. If anything is wanted, I must be asked for it. I have a horror of waste. What are you accustomed to take in the morning?"

"Coffee with milk, Madame."

"Coffee with milk? You do not stint yourself. Yes, in these days they all take coffee with milk. Well, that is not the custom in my house. You will take soup; it is better for the stomach. What did you say "

Jeanne had said nothing. But it was evident she was making an effort to say something. At last she made up her mind.

"I ask Madame's pardon, but what does Madame give us to drink?"

"Six quarts of cider a week."

"I cannot drink cider, Madame. The doctor has forbidden me to."

"Ah! the doctor has forbidden you to. Well, I will give you six quarts of cider. If you want wine, you will buy it. That concerns you. What pay do you expect?"

She hesitated, looked at the carpet, the clock, and the ceiling, rolled her umbrella in her hands, and said, timidly:

"Forty francs."

"Forty francs!" exclaimed Madame. "Why don't you say ten thousand francs, and done with it? You must be crazy. Forty francs! Why, it is unheard of! We used to pay fifteen francs, and got much better service. Forty francs! And you do not even know how to fatten poultry! You do not know how to do anything! I pay thirty francs, and I think that altogether too much. You have no expenses in my house. I am not exacting as to what you wear. And you are washed and fed. God knows how well you are fed! I give out the portions myself.''

Jeanne insisted:

''I have had forty francs in all the places where I have worked.''

But the lady had risen. And, in a dry and ugly voice, she exclaimed:

''Well, you had better go back to them. Forty francs! Such impudence! Here are your recommendations — your recommendations from dead people. Be off with you!''

Jeanne carefully wrapped up her recommendations, put them back into the pocket of her dress, and then said, imploringly, in a timid and sorrowful voice:

''If Madame will go as high as thirty-five francs, we could come to terms.''

''Not a sou. Be off with you! Go to Algeria to find again your Mme. Robert. Go where you like. There is no lack of vagabonds like you; there are heaps of them. Be off with you.''

With sad face and slow step Jeanne left the bureau, after curtseying twice. I saw from her eyes and lips that she was on the point of crying.

Left alone, the lady shouted furiously: ''Ah! these domestics, what a plague! It is impossible to be served these days.''

To which Mme. Paulhat-Durand, who had finished sorting her cards, answered, majestic, crushed, and severe:

''I had warned you, Madame; they are all like that. They are unwilling to do anything, and expect to earn hundreds and thousands. I have nothing else to-day. All the others are worse. To-morrow I will try to find you something. Oh! it is very distressing, I assure you."

I got down from my post of observation the very moment that Jeanne Le Godec was re-entering the ante-room, amid an uproar.

"Well?" they asked her.

She went and sat down on her bench at the rear of the room, and there, with lowered head, folded arms, heavy heart, and empty stomach, she remained in silence, her two little feet twitching nervously under her gown.

But I saw things sadder still.

Among the girls who came daily to Mme. Paulhat-Durand's I had noticed one especially, in the first place because she wore a Breton cap, and then because the very sight of her filled me with unconquerable melancholy. A peasant girl astray in Paris, in this frightful, jostling, feverish Paris,—I know nothing more lamentable. Involuntarily it invites me to a survey of my own past, and moves me infinitely. Where is she going? Where does she come from? Why did she leave her home? What madness, what tragedy, what tempest has pushed her forth, and stranded her, a sorrowful waif, in this roaring human sea? These questions I asked myself every day, as I examined this poor girl sitting in her corner, so frightfully isolated.

She was ugly with that definitive ugliness which excludes all idea of pity and makes people ferocious, because it is really an offence to them. However disgraced she may be by nature, a woman rarely reaches the point of total and absolute ugliness, utter degeneracy from the human estate. Generally she has something, no matter what,—eyes, a mouth, an undulation of the body, a bending of the hips, or less than that, a movement of the arms, a coupling of the wrist, a freshness of skin, upon which others may rest their eyes without being offended. Even in the very old a certain grace almost always survives the deformation of the body, the death of sex, and the seamy flesh betrays some souvenir of what they formerly were. The Breton had nothing of the kind, and she was very young. Little, long-waisted, angular, with flat hips, and legs so short that it seemed as if she really called to mind those barbarian virgins, those snub-nosed saints, shapeless blocks of granite that have been leaning for centuries, in loneliness, on the inclined arms of Armorican Calvaries. And her face? Ah! the unfortunate! An overhanging brow; pupils so dim in outline that they seemed to have been rubbed with a rag; a horrible nose, flat at the start, gashed with a furrow down the middle, and suddenly turning up at its tip, and opening into two black, round, deep, enormous holes, fringed with stiff hair. And over all this a gray and scaly skin,—the skin of a dead adder, a skin that, in the light, looked as if it had been sprinkled with flour. Yet the unspeakable creature had one beauty that many beautiful women would have envied,—her hair, magnificent, heavy, thick hair, of a resplendent red reflecting gold and purple. But, far from being a palliation of her ugliness, this hair only aggravated it, making it more striking, fulgurating, irreparable.

This is not all. Every movement that she made was clumsy. She could not take a step without running against something; everything she took into her hands she was sure to let fall; her arms hit against the furniture, and swept off everything that was lying on it. When walking, she stepped on your toes and dug her elbows into your breast; then she excused herself with a harsh and sullen voice, a voice that breathed into your face a tainted, corpse-like odor. As soon as she entered the anteroom there at once arose among us a sort of irritated complaint, which quickly changed into insulting recriminations and ended in growls. The wretched creature was hooted as she crossed the room, rolling along on her short legs, passed on from one to another like a ball, until she reached her bench at the end of the room. And every one pretended to draw away from her, with significant gestures of disgust, and grimaces that were accompanied with a lifting of handkerchiefs. Then, in the empty space instantaneously formed behind the sanitary cordon that isolated her from us, the dismal girl sat leaning against the wall, silent and detested, without a complaint, without revolt, without seeming to understand that all this contempt was meant for her.

Although, not to be unlike the others, I sometimes took part in this cruel sport, I could not help feeling a sort of pity for the little Breton. I understood that here was a being predestined to misfortune, — one of those beings who, whatever they may do and wherever they may go, will be eternally repulsed by men, and also by beasts,—for there is a certain height of ugliness, a certain form of infirmity, that the beasts themselves do not tolerate.

One day, overcoming my disgust, I approached her, and asked:

"What is your name?"

"Louise Randon."

"I am a Breton . . . from Audierne. And you, too, are a Breton, are you not?"

Astonished that anyone was willing to speak to her, and fearing some insult or practical joke, she did not answer directly. She buried her thumb in the deep caverns of her nose. I repeated my question:

"From what part of Britanny do you come?"

Then she looked at me, and, seeing undoubtedly that there was no unkindness in my eyes, she decided to answer:

"I am from Saint-Michel-en-Grève, near Lannion."

I knew not what further to say to her. Her voice was repulsive to me. It was not a voice; it was something hoarse and broken, like a hiccup,—a sort of gurgle. This voice drove away my pity. However, I went on.

"You have relatives living?"

"Yes; my father, my mother, two brothers, four sisters. I am the oldest."

244

"And your father? What does he do?"

"He is a blacksmith."

"You are poor."

"My father has three fields, three houses, three threshing-machines" . . .

"Then he is rich?"

"Surely he is rich. He cultivates his fields and rents his houses, and goes about the country with his threshing-machines and threshes the peasants' wheat. And my brother shoes the horses."

"And your sisters?"

"They have beautiful lace caps and embroidered gowns."

"And you?"

"I have nothing."

I drew further away, that I might not get the mortal odor of this voice.

"Why are you a domestic?" I resumed.

"Because" . . .

"Why did you leave home?"

"Because" . . .

"You were not happy?"

She spoke very quickly, in a voice that rushed and rolled the words out, like pebbles.

"My father whipped me; my mother whipped me; my sisters whipped me; everybody whipped me; they made me do everything. I brought up my sisters."

"Why did they whip you?"

"I do not know; just to whip me. In all families there is some one who is whipped . . . because . . . well, one does not know."

My questions no longer annoyed her. She was gaining confidence.

"And you?" she said to me, "did not your parents whip you?"

"Oh! yes."

"Of course; that is how things are."

Louise was no longer exploring her nose; her two hands, with their close-clipped nails, lay flat upon her thighs. Whispering was going on around us. Laughs, quarrels, and lamentations prevented the others from hearing our conversation.

"But how did you happen to come to Paris?" I asked, after a silence.

"Last year," answered Louise, "there was a lady from Paris at Saint-Michel-en-Grève, who was taking the sea-baths with her children. She had discharged her domestic for stealing, and I offered to go to work for her. And so she took me with her to Paris, to take care of her father, an old invalid whose legs were paralyzed."

"And you did not stay in your place? In Paris it is not the same thing."

"No," she exclaimed, energetically. "I could have remained; it was not that. But I was not treated right."

Her dull eyes lighted up strangely. Something like a gleam of pride passed over them. And her body straightened up, and became almost transfigured.

"I was not treated right," she repeated. "The old man made advances to me."

For a moment I was stunned by this revelation. Was it possible? Then a desire, even that of a low and nasty old man, had been felt for this bundle of shapeless flesh, this monstrous irony of nature? A kiss had wished to place itself upon these decaying teeth and mingle with this rotten breath? Ah! what filthy things men are! What a frightful madness, then, is love! I looked at Louise. But the flame had gone out of her eyes. Once more her pupils looked like dead gray spots.

"That was some time ago?" I asked.

"Three months."

"And since then you have found no place?"

"Nobody wants me. I do not know why. When I enter the bureau, all the ladies cry out at the sight of me: 'No, no;

I don't want *her*.' There must surely be some spell over me. For, you know, I am not ugly; I am very strong; I know my work; and my will is good. If I am too small, it is not my fault. Surely, some one has thrown a spell over me."

"How do you live?"

"In a lodging-house. I do all the chambers, and I mend the linen. They give me a mattress in the garret, and a meal in the morning."

There were some, then, that were more unforunate than myself! This egotistic thought brought back the pity that had vanished from my heart.

"Listen, my little Louise," I said, in a voice which I tried to make as tender and convincing as possible. "Places in Paris are very hard. One has to know many things, and the masters are more exacting than elsewhere. I am much afraid for you. If I were you, I would go home again."

But Louise became frightened.

"No, no," she exclaimed, "never! I do not want to go home. They would say that I had not succeeded, that nobody wanted me; they would laugh at me too much. No, no, it is impossible; I would rather die!"

Just then the door of the ante-room opened. The shrill voice of Mme. Paulhat-Durand called:

"Mademoiselle Louise Randon!"

"Are they calling me?" asked Louise, frightened and trembling.

"Why, yes, it is you. Go quickly, and try to succeed this time."

She arose, gave me a dig in the ribs with her outstretched elbows, stepped on my feet, ran against the table, and, rolling along on her too short legs, disappeared, followed by hoots.

I mounted my stool, and pushed open the casement-window, to watch the scene that was about to take place. Never did Mme. Paulhat-Durand's *salon* seem to me gloomier; yet God knows whether it had frozen my soul, every time I had entered

it. Oh! that furniture upholstered in blue rep, turned yellow
by wear; that huge book of record spread like the split carcass
of a beast, on the table, also covered with blue rep spotted with
ink. And that desk, where M. Louis's elbows had left bright
and shining spots on the dark wood. And the sideboard at
the rear, upon which stood foreign glass-ware, and table-ware
handed down from ancestors. And on the mantel, between two
lamps which had lost their bronze, between photographs that
had lost their color, that tiresome clock, whose enervating tic-
tac made the hours longer. And that dome-shaped cage in
which two homesick canaries swelled their damaged plumage.
And that mahogany case of pigeon-holes, scratched by greedy
nails. But I had not taken my post of observation for the purpose of taking an inventory of this room, which I knew, alas!
too well,—this lugubrious interior, so tragic, in spite of its
bourgeois obscurity, that many times my maddened imagination transformed it into a gloomy butcher-shop for the sale of
human meat. No; I wanted to see Louise Randon, in the
clutches of the slave-traders.

There she was, near the window, in a false light, standing
motionless, with hanging arms. A hard shadow, like a thick
veil, added confusion to the ugliness of her face, and made still
more of a heap of the short and massive deformity of her body.
A hard light illuminated the lower locks of her hair, enhanced
the shapelessness of her arms and breast and lost itself in the
dark folds of her deplorable skirt. An old lady was examining
her. She was sitting in a chair with her back toward me,—a
hostile back, a ferocious neck. Of this old lady I saw nothing
but her black cap, with its ridiculous plumes, her black cape,
whose lining turned up at the bottom in grey fur, and her black
gown, which made rings upon the carpet. I saw especially
lying upon one of her knees, her hand gloved with black floss-
silk, a knotty and gouty hand that moved slowly about, the
fingers stretching out and drawing back, clutching the material
of her dress, as talons fasten upon living prey. Standing near

the table, very erect and dignified, Mme. Paulhat-Durand was waiting.

It seems a small matter, does it not? the meeting of these three commonplace beings, in this commonplace setting. In this very ordinary fact there was nothing to cause one to stop, nothing to move one. Nevertheless it seemed to me an enormous drama, these three persons, silently gazing at one another. I felt that I was witnessing a social tragedy, terrible, agonizing, worse than a murder! My throat was dry. My heart beat violently.

"I do not get a good view of you, my little one," said the old lady, suddenly. "Do not stay there; I do not get a good view of you. Go to the rear of the room, that I may see you better."

And she cried, in an astonished voice:

"My God! how little you are!"

In saying these words, she had moved her chair, and now I had a sight of her profile. I expected to see a hooked nose, long teeth protruding from the mouth, and the round and yellow eye of a hawk. Not at all; her face was calm, rather amiable. In truth, there was no expression at all in her eyes, either kind or unkind. She must have been an old shop-keeper, retired from business. Merchants have this faculty of acquiring a special physiognomy, revealing nothing of their inner nature. In proportion as they grow hardened in their business, and as the habit of unjust and rapid gains develops low instincts and ferocious ambitions, the expression of their face softens, or, rather, becomes neutralized. That in them which is bad, that which might inspire distrust in their customers, hides itself in the privacies of their being, or takes refuge on corporeal surfaces that are ordinarily destitute of any expression whatever. In this old lady the hardness of her soul, invisible in her eyes, in her mouth, in her forehead, in all the relaxed muscles of her flabby face, was exhibited prominently in her neck. Her neck was her real face, and this face was terrible.

249

Louise, obeying the old lady's command, had gone to the rear of the room. The desire to please gave her a really monstrous look and a discouraging attitude. Scarcely had she placed herself in the light, when the old lady cried:

"Oh! how ugly you are, my little one!"

And calling Mme. Paulhat-Durand to witness:

"Can there really be creatures on earth as ugly as this little one?"

Ever solemn and dignified, Mme. Paulhat-Durand answered:

"Undoubtedly she is not a beauty, but Mademoiselle is very honest."

"Possibly," replied the lady. "But she is too ugly. Such ugliness is in the last degree disagreeable. What? What did you say?"

Louise had not uttered a word. She had simply blushed a little, and lowered her head. Her dull eyes were surrounded with a red streak. I thought she was going to cry.

"Well, let us look into this," resumed the lady, whose fingers at this moment, furiously agitated, were tearing the material of her gown, with the movements of a cruel beast.

She questioned Louise regarding her family, her previous places, and her capacities for cooking, sewing and doing housework. Louise answered, "Yes, indeed," or "No, indeed," hoarsely and spasmodiaclly. The examination, fastidious, unkind, criminal, lasted twenty minutes.

"Well, my little one," concluded the old lady, "the clearest thing about you is that you do not know how to do anything. I shall have to teach you everything. For four of five months you will be of no use to me. And besides, such ugliness is not prepossessing. That gash in your nose? Have you received a blow?"

"No, Madame, it has always been there."

"Well, it is not very attractive. What pay do you expect?"

"Thirty francs, washing, and wine," declared Louise, resolutely.

The old woman started.

"Thirty francs! Have you never, then, looked at yourself? It is senseless! What? Nobody wants you; nobody will ever want you. If I take you, it is because I am kind, it is because I really pity you. And you ask me thirty francs! Well, you have audacity, my little one. Undoubtedly your comrades have been giving you bad advice. You do wrong to listen to them."

"Surely," said Mme. Paulhat-Durand, approvingly, "When they get together, they get very big ideas."

"Well," offered the old lady, in a tone of conciliation, "I will give you fifteen francs. And you will pay for your own wine. It is too much. But I do not wish to take advantage of your ugliness and distress."

She softened. Her voice became almost caressing.

"You see, my little one, this is a unique opportunity, such as you will not find again. I am not like the others; I am alone, I have no family, I have no one. My servant is my family. And what do I ask of my servant? To love me a little, that is all. My servant lives with me, eats with me . . . apart from the wine. Oh! I am indulgent to her. And then, when I die,—for I am very old and often sick,—when I die, surely I shall not forget the girl who has been devoted to me, served me well, and taken care of me. You are ugly, very ugly, too ugly. Well, I shall get used to your ugliness, to your face. There are some pretty women who are very ill-disposed, and who rob you beyond question. Ugliness is sometimes a guarantee of morality in the house. Of course, you will bring no men to my house? You see, I know how to do you justice. Under these conditions, and as kind as I am, what I offer you, my little one,—why, it is a fortune; better than a fortune, it is a family!"

Louise was shaken. Certainly, the old lady's words caused unknown hopes to sing in her head. With her peasant's rapacity, she had visions of strong-boxes filled with gold, and fabulous wills. And life in common, with this good mistress, the table shared, frequent trips to the squares and the suburban woods,—these things seemed marvelous to her. And they frightened her also, for doubts, an unconquerable and native mistrust, dimmed the brilliancy of these promises. She knew not what to say or do; she knew not what course to take. I felt a desire to cry out to her: "Do not accept." For I could see this hermit-like life, the exhausting tasks, the bitter reproaches, the disputed food, and the stripped bones and spoiled meat thrown to her hunger, and the eternal, patient, torturing exploitation of a poor, defenceless being. "No, do not listen to her; go away!" But I repressed this cry, which was on my lips.

"Come a little nearer, my little one," ordered the old lady. "One would think that you were afraid of me. Come, do not be afraid of me; come nearer. How curious it is! Already you seem less ugly. Already I am getting used to your face."

Louise approached slowly, with stiffened members, trying hard not to run against the chairs and furniture, endeavoring to walk with elegance, the poor creature! But she had scarcely placed herself beside the old lady, when the latter repulsed her with a grimace.

"My God!" she cried, "what is the matter with you? Why do you smell so bad? Is your body rotten? It is frightful! It is incredible! Never did any one smell as you smell. Have you, then, a cancer in your nose, or perhaps in your stomach?"

Mme. Paulhat-Durand made a noble gesture.

"I had warned you, Madame," she said. "That is her great fault. It is that which keeps her from finding a place."

The old lady continued to groan.

"My God! My God! is it possible? Why, you will taint the whole house; you cannot stay near me. This changes the case entirely. And when I was beginning to feel sympathy for you! No, no; in spite of all my kindness, it is not possible, it is no longer possible!''

She had pulled out her handkerchief, and was trying to dissipate the putrid air, as she repeated:

"No, really, it is no longer possible!"

"Come, Madame," intervened Mme. Paulhat-Durand, "make an effort. I am sure that this unhappy girl will always be grateful to you."

"Grateful? That is all well enough. But gratitude will not cure her of this frightful infirmity. Well, so be it! But I can give her only ten francs. Ten francs, no more! She can take it or leave it."

Louise, who had so far kept back her tears, was choking.

"No . . . I will not . . . I will not . . . I will not."

"Listen, Mademoiselle," said Mme. Paulhat-Durand, dryly. "You will accept this place. If you don't, I will not undertake to get another for you. You can go and ask for places at the other bureaus. I have had enough. And you are doing injury to my house."

"It is evident," insisted the old lady. "And you ought to thank me for these ten francs. It is out of pity, out of charity, that I offer them to you. How is it that you do not see that I am doing a good work, of which no doubt I shall re-pent, as I have repented of others?"

Then, addressing Mme. Paulhat-Durand, she added:

"What do you expect? I am so constituted. I cannot bear to see people suffer. In the presence of misfortune I be-come utterly stupid. And at my age one does not change, you know. Come, my little one, I take you with me."

Just then a sudden cramp forced me to descend from my post of observation. I never saw Louise again.

The next day but one Mme. Paulhat-Durand had me cere-moniously ushered into the bureau, and, after having examined me in rather an embarrassing fashion, she said to me:

"Mademoiselle Célestine, I have a good place for you, a

very good place. Only you have to go into the country,—oh! not very far."

"Into the country? I do not go there, you know."

She insisted.

"You do not know the country. There are excellent places in the country.

"Oh! excellent places! What a humbug!" I said. "In the first place, there are no good places anywhere."

Mme. Paulhat-Durand smiled amiably and affectedly. Never had I seen such a smile on her face.

"I beg your pardon, Mademoiselle Célestine, there are no bad places."

"Indeed, I know it well. There are only bad masters."

"No, only bad servants. See, I offer you all the best houses; it is not my fault, if you do not stay in them."

She looked at me in a way that was almost friendly.

"Especially as you are very intelligent. You have a pretty face, a pretty figure, charming hands not at all ruined by work, and eyes that are not in your pockets. Good fortune might easily come to you. One does not know what good fortune could come to you . . . with conduct."

"With misconduct, you mean."

"That depends on how you look at it. For my part, I call it conduct."

She was melting. Little by little, her mask of dignity fell. I was now confronted simply with the former chambermaid, expert at all rascalities. Now she had the piggish eye, the fat and flabby movements, the sort of ritual lapping of the mouth characteristic of the procuress, and which I had observed on the lips of "Madame Rebecca Ranvet, Millinery." She repeated:

"For my part, I call it conduct."

"It? What?" I exclaimed.

"Come, Mademoiselle, you are not a beginner, and you are acquainted with life. One can talk with you. It is a question of a single gentleman, already old, not extremely far from Paris, and very rich,—yes, in fact, rich enough. You will keep his house,—something like a governess, do you understand? Such places are very delicate, much in demand, and highly profitable. This one offers a certain future for a woman like you, as intelligent as you are, as pretty as you are,—especially, I repeat, with conduct.''

This was my ambition. Many times I had built marvelous futures on an old man's fancy, and now this paradise that I had dreamed of was before me, smiling, calling me. By an inexplicable irony of life, by an imbecile contradiction, the cause of which I cannot understand, I squarely refused this good fortune which I had wished for so many times, and which at last presented itself.

"An old rake! Oh! no! Besides, men are too disgusting to me,—the old, the young, all of them.''

For a few seconds Mme. Paulhat-Durand stood in amazement. She had not expected this sally. Resuming her severe and dignified air, which placed so great a distance between the correct *bourgeoise* that she wished to be and the bohemian girl that I am, she said:

"Ah! Mademoiselle, what do you think, then? What do you take me for? What are you imagining?''

"I imagine nothing. Only I repeat that I have had enough of men.''

"Do you really know of whom you are speaking? This gentleman, Mademoiselle, is a very respectable man. He is a member of the Society of Saint-Vincent-de-Paul. He has been a royalist deputy.''

I burst out laughing.

"Yes, yes, of course. I know your Saint-Vincent-de-Pauls, and all the devil's saints, and all the deputies. No, thank you!''

Then, suddenly, without transition, I asked:

"Just what is your old man? To be sure, one more or

less will make no difference. It is not a matter of great consequence, after all.''

But Mme. Paulhat-Durand did not unbend. She declared, in a firm voice:

''It is useless, Mademoiselle. You are not the serious woman, the trusty person, that this gentleman needs. I thought you were more suitable. With you, one cannot be sure of anything.''

I insisted a long time, but she was inflexible. And I went back to the ante-room in a very uncertain state of mind. Oh! that ante-room, so sad and dark, always the same! These girls sprawling and crushed upon the benches, this market for human meat to tempt *bourgeois* voracity, this flux of filth and this reflux of poverty that bring you back there, mournful waifs, wreckage from the sea, eternally tossed hither and thither.

''What a queer type I am!'' thought I. ''I desire things . . . things . . . things . . . when I think them unrealizable, and, as soon as they promise realization, so soon as they present themselves to me in clearer outline, I no longer want them.''

There was something of this, certainly, in my refusal; but there was also a childish desire to humiliate Mme. Paulhat-Durand a little, and to take a sort of vengeance upon her by catching the contemptuous and haughty creature in the very act of catering to lust.

I regretted this old man, who now exercised over me all the seductions of the unknown, all the charms of an inaccessible ideal. And I found pleasure in picturing him to my fancy,— a spruce old man, with soft hands, a pretty smile, a pink and shaven face, and gay, and generous, and good-natured, not so much a maniac as M. Rabour, allowing himself to be led by me, like a little dog.

''Come here. Come, come here.''

And he came, caressing, frisking about, with a kind and submissive look.

''Now sit up.''

And he sat up, in such a funny way, with his forepaws beating the air.

"Oh! the good bow-wow!"

I gave him sugar; I stroked his silky skin. He no longer disgusted me. And again I reflected:

"How stupid I am, all the same! A good doggy, a fine garden, a fine house, money, tranquillity, an assured future,—to think that I have refused all these, and without knowing why. And never to know what I want, and never to will what I desire! At bottom I am afraid of man,—worse than that, I have a disgust for man,—when he is far away. When he is near me, I am capable of anything. I have no power of resistance save against things that are not to happen and men whom I shall never know. I really believe that I shall never be happy."

The ante-room was oppressive to me. This obscurity, this dim light, these sprawling creatures, made my ideas more and more lugubrious. Something heavy and irremediable hovered over me. Without waiting for the bureau to close, I went away, with heavy heart and choking throat. On the stairs I met M. Louis. Clinging to the banister, he was ascending the steps, slowly and painfully. We looked at each other for a second. He did not say anything, and I too found no word; but our looks said all. I listened to him a moment, as he went up the steps; then I plunged down the stairway. Poor little wretch!

In the street I stood for a moment as if stunned. I looked about for love's recruting-agents, for the round back and black costume of "Mme. Rebecca Ranvet, Millinery." Ah! if I had seen her, I would have gone to her, I would have delivered myself to her. But there was no such person there. The people passing were busy and indifferent, and paid no attention to my distress. Then I stopped at a wine-shop, where I bought a bottle of brandy, and, after strolling about for a while, still stupid and with heavy head, I went back to my hotel.

Toward evening, late, I heard a knock at my door. I lay stretched upon my bed, half naked, stupefied by drink.

"Who is there?" I cried.

"It is I."

"Who are you?"

"The waiter."

I rose, with my loosened hair falling from my shoulders, and opened the door.

"What do you want?"

The waiter smiled. He was a tall fellow with red hair, whom I had met several times on the stairs, and who always looked at me strangely.

"What do you want?" I repeated.

The waiter smiled again, apparently embarrassed and, rolling in his fat fingers the bottom of his blue apron, covered with grease spots, he stammered:

"Mam'zelle . . . I" . . .

He surveyed my person with a sort of dismal desire.

"Well, come in, you brute," I cried, suddenly.

And pushing him into my room, I closed the door again, violently.

Oh! misery me!

The waiter was discharged. I never knew his name!

I should not like to leave the subject of Mme. Paulhat-Durand's employment-bureau, without giving my recollection of a poor devil whom I met there. He was a gardener, who had been a widower for four months, and who was looking for a place. Among the many lamentable faces that passed through the bureau I saw none as sad as his, none that seemed to me more overwhelmed by life. His wife had died of a miscarriage . . . of a miscarriage? . . . the night before the day when, after two months of poverty, they were at last to take positions on an estate,—he in charge of the garden, she in charge of the barn-yard. Whether from ill-luck, or from weariness and from disgust of life, he had found nothing since this great misfortune; he had not even looked for anything. And during this period of idleness his little savings had quickly melted away. Although he was very suspicious, I succeeded in taming him a little. I put into the form of an impersonal narrative the simple and poignant tragedy that he related to me one day when I, greatly moved by his misfortune, had shown more interest and pity than usual. Here it is.

When they had examined the gardens, the terraces, the conservatories, and the gardener's house at the park entrance, sumptuously clothed with ivies, climbing plants, and wild vines, they came back slowly, without speaking to each other, their souls in anguish and suspense, toward the lawn where the countess was following with a loving gaze her three children, who, with their light hair, their bright trinkets, and their pink and prosperous flesh, were playing in the grass, under the care of the governess. At a distance of twenty steps they halted respectfully, the man with uncovered head and holding his cap in his hand, the woman, timid under her black straw hat, embarrassed in her dark woollen sack, and twisting the chain of a little leather bag, to give herself confidence. The undulating greensward of the park rolled away in the distance, between thick clusters of trees.

"Come nearer," said the countess, in a voice of kind encouragement.

The man had a brown face, skin tanned by the sun, large knotty hands of the color of earth, the tips of the fingers deformed and polished by the continual handling of tools. The woman was a little pale, with a gray pallor underlying the freckles that besprinkled her face,—a little awkward, too, and very clean. She did not dare to lift her eyes to this fine lady, who was about to examine her inconsiderately, overwhelm her with torturing questions, and turn her inside out, body and soul, as others had done before. And she looked intently at the pretty picture of the three babies playing in the grass, already showing manners well under control and studied graces.

They advanced a few steps, slowly, and both of them, with a mechanical and simultaneous movement, folded their hands over their stomachs.

"Well," asked the countess; "you have seen everything?"

"Madame the Countess is very good," answered the man. "It is very grand and very beautiful. Oh! it is a superb estate. There must be plenty of work, indeed!"

"And I am very exacting, I warn you,—very just, but very exacting. I love to have everything perfectly kept. And flowers, flowers, flowers, always and everywhere. However, you have two assistants in summer, and one in winter. That is sufficient."

"Oh!" replied the man, "the work does not worry me; the more there is, the better I like it. I love my calling, and I know it thoroughly,—trees, early vegetables, mosaics, and everything. As for flowers, with good arms, taste, water, good straw coverings, and—saving your presence, Madame the Countess— an abundance of manure, one can have as many as one wants."

After a pause, he continued:

"My wife, too, is very active, very skilful, and a good manager. She does not look strong, but she is courageous, and never sick, and nobody understands animals as she does. In the place where we last worked there were three cows and two hundred hens."

The countess nodded approvingly.

"How do you like your lodge?"

"The lodge, too, is very fine. It is almost too grand for little people like us, and we have not enough furniture for it. But one need not occupy the whole of it. And besides, it is far from the château, and it ought to be. Masters do not like to have the gardeners too near them. And we, on the other hand, are afraid of being embarrassed. Here each is by himself. That is better for all. Only" . . .

The man hesitated, seized with a sudden timidity, in view of what he had to say.

"Only what?" asked the countess, after a silence that increased the man's embarrassment.

The later gripped his cap more tightly, turned it in his fat fingers, rested more heavily on the ground, and making a bold plunge, exclaimed:

"Well, it is this. I wanted to say to Madame the Countess that the wages do not correspond with the place. They are too low. With the best will in the world it would be impossible to make ends meet. Madame the Countess ought to give a little more."

"You forget, my friend, that you are lodged, heated, lighted; that you have vegetables and fruits; that I give a dozen eggs a week and a quart of milk a day. It is enormous."

"Ah, Madame the Countess gives milk and eggs? And she furnishes light?"

And he looked at his wife as if to ask her advice, at the same time murmuring:

"Indeed, that is something! One cannot deny it. That is not bad."

The woman stammered:

"Surely that helps out a little."

Then, trembling and embarrassed:

"Madame the Countess no doubt gives presents also in the month of January and on Saint Fiacre's day?"

"No, nothing."

"It is custom, however."

"It is not mine."

In his turn the man asked:

"And for the weasels and pole-cats?"

"No, nothing for those either; you can have the skins."

This was said in a dry, decisive tone, that forbade further discussion. And suddenly:

"Ah! I warn you, once for all, that I forbid the gardener to sell or give vegetables to any one whomsoever. I know very well that it is necessary to raise too many in order to have enough, and that three-fourths of them are wasted. So much the worse! I intend to allow them to be wasted."

"Of course, the same as everywhere else!"

"So it is agreed? How long have you been married?"

"Six years," answered the woman.

"You have no children?"

"We had a little girl. She is dead."

"Ah! that is well; that is very well," approved the countess, in an indifferent tone. "But you are both young; you may have others yet."

"They are hardly to be desired, Madame the Countess, but they are more easily obtained than an income of three hundred francs."

The countess's eyes took on a severe expression.

"I must further warn you that I will have no children on the premises, absolutely none. If you were to have another child, I should be obliged to discharge you at once. Oh! no children! They cry, they are in the way, they ruin everything, they frighten the horses and spread diseases. No, no, not for anything in the world would I tolerate a child on my premises. So you are warned. Govern yourselves accordingly; take your precautions."

Just then one of the children, who had fallen, came, crying, to take refuge in his mother's gown. She took him in her arms, lulled him with soothing words, caressed him, kissed him tenderly, and sent him back to rejoin the two others, pacified and smiling. The woman suddenly felt her heart growing heavy. She thought that she would not be able to keep back her tears. Joy, tenderness, love, motherhood, then, were for the rich only? The children had begun to play again on the lawn. She hated them with a savage hatred; she felt a desire to insult them, to beat them, to kill them; to insult and kill also this insolent and cruel woman, this egoistic mother, who had just uttered abominable words, words that condemned not to be born the future humanity that lay sleeping in her womb. But she restained herself, and said simply, in response to a new warning, more imperative than the other:

"We will be careful, Madame the Countess; we will try."

"That's right; for I cannot too often repeat it to you,—this is a principle here, a principle upon which I cannot compromise."

And she added, with an inflection in her voice that was almost caressing:

"Moreover, believe me, when one is not rich, it is better to have no children."

The man, to please his future mistress, said, by way of conclusion:

"Surely, surely. Madame the Countess speaks truly."

But there was hatred within him. The sombre and fierce gleam that passed over his eyes like a flash gave the lie to the forced servility of these last words. The countess did not see this murderous gleam, for she had fixed her eyes instinctively on the person of the woman whom she had just condemned to sterility or infanticide.

The bargain was quickly concluded. She gave her orders, detailed minutely the services that she expected of her new gardeners, and, as she dismissed them with a haughty smile, she said, in a tone that admitted of no reply:

"I think that you have religious sentiments, do you not? Here everybody goes to mass on Sunday, and receives the sacrament at Easter. I insist upon it absolutely."

They went away without speaking to each other, very serious, very sober. The road was dusty and the heat oppressive, and the poor woman walked painfully, dragging her legs after her. As she was stifling a little, she stopped, placed her bag upon the ground, and unlaced her corsets.

"Ouf!" she exclaimed, taking in deep breaths of air.

And her figure, which had been long compressed, now swelled out, revealing the characteristic roundness, the stain of motherhood, the crime. They continued on their way.

A few steps further on they entered an inn by the roadside, and ordered a quart of wine.

"Why didn't you say I was pregnant?" asked the woman.

The man answered:

"What? That she might show us the door, as the three others have done?"

"To-day or to-morrow makes but little difference."

Then the man murmured between his teeth:

"If you were a woman,—well, you would go this very evening to Mother Hurlot. She has herbs."

But the woman began to wep. And in her tears she groaned:

"Don't say that; don't say that! That brings bad luck."

The man pounded the table, and cried:

"Must we, then die, my God!"

The bad luck came. Four days later the woman had a miscarriage . . . a miscarriage? . . . and died in the frightful pains of peritonitis.

And, when the man had finished his story, he said to me:

"So now here I am, all alone. No wife, no child, nothing. I really thought of revenging myself; yes, for a long time I thought of killing those three children that were playing on the lawn, although I am not wicked, I assure you. But that woman's three children, I swear to you, I could have strangled with joy, with real joy! Oh, yes. But then, I did not dare. What do you expect? We are afraid; we are cowards, we have courage only to suffer!"

XVI.

November 24.

No letter from Joseph. Knowing how prudent he is, I am not greatly astonished at his silence, but it causes me a little suffering. To be sure, Joseph is not unaware that the letters go through Madame's hands before reaching ours, and doubtless he does not wish to expose himself or me the danger of their being read by her, or even have the fact that he writes to me made a subject of Madame's malicious comments. Yet, with his great mental resources, it seems to me that he could have found a way of sending me news. He is to return to-morrow morning. Will he return? I am not without anxiety, and cannot keep from thinking about it. Why, too, was he unwilling to give me his Cherbourg address? But I do not wish to think of all these things, that split my head and put me into a fever.

Here everything goes on in the same way, except that there are fewer events and still greater silence. Joseph's work is done by the sacristan, out of friendship. He comes every day, punctually, to groom the horses and to tend to the garden-frames. Impossible to get a single word out of him. He is more silent and suspicious than Joseph, and his manners are more doubtful. He is more ordinary, too, and lacks his greatness and power. I see him only when I have an order to deliver to him. He is a queer type, too. The grocer tells me that, when young, he studied for the priesthood, and was expelled from the seminary on account of his indelicacy and immorality. May it not have been he who outraged the little Claire in the woods? Since then, he has tried his hand at all trades. Now a pastry-cook, now a church-singer, now a peddler, a notary's clerk, a domestic, the town drummer, an auctioneer, and an

CELESTINE

employee in the sheriff's office, for the last four years he has
been sacristan. To be sacristan is to be also something of a
priest. Moreover, he has all the slimy and crawling manners
of the ecclesiastical bugs. Surely he would not recoil from the
vilest tasks. But is he his friend? Is he not, rather, his accomplice?

Madame has a sick headache. It seems she has one regularly every three months. For two days she remains shut up
in her room, with drawn curtains and without light, only
Marianne being allowed to enter. She does not want me.
Madame's sickness means a good time for Monsieur. Monsieur
makes the most of it. He does not leave the kitchen.

Captain Mauger, who does not speak to me any more, but
casts furious glances at me over the hedge, has become reconciled with his family,—at least, with one of his nieces, who
has come to live with him. She is not bad-looking,—a tall
blonde with a nose that is too long, but with a fresh complexion and a good figure. People say she is to keep the house,
and take Rose's place.

As for Mme. Gouin, Rose's death must have been a blow
to her Sunday mornings. She saw at once that she could not
get along without a leading lady. Now, it is that pest of a
haberdasher who leads off in the gossip, and undertakes to
maintain the admiration of the girls of Mesnil-Roy for the
clandestine talents of this infamous grocer. Yesterday being
Sunday, I went to the grocery-shop. It was a very brilliant
occasion; they were all there. There was very little said about
Rose, and, when I told the story of the wills, there was a general shout of laughter. Ah! the captain was right when he
said to me: "Everything can be replaced." But the haberdasher has not Rose's authority, for she is a woman concerning
whom, from the point of view of morals, there unhappily is
nothing to be said.

In what a hurry I am to see Joseph! With what nervous
impatience I await the moment when I shall know what I must

hope or fear from destiny! I can no longer live as I am living now. Never have I been so distressed by this mediocre life that I live, by these people whom I serve, by all these dismal mountebanks around me, among whom I am growing more stupid from day to day. If I were not sustained by the strange feeling that gives a new and powerful interest to my present life, I think it would not be long before I, too, should plunge into the abyss of stupidity and vileness which I see continually widening around me. Ah! whether Joseph succeeds or not, whether he changes his mind about me or not, I have come to a final decision; I will no longer stay here. A few hours more, another whole night of anxiety, and then I shall be settled regarding my future.

I am going to spend this night in a further revival of old memories, perhaps for the last time. It is the only way that I have of avoiding the anxieties of the present and not splitting my head over the dreams of to-morrow. In reality these recollections amuse me, and deepen my contempt. What singular and monotonous faces, all the same, I have met on my path of servitude! When I see them again, in my mind's eye, they do not make on me the impression of really living beings. They live, or at least give the illusion of life, only through their vices. Take away the vices that sustain them as bandages sustain mummies, and they are no longer even phantoms . . . they are nothing but dust . . . ashes . . . death.

Oh! that was a famous house, for instance, to which, a few days after my refusal to go into the service of the old gentleman in the country, I was sent, with all sort of admirable references, by Mme. Paulhat-Durand. My masters were a very young couple, without animals or children, living in an ill-kept interior, though the furniture was stylish and there was a heavy elegance about the decorations. Luxury and great waste! A single glance as I entered showed me all; I saw clearly with whom I had to deal. It was my dream! Now then, I was going to forget all my miseries,—M. Xavier, and the good sisters of Neuilly, and the killing sessions in the ante-room of the employment bureau, and the long days of anguish, and the long nights of solitude and debauchery.

Now then, I was going to plan for myself an agreeable life, with easy work and certain profits. Made happy by this prospect, I promised myself that I would correct my caprices, repress the ardent impulses of my frankness, in order to stay in this place a long, long time. In a twinkling my gloomy ideas vanished; and my hatred of the *bourgeois* flew away, as if by enchantment. I again became madly and hilariously gay, and, seized anew with a violent love of life, I began to think that the masters are sometimes good. The personnel was not numerous, but it was select,—a cook, a *valet de chambre*, an old butler, and myself. There was no coachman, the masters having abolished their stable a short time before, preferring to hire their teams from a livery-man. We became friends directly. That very evening, they gave me welcome by opening a bottle of champagne.

"My!" I exclaimed, clapping my hands; "they do things well here."

The *valet de chambre* smiled, and shook a bunch of keys musically in the air. He had the keys to the cellar; he had all the keys. He was the trusted servant of the house.

"Say, will you lend them to me?" I asked, by way of a joke.

Giving me a tender look, he answered:

"Yes, if you are nice with Baby. You will have to be nice with Baby."

Oh! he was a *chic* man, and he knew how to talk to women. He had an English name,—William. What a pretty name!

During the meal, which lasted for some time, the old butler did not say a word, but ate and drank a great deal. They paid no attention to him, and he seemed a little dopy. As for William, he was charming, gallant, and assiduous; he paid me delicate attentions under the table; and, when we were drinking our coffee, he offered me Russian cigarettes, of which his pockets were full. Then, drawing me to him,—the tobacco had made me a little dizzy, and I was a little drunk too, and my hair was disarranged,—he seated me upon his knees, and whispered audacious things in my ear. Oh! but he was bold!

Eugénie, the cook, did not seem scandalized by these remarks and these performances. Anxious and dreamy, she kept her neck continually inclined toward the door, pricked up her ears at the slightest sound, as if she were expecting some one, and, with a very uncertain eye, kept on guzzling wine, glass after glass. She was a woman of about forty-five, with a large bust, sensual lips, languishing and passionate eyes, and an air of great kindness mingled with melancholy. At last there came a discreet knock at the door. Eugénie's face lighted up; she rose with a bound, and went to open the door. Not being familiar with the habits of this servants' hall, I wanted to assume a more decorous attitude, but William held me more tightly than before, pressing me close against him with a firm embrace.

"That's nothing," he remarked, quietly. "That is the little one."

Meantime a young man had entered, almost a child. Very slender, very blonde, with a grey white skin underlying the dark beginnings of a beard, scarcely eighteen, he was as pretty as a love. He wore an entirely new and elegant jacket, which set off his trim and slender bust, and a pink cravat. He was the son of the janitor in the next house. He came, it seems, every evening. Eugénie adored him, was mad over him. Every day she put aside, in a big basket, tureens full of *boullion,* fine slices of meat, bottles of wine, cakes, and delicious fruits, which the little one carried to his parents.

"Why are you so late to-night?" asked Eugénie.

The little one excused himself in a drawling voice.

"I had to look out for the lodge. Mamma had gone on an errand."

"Your mother, your mother . . . are you telling me the truth, young scamp?"

She sighed, and, with her eyes gazing into the child's eyes, and her two hands resting on his shoulders, she continued, in a mournful tone:

"When you are late, I am always afraid something has happened. I do not want you to be late, my darling. You will say to your mother that, if that continues,—well, I will give you nothing more . . . for her."

Then, with quivering nostrils and her whole body shaken by a thrill, she said:

"How pretty you are, my love! Oh! your little phiz! your little phiz! Why did you not wear your pretty yellow shoes? I want you to look your best when you come to see me. And those eyes, those big eyes, you little brigand! Ah! I'll bet they have been looking at another woman. And your lips! your lips! What have those lips been doing?"

He smilingly reassured her, with a slightly swaying motion of his body.

"No, indeed, I assure you, Nini, that's straight. Mamma had gone on an errand,—yes, truly."

Eugénie repeated several times:

"Oh! you scamp, you scamp, I do not want you to be looking at other women. Your little phiz for me, your little mouth for me, your big eyes for me! Say, do you really love me?"

"Oh, yes, surely."

"Say it again."

"Oh! surely."

She leaped upon his neck, and, panting, led him into the adjoining room, stammering words of love.

William said to me:

270

"How she holds him! And what a pile this little chap costs her! Last week she gave him a complete new outfit. You would not love me like that."

This scene had stirred me deeply, and I promptly vowed a sister's friendship for the poor Eugénie. This boy resembled M. Xavier. At least there was a moral similarity between these two beings,—so pretty, though so rotten. And this reminder made me sad,—oh! infinitely sad! I saw myself again in M. Xavier's room, the night when I gave him the ninety francs. Oh! your little phiz! your little mouth! your big eyes! They were the same cold and cruel eyes, there was the same undulation of the body, there was the same vice shining in the pupils and imparting a sort of benumbing poison to the lips.

I released myself from William's arms, and, as I was arranging my disordered hair, I remarked:

"Well, I must say, you don't lose any time."

Of course I did not want to change anything in the habits of the house, or in the service. William did the housework, in a go-as-you-please fashion. A stroke of the broom here, a stroke of the duster there, and the thing was done. The rest of the time he babbled, ransacked drawers and closets, and read the letters that were dragging about on every hand and in every corner. I did as he did. I allowed the dust to accumulate upon and under the furniture, and I took good care not to disturb the disorder of the *salons* and the chambers. If I had been in the masters' place, I should have been ashamed to live in so untidy an interior. But they did not know how to command, and, being timid and fearing scenes, they never dared to say anything. If sometimes, after an omission that was too patent or too embarrassing, they ventured to stammer: "It seems to me that you have not done this or that," we had only to answer, in a tone whose firmness did not exclude insolence: "I really ask Madame's pardon; Madame is mistaken. And, if Madame is not content" . . . Then they insisted no further, and that was the end of it. Never in my life have I met masters having less authority over their servants, or such ninnies! Really, one is not to be led by the nose as they were.

It is necessary to do William his justice,—that he had known how to put things on a good footing in the box. William had a passion that is common among servants,—the passion for the races. He knew all the jockeys, all the trainers, all the book-makers, and also some pretty sporty gentlemen, barons and viscounts, who showed a certain friendship for him, knowing that he had astonishing tips from time to time. This passion, whose maintenance and satisfaction require numerous suburban excursions, does not harmonize with a restricted and sedentary calling, like of a *valet de chambre*. Now William had regu-lated his life in this way; after breakfast, he dressed and went out. How *chic* he was in his black and white check pantaloons, his highly-polished shoes, his putty-colored overcoat, and his hats! Oh! William's hats, hats the color of deep water, in which skies, trees, streets, rivers, crowds, hippodromes, suc-ceeded one another in prodigious reflections! He came back just in time to dress his master, and often, in the evening, after dinner, he went out again, saying that had an important ren-dezvous with the English. I did not see him again until very late at night, when he always came home a little drunk, from having taken too many cocktails. Every week he invited friends to dinner,—coachmen, *valet de chambre*, race-track people,— these latter very comical and weird with their twisted legs, their deformed knees, and their appearance of crapulous cynic-ism and ambiguous sex. They talked horses, turf, women, told all sorts of disagreeable stories about the morals of their masters, and then, becoming excited by the fumes of the wine, began on politics. William was a superbly uncompromising and terribly violent reactionary.

"The man for me," he cried, "is Cassagnac. A rude lad, Cassagnac! They are afraid of him. How he can write! What raps he gives! Yes, let the dirty rascals tackle this strenuous chap if they dare!"

And suddenly, at the height of the noise, Eugénie rose, paler and with shining eyes, and rushed for the door. The little one entered, his face wearing an expression of astonishment at sight of these unusual people, of these empty bottles, of this reckless pillage of the table. Eugénie had saved a glass of champagne and a plate of goodies for him. Then they both disappeared into the adjoining room.

"Oh! your little phiz, your little mouth, your big eyes!" That night the parents' basket contained larger and better portions. Of course these worthy people should profit by the feast.

William often spoke to me of Edgar, the celebrated stud-groom of the baron de Borgsheim. He was proud to know him; he admired him almost as much as he admired Cassagnac. Edgar and Cassagnac were the two great enthusiasms of his life. I think it would have been dangerous to joke him about them, or even to discuss them with him. When he came home at night, late, William excused himself by saying to me, "I was with Edgar." It seemed that to be with Edgar constituted not only an excuse, but a glory.

"Why don't you bring your famous Edgar to dinner, that I may see him?" I asked of him one day.

William was scandalized at this idea, and he declared loftily: "What! do you imagine that Edgar would dine with simple servants?"

It was from Edgar that William got his incomparable method of polishing his hats. Once, at the Auteuil races, Edgar was approached by the young marquis de Plérin.

"Say, my lad," begged the marquis, "how do you get your hats?"

"My hats, Monsieur the Marquis?" responded Edgar, highly flattered, for the young Plérin, a robber at the races and a trickster at the gaming-table, was then one of the most famous personalities of Parisian society. "It is very simple;

only it is like picking the winner,—you must know how. Well, this is the trick. Every morning I make my *valet de chambre* run for a quarter of an hour. He sweats, of course. And the sweat contains oil. Then, with a very fine silk handkerchief, he wipes the sweat from his brow, and rubs my hats with it. A stroke or two with the iron finishes the job. But it takes a clean and healthy man, preferably a man with nut-brown complexion,—for some blondes smell strong, and all sweats are not suitable. Last year I gave the receipt to the prince of Wales.''

And, as the young marquis de Plérin thanked Edgar and slyly shook his hand, the latter added, confidently:

''Take Baladeur at seven to one. He is to be the winner, Monsieur the Marquis.''

It is really funny when I think of it, but I finally came to feel flattered myself that William had such a relation. To me, too, Edgar was something admirable and inaccessible, like the emperor of Germany, Victor Hugo, or Paul Bourget. That is why I think it advisable to fix in these pages, from all that William told me, the portrait of this more than illustrious, this historic personage.

Edgar was born in London, in a frightful den, between two hiccups of whiskey. As a boy he was a vagabond, a beggar, a thief, and a jail-bird. Later, having the requisite physical deformities and the most crapulous instincts, he was pitched on for a groom. From ante-room to stable, rubbing against all the trickery, all the rapacity, all the vice prevailing among the servants of a grand establishment, he became a ''lad'' in the Eaton stud. And he strutted about in a Scotch cap, a yellow and black striped waistcoat, and light pantaloons, loose at the knees in the form of a screw. When scarcely an adult, he looked like a little old man, with frail limbs and furrowed face, red at the cheek-bones, yellow at the temples, with worn-out and grimacing mouth, with thin hair brushed over his ears in the form of a greasy spiral. In a society which the odor of horse-dung causes to swoon with delight Edgar was already a personage less anonymous than a workingman or a peasant,—almost a gentleman.

At Eaton he learned his trade thoroughly. He knows how to groom a stylish horse, how to take care of it when it is sick, and what detailed and complicated toilets are most suitable to the color of its coat. He knows the secret of the intimate washings, the refined polishings, the expert pedicurings, and the ingenious processes of make-up, by which the beasts of the race-track, like the beasts of love, are set out and beautified. In the bar-rooms he knew important jockeys, celebrated trainers, and the big-bellied baronets, and blackleg dukes and bums, who are the *cream* of this muckheap and the *flower* of this horse-dung. Edgar would have liked to become a jockey, for he soon saw all the tricks that could be played and the money that could be made. But he had grown too large. Though his legs had remained thin and bowed, he had acquired something of a corporation. He was too heavy. So, being unable to don the jockey's coat, he decided to wear the coachman's livery.

To-day Edgar is forty-three years old. He is one of the five or six English, Italian, and French stud-grooms of whom they talk in elegant society with wondering admiration. His name triumphs in the sporting papers, and even in the paragraphs of the society and literary journals. The baron de Borgsheim, his present master, is proud of him,—more proud of him than he would be of a financial operation that had ruined a hundred thousand janitors. Swelling up with an air of definitive superiority, he says: "My stud-groom!" as a collector of pictures would say: "My Rubens!" And, in fact, the lucky baron has reason to be proud, for since he came into possession of Edgar, he has made great strides in fame and respectability. Edgar has gained for him that admission to uncompromising *salons* which he so long coveted. Through Edgar he has at last overcome the resistance of society to his race. At the club they talk of the famous "victory of the baron over England." The English have taken Egypt from us, but the baron has taken Edgar from the English, and that restores the equilibrium. If he had conquered the Indies, he would not have been more loudly acclaimed. This admiration is accompanied, by deep jealousy. They would like to get Edgar away from him, and so there goes on around Edgar all sorts of intrigues, and corrupting conspiracies, and flirtations, like those that go on around a beautiful woman. As for the newspapers, they, in their respectful enthusiasm, have reached a point where they are no longer able to tell exactly which of the two, Edgar or the baron, is the admirable stud-groom, and which the admirable financier. They confound the two in the mutual glories of one and the same apotheosis.

Provided you have been curious enough to circulate among aristocratic crowds, you certainly must have met Edgar, who is one of their most precious ornaments and one who is most commonly displayed. He is a man of average height, very ugly,—that comical English ugliness,—and having an immoderately long nose, with doubly royal curves, which oscillate between the Semitic curve and the Bourbon curve. His lips, very short and turned-up, reveal black holes between decayed teeth. His complexion is lightened in the scale of the yellows, relieved at the cheek-bones with some hatchings in bright lake. Without being obese, like the majestic coachman of the olden time, he is now endowed with a comfortable and regular *embonpoint* which covers with fat the vulgar protuberances of his frame. And, slightly throwing out his chest, he walks with an elastic step, his elbows bent at the regulation angle. Scorning to follow the fashion, desirous rather of setting it, he dresses richly and fantastically. He has blue frock-coats, with watered-silk facings, excessively tight-fitting and too new; pantaloons of English cut that are too light; cravats that are too white; jewels that are too big; handkerchifs that are too fragrant; shoes that are too highly polished; hats that are too shining. How long the young swells have envied Edgar the unusual and fulgurating brilliancy of his headgear!

276

At eight o'clock in the morning, wearing a little round hat and a putty-colored overcoat as short as a jacket, with an enormous yellow rose in his button-hole, Edgar descends from his automobile, in front of the baron's mansion. The grooming is just finished. After having cast an ill-humored look around the yard, he enters the stables and begins his inspection, followed by the anxious and respectful hostlers. Nothing escapes his suspicious and sidewise glances,—a bucket not in its place, a spot on the steel chains, a scratch on the silvers and brasses. And he growls, flies into a passion, and threatens in a phlegm-choked voice, his bronchial tubes being still obstructed by the fermentation of the champagne drunk the night before. He enters each box, and passes his white-gloved hand over the manes, necks, bellies, and legs of the horses. If he finds the slightest trace of dirt on his glove, he jaws the hostlers; there is a flood of filthy words and insulting oaths, and a tempest of furious gestures. Then he examines minutely the horses' hoofs, smells of the oats in the marble mangers, feels of the litter, and long and carefully studies the form, color, and density of the dung, which never suits him.

"What kind of dung do you call that, I should like to know? It is the dung of a cab-horse. Be sure that I see nothing like it to-morrow, pack of good-for-nothings that you are!"

Sometimes the baron puts in an appearance, glad of a chance to talk with his stud-groom. Scarcely does he notice his master's presence. The latter's timid questions he answers with curt and snarling words. Never does he say "Monsieur the Baron." The baron, on the contrary, is almost tempted to say: "Monsieur the coachman!" Afraid that he may irritate Edgar, he does not stay long, and retires discreetly.

Having finished his review of the stables, the carriage-houses, and the harness-rooms, and having given his orders in a tone of military command, Edgar gets into his automobile again, and starts rapidly for the Champs-Elysées, where at first he makes a short stop in a little bar-room, among race-track people, skunk-faced tipsters, who drop mysterious words into his ears, and show him confidential dispatches. The rest of the morning is devoted to visits to sundry trades-people, to give them new orders and receive commissions, and to horse-dealers, with whom such conversation as the following take place:

"Well, Master Edgar?"

"Well, Master Poolny?"

"I have a buyer for the baron's bays."

"They are not for sale."

"Fifty pounds for you."

"No."

"A hundred pounds, Master Edgar."

"We will see, Master Poolny."

"That is not all, Master Edgar."

"What else, Master Poolny?"

"I have two magnificent sorrels for the baron."

"We do not need them."

"Fifty pounds for you."

"No."

"A hundred pounds, Master Edgar."

"We will see, Master Poolny."

A week later Edgar has spoiled the paces of the baron's bays in just the right degree, not too much or too little, and then, having demonstrated to the baron that it is high time to get rid of them, sells them to Poolny, who sells to Edgar the two magnificent sorrels. Poolny restores the bays to good condition by sending them to pasture for three months, and two years later perhaps sells them again to the baron.

At noon Edgar's work is done. He returns for lunch to his apartments in the Rue Euler, for he does not live in the baron's mansion, and never drives the baron. His apartments consist of a ground-floor, heavily upholstered in embroidered plush of the loudest shades, the walls being covered with English lithographs of hunts, steeplechases, famous cracks, and various portraits of the prince of Wales, one of which was presented to Edgar by the prince himself, and bears a dedication from him. Then there are canes, whips, stirrups, bits, and tally-ho horns, arranged in a panoply, with an enormous bust of Queen Victoria, made of polychromatic and loyalist terra cotta, in the centre, between two gilded pediments. Then, free from care, strangling in his blue frock-coats, his head covered with his radiant beacon, Edgar devotes the rest of his day to his own affairs and to his own pleasures. His affairs are numerous, for he is in partnership with a club cashier, a bookmaker, and a horse photographer, and he has three horses in training near Chantilly. Nor are his pleasures lacking; the most famous little women know the way to the Rue Euler, where, on days when they happen to be short, they are sure to find a cup of tea and five louis.

In the evening, after having shown himself at the Ambassadeurs, at the Cirque, and at the Olympia, very correct in his silk-faced dress-coat, Edgar repairs to the *Ancien,* and there spends a long time in getting drunk, in the company of coachmen who assume the airs of gentlemen, and of gentlemen who assume the airs of coachmen.

And every time that William told me one of these stories he concluded, with a voice of admiring wonder:

"Oh! this Edgar! there is a man for you, indeed."

My masters belonged to what it is agreed to call the high society of Paris; that is to say, Monsieur was a penniless nobleman, and nobody knew exactly where Madame came from. Many stories were afloat regarding her origin, each more disagreeable than the others. William, very familiar with the scandals of high society, pretended that the madame was the daughter of an old coachman and an old chambermaid, who, by pinching and general misbehavior, got together a small capital, established themselves as usurers in a disreputable quarter of Paris, and rapidly made a large fortune by lending money, mainly to prostitutes and house-servants. They struck it rich, indeed!

It was certainly true that Madame, in spite of her apparent elegance and her very pretty face, had queer manners and vulgar habits that were very disagreeable. The dirty creature was fond of boiled beef, and bacon and cabbage; and, like the cabmen, it was her delight to pour red wine into her soup. I was ashamed of her. Often, in her quarrels with Monsieur, her anger stirred the mud that still remained in the depths of her being, not yet thoroughly cleaned by her suddenly-acquired luxury,—ah! words that I, who am not a lady, often regret having uttered. But there you are! One does not imagine how many women there are, with angels' mouths, and starry eyes, and three-thousand-franc dresses, make filthy gestures, and are disgusting by their vulgarity,—in fact, strumpets of the lowest type.

"Great ladies," said William, "are like the best sauces,—it is better not to know how they are made."

William was given to these disenchanting aphorisms. And, being all the same a very gallant man, he added, as he took me about the waist:

"A little girl like you is less flattering to a lover's vanity. But she is more serious, all the same."

I must say that Madame spent all her wrath and showered all her coarse words upon Monsieur; with us, I repeat, she was rather timid.

Moreover, amid the disorder of her house, amid all the reckless waste she tolerated, Madame showed queer streaks of avarice that were quite unexpected. She haggled with the cook over two sous spent for salad, economized in the matter of the servants' washing, raised objections to a bill of three francs, and did not rest until, after endless complaints and correspondence, and interminable negotiations, she had secured a refunding of fifteen centimes unwarrantably collected by an expressman for the transportation of a package. Every time she took a cab, there was a quarrel with the coachman, to whom she gave no tip, and whom she even found a way of cheating. And yet she left her money about everywhere, with her jewels and her keys, on the mantels and on the furniture. She recklessly ruined her richest costumes and her finest linen, she suffered herself to be impudently robbed by dealers in articles of luxury, and accepted without a frown the books of the old butler, as Monsieur, for that matter, accepted those of William. And yet God knows what frauds they contained! Sometimes I said to William:

"Really, you pinch too much; some day you will get into trouble."

To which William replied, very calmly:

"Oh! let me alone; I know what I am about, and how far I can go. When one has masters as stupid as these are, it would be a crime not to take advantage of them."

But the poor fellow scarcely profited by these continual larcenies, which, in spite of the astonishing tips he had, continually went to fill the pockets of the bookmakers.

Monsieur and Madame had been married for five years. At first they went into society a great deal, and gave dinners. Then gradually they restricted their goings-out and their receptions, and lived almost alone, saying that they were jealous of each other. Madame reproached Monsieur with flirting with the women; Monsieur accused Madame of looking too much at the men. They loved each other much,—that is to say, they quarreled all day long, like a little *bourgeois* household. The truth is that Madame had not succeeded in society, and that her manners had cost her not a few insults. She was angry with Monsieur for not having been able to impose her upon society, and Monsieur was angry with Madame for having made him ridiculous in the eyes of his friends. They did not confess to each other the bitterness of their feelings, finding it simpler to charge their dissensions to the score of love.

281

CELESTINE

Every year, in the middle of June, they started for the country, Madame having, it seems, a magnificent château in Touraine. The personnel was re-enforced with a coachman, two gardeners, a second chambermaid, and some barnyard-scullions. There were cows, peacocks, hens, and rabbits. How delightful! William told me the details of their country life with a bitter and grumbling ill-humor. He did not like the country; the fields, the trees, and the flowers made him tired. Nature was endurable to him only with bar-rooms, race-tracks, bookmakers, and jockeys. He was exclusively Parisian.

"Do you know anything more stupid than a chestnut tree?" he often said to me. "Take Edgar, for instance; is he a *chic* man, a superior man; does he like the country?' '

I became enthusiastic:

"Oh! but the flowers in the broad lawns! And the little birds!"

William sneered:

"The flowers? They are pretty only on hats and in the millinery shops. And the little birds? Oh, don't talk about them! They prevent you from sleeping in the morning. They sound like bawling children. Oh! no. Oh! no. I have enough of the country. The country is fit only for peasants."

And, straightening up, with a noble gesture, he concluded, in a proud voice:

"I must have sport. I am not a peasant; I am a sports-man."

Nevertheless I was happy, and I awaited the month of June with impatience. Oh! the marguerites in the meadows; the little paths under the trembling leaves; the nests hidden in the ivies against the old walls; and the nightingales on moonlight nights; and the sweet conversations, hand in hand, on the brinks of wells, lined with honeysuckles and carpeted with maiden's-hair and moss; and the bowls of foaming milk; and the broad-brimmed straw hats; and the little chickens; and the masses heard in the village churches, with their towering steeples; and everything that moves and charms you, and makes an impression on your heart, like one of those pretty ballads they sing in the music-halls!

Although I am fond of fun, I have a poetical nature. The old shepherds, the outspread hay, the birds that pursue one another from branch to branch, and the brooks that run singing over light pebbles, and the handsome lads, with complexions made purple by the sun, like grapes on very old vines,—the handsome lads with robust limbs and powerful chests,—all these things make me dream pleasant dreams. In thinking of these things, I become almost a little girl again, my soul inundated and my heart refreshed by innocence and candor, as a little rain refreshes the little flower too much burned by the sun, too much dried by the wind. And at night, while waiting for William, becoming enthusiastic over the prospects of this future of pure joys, I made verses:

> Petite fleur,
> O toi, ma sœur,
> Dont la centeur
> Fait mon bonheur . . .

> Et toi, ruisseau,
> Lointain coteau,
> Frêle arbrisseau,
> Au bord de l'eau,

> Que puis-je dire,
> Dans mon délire?
> Je vous admire . . .
> Et je soupire . . .

> Amour, amour,
> Amour d'un jour,
> Et de toujours! . . .
> Amour, amour! . . .

As soon as William returned, all poesy flew away. He brought me the heavy odor of the barroom, and his kisses, which smelt of gin, quickly broke the wings of my dream. I never wanted to show him my verse. What was the use? He would have laughed at me, and at the sentiment that inspired them. And undoubtedly he would have said to me:

"Take Edgar, now! He is an astonishing man. Does he make verses?"

My poetical nature was not the only cause of my impatience to start for the country. My stomach was out of order, in consequence of the long period of poverty through which I had just passed, and perhaps also in consequence of the too abundant and exciting food that I was now enjoying, and the champagne and the Spanish wines that William forced me to drink. I was really suffering. Often, in the morning, on getting out of bed, I was seized with vertigo. During the day my legs bent under me, and I felt pains in my head, like the blows of a hammer. I really needed a quieter life, to restore me a little.

Alas! it was written that all this dream of happiness and health was also to be dashed.

"Oh! hell!" as Madame would say.

The scenes between Monsieur and Madame always began in Madame's dressing-room, and always grew out of trifling pretexts, out of nothing. The more trifling the pretext, the more violent was the scene. After which, having vomited all that their hearts contained of long pent-up bitterness and wrath, they sulked for entire weeks. Monsieur retired into his room, where he played solitaire and rearranged his collection of pipes in new harmonies. Madame remained all the time in her room, where, stretched upon a long chair, she read love stories, interrupting her reading only to rearrange her closets and her wardrobe, with rage and frenzy,—such a pillage! They met only at meals. At first, not being familiar with their manias, I thought they were going to throw plates, knives, and bottles

284

at each other's heads. Nothing of the kind, alas! It was at these times that they were the best behaved, and that Madame contrived to appear like a woman of society. They talked about their little affairs as if nothing had happened,—a little more ceremoniously than usual, with a little more cold and stilted politeness,—that was all. One would have said they were dining in town. Then, the meal finished, with serious air, sad eyes, and very dignified, they retired to their respective rooms. Madame began again on her novels and drawers, Monsieur on his solitaire and his pipes. Sometimes Monsieur went to pass an hour or two at his club, but rarely. And they exchanged a furious correspondence, hen-shaped or heart-shaped love-letters, with the transmission of which I was entrusted. All day long I played the letter-carrier, bearing terrible ultimatums, threats, supplications, pardons, and tears, from the room of Madame to that of Monsieur. It was enough to make one die of laughter.

After a few days, they became reconciled, just as they had fallen out, without any apparent reason. And there were sobs, and "Oh, you naughty boy!" "Oh! you naughty girl!" and "It is over, do I not tell you it is over?" And they went away to have a little fête at the restaurant, and the next day arose very late, much fatigued.

I at once understood the farce that the two poor actors were playing for themselves. And, when they threatened to leave each other, I knew very well that they were not sincere. They were riveted to each other,—he by his interest, she by her vanity. Monsieur clung to Madame's money, Madame held fast to Monsieur's name and title. But, as in reality they detested each other, precisely because of this dupe's bargain that bound them, they felt the need of saying so to each other from time to time, and of giving to their disappointment, their spite, and their contempt an expression as base as their souls.

"What are such lives good for?" said I to William.

"For Baby!" answered William, who, under all circumstances, found the accurate and final word.

CELESTINE

For immediate and material proof he drew from his pocket a magnificent cigar, pinched that very morning, carefully cut off the tip, and then, lighting it with satisfaction and tranquillity, declared, between two fragrant whiffs:

"One should never complain of the stupidity of his masters, my little Célestine. It is the only guarantee of happiness that we servants have. The more stupid the masters, the more fortunate the servants. Go and get me the fine champagne."

Half stretched out in a rocking-chair, with legs cocked up and crossed, with the cigar in his mouth, and a bottle of old Martell within reach of his hand, he slowly and methodically unfolded the "Autorité," and said, with admirable good nature:

"You see, my little Célestine, one must be stronger than the people whom one serves. That is the whole secret. God knows whether Cassagnac is a terrible man. God knows whether his ideas suit me to a T, and whether I admire this tall devil. Well, do you know? I would not like to be his servant,—not for anything in the world. And what I say of Cassagnac I say also of Edgar. Remember this, and try to profit by it. To serve in the houses of intelligent people who are 'on to us' is to be duped, my little pet."

And, enjoying his cigar, he added, after a silence:

"When I think that there are servants who pass their lives in running down their masters, in annoying them and threatening them! What brutes! When I think that there are some who would like to kill them! Kill them! And what then? Do we kill the cow that gives us milk, and the sheep that gives us wool? No, we milk the cow, and shear the sheep . . . skilfully . . . gently."

And he silently plunged into the mysteries of conservative politics.

Meanwhile Eugénie was prowling around the kitchen, amorous and flabby. She did her work mechanically, like a sumnambulist, far from the people up-stairs, far from us, far

286

from herself, with no eye for their follies or ours, and with silent words of sorrowful admiration always on her lips.

"Your little mouth, your little hands, your big eyes!"

All this often saddened me,—I don't know why,—saddened me to the point of tears. Yes, this strange house, in which all the beings in it, the silent old butler, William, and myself, seemed to me disquieting, empty, and dismal, like phantoms, sometimes filled me with unspeakable and oppressive melancholy.

The last scene that I witnessed was particularly droll.

One morning Monsieur entered the dressing-room at the moment when Madame was trying on a new corset in my presence, a frightful mauve satin corset with yellow flowerets and yellow silk lacings. Madame's taste will never choke her.

"What?" said Madame, in a tone of gay reproach. "Is that the way one enters women's rooms, without knocking?"

"Oh! women?" chirped Monsieur. "In the first place, you are not women."

"I am not women? What am I, then?"

Monsieur rounded his lips,—My! what a stupid air he had! —and very tenderly, or pretending tenderness, he buzzed:

"Why! you are my wife, my little wife, my pretty little wife. There is no harm in entering the room of one's little wife, I suppose."

When Monsieur played the imbecile lover, it was because he wanted to get some money out of Madame. She, still suspicious, replied:

"Yes, there is harm."

And she minced:

"Your little wife? Your little wife? It is not so sure that I am your little wife."

"What! It is not so sure?"

"Indeed, one never knows. Men are so queer."

"I tell you, you are my little wife,—my dear, my only little wife . . . ah!"

"And you . . . my baby . . . my big baby . . . his little wife's only big baby . . . na!"

I was lacing Madame, who, with bare arms raised, was looking into the mirror. And I had a great desire to laugh. How they tired me with their "little wife" and their "big baby"! What a stupid air they both had!

After picking up skirts, stockings, and towels, and distributing brushes, jars, and bottles, Monsieur took a fashion journal which was lying on the dressing-table, and sat down on a sort of plush-covered stool. He asked:

"Is there a rebus in this number?"

"Yes, I think there is a rebus."

"Have you guessed it?"

"No, I have not guessed it."

"Ah! ah! let's have a look at it."

While Monsieur, with wrinkled brow, was absorbed in the study of the rebus, Madame said, a little dryly:

"Robert?"

"My darling."

"Then you notice nothing?"

"No. What? In this rebus?"

She shrugged her shoulders, and pursed up her lips.

"It is not a question of the rebus. Then you notice nothing? Well, you never notice anything."

Monsieur surveyed the room from carpet to ceiling, from dressing-table to door, with an annoyed and a very round look, which was excessively comical.

"No, indeed! What is it? Is there anything new here, then, that I have not noticed? I see nothing, upon my word."

Madame became very sad, and she groaned:

"Robert, you no longer love me."

"What! I no longer love you! Indeed, that is putting it a little too strong!"

He rose, brandishing the fashion journal.

"What! I no longer love you!" he repeated. "Well, that's an idea! Why do you say that?"

"No, you no longer love me . . . because, if you still loved me, you would have noticed something."

"But what thing?"

"Well, you would have noticed my corset."

"What corset? Oh! yes, this corset. 'Tis true, I had not noticed it. How stupid I am! Why, yes, it is very pretty, you know, . . . ravishing."

"Yes, you say that now, and don't mean it. I am too stupid, myself. I tire myself out in trying to make myself beautiful,—in trying to find things to please you. And you care nothing about it. Besides, what am I to you? Nothing; less than nothing! You come in here, and what do you see? That dirty newspaper. In what are you interested? In a rebus! Ah, a pretty life you give me here! We do not see anybody; we do not go anywhere; we live like wolves, like poor people."

"Oh! come, come, I beg of you. Don't get angry. Come! As poor people, indeed!"

He tried to approach Madame, to take her about the waist, to kiss her, but she repulsed him severely.

"No, let me alone. You provoke me."

"Oh! come, my darling, my little wife."

"You provoke me, do you hear? Let me alone. Do not approach me. You are a gross egoist, a clumsy puppy; you don't know how to do anything for me; you are a dirty type, there!"

"Why do you say that? It is madness. Come, don't fly into a passion like that. Well, yes, I was wrong. I ought to have seen this corset right away,—this very pretty corset. Why did I not see it right away? I do not understand it. Look at me; smile at me. My! how pretty it is! And how it becomes you!"

Monsieur dwelt too persistently upon the subject. He irritated me, although I had no interest in the quarrel. Madame stamped on the carpet, and, becoming more and more nervous, with pale lips and clenched hands, she rattled on:

"You provoke me, you provoke me! Do you understand? Clear out!"

Monsieur continued to stammer, beginning now to show signs of exasperation.

"My darling! It is not reasonable. Just for a corset! It is out of all proportion. Come, my darling, look at me, smile at me. It is stupid to make such a fuss over a corset."

"Ah! *Tu m'emmerdes!*" vomited Madame, in the voice of a washerwoman. *"Tu m'emmerdes!* Clear out!"

I had finished lacing my mistress. I arose at this word, delighted at having surprised their two beautiful souls in all their nakedness, and at the thought of the humiliation that they would feel in my presence afterward. They seemed to have forgotten that I was there. Desiring to see how the scene would end, I kept perfectly still, and made myself as small as possible.

Monsieur, who had been holding in for a long time, now got angry in his turn. He made the fashion journal into a big ball, and flung it with all his might against the dressing-table; and he cried:

"Zut! Flûte! This is really getting too tiresome! It is always the same thing. One cannot say anything or do anything without being received like a dog. And always brutalities and coarse language. I have enough of this life; I have had enough of these fishwife's manners. And shall I tell you the truth? Your corset,—well, your corset is vile. It is a prostitute's corset."

"Wretch!"

With bloodshot eye, foaming mouth, and clenched and threatening fist, she advanced toward Monsieur. And such was her rage that the words came from her mouth in a sort of hoarse belching.

"Wretch!" she roared again. "And it is you who dare

to speak to me in this way,—you? Oh! but it is unheard of. When I picked him up in the mud, this poverty-stricken fine gentleman, covered with dirty debts, posted at his club,—when I saved him from the mire, he was not so proud! Your name, I suppose? Your title? Oh! clean they were, indeed, this name and title, on which the usurers were unwilling to advance you another hundred sous. You can take them back, and welcome. And he talks of his nobility, of his ancestors, this Monsieur whom I have bought and whom I support! Well, the nobility will have nothing more from me,—not that! And, as for your ancestors, you scoundrel, you can try to hang them up. You will see whether you can borrow even ten sous on their ugly mugs,—mugs of veterans and valets. Nothing more, do you hear? Never, never! Back to your gaming-tables, trickster! Back to your prostitutes, tramp!''

She was frightful. Monsieur, timid, trembling, with cowardly back and humiliated eye, retired before this flood of filth. He reached the door, noticed me, and fled, and Madame again cried after him, in the passage-way, in a voice which had become more hoarse and horrible:

''Tramp! Dirty tramp!''

And she sank upon her long chair, overcome by a terrible nervous attack, which I finally quieted by making her inhale an entire flask of either.

Then Madame began again the reading of her love stories and the rearrangement of her drawers. Monsieur was more absorbed than ever in the complexities of solitaire and in the revision of his collection of pipes. And the correspondence began again. Timid and widely-spaced at first, it was soon going on fast and furiously. I became utterly tired out with running from the room of one to the room of the other, bearing heart-shaped or hen-shaped threats. But oh! what fun I had!

Three days after this scene, while reading a missive from Monsieur, on pink paper and bearing his coat of arms, Madame turned pale, and suddenly asked me, in a gasping voice:

"Célestine, do you really think that Monsieur wants to kill himself? Have you seen him with weapons in his hands? My God! If he were to kill himself?"

I burst out laughing in Madame's face. And this laugh, which had escaped me in spite of myself, increased, let itself loose, poured itself out. I thought I should die, choked by this laugh, strangled by this cursed laugh that rose, like a tempest, in my breast, and filled my throat with irrepressible hiccups.

For a moment Madame sat aghast.

"What is it? What is the matter with you? Why do you laugh like that? Be still, then. Will you be still, nasty creature?"

But the laugh held me fast; it would not let go. At last, between two gasps, I cried:

"Oh! no, your goings on are too funny, too stupid! Oh! la la! Oh! la la! How stupid it is!"

Of course I quit the house that night, and found myself once more on the street pavement.

What a dog of a trade! What a dog of a life!

The blow was a hard one, and I said to myself, but too late, that never should I find another place like that. There I had everything,—good wages, profits of all sorts, easy work, liberty, pleasures. I had only to let myself live. Another, less crazy than I, would have been able to put much money aside, and gradually accumulate a complete and beautiful wardrobe. One could marry, buy a little business, have a home of one's own, secure against want and ill-luck,—almost a lady. But now the series of miseries must begin over again, and I submit anew to the offences of chance. I was much put out by this accident, and furious; furious against myself, against William, against Eugénie, against Madame, against everybody. Curious and inexplicable thing,—instead of clinging and holding fast to my place, which would have been easy with a type like Madame, I had buried myself deeper in my stupidity, and, cheeking it through, I had rendered irreparable that which could have been repaired. What strange things take place in one at certain moments! It passes understanding. It is like a fit of madness which falls upon you, you know not whence, you know not why,—which seizes you, shakes you, excites you, and forces you to cry out and shower insults. Under the influence of this fit of madness, I had heaped outrages upon Madame. I had reproached her with her father, with her mother, and with the imbecile falsehood of her life; I had treated her as one does not treat a prostitute; I had spat upon her husband. And this frightens me, when I think of it. I feel ashamed of these sudden descents into baseness, of these filthy intoxications, in which my reason so often staggers, and which impel me to violence and murder. Why did I not kill her that day? Why did I not strangle her? I do not know. God knows, however, that I am not wicked. Today I see again this poor woman, in my mind's eye; I see again her sad and disorderly life, with her coward, her dismal coward, of a husband. And I feel an immense pity for her; and I would like her to have strength enough to leave him and be happy.

After the terrible scene I hurried down to the servants' hall. William was mildly polishing the silverware, and smoking a Russian cigarette.

"What is the matter with you?" asked he, in the most tranquil fashion in the world.

"I must go away; I must quit the box to-night," I gasped. I could scarcely speak.

"What! you are going?" exclaimed William, without the least emotion. "And why?"

In short and hissing phrases, and mimicking their manners, I related the entire scene between Madame and Monsieur. William, very calm and indifferent, shrugged his shoulders.

"It is too stupid, indeed!" said he. "One should not be as stupid as that!"

"And that is all you find to say to me?"

"What else do you expect me to say to you? I say that it is stupid. There is nothing else to say."

"And you? What are you going to do?"

He looked at me obliquely. There was a sneer on his lips. Ah! how ugly was his look, in that moment of distress; how ugly and hideous was his mouth!

"I?" said he, pretending not to understand that, in this question, there were prayers for him.

"Yes, you. I asked you what you were going to do."

"Nothing. I have nothing to do. I am going to continue. Why, you are crazy, my girl. You do not expect" . . .

I burst out:

"You are going to have the courage to remain in a house from which I am driven out?"

He rose, relighted his cigarette, and said, icily:

"Oh! no scene, you know. I am not your husband. You have seen fit to commit a stupidity. I am not responsible for it. What do you expect? You must take the consequences. Life is life."

I became indignant.

"Then you are going to drop me? You are a wretch, a scoundrel, like the others, do you know it?"

William smiled. He was really a superior man.

"Oh! don't say useless things. I have made you no promises. Nor have you made me any. People meet; that is well. They part; that is well, too. Life is life."

And he added, sententiously:

"You see, Célestine, in life there must be conduct; there must be what I call administration. You have no conduct; you have no administration. You allow yourself to be carried away by your nerves. In our business nerves are a very bad thing. Remember this well: life is life."

I think I should have thrown myself upon him and torn his face, his emotionless and cowardly face of a flunky, with furious digs of my nails, if tears had not suddenly come to soften and relax my overstrained nerves. My wrath fell, and I begged:

"Oh, William! William! my little William! my dear little William! how unhappy I am!"

William tried to revive my drooping spirits a little. I must say that made use of all his powers of persuasian and all his philosophy. During the day he generously overwhelmed me with lofty thoughts, with grave and consoling aphorisms, in which these words, provoking and soothing at the same time, continually recurred:

"Life is life."

I must do him justice. This last day he was charming, though a little too solemn, and he did things very well. In the evening, after dinner, he put my trunks on a cab, and escorted me to a lodging-house where he was known, paying a week's rent in advance out of his own pocket, and recommending the proprietor to take good care of me. But he could not stay himself, for he had an appointment with Edgar!

"You understand, of course, that I cannot disappoint Edgar. And perhaps, too, he might know of a place for you. A place gotten through Edgar,—ah! that would be astonishing."

On leaving me, he said:

"I will come to see you to-morrow. Be wise; no more stupidities. They do you no good. And get this truth well into your head, Célestine,—that life is life!"

The next day I waited for him in vain. He did not come.

"It is life," I said to myself.

But the following day, being impatient to see him, I went to the house. I found in the kitchen only a tall blonde girl, bold and pretty,—prettier than I.

"Eugénie is not here?" I asked.

"No, she is not here," answered the tall girl, dryly.

"And William?"

"Nor William either."

"Where is he?"

"How do I know?"

295

"I want to see him. Go tell him I want to see him."

The tall girl looked at me scornfully.

"Say, am I your servant?"

I understood it all. And, being tired of struggling, I went away.

"It is life."

This phrase pursued me, obsessed me, like a music-hall refrain.

And, as I went away, I could not help thinking, not without a feeling of sorrowful melancholy, of the joy with which I had been welcomed in that house. The same scene must have taken place. They had opened the usual bottle of champagne. William had taken the blonde girl on his knees, and had whispered in her ear:

"You will have to be nice with Baby."

The same words, the same movements, the same caresses, while Eugénie, devouring the janitor's son with her eyes, led him into the adjoining room.

"Your little phiz, your little hands, your big eyes!"

I walked on, utterly irresolute and stupefied, repeating to myself with stupid obstinacy:

"Yes, indeed, it is life; it is life."

For more than an hour, in front of the door, I paced up and down the sidewalk, hoping that William might come in or go out. I saw the grocer enter, a little milliner with two big band-boxes, and the delivery-man from the Louvre; I saw the plumbers come out, and I know not who or what else,—shades, shades, shades. I did not dare to go into the janitor's lodge in the next house. The janitress undoubtedly would not have received me well. And what would she have said to me? Then I went away for good, still pursued by the irritating refrain:

"It is life."

The streets seemed to me intolerably sad. The passers-by made upon me the impression of spectres. When I saw in the distance a hat shining on a gentleman's head, like a lighthouse in the night, like a gilded cupola in the sunshine, my heart leaped. But it was never William. In the lowering, pewter-colored sky, no hope was shining.

I returned to my room, disgusted with everything.

Ah! yes, the men! Be they coachmen, *valets*, dudes, priests, or poets, they are all the same. Low-lived wretches!

I think that these are the last recollections that I shall call up. I have others, however,—many others. But they all resemble each other, and it tires me to continually write the same stories, and to unroll, in a continuous and monotonous panorama, the same faces, the same souls, the same phantoms. And then I feel that I have no mind left for it, for I am becoming more and more distracted from the ashes of this past by the new preoccupation of my future. I could have told also of my stay in the Countess Fardini's mansion. But what is the use? I am too weary, and also too distressed. There, amid the same social phenomena, there was one vanity that disgusts me more than any other,—literary vanity; one species of stupidity that is lower than any other,—political stupidity.

There I knew M. Paul Bourget in all his glory; it is needless to say more. Ah! there you have the philosopher, the poet, the moralist, befitting the pretentious nullity, the intellectual hollowness, the falsehood, of that sphere of society in which everything is artificial,—elegance, love, cooking, religious feeling, patriotism, art, charity, and vice itself, which, making a pretext of politeness and literature, wraps itself in mystical tinsel and covers itself with sacred masks; that sphere of society in which there is to be found but one sincere desire,—the fierce desire for money, which gives to these ridiculous mountebanks something even more odious and grim than their ridiculousness. That is the only thing that makes of these poor phantoms living human creatures.

There I knew Monsieur Jean, he too a psychologist and a moralist, a moralist of the servants' hall, a psychologist of the ante-room, scarcely more of a *parvenu* in his way, or more of a ninny, than he who reigned in the *salon*. Monsieur Jean emptied chamber-vessels; M. Paul Bourget emptied souls. Between the servants' hall and the *salon* there is not such a distance of servitude as we think. But, since I have put Monsieur Jean's photograph in the bottom of my trunk, let his memory remain, similarly buried, in the bottom of my heart, under a thick layer of oblivion.

It is two o'clock in the morning. My fire is going out, my lamp is smoking, and I have no more wood or oil. I am going to bed. But there is too much fever in my brain; I shall not sleep. I shall dream of him who is on the way to me. I shall dream of what is to happen to-morrow. Outside, the night is calm and silent. A sharp, cold air is hardening the ground, beneath a sky sparkling with stars. And somewhere in this night Joseph is on his way. Through space I see him,—yes, really, I see him, serious, dreaming, enormous, in his compartment in a railway carriage. He is smiling at me; he is drawing nearer to me; he is coming toward me. He is bringing me, at last, peace, liberty, happiness. Happiness?

I shall see him to-morrow.

XVII.

It is eight months since I have written a single line in this diary,—I have had something else to do and to think of,—and it is exactly three months since Joseph and I left the Priory, and established ourselves in the little café at Cherbourg, near the harbor. We are married; business is good; I like the trade; I am happy. Born by the sea, I have come back to the sea. I did not miss it but it gives me pleasure, all the same, to find it again. Here one does not see the desolate landscapes of Audierne, the infinite sadness of its costs, the magnificent horror of its beaches that howl so mournfully. Here nothing is sad; on the contrary, everything contributes to gaiety. There is the joyous sound of a military city, the picturesque movement and varied activity of a military harbor. Crowds in a hurry to enjoy between two periods of far-off exile; spectacles incessantly changing and diverting, in which I inhale that natal odor of coal tar and sea-weed which I love, although I never found it agreeable in my childhood. I have seen again the lads of my native province, now serving on State men-of-war. We have scarcely talked together, and I have not dreamed of asking them for news of my brother. It is so long ago! To me it is as if he were dead. Good day! . . . good evening! . . . be good. When they are not drunk, they are too stupid! When they are not stupid, they are too drunk. And they have heads like those of old fishes. Between them and me there has been no other emotion, no other effusion. Besides, Joseph does not like me to be familiar with simple seamen, dirty Bretons who haven't a sou, and who get drunk on a glass of kill-me-quick.

But I must relate briefly the events that preceded our departure from the Priory.

299

CELESTINE

It will be remembered that, at the Priory, Joseph slept in the out-buildings, over the harness-room. Every day, summer and winter, he rose at five o'clock. Now, on the morning of December 24, just a month after his return from Cherbourg, he noticed that the kitchen-door was wide open.

"What!" said he to himself. "Can they have risen already?"

He noticed at the same time that a square of glass had been cut out of the glass door, with a diamond, near the lock, in such a way as to admit the introduction of an arm. The lock had been forced by expert hands. Bits of wood, glass, and twisted iron were strewn along the stone flagging. Within, all the doors, so carefully bolted at night under Madame's eyes, were open also. One felt that something frightful had happened. Greatly impressed,—I tell the story of his discovery as he told it himself before the magistrates,—Joseph passed through the kitchen, and then through the passage-way into which opened, at the right, the fruit-room, the bath-room, and the ante-room; at the left, the servants' hall, and dining-room, and the little *salon;* and, at the end, the grand *salon.* The dining-room presented a spectacle of frightful disorder, of real pillage. The furniture was upset; the sideboard had been ransacked from top to bottom; its drawers, as well as those of the two side-tables, were turned upside down on the carpet; and on the table, among empty boxes and a confused heap of valueless articles, a candle was burning itself out in a brass candlestick. But it was in the servants' hall that the spectacle became really imposing. In the servants' hall—I believe I have already noted the fact—there was a very deep closet, protected by a very complicated system of locks, the secret of which was known only to Madame. There slept the famous and venerable silver service, in three heavy boxes, with steel corners and cross-pieces. The boxes were screwed to the floor, and held fast against the wall by solid iron clamps. But now the three boxes, torn from their mysterious and inviolable tabernacle, lay yawning and empty, in the middle of the room. At sight of these, Joseph gave the alarm. With all the strength of his lungs, he shouted up the stairs:

"Madame! Monsieur! Come down right away. We are robbed! we are robbed!"

There was a sudden avalanche, a frightful plunge down the stairs. Madame, in her chemise, with her shoulders scarcely covered by a light neckerchief. Monsieur, in his drawers and shirt. And both of them, dishevelled, pale, and grimacing, as if they had been awakened in the middle of a nightmare, shouted:

"What is the matter? What is the matter?"

"We are robbed! we are robbed!"

"We are robbed, what? We are robbed, what?"

In the dining-room, Madame groaned:

"My God! My God!"

While, with distorted mouth, Monsieur continued to scream:

"We are robbed, what? what?"

Guided by Joseph into the servants' hall, Madame, at sight of the three boxes unsealed, made a great gesture, uttered a great cry:

"My silver service! My God! Is it possible? My silver service!"

And, lifting the empty compartments, and turning the empty cases upside down, she sank, frightened and horrified, upon the floor. Scarcely had she strength enough to stammer, in the voice of a child:

"They have taken everything! They have taken everything . . . everything . . . everything . . . everything! Even the Louis XVI cruet."

While Madame was looking at the boxes as if she were looking at a dead child, Monsieur, scratching his neck, and rolling haggard eyes, moaned persistently in the far-away voice of a demented person:

"Name of a dog; Ah! name of a dog! Name of a dog of name of a dog!"

And Joseph, too, with atrocious grimaces, was exclaiming: "The cruet of Louis XVI! The cruet of Louis XVI! Oh! the bandits!"

Then there was a minute of tragic silence, a long minute of prostration,—that silence of death, that prostration of beings and things, which follows the fracas of a terrible downfall, the thunder of a great cataclysm. And the lantern, swinging in Joseph's hands, cast a red, trembling, sinister gleam over the whole scene, over the dead faces and the empty boxes.

I had come down, in response to Joseph's call, at the same time as the masters. In presence of this disaster, and in spite of the prodigious comicality of these faces, my first feeling was one of compassion. It seemed to me that this misfortune fell upon me too, and that I was one of the family, sharing its trials and sorrows. I should have liked to speak consoling words to Madame, whose dejected attitude it gave me pain to see. But this impression of solidarity or of servitude quickly vanished.

In crime there is something violent, solemn, justiciary, religious, which frightens me, to be sure, but which also leaves in me—how shall I express it?—a feeling of admiration. No, not of admiration, since admiration is a moral feeling, a spiritual excitement, whereas that which I feel influences and excites only my flesh. It is like a brutal shock throughout my physical being, at once painful and delicious,—a sorrowful and swooning rape of my sex. It is curious, doubtless it is peculiar, perhaps it is horrible,—and I cannot explain the real cause of these strange and powerful sensations,—but in me every crime, especially murder, has secret relationships with love. Yes, indeed! A fine crime takes hold of me just as a fine man does.

I must say that further reflection suddenly transformed

302

into a hilarious gaiety, a childish content, that grave, atrocious, and powerful enjoyment of crime which succeeded the impulse to pity that at first so inappropriately startled my heart. I thought:

Here are two beings who live like moles, like larvæ. Like voluntary prisoners, they have voluntarily shut themselves up in the jail of these inhospitable walls. All that constitutes the joy of life, the smile of a house, they repress as something superfluous. Against everything that could excuse their wealth, and pardon their human uselessness, they guard as they would guard against filth. They let nothing fall from their parsimonious table to satisfy the hunger of the poor; they let nothing fall from their dry hearts to relieve the pain of the suffering. They even economize in making provision for their own happiness. And should I pity them? Oh! no. It is justice that has overtaken them. In stripping them of a portion of their goods, in giving air to the buried treasures, the good thieves have restored equilibrium. What I regret is that they did not leave these two maleficent beings totally naked and miserable, more destitute than the vagabond who so often begged at their door in vain, sicker than the abandoned creature dying by the roadside, within two steps of this hidden and accursed wealth.

This idea of my masters, with wallets on their backs, having to drag their lamentable rags and their bleeding feet over the stony highways, and to stand with outstretched hands at the implacable threshold of the evil-minded rich, enchanted me, and filled me with gaiety. But my gaiety became more direct, and more intense, and more hateful, as I surveyed Madame, stranded beside her empty boxes, deader than if she had been really dead,—for she was conscious of this death, the most horrible death conceivable to a being who had never loved anything but the valuation in money of those invaluable things,— our pleasures, our caprices, our charities, our love, the divine luxury of the soul. This shameful sorrow, this crapulous dejection, was also a revenge for the humiliations and severities that I have undergone, that came to me from her, in every word that issued from her mouth, in every look that fell from her eyes. This deliciously grim enjoyment I tasted to the full. I would have liked to cry out: "Well done! Well done!" And, above all, I would have liked to know these admirable and sublime thieves, in order to thank them in the name of all the ragamuffins, and to embrace them, as brothers. Oh! good thieves, dear figures of justice and pity, through what a series of intense and delightful sensations you have made me pass!

Madame was not slow in recovering her self-possession. Her combative, agressive nature suddenly reawakened in all its violence.

"And what are you doing here?" she said to Monsieur, in a tone of anger and supreme scorn. "Why are you here? How ridiculous you are, with your big puffy face, and in your shirt-tail! Do you think that will get us back our silver service? Come! shake yourself; stir yourself; try to understand. Go for the police, for the justice of the peace. Ought they not to have been here long ago? Oh! my God! what a man!"

Monsieur, with bent back, started to go. She interrupted him:

"And how is it that you heard nothing? What! they turn the house upside down, break in doors, force locks, empty walls and boxes, and you hear nothing? What are you good for, big blockhead?"

Monsieur ventured to answer:

"But you, too, my pet, you did not hear anything."

"I? It is not the same thing. Is it not a man's business to hear? And besides, you provoke me. Clear out!"

And, as Monsieur went up-stairs to dress, Madame turned her fury upon us.

"And you? What are you doing, standing there like so many bundles, and looking at me? It is all the same to you, I suppose, whether your masters are plundered or not? And you too heard nothing? What luck! It is charming to have such servants. You think of nothing but eating and drinking, pack of brutes that you are!''

Then, addressing Joseph directly, she asked:

''Why didn't the dogs bark? Say, why not?''

This question seemed to embarrass Joseph for a fraction of a second, but he quickly recovered himself.

''I don't know, Madame,'' said he, in a most natural tone. ''It is true that the dogs didn't bark. That is curious, indeed!''

''Did you let them loose last night?''

''Certainly I let them loose, as I do every night. That is curious! Yes, indeed! that is curious! It must be that the robbers knew the house . . . and the dogs.''

''Well, Joseph, how is it that you, so devoted and punctual as a rule, did not hear anything?''

''It is true that I heard nothing. That is another singular thing. For I do not sleep soundly. If a cat crosses the garden, I hear it. It is not natural, all the same. And those confounded dogs especially! Indeed, indeed!''

Madame interrupted Joseph:

''Stop! Leave me in peace. You are brutes, all of you! And Marianne. Where is Marianne? Why isn't she here? She is sleeping like a chump, undoubtedly.''

And, going out of the servants' hall, she called up the stairs:

''Marianne! Marianne!''

I looked at Joseph, who looked at the boxes. Joseph's face wore a grave expression. There was a sort of mystery in his eyes.

I will not try to describe this day, with all its varied incidents and follies. The prosecuting attorney, summoned by dispatch, came in the afternoon, and began his investigation. Joseph, Marianne, and I were questioned, one after the other,

—the first two for the sake of form, I with a hostile persistence which was extremely disagreeable to me. They visited my room, and searched my commode and my trunks. My correspondence was examined in detail. Thanks to a piece of good luck that I bless, the manuscript of my diary escaped them. A few days before the event I had sent it to Cléclé, from whom I had received an affectionate letter. But for that the magistrates perhaps would have found in these pages a foundation for a charge against Joseph, or at least for suspicion of him. I still tremble at the thought of it. It goes without saying that they also examined the garden paths, the platbands, the walls, the openings in the hedges, and the little yard leading to the lane, in the hope of finding foot-prints and traces of wall-scaling. But the ground was very dry and hard; it was impossible to discover the slightest imprint, the slightest clue. The fence, the walls, the openings in the hedges, kept their secret jealously. Just as in the case of the outrage in the woods, the people of the neighborhood hurried forward, asking to testify. One had seen a man of light complexion "whose looks he did not like;" another had seen a man of dark complexion "who had a funny air." In short, the investigation proved fruitless. No scent, no suspicion.

"We shall have to wait," declared the prosecuting attorney, mysteriously, as he left that night. "Perhaps the Paris police will put us on the track of the guilty."

During this fatiguing day, amid the goings and comings, I had scarcely the leisure to think of the consequences of this drama, which for the first time put a little animation and life into this dismal Priory. Madame did not give us a minute's rest; we had to run hither and thither,—without reason, moreover, for Madame had lost her head a little. As for Marianne, she seemed to take no notice of anything, and to be unaware that anything had happened to upset the house. Like the sad Eugénie, she followed her own idea, and her own idea was very far from our preoccupations. When

Monsieur appeared in the kitchen, she became suddenly like one intoxicated, and she looked at him with ecstatic eyes.

"Oh! your big phiz! Your big hands! Your big eyes!"

In the evening, after a silent dinner, I had an opportunity to reflect. The idea had struck me immediately, and now it was fortified within me, that Joseph was not a stranger to this bold robbery. I even went so far as to hope that between his Cherbourg trip and the preparation of this audacious and incomparably executed stroke there had been an evident connection. And I remembered the answer he made to me, on the eve of his departure:

"That depends . . . on a very important matter."

Although he endeavored to appear natural, I perceived in his movements, in his attitude, in his silence, an unusual embarrassment, visible only to me.

I took so much satisfaction in this presentiment that I did not try to put it aside. On the contrary, I felt an intense joy in contemplating the idea. Marianne having left us alone a moment in the kitchen, I approached Joseph, and, in a coaxing, tender voice, moved by an inexpressible emotion, I asked him:

"Tell me, Joseph, that it was you who outraged the little Claire in the woods. Tell me that it was you who stole Madame's silver service."

Surprised, stupefied by this question, Joseph looked at me. Then, suddenly, without answering, he drew me to him, and, making my neck bend under a kiss that fell like a blow of a club, he said to me:

"Don't talk about that, since you are to come with me to the little café, and since our two souls are alike."

I remember having seen in a little *salon* at the Countess Fardin's a sort of Hindoo idol, horribly and murderously beautiful. At this moment Joseph resembled it.

Days passed, and months. Naturally the magistrates were unable to discover anything, and finally they abandoned the investigation. Their opinion was that the crime was the work of expert burglars from Paris. Paris has a broad back. Go look for them in the heap!

This negative result made Madame indignant. She railed violently at the magistracy, which could not recover her silver service. But nevertheless she did not give up hope of finding "the cruet of Louis XVI," as Joseph called it. Every day she concocted new and outlandish schemes, which she sent to the magistrates, who, tiring at last of all this nonsense, did not even answer her. At last I was reassured concerning Joseph; for I was always afraid that some catastrophe would overtake him.

Joseph had again become silent and devoted, the family servant, the rare pearl. I cannot help puffing with laughter at the recollection of a conversation which, on the very day of the robbery, I overheard behind the door of the *salon*, between Madame and the prosecuting attorney, a dry little man, with thin lips and bilious complexion, whose profile was as sharp as the edge of a sword.

"You do not suspect anybody among your people?" asked the prosecuting attorney. "Your coachman?"

"Joseph!" cried Madame, scandalized, "a man who is so devoted to us, who has been in our service for more than fifteen years! Honesty itself, Monsieur; a pearl! He would throw himself into the fire for us."

Anxious, with wrinkled brow, she reflected:

"Unless it were this girl, the chambermaid. I do not know her. Perhaps she has very bad relations in Paris. Several times I have caught her drinking the table-wine and eating our prunes. A servant who drinks his master's wine is capable of anything."

And she murmured:

"One should never take servants from Paris. She is singular, indeed."

Just fancy the mean thing!

That is the way with suspicious people. They suspect everybody, save him who robs them, of course. For I was more and more convinced that Joseph had been the soul of this affair. For a long time I had watched him, not from any hostile feeling, as you know, but from curiosity; and I was certain that this faithful and devoted servant, this unique pearl, was foraging in the house for all he was worth. He stole oats, coal, eggs, all sorts of little things that could be sold without giving any trace of their origin. And his friend, the sacristan, did not come to the harness-room in the evening for nothing, and simply to discuss the benefits of anti-Semitism. Being a circumspect, patient, prudent, methodical man, Joseph was not unaware that petty larcenies, committed daily, foot up largely at the end of the year, and I am persuaded that in this way he tripled and quadrupled his wages,—a thing never to be disdained. I know very well that there is a difference between these little thefts and such an audacious pillage as that of the night of December 24. That proves that he liked also work on the grand scale. How do I know that Joseph was not then a member of a gang? Ah! how I should have liked to know all that, and how I should like to know it still.

After the evening when he gave me the kiss that to me was equivalent to a confession of the crime, when his confidence went out to me in a moment of passion, Joseph steadily denied. In vain did I turn him this way and that, set traps for him, and wheedle him with soft words and caresses; he would not contradict himself. And he entered into the madness of Madame's hopes. He too concocted schemes, and tried to imagine the robbery in all its details; and he beat the dogs that did not bark, and he threatened with his fist the unknown thieves, the chimerical thieves, as if he saw them running at the horizon. I did not know what to think about this impenetrable man. One day I believed him guilty; another day I believed him innocent. And it was horribly provoking.

We met again in the harness-room in the evening, as before.

"Well, Joseph?"

"Ah! it is you, Célestine!"

"Why don't you speak to me any more? You seem to shun me."

"Shun you? I? Oh! heavens!"

"Yes, since that famous morning."

"Don't talk of that, Célestine; you have too bad ideas."
And he sadly wagged his head.

"Come, Joseph, you know that I do that for fun. Would I love you, if you had committed such a crime? My little Joseph" . . .

"Yes, yes. You are trying to wheedle me. It is not well."

"And when are we to start? I cannot live here any longer."

"Not directly. We must wait awhile."

"But why?"

"Because . . . that cannot be done at once."

A little piqued, I said in a tone of slight anger:

"It is not nice of you. You evidently are in no hurry for me."

"I?" cried Joseph, with ardent grimaces. "Why, I am crazy over you."

"Well, then, let us start."

But he was obstinate, refusing to explain further.

"No, no; that cannot be done yet."

Very naturally I reflected:

"He is right, after all. If he has stolen the silver service, he cannot go away now, or set up in business. Perhaps it would awaken suspicion. Some time must be allowed to pass, so that this mysterious affair may be forgotten."

Another evening I proposed:

"Listen, my little Joseph; I know a way of leaving here. We could get up a quarrel with Madame, and force her to discharge us both."

But he protested sharply.

"No, no," he exclaimed. "None of that, Célestine. No, indeed! For my part, I love my masters. They are good masters.

We must part with them on good terms. We must go away from here like worthy people, like serious people. The masters must be sorry to have us leave; they must weep to see us go.''

With a sad gravity, in which I perceived no trace of irony, he declared:

"I, you know, shall be greatly grieved at leaving here. I have been here for fifteen years. One gets attached to a house in that time. And you, Célestine, will it give you no pain?''

"Oh! no," I shouted, laughing.

"It is not well; it is not well. One should love one's masters. Masters are masters. And let me give you some advice. Be very nice, very gentle, very devoted; do your work well; don't talk back. In short, Célestine, we must leave on good terms with them,—with Madame, especially.''

I followed Joseph's advice, and, during the months that we had to remain at the Priory, I promised myself that I would be a model chambermaid,—that I would be a pearl, too. I lavished upon them all my intelligence, all my willingness, all my delicacy. Madame became human with me; little by little, she became really my friend. I do not think it was my care alone that brought about this change in Madame's character. Madame's pride, and even her reasons for living, had received a blow. As after some great sorrow, after the overwhelming loss of some cherished darling, she no longer struggled, but gently and plaintively abandoned herself to the dejection of her conquered nerves and her humiliated pride, seeming to seek from those about her only consolation, pity, and confidence. The hell of the Priory was transformed for everybody into a real paradise.

It was in the height of this family peace, of this domestic calm, that I announced one morning to Madame that I was under the necessity of leaving her. I invented a romantic story; I was to return to my native province, there to marry a worthy fellow who had long been waiting for me. In words of tender-

311

ness I expressed my pain, my regrets, my appreciation of Madame's kindness, etc. Madame was overwhelmed. She tried to keep me by appealing to my sentiments and to my interest. She offered to increase my wages, and to give me a fine room on the second floor. But, finding me determined, she had to be resigned.

"I have become so accustomed to you now," she sighed. "Ah! I have no luck."

But it was much worse when, a week later, Joseph came, in his turn, to explain that, being too old and tired, he could no longer continue his service, and must seek the rest that he needed.

"You, Joseph?" cried Madame. "You, too? It is not possible. A curse must have fallen on the Priory. Everybody abandons me; everything abandons me."

Madame wept. Joseph wept. Monsieur wept. Marianne wept.

"You take with you all our regrets, Joseph."

Alas! he took not only regrets; he took also the silver service.

Once away, I was much perplexed. I had no scruple about enjoying Joseph's money, the stolen money,—no, it was not that,—where is the money that is not stolen?—but I feared lest my feeling might prove only a fleeting curiosity. Joseph had acquired over me, over my mind as well as my flesh, an ascendency that perhaps would not last. And perhaps it was only a momentary perversion of my senses. There were moments, too, when I asked myself if it was not my imagination, carried to the heights of exceptional dreams, which had created Joseph as I saw him; if really he was anything more than a simple brute, a peasant, incapable even of a fine act of violence, of a fine crime. The consequences of this act frightened me. And then, is it not really inexplicable? This idea that I was no longer to be in the service of others caused me some regret. Formerly I thought that I should welcome the news of my liberty with

312

great joy. Well, no! Through being a domestic, one gets it into his blood. Suppose I should suddenly miss the spectacle of *bourgeois* luxury? I foresaw my own little interior, severe and cold, like a workman's interior, my mediocre life, deprived of all these pretty things, of all these pretty stuffs so soft to touch, of all these pretty vices which it was my pleasure to serve, to dress, to adorn, to plunge into, as into a perfumed bath. But it was too late to draw back.

Ah! who could have told me, on the gray, sad, and rainy day on which I arrived at the Priory, that I would end with this strange, silent, and crusty man, who looked at me with such disdain?

Now we are in the little café. Joseph has grown young again. He is no longer bent and clumsy. And he walks from one table to another, and he runs from one room to the other, with supple leg and elastic spine. His shoulders, which so frightened me, have taken on good nature; his neck, sometimes so terrible, has something about it that is fraternal and restful. Always freshly shaven, with skin as dark and shining as mahogany, with a skull cap on his head, and wearing a blue and very clean woolen shirt, he has the air of an old sailor, of an old sea-dog who has seen extraordinary things and passed through extravagant countries. What I admire in him is his moral tranquillity. There is no longer any anxiety in his look. One sees that his life rests on solid foundations. More violently than ever, he is for the family, for property, for religion, for the navy, for the army, for the country. He astonishes me!

When we married, Joseph gave me a marriage portion of ten thousand francs. The other day the maritime commissary knocked down to him at fifteen thousand francs a lot of wreckage, for which he paid cash, and which he has sold again at a big profit. He also does a little banking business,—that is, he lends money to fishermen. And already he is thinking of branching out, by taking the next house. Perhaps we shall start a music-hall there.

313

It puzzles me that he has so much money. And how much is his fortune? I do not know. He does not like me to talk to him about that. He does not like me to talk to him about the time when we were servants. One would say that he has forgotten everything, and that his life really began only on the day when he took possession of the little café. When I ask him a question that torments me, he seems not to understand what I say. And then terrible gleams flash through his eyes, as they used to do. Never shall I know anything of Joseph; never shall I know the mystery of his life. And perhaps it is this mystery which so attaches me to him.

Joseph looks out for everything in the house, and there is no hitch anywhere. We have three waiters to serve the customers, a maid-of-all-work for the kitchen and the household, and everything goes as to the beat of a magic wand. It is true that in three months we have changed our servant four times. How exacting these Cherbourg servants are! how thieving, and how shameless! No, it is incredible, and it is disgusting.

As for me, I superintend the cash, enthroned behind the bar, amid a forest of colored bottles. I am there also on show, and to chat. Joseph wishes me to be finely arrayed; he never refuses me anything for the adornment of my person, and he likes me to show my skin in the evening, in a tantalizing dress, somewhat low in the neck. It is necessary to excite the customer, to keep him in a state of constant desire. There are already two or three fat quartermasters, two or three engineers of the squadron, very well fixed, who pay me assiduous court. Naturally, to please me, they spend a good deal. Joseph spoils them especially, for they are terrible drinkers. We have also taken four boarders. They eat with us, and every evening pay for wine and cordials, which all hands drink. They are very gallant with me, and I do my best to excite them. But I am careful not to let my manners go farther than the encouragement of commonplace ogling, equivocal smiles, and illusory promises. Moreover, I have no intentions. Joseph is enough for me, and I really think I should suffer by the change, even if I had the opportunity to deceive him with the admiral. It is really funny; ugly as he is, nobody is as handsome as my Joseph. Oh! the old monster! What a hold he has taken on me! And to think that he has always lived in the country, and has been all his life a peasant!

But where Joseph especially triumphs is in politics. Thanks to him, the little café, whose sign, "To the French Army," shines over the whole neighborhood, in big letters of gold by day, in big letters of fire by night, is now the official rendezvous of the conspicuous anti-Semites and the noisiest patriots of the town. These come here to fraternize, in heroic sprees, with sub-officers of the army and non-commissioned officers of the navy. There have already been some bloody fights, and several times, apropos of nothing, the sub-officers have drawn their swords, threatening to kill imaginary traitors. The night that Dreyfus landed in France I thought that the little café would tumble down under the cries of "Long Live the Army!" and "Death to the Jews!" That night Joseph, who is already popular in the town, had a mad success. He mounted a table, and shouted:

"If the traitor is guilty, let him be sent back. If he is innocent, let him be shot."

On every hand they shouted:

"Yes, yes! Let him be shot! Long live the army!"

This proposition had carried the enthusiasm to the height of paroxysm. Above the shouting, in the café, could be heard only the clashing of swords and the pounding of fists on the marble tables. Some one, having ventured to say nobody knows what, was hooted, and Joseph, rushing upon him, smashed his mouth with a blow of his fist, and broke five teeth for him. Struck repeatedly with the flat of a sword, torn, covered with blood, and half dead, the unforunate man was cast, like so much filth, into the street, always to the cries of "Long Live the Army! Death to the Jews!"

There are moments when I am afraid in this atmosphere of debauchery, among all these bestial faces, heavy with alcohol and murder. But Joseph reassures me.

"That's nothing," he says. "That is good for business."

Yesterday, coming back from the market, Joseph announced, gaily rubbing his hands:

"Bad news. There is talk of a war with England."

"Oh! my God!" I cried. "Suppose Cherbourg should be bombarded?"

"Pooh! Pooh!" sneered Joseph. "Only I have thought of something; I have thought of a stroke, a rich stroke."

In spite of myself I shuddered. He must be contemplating some immense rascality.

"The more I look at you," he said, "the more I say to myself that you have not the head of a Breton. Oh! no, you have not the head of a Breton. You have rather an Alsatian head. Hey? That would make a fine show behind the bar."

I was disappointed. I thought that Joseph was going to propose some terrible thing. I was proud already at the thought of being admitted to partnership in a bold undertaking. Whenever I see him in reflective mood, my ideas are immediately inflamed. I imagine tragedies, nocturnal wall-scalings, robberies, drawn knives, people in the agony of death on the forest heath. And it was nothing but a petty and vulgar piece of advertising.

With his hands in his pockets, and his blue skull-cap on his head, he swayed to and fro, in a droll fashion.

"Do you understand?" he insisted. "At the outbreak of a war a very pretty Alsatian, finely dressed, would inflame hearts and excite patriotism. And there is nothing like patriotism to get people drunk. What do you think of it? I would put you in the newspapers, and perhaps even on posters."

"I prefer to remain in the costume of a lady," I answered, a little dryly.

Thereupon we began to quarrel. And for the first time we came to violent words.

316

"You did not put on so many airs when you were intimate with everybody," cried Joseph.

"And you? . . . When you . . . Oh! you had better let me alone, because I could say too much."

"Strumpet!"

"Thief!"

A customer came in. The discussion ceased. And at night there was a reconciliation, with kisses.

I am going to have a pretty Alsatian costume made for me, of silk and velvet. Really I am powerless against Joseph's will. In spite of this little fit of revolt, Joseph holds me, possesses me, like a demon. And I am happy in being his. I feel that I shall do whatever he wishes me to do, and that I shall go wherever he tells me to go . . . even to crime!

March, 1900.

Irene

by Albert de Routisie

Don't wake me up, for God's sake, you bastards, don't wake me up, look out I bite I see red. How revolting daylight again more nastiness instability sourness. I want to go back into the blind sea enough lightning what's the meaning of these constant storms they want to make me live the life of thunder they've replaced my ears with pieces of sheet metal there are firedamp explosions with each breath of my chest my miners are fleeing through the galleries of anguish it's blowing up there's one explosion after another. But it's not daylight it's dynamite. They're sticking swords through my eyelids they're digging fingers into my throat they're rubbing my skin with the

3

gravel of waking. Don't pull off my fingernails plunged into the compost of dreams my flesh sticks to the darkness night is in my mouth my blood won't flow. I'm asleep for God's sake I'm asleep.

Brutes I'm going to yell I'm yelling brutes sons of sows buggered by prayer stools abortions of dirty underwear latrine mud runs in whores' stockings domestic toads purulent mucous membranes vermin let go of me rhododendron-blight armpit-hairs candles louse-clippings rat-grease chips chips black dejecta let go of me I'll kill you I'll grind you I'll pull off your balls I'll chew your nose I'll I'll trample you.

Dead dead they're going to wake me up they're waking me. Come to me waterfalls whirlwinds cyclones. Onyx the depths of mirrors the holes of pupils mourning dirt photography roaches crime ebony betel man-faced African sheep priestly rabble come to me cuttlefish-ink crankcase-oil tobacco-juice decaying teeth north winds plague come to me garbage and melancholy thick birdlime paranoia fear come to me from the hissing shadows from the cavalcades of conflagrations of coal towns and peat bogs and the stinking exhalations of railroads in brick cities everything that resembles the make-up of moonless nights everything that's torn up before the eyes into spots into flies into cinders into mirages of death into howls into despair spittle of cachou crabs of licorice rages magic residues muscats seals colloidal gold bottomless pit. Come to me blackness.

Asses dung vomit fags fags rotten pigs horse-chestnuts urine-brine excrement bloody spit menstrual fluid ugh caterpillar-sweat glue snot slobber you you pus and old semen abominable discharges swellings burst bladders moldy cunts shitty lungs garlic-belches.

If you've loved only once in the world don't wake me up if you've loved!

The bad state of my affairs having made me almost destitute, even more than poverty the haunting memory of a terrible episode that I would just as soon have forgotten made me accept an invitation from some relatives who lived in the provinces. C——, where I arrived with my phantoms, did not offer me precisely the diversion I had expected. I am not made for family life. I reduced it to a minimum. I appeared at meal times. I consumed the rest of the time in leisurely walks, and even more in long reveries in my room, away from the window, from which I could see only a bleak stretch of empty street, lined by those gray houses which bear on their faces all the dreariness of eastern France. The town went to bed early and got up early just to wake me with the slamming of its shutters, for by the time I got to the window there was no longer a living soul in the street, except for artillery officers' orderlies walking horses with the saintlike air of flunkeys. Three or four cafés did not really open before eleven o'clock or so, till then dirty water was sloshed between your feet on the pretext of washing the floor, then the sand flew, you got it in your mouth with quick sorry-excuse-mes; they were wretched places whose sagging seats might not have been too bad if it had not been for the incredible filth of the tables and the truly painful gloom of the mirrors, which flies had transformed into unspeakable fingernails, like those of the waiters. The most acceptable of these pleasure spots was on a surly square, not far from the military quarter, an establishment where there was red velvet, and checkered patterns on the mirror frames. One was quickly deafened by the noise of the billiard table, however, for as bad luck would have it the room had an unfortunate echo that applauded the caroms. After two sojourns in that Eden I began to recognize the faces of the habitués, five or six people including three officers and their mistresses, who counted for nothing. The hideous truth about the lives of the citizens of C—— was rapidly revealed to me by loud voices. The arrival of a new tax collector was a topic of conversation for three days. I learned that Professor So-and-So's wife was not an honorable person. There was gossip about a watchmaker's wife but nothing specific was stated. As for the postmistress, however, someone had been seen passing by her window, and he could be named, it was no mystery. I stopped going to the café.

The countryside, the woods, kept me occupied a while longer. Then I took a violent dislike to them and confined myself to my room. The prodigious slowness of time, the horrible punctuality of the meals, my reading of what I found in the library of the house, and especially a relentless memory, gave me a rapid desire to flee that miserable place. But how could I? Everything came back to an image that possessed me and that I was determined to drive away once and for all. I had no complaint against that woman, really, except that she did not love me. Even if she had believed she did. Even if she had said so. Never mind. She was so incredibly like a pearl. Physically. The luster of a pearl. To drive away that luster I tried to think about other women. I began going out again, and looking. Fat lot of good it did. The French provinces. The ugliness of French women. The stupidity of their bodies, their hair. Dishwater. So much for that.

That damned prick of mine, there was the hitch. At first it seems like nothing. You don't care about it. Then time passes. It makes a weight. Standing up, sitting down again. It makes me feel sick. Not exactly, but after lunch, a . . . a queasy stomach, a need to move laboriously. Yet I have a calm temperament. Even. Nothing tremendous. As far as possible from amorous exploits. Once I've done it, I don't always feel like doing it again. Often I don't get a good erection. But I can't stand prolonged continence. Maybe it's a matter of circulation. Anyway, it plays hell with me. Impossible to think about anything. In C—— it would have been better to jerk off. Considering what there was in the way of ass. Officers' mistresses who were bored while their ball-carriers were on the drill field. I'd have had to buy them a drink, and chat with them. It would have made me better informed about the garrison. But I'd had enough of false intrigues, hollow virtues, fake defenses. No, I didn't have the patience. It would have been better to jerk off. It's nice to say, probably for you that makes everything all right. Me. So I handled myself a little, then since there was no air in that blasted room I leaned out the window and scrutinized the street. Ah, amorous inspiration wasn't rising from the pavement with that niggardly smell of cook-ing which characterizes our heroic Lorraine. It did me no good to look at myself in the mirror, full face, three-quarters, profile. To run my hand over my balls. To squeeze my prick hard enough to cry. That's how I am, might as well make the best of it. I stood there with that congested, terrible ridiculous appendage. I looked at myself with shame. And a certain rage. I stuck wet handkerchiefs in my pants. Meal times regularly found me in an impossible posture, and I had to go through complicated gymnastics before I could go downstairs to table without thoroughly offending family modesty.

A dream brought a little respite to my continuous overexcitement: six women austerely dressed above the waist had surrounded me while I was engaged in tying the ropes that held the scaffolding of a house under construction to a ring to which a horse had

11

also been tied. They moved around me in a circle, bending down, with their arms around each other's waists. Each was fingering the clitoris of the woman on her left and wiggling her tongue in the ass of the one on her right, who writhed to make better contact. In my dream it was perfectly natural, and they kept turning around me. And they rubbed their swollen vulvas against me. Dressed in a pair of scanty linen shorts, I felt myself reaching a mythological volume. An old woman who was there, wearing a rosary adorned with numerous religious medals, took my prick in her mouth, and I awoke in great embarrassment. Talk about something that gives you a hangover. Then that discomfort in the sheets, the sticky hair, the time it takes you to make up your mind to get out of bed and wash. The respite lasted only twenty-four hours. Besides a horrible feeling of waste, disgust, and everything else. Three days later another dream. Lying in my garbage I decided to go to the brothel.

Family jokes about that honorable edifice had told me the name of the street where it was located. I easily found it in the poorest quarter of the town, a working-class quarter whose morals didn't have to be supervised by the municipality because it was "not inhabited by the bourgeoisie." It was a quarter of empty houses. During the day the men and women worked in factories. In a street that angled off sharply I saw the house, which had only two barred windows on that street and a thick, studded door at the end of a long gray wall. A real prison, if it hadn't had its lantern. It was just after lunch. The assistant madam, a tall, gawky woman, apologized for presenting only three girls to me: two were engaged, two were still taking a nap. A stale smell of food lingered on their skin. A sad August with shallots. Dreary. The fattest of the three was simpering with a scarf, she looked like a big fidgeting turd. Putrid blonde hair. And short little hands that hadn't been washed after lunch. She probably stuffed herself. The second one had what's called a dreamy face, because she had a big jaw that didn't close right. Her little shoes were obviously too tight for her enormous housemaid feet. She must have had corns. I preferred the third one. She would have been a chestnut blonde if her peroxide hadn't been badly applied so that it revealed a relative secret at the roots of her hair. Her little face of a cat that had fornicated with a rat, on a long, slovenly body that looked as if it would taste like

IRENE

Fallières Phosphatine, didn't leave me insensitive. Besides, I'd been stiff as a board for the last two hours. She called me her fat tomcat despite my skeleton-like appearance, and immediately sprayed spit in my mouth rather winsomely. The two other ladies had resumed their occupations, one was crocheting, the other was reading *La Vie de Guynemer* by Henry Bordeaux. We went upstairs. It turned out that she'd been bored, she didn't like to read, she didn't know how to crochet. So I'd come at a good time. She drew attention both to an orange and gold Chinese vase containing big cloth irises that were curled downward, showing their wire, and to her breasts. They were already very close together, but she pushed them still closer, with one hand, until they touched, because she thought that natural scantiness was her most attractive feature. Her mound was prettily shaded by hairs that had kept their own color. Her labia, a little long, drooped. For her rather long body, her shoulders were quite round, and her neck was barely beginning to show pudgy folds, exaggerated by cream. On the bed she suddenly looked like a pile of macaroni. She was restless, she wanted to do something imaginative. She roguishly showed me her ass. She rolled over. She squirmed and said, "You're getting all worked up, oh, what a lecher," etc. It was useless. Nothing had the slightest effect on me now, a cannon shot couldn't have made my erection go down. She said she wanted to get herself worked up and grabbed me as I was undoing my clothes, with my pants down and my shoes still on. From the bed she'd thrown herself onto she moved her mouth forward like an animal absolutely different from herself. I saw a blue tooth in it, because of a cheap filling. She held my prick energetically. As soon as her tongue touched it, sperm spurted up to her eyes. I'd hardly felt what had happened there. In fact, it was no better than a dream.

She was annoyed. Now she would have to go back downstairs and stare at the wall. She washed her face in the water that was already in the bidet. Sounds were coming from the next room. "They seem to be doing all right in there," I said, to say something. She lit up like a fireworks display that suddenly understands what it's writing on the sky. She squeezed her breasts against each other again, she would have sewed them together if she could, and motioned me to follow her. She led me to the door, looked through the keyhole and explained, "It's the

15

nymphomaniac, that's what we call her. She likes it so much it's a habit with her, she takes on three at a time, here, look." On the bed I saw, not very clearly, a disheveled artilleryman lying on his back. Strad-dling him was a bulky girl with sagging breasts, rolls of fat over her ribs, a wide goitrous neck, big eyes and a little mouth like a saber cut. She was writhing like a soul in hell. Facing her, the two other cus-tomers, two troopers with blank eyes and no fore-heads, were peacefully playing with themselves on their chairs, with a stupid look on their faces, waiting their turn. "Yes, she likes it so much they all give her less, you understand, but since they go with her three at a time she makes more. It works out better for all of them. Not for us, though. But she's in good with Madame. She's a dyke too so you understand. I'm telling you she never stops. In fact, it's disgusting. When she doesn't have anybody, she rubs herself. She's not a woman, she's a river. You can tell the chairs she sits on by the spots on them. Even at the table. I used to sit by her but I had to change places, it turned my stomach." One of the soldiers sitting in the room was getting impatient. On his pig-face I saw a little rain of sweat which, by a sympathetic phenomenon, reproduced a clearly visible analogous

sprinkling on the plump buttocks of the nymphomaniac, whose light blue garters I noticed. He stood up,
and treading heavily, because of his boots, went over
to the bed where his comrade was grunting, so
astounded at giving a whore such pleasure that he'd
forgotten to move. Anyway she was moving enough
for both of them. I also noted that on the mantelpiece
the same vase instead of irises contained satinflowers
and, an unprecedented anomaly to the best of my
knowledge, a calendar from the Galeries Nancéiennes
almost made it possible to know what day of the
month it was.

The impatient soldier had taken hold of the
woman, she was twisting and turning, "Stop it, you're
tickling me," and it made her thrust more vigorously
with her ass. This tempted the interrupter, and I
saw him, with incredible precision and a rapidity that
bordered on the miraculous and probably owed much
to the excellent pyrotechnic training given in the
garrison at C——, jump onto the quilt without letting go of either his prick or the woman, yet without
disengaging the latter, whose partner was solidly
plugged into her, and in the same movement insert
said prick between the little minx's buttocks so felic-

itously that it plunged straight into her asshole, while its owner, sliding back a little, found himself sitting on the foot of the bed with his legs stretched out along the original occupant, caressing his armpits with his boots. The first man yelled, and the trio swayed while the woman blissfully bounced on both pricks, constantly releasing her usual disquieting juices. The third trooper was still amusing himself with broad, nonchalant gestures. The nymphomaniac called him. "Psst, sweetheart, get on the bed. No, in front of me. Yes. Stay standing, bend your knees a little. You sure are big." He got in position, and she set about sucking him off. I stopped looking. "Well," said my companion, tickling me, "doesn't it get you stirred up again to see things like that?" Not at all, as a matter of fact. I pulled up my pants. What sadness there is in all the erotic performances! I think of the awkwardness of dogs in the street, flocking together and all trying to outfuck each other. The dogs in the next room wore boots, that was all. Then the whole thing always goes back to the same architectural platitude. When they've built a pyramid with their bodies, they've reached the end of their imagination. They all fire their shots, more or less at random, and finally the compound marionette collapses and flattens in sweat, body hair, and sperm. A grotesque, deflated balloon. When I think that those antics were a fad in "society" some time ago. But then they did it in an artistic manner. The height of elegance was to build a cathedral. Certain people whose names are on everyone's lips are even said to have made a reproduction of the Cathedral of Chartres in their town house one night, without leaving out a single Gothic arch! They had to keep changing the flying buttresses because they wouldn't wait till the last stone was put in place before following their inclinations.

My companion didn't feel like going back down to the parlor. She liked the bedrooms, the child, she felt they were homier. And she was under orders not to stay in them between customers, on the pretext that it was something that wasn't done in a well-run house. "Actually I understand you, I don't like all that fancy stuff either, but wait till you see the next room!" She immediately caught herself. "No, no, I can't show you. Such a refined man—he's chosen me twice—and then there's his reputation!" I stopped getting dressed, her last phrase interested me. She made me swear I was a stranger staying in C—— for only a little while and that I didn't know anyone's face there, then she led me to the second door on the left, where behind a tapestry cleverly unraveled by a curiosity that was no doubt habitual a little peephole made it possible to see into the next room unknown to the customer, too confident in the efficacy of the Gobelin tapestry. I first saw a woman who struck me as unquestionably the most beautiful one in that indiscreet bordello. She had dark hair, forget-me-not eyes and tiny little breasts with nipples as long as cigars. She had very wide hips and absolutely round buttocks. Her black stockings perfectly suited her slender, agitated legs. She was playing with little red slippers, constantly putting them on and taking them off while she watched her customer undress. The latter, a short, stocky man who was beginning to lose his hair, turned around. He had a big, fan-shaped blond beard. My God, it was the mayor of the town, I'd seen him one evening at my relatives' house. "He's a very respectable man," my accomplice explained to me. "He can't always go to Paris, you understand, so he comes here, but he keeps it a secret. He can't keep a woman in this town. Besides the fact that it costs a lot of money, nobody would vote for him. So what else can he do?" For the moment the mayor, in his shirttails, was spreading a folded drawsheet on the bed. I expressed surprise. "You'll see for yourself. He has a little weakness. As soon as he comes he shits, oh not much, but a little. He can't help it. A little bit of soft, liquid shit. Like a baby. You'll see." She was wrong, I wasn't going to see, I straightened up and walked away from the observation post. She then lavished all sorts of seductive wiles on me that I understood very well. The money slipped into her shoe and I slipped into the street.

This little excursion didn't solve anything: I slept peacefully for one night. The next day it began all over again. And the idea of going back to the whore-house disgusted me. Besides, I had no desire to be exhibited to the neighbors through keyholes or peep-holes. My dreams came back. They didn't tire me at all. A few family scenes added to my bad humor. There was a little wrangle over a vanished fork in which I sided with the maid. Alas, the maid was old and ugly, and smelled bad.

Whatever I think naturally expresses itself. Each man's language varies with each man. I, for example, do not think without writing, I mean that writing is my method of thinking. The rest of the time, not writing, I have only a reflection of thought, a kind of grimace of myself, like a memory of what it is. Others rely on different procedures. Thus I greatly envy erotics, whose eroticism is their expression. A magnificent language. It is really not mine.

Notwithstanding what I think of the limitations of erotic experience, of the inescapable, unavoidable repetition of an elementary theme that is perfectly reducible to any other indifferent action, I have the deepest respect for those to whom this limitation seems to be freedom itself. They are the true masters of the physical world, the perfect executioners of a kind of metaphysic of annihilation in which, for me, the spectator, all morality is summed up. He among you who has not dreamed of the idea of death in the midst of fornication, let him interrupt me here. I am well aware that everything in the possible complica- tions of sensual pleasure that is irremediably poor for unfortunate individuals of my stamp has for others the prodigious metaphorical value which I attribute only to words. I mean which words impose on me. I am probably deaf to that special, immense poetry. I can conceive it. Hence the terrible *finiteness* of my sensations and, worse, of my life. Eroticism: that word has often led me into a field of bitter reflections. I am known as a proud man. Let it pass. During the period of which I am speaking, I let my thoughts wander at great length, in the solitude of my room, before the distressing flowered wallpaper, over erotic subjects and their importance in my eyes. The erotic idea is the worst mirror. The glimpses of oneself that one catches in it are enough to make one shudder. An ordinary pervert, how I would like to be an ordinary pervert. This wish told me a great deal about my deep concept of all truth. I do not like very much to think about a person's sexual adventures, yet I must acknowledge that mine are all over. Now and then the newspapers give us rather incomplete stories which go from commonplace crimes of passion to stupefying excesses, to admirable aberrations which, for my part, plunge me into abysses of regret and reverie. I then take my own measure, and I do not feel proud. I am not a magician, and that realization is not without sadness. The magic of pleasure is perhaps the most extraordinary, with the material, the marvelously material aspect that it involves. And its disconcerting confirmation, sperm like the snow of mountaintops.

It pleases me . . . Those words stop me. It would not please me if it were to be more of the same. To mix someone up in all this whom nothing seemed to mix up in it at the time, someone who, I now know, meant much more to me than I was willing to believe. It is to you that I address myself, my friend, my very dear friend, to you whose name cannot appear here, and who amid such considerations would have such good reason to be surprised that I should dare even to allude to your existence, to the strange rela-

tions which, however, united us elsewhere and probably forever, united something of you and something
of me. I shall see to it that this comes before your
eyes. I shall not bring it to you to read, as it would
be permissible for me to do. No, I know the way.
Someone else, unconsciously, will show you this, and
you will read it. You will read it alone. And at first
you may think I am addressing myself to another
woman. To what other woman really. Do you not
recognize a tone, which I have lost since I no longer
talk to you, since I no longer talk to you really. It is
in your character not to recognize yourself immediately. But when I remind you of the value you attached to a very special abandon, which other women
regard as a trifling favor, when I remind you that I
had confided to you how precious that favor was to
me, more precious than everything which after all I
expected of you, expected of you terribly, when I
remind you of the public place where *that* which is
nothing to the world occurred, of the noise, the
neighbors, the insipid orchestra, the gold of the pillars, the untouched glasses in front of us, my long
hope, then how could you dare, I nearly let slip your
name here, a name like the wind when it falls at your
feet, how could you dare not recognize yourself? It

was by you that amid physical harassments I was solely, and purely, haunted. You put your very cool hands on my forehead. When by myself, I felt your presence. You came back. A strange thought; it seemed to me that because of that you were dead, and I had terrible apprehensions at mail time which restrained me from going downstairs, near your fading image. How words betray us, when I said your image I did not want to make you believe I saw you. No. If I had seen you! I sometimes tried desperately to see you, by closing my eyes, or on the contrary opening them very wide on the shadows of the room. But you were there suddenly. Your walk. Your dress. It seemed that you chose to come precisely at the time when I was writing at my narrow table, with only the wall before me. Then the room with all its nooks and corners, and the area where the carpet was turning blue, belonged entirely to you. I knew you were walking back and forth behind my back, mute. Sometimes you came close to me. My heart would pound. I knew that to turn around would be to make you vanish. I did not turn around. I wrote. Little by little you became bolder. I felt your breath. I did not turn around.

IRENE

Those strange tacit rendezvous! There had been
no need to set a time for them. I could not have
cheated with you if I had wanted to. If someone had
then asked me to leave that accursed provincial town
. . . to be quite truthful, I would have gone, I would
have left you. But no one, and especially not you,
not you, can measure the despair it would have in-
volved. Evenings prolonged with a dim light still
brought you back, but changed. You were no longer
that companion of the afternoon, that elusive person
who put disarranged objects back in their usual places
without a word. You were sadder, more distant. You
never approached me in the shadows. I did not think
of asking you to.

One evening, however, I was wearier than usual
and you had not come. How it irritates me to say so
crudely what previously did without all the customary terms that accompany human movements
from one place to another. Come. It had everything
to do with coming. I knew you would not come, that
you never came. Yet sometimes you were there,
sometimes you were not. Come? At times we manage to lose all sense of the commonest conditions.
Suddenly your absent person underwent a singular
eclipse, as though it had obscured itself. You would

disappear again, without having yet appeared. And this by the immense effect of your eyes, which filled not only my memory but the room, the real room, with its chairs, the bed, the walls, the ceiling, my suitcase. Your boundless eyes. I no longer know to-day, even though I occasionally encounter you, what color your eyes are. Yes, I have forgotten your eyes to the point where seeing them again is a matter of such indifference to me. Indifference . . . oh no, words do not express love any more than they do the death of love. Your eyes that evening were a very pale blue, and in a single one of their glints the room huddles, the room in which I was not writing.

So I wrote. Time must have been burned by some sort of infernal caustic. The only one I know is thought, and I have said that writing is my only method of thinking. I wrote. I have always envied erotic individuals, those free people. They do not write. I did not really expect the kind of obsession that gripped me to be truly dissipated by anything but time. Poverty, and a terrible regret. I could hope for a little money toward the end of the summer. I had to hold out till then, physically, intellectually. I wrote. I followed what took shape there, like a traveler looking through a train window without great joy, watching an endless landscape slide past in which everything holds together, varies, and finally becomes all alike again, comes down to an unfolded folding post card. He does not have the illusion of having chosen that region from among a thousand others in order to reel off its chilling aspects. I did not have that illusion, and yet I did not turn my eyes away from the paper on which the market prices of imaginary securities were unwinding. A great confusion brought me back toward a region that was becoming precise. Through slowly dissipated fogs, a face strove to oppose my obsessions, an unreal face, and not the most beautiful one possible, but a face that drew a certain conjuring force from a previous and quite similar procedure. Around it, the elements of a world were falling into place. An odd structure. I looked back to the period when I had built that setting for the first time, placing various specters in it, most of which had never taken substance. I found myself the same in it as today. Already isolation, sadness, the impossibility of coming to rest, of accepting one fate among so many others that would have been equally unappealing to me. I was already undergoing the special pressure of an obtrusive body that took precedence over what I considered higher concerns. Already trying by some subterfuge to transform that tiresome and stupid hallucination and make it the substratum of some experimental adventure, already what filth, what poverty of the senses, what a miserable, rotten life. It was two years, three years earlier, what does it matter. I had at last left everything, so I thought, in the preceding weeks. The country. The country, despite its sun, early that year, did not sustain me well. Watching the water swirl in the very cold river I was going to swim in; hours in the already high grass, lying on my back, waiting for evening; the first flies; evening at last, with its great violet smell. A head cannot remain empty. Along the roads I traveled, walking up little valleys without any distinguishing feature, there were inns of a sort, with apple brandy. Not in all of them was the waitress talkative. One gets tired of calendar lithographs. On the square-ruled paper that is given to you parsimoniously, I became caught up in the game of new associations. My sentences swept me away. They were wide enough to carry along in their folds a few first names that stirred nothing, then came back, less modestly, and awoke. It was thus that, in the establishment of a wagoner named Gentil-Daniel, I became acquainted with Irène. She appeared in the conchshell of a sentence, suddenly. Beginning with the wind a kind of scene had constructed itself and might have continued. It broke down in front of that woman. I thought about her for a long time.

In C——, rereading what is going to follow, I found myself thinking about her again, and I thus passed from the power of one phantom to that of another. But the second one, through years of oblivion, had enriched itself with a specific body. It was no doubt everything that did not accompany the eyes whose disproportionate gaze I fled in the evening, everything that did not resemble those hazardous bodies, that I would have found again in crossing the town. It was by no means an ideal. Since I have not changed?

The kitchen servants looked at each other. A great wind that came out of the black, hollow sea, that came out of the sea full of naked drowned bodies, a great wind lifted, billowed the percale curtain with the sound of a sudden reef in the topsail. Bad looks had been seen on the road: faces of dust, irascible. All at once a supernatural night takes the country-side by the throat of the salt hills, by the hollows of the marshes where as is too well known the firedamp wanders which I swear is the returning souls of those engulfed in quicksand or to be fair and report the opinion common to all those who have shaken off forever the mouse-colored cloak of superstition the

33

unexplained and detonating combustion of the methane gas of peat bogs, and that is nothing to worry about, even in the supernatural night that suddenly swoops down toward the four o'clock of blue groves with damp dells, while there prowls somewhere a man, magnificent if one is to believe the carter back from the station, under the first broad drops of rain and in the disorder of the grass shivering with the foreseeing panic of insects. Curtain, you sigh like a breast. It sounds like. It sounds like the approach of love. When an imminent storm is already rolling its powerful wrestler's shoulders in the dark setting of the clouds, when a storm weighs down on an oppressed land where uneasiness stretches in isolated houses that maidservants were just washing with their wooden shoes off and a dishrag at the end of the broom pushed by their bare feet, when trickling sweat is already taking a whole people by the armpits, and when idle women put down the work they have voluntarily imposed on themselves to watch farmhands armed with pitchforks or hoes coming and going, whistling to put up a bold front and opening their shirts over their moist skin without knowing why, and to follow with their eyes, their eyes heavy and lusterless as billiard balls, the embarrassed bodies of those young men whose clothes seem to want to abandon them in the great perspiration of the electric springtime, then the percale curtain that has been swelling with all its strength, with all the power of the atmosphere, falls back with a clap, with a pure smack. It is said that doors and windows should be closed at the approach of the storm. Drafts must be avoided at all cost: they attract lightning, they attract the deadly discharge onto girls possessed by the spirit of sin in the cursed dwellings through which pass, without understanding anything about that leaden light or the flashing looks with which you burn them, Irene, unshaven plowmen and drivers haunted by memories of the town where women immediately in their underwear smile behind the blinds to the nasal sound of a phonograph. You must, Irene, avoid placing a burning mouth on the windowpane while those domestic figures, so long visited by your desires, are passing in the yard. The semblance of a kiss will no doubt draw the ardent tongue of the storm into your gaping lips better than a draft could do. Irene touches her hair and imagines the lightning hurling itself at her. She distractedly hears people at the other end of the room laughing and talking about the stranger who is making his way northward beneath the menace of the sky, in the midst of the man-eating mud. The damp floor gives off a smell of soap and resin. The animals are being taken into the barns: the roads in all directions are clogged with the woolly thrust of the flocks. The mares in the stable call desperately for a refused sweet. The dogs pace anxiously in front of the porch. The paralytic grand-father signals that he wants to speak. He is jostled. He wants to speak, he wants to speak, to speak ter-ribly. The others think of the goats rather than of him. He's nothing but a bother to us. He hasn't been able to talk for ten years now. He wants to speak. He slobbers. He looks at Irene, who blushes. The tenant farmer's son Gaston, who is doing his military service in the eastern part of the country, comes into the room singing. All eyes turn to an open wardrobe in which linen is sleeping. The yellow earth of the hills must already be sticking to the traveler's steps. The grandfather points to Irene. What's wrong with him now that old lunatic. What stupid things must go on in his mind. All the farmhands are going through the room on their way to the kitchen. Pierre, Joseph, Prudent . . . they joke with each other, elbow each other, hit each other in the stomach, in an aroma of wet hair. Gaston pinches Prudent's balls. They fight a little. One of them slips on an old piece of black soap: that makes him swear. What would you say in the marsh, then. Christ's whore, for sure, or Virgin of my ass. Gaston don't laugh, oh don't laugh at that blasphemy. Agile syphilis, and he will know nothing about it for another two weeks, is already stretching deep in his blood, ready to draw strange red flowers on his skin and livid lizards in the meanders of his nerves. If that isn't a pity. He caught the disease that will some day make him like the grandfather, choking in his chair, quiet, chatterbox! in the most common way at Nancy, and yet he is an infantryman, in a wretched dirty blue room above a bar, while the red permanganate tablets from which he absurdly expected effective protection were simmering over a little gas burner. The imploring eyes of his mother as she passes by with a pile of plates in her arms greatly excite the soldier on leave. He spits on the floor and shouts: *By God's prick!* Thunder covers the name of the Creator and the blasphemer's laughter. Rain loudly lashes the windowpanes. Irene sees the following flash of lightning in the grandfather's eyes and puts her hands over her ears. What is she afraid of? An oath or the outburst of celestial anger? She leans against the bread bin and its mouldings knead her gently.

"I've lost count of the years. At first I used to watch for the hand that would tear a sheet off the black calendar at the edge of my field of vision. Monday, Tuesday, I no longer understood those human distinctions very well. The days of the week were so much alike in my body. The day of the month made a song that was more distinct to my weakened eyes. That number growing on the wall never reached the value I would have liked to give it. Each month I madly hoped we would cross forever the frontier beyond which man begins counting from his thumb again. Then what happened? Did someone push my chair a little, did my field of vision become still narrower? I no longer saw the calendar, I mixed up the days and the months. The seasons enabled me to keep my bearings; finally I lost count of the years.

"I was twenty-five when I sat down forever. My daughter's child is old enough to arouse love in me. That makes me well over sixty, and that fire hasn't gone out, can't go out in the heart of my immobility. At first, when I still hoped for a distant recovery, and yet I've seen senile people and cripples, I made superhuman efforts to tell my wife with my eyes when she brushed against me that I was still, that I was precisely at that moment a man. She would put her hand on my shoulder and say, 'He's restless, how restless he is,' with a sweet, glowing hope, perceptible only to me, that a good congestion would eventually do away with me. She stayed for hours at a time, dispensing calm and advice to me, close, very close to me, without seeing, I never knew if she saw, without seeing the mingled bloody hatred and desire in the tragic pupils of my eyes. They danced in silence and quietude to move her. A tide of images rose in them, little by little it interposed itself between the world and me. Bodies, bodies, bodies of all the people around, my nailed hands ripped off your clothes, ripped off the clothes that revealed your damning

shapes, and at the same time ripped off your tempting skin, flayed you, and left on your whiteness and
on my corneas great streaks of red to die a foul death
without a confessor, a divine and roaring death secretly invoked by my convulsed flesh on the shore of
pleasure impossible to leave, forbidden to a man who
no longer has the use of his hands nailed to either
side of his inert thighs between which ludicrously
stands, enormous—in heaven's name suck, jerk off
or fuck!—a prick ready to burst through the walls,
and rising stiffly to the stars. One fine morning my
pious wife had the idea of reading the prayers for
the dying to me when my eyes betrayed a savage preoccupation. Sometimes she made my daughter sit at
my feet, and then, in my jumbled mind, incest joined
its thundering voice to the gale of blasphemies that
swept through me. 'Never forget your father, Victoire, or how patient I was in his misfortune,' the
good mother would murmur, 'or how I took care of
him, or how I loved him. Invalids already have one
foot in heaven. They share in the eternal peace of
the Good Lord in the clouds. The spirit of sin gradually leaves them. They don't die all at once, they
don't become angels all at once; but grace seeps into
them like a rising tide. Victoire, my darling, look into

your father's eyes and you'll see the heavenly blue slowly rising.' And Victoire would raise her eyes to me, the eyes of a naïve, obscurely troubled child. I saw a budding mystery in them, like the secrets of the great woods when the first violets breathe beneath the leafy branches. Then from the edges of her pure eyelids my gaze would glide over all her pearly skin, lingering on her lips for a moment in passing. A spot on them revealed the ink she had drunk in secret. The string of her scapular showed above her chemisette on the back of her narrow neck. Her two agile little hands sometimes touched my knees.

"No, I never knew if my wife saw. There were moments when I could have sworn that a kind of shiver passed between us that was not memory. Yes, and then immediately there was nothing more. Had I imagined it? I mistook my fever for hers. She was there, dignity personified, coming and going, all in black, because that was more in keeping with her situation. Oh how I raged against that anticipatory mourning! I wished I could dress her like an acrobat, strip her naked, put make-up on her, leave her with nothing but black stockings. She told her beads and sometimes kissed me on the forehead. The monster! But she brought my daughter to me, and I seemed to glimpse an expression of sly complicity on her face, and I no longer knew what to think. All the more because another feeling took possession of my senses and I tried to smile at Victoire. No, I'd only been dreaming again: my wife still spoke in that cold voice I knew so well. She told me the news. Her usual piti-less pity. One afternoon, though, I still remember, she came in to give me a drink. All of August was pressing down on the room. The air hadn't slammed the doors for weeks. A chicken was being plucked in the yard. It came over me suddenly. A strong gust. A motionless hurricane between our faces close be-side each other. I fiercely felt my inaccessible wife's ripe beauty, ready to disintegrate. The magnificent texture of her slightly moist skin, her brunette odor, her immense warmth. Did I understand? It seemed to me that she drew away from me with her eyes closed, that she stiffened, what silence. It seemed to me. It seemed to me. She fled, turning her head away. After all, it was merely sadness, for me or for herself. For herself, probably.

IRENE

"Meanwhile Victoire was growing up. Her eyes avoided mine. She furtively watched the farmhands. At first she hid nothing from me. She would sit beside me looking through illustrated books and sometimes spend a good quarter of an hour before the same picture, with a little mustache. Once she was right there, in my window recess. She had been sewing, and the sight of something outside had interrupted her. She stayed the way she was, with her needle in the air and her mouth half open; I saw her round arm. In the light her breasts quivered. I sensed them under her plaid dress: scarcely formed, unconscious, as though blind. I sensed those child breasts becoming hard, hard. She bent her neck, her lips trembled. Then her hand began sewing again, ardently. She didn't look up when one of the farmhands came in from the yard with a big innocent face and walked through the room, buttoning his pants. When the kitchen door closed behind my back, Victoire's eyes slowly rose from her sewing and moved toward the end of the room, but on the way they encountered mine. That was the beginning of my own daughter's hatred of me.

"Victoire and her mother were not the only ones

to rekindle those smoldering desires that the slightest thing could bring back to life. There were servant girls whose sole presence turned over my insides the way a plow turns over the earth. Only the new ones paid any attention to me. When they got used to me, they became indifferent. When I was still very young, it used to trouble some of them to see that frozen strength in me. There were some whose eyes would stray. Then they would hurry away, fearful; or else laugh. One of them, once. She'd realized what went on inside me. A big slow girl with big slow hands. A scullery maid. When there was no one else in the room, she would stand in front of me. Her face darkened. She let time flow. Then she spread her thighs far apart. She came back like that two or three times a day. She looked around the room. With one hand she straightened her hair. She never even brushed her sleeve against me during the six months she was on the farm. One morning during harvest time when everyone was in the fields, she came in as usual and planted herself in front of me. But she had something on her mind. She shook her head. She was debating a profound question. Suddenly she pulled up her skirt and showed me her mound. A pretty light brown mound, well rounded. She was wearing gray cotton stockings held up by strings. Her skirt dropped and she walked out, talking to herself: 'I'll have to see where I put the milk.' Three days later she left the farm, she had received a letter.

"Every spring I observed the resurgence of passion among the men and women on the farm. They didn't bother to hide anything from me. I knew about their affairs, their deceptions, their vices. From my corner I saw couples made and unmade, and sometimes curious triangles and complex arrangements. They didn't let my presence stop them from kissing each other: 'The old man? He won't say anything, he can't say anything,' and there were even some who were amused by my presence. Amused? In any case, there's no doubt that the tenant farmer, Gaston's father, made sure I saw him with different women several years in a row. He stood by the window, as though he were getting a breath of fresh air. Sometimes he even smoked his pipe. The woman would look at me as she worked on him, squatting on the floor. Or else she couldn't look at me. He stood watching the yard. He often called out to someone. That made the woman afraid. He would poke her with his knee.

[*Le Con d'Irène*]

"I got a positive pleasure from seeing men and women together. It seemed to me that the example overcame my infirmity. It excited me terribly. It even happened that such sights took me further than I would have thought. It always threw me into great embarrassment. But more and more I liked that embarrassment itself. More and more I liked what had made me ashamed at the beginning of my paralysis. I came to watch the men, to want them to desire the servant girls, or my daughter. I undressed them to see the effect that the sight of a breast or a shoulder couldn't fail to have on them.

"One winter my wife died buried in her mourning. I was taken to her body. She was tight-lipped. She was taking her secret with her. I wished I could shout out mine, I tortured my intractable face. People nudged each other. 'It's sad, the poor old man. She was so good to him.' Her death simplified my life a little. Victoire no longer felt bound by her mother's pretenses. She even laughed when the farmhands joked about me. I thought, 'Instead of wasting your time on me, take her.' Toward May, probably April, May, the tenant farmer came back to the window, and it was Victoire at his feet. She thought she was playing an outrageous trick on me. She laughed maliciously. I looked at her closely: I saw the same pure eyes as before, her little body, developed now. She still wore a scapular. The scene was repeated several times. I was agitated by a singular pleasure that she mistook for rage. Once when she stood up she passed very close to me and showed me her chapped lips.

"After everything here came to belong to her, Victoire, my daughter Victoire got married. She's had lovers, she's had children. She's never stopped pursuing me with her hatred. And I've acquired a taste for her hatred that she can't guess. I love her, I've never loved anyone in the world but her, I give you my word. She's showed herself to me in the arms of all the men she's had, I really think all of them. I've even seen her with servant girls. She's become a real woman, solid. She's wilted a little. She's past forty. She's my daughter. There's a long story in the depths of the looks we cross. I love her tenacious hatred, and I feel it every day. I love the contempt that shows through in every word she says to me. She subdues men. The tenant farmer of her youth is still in her service. He's married too. He's like a well-trained dog before her. A masterful woman. Ah, if her mother had been like that.

"It's been forty years now, no less, that I've been nailed down in the midst of passions while they gnaw at me without destroying the dike that separates me from the world. A great indifferent commiseration surrounds the chairs of the helpless. Idiotic spectators, you will never understand anything. I wouldn't give up my place for all the gold in the world. Preserved from all the puerile concerns of men, I devote all my time here to sensuality. My reduced senses have attained extreme refinement, and I have come to know pleasure in its purity. Age has touched my body very little. Although my hair has turned white, I have not worn out my life in the bed of a woman who lies dying every night in her wrinkled skin. What true freedom in my apparent slavery. In the days when I had the power to walk and speak, I had to take account of others. I didn't dare to think, everything seemed criminal to me. I limited myself. I dreaded the questions that were put to me. A great injustice puts one at ease. Today there's no longer any misfortune that could affect me, no event that could disconcert me. Thus I've learned to take plea sure in myself, and in others. I don't think of dying. I'm not bored. It's no harder not to be bored than not to speak, and I can no longer speak. Now and then the violent desire to be like everyone else returns to me. Those brief crises make me better aware of my good fortune. What's the worst thing that could happen to me? The house burning down? Almost no part of my body is subject to physical suffering. It would be a beautiful sight, and I'm not far from wishing the house *would* burn down, just so I could discover the instinctive reactions in all those men, in those women, in Victoire, and her daughter Irene, and die in the midst of the spectacle of these dizzying revelations, of that disheveled, half-naked populace, running at the top speed of their lives and feelings. If you only knew, you young people who laugh at the invalid, the kind of secret joy, the tremor that's awakened in my numbed flesh by the light sound of your derision. Ah, laugh, go on laughing, young louts in your twenties. I *hold* you by the very pleasure I feel in listening to you. Go on laughing at me, go on, please, laugh till you turn red, till you choke, till you suffocate. There. There. How their skin tightens. They too think I'm angry then. They begin by heartily detesting me. Dirty old man, they think, he'd try to stop everybody from having any fun if he weren't rotting in his own slobber. They insult me: they give it a try, they know that Victoire, Madame Victoire, won't mind. The boldest ones jostle me. Unfortunately they don't dare to mistreat me too much. There are times when I think some of them are going to beat me. But they don't. Not this time anyway. I used to be handsomer than any of you, and stronger, and more intelligent. I've been loved. You would have paid me your respects in those days. I've lived in the city. An educated man, you brute beasts. I was enamored of insoluble prob-lems. I'd tell you too much about it if I could talk. But, blessed be the name of syphilis, I can't talk. You'll never guess *who* has been here for forty years. Ah, why don't you slap me, what foolish supersti-tion of weakness holds you back? My life makes me dizzy. I feel an immense, dominating joy in my pants, which I dirty: beat me, I tell you, I'm perhaps some-thing better, something more than Alexander or Julius Caesar!"

Fish fish it is I, I call you: pretty agile hands in the water. Fish you resemble mythology. Your loves are perfect and your ardors inexplicable. You do not approach your females and enthusiasm comes to you with the mere idea of the semen that follows you like a thread, with the idea of the mysterious deposit that made another mute, anonymous exaltation in the shadows of the gleaming waters. Fish you do not exchange love letters, you find your desires in your own elegance. Lithe masturbators of both sexes, fish I bow to the intoxication of your senses. Would to heaven, would to earth that I had the power thus to come out of myself. How many crimes avoided, how many tragedies withdrawn into the prompter's box. Your transparent transports, death of Christ, ah how I envy them. Dear divinities of the depths, I stretch and writhe if I think for a moment of the moment of your minds in which is formed the beautiful aquatic plant of sensuality whose branches spread out in your subtle beings, while the water vibrates around your solitudes and gives forth a song of ripples toward the banks. Fish fish, quick images of pleasure, pure symbols of involuntary pollutions, I love you and invoke you, fish like hot-air balloons. Throw into the hollow of your wakes a ballast of passion, the sign of your intellectual grandeur.

Fish fish fish fish
But man also sometimes makes love.

The gaze of lovers marks off between the two limits of the couple a zone where attention is concentrated and personalities dissolve. It is at these boundaries, when the light of desires is decomposed from delirium red to consciousness purple that the perceptible mira-cle imperceptibly occurs. Then then . . . but let us not anticipate.

For the moment let me bring you, reader—you who paid so dearly last week for the right to witness through a periscope a rather brief scene which from the cellar where you had been hidden you took for a genuine exaltation of the human soul, but which was not one at all: that pale suburban team that had

55

been camouflaged in advance for fear that pity would seize you, you or someone else, for it was not specifically you that one expected, at the sight of what debauchery and bad food can do when they put their minds to it, that team had learned from sad everyday experience the art of feigning sensual pleasure without feeling its bite—into Irene's bedroom, yes it is Irene who is making love. I easily recognize her even naked, her breasts are a little long for my taste. As for the man, he has his back to me: I am unable to attach a name to him and besides if I have had occasion to encounter that body somewhere, it was no doubt under clothes and for me clothes make a man's personality if not a woman's. If a naked man has whiskers, I seem to see Jesus Christ. But the man who was spreading his thighs above Irene and riding her hard, when he lifts himself I see four breasts that hesitate to abandon each other, judging from the little lateral movements of his jaws, was clean-shaven. Unless he had an imperial or a close-cropped mustache. Leaning on his left arm with his right hand on Irene's right side. Grabbing her left shoulder from behind with his right hand. Giving the impression of being greatly excited. Murmuring oh do you feel me. Irene seeming fearful at first, holding back at first, then letting herself go, following, provoking, exaggerating the race. Now she is carried away.

It is the male's turn to restrain the wench. Hold on there, not so fast. He does not want to come yet, he wants to enjoy at leisure the desire he feels. It impels him, he curbs it. In the depths of pleasure there remains only a weak memory, a regretful reflection, of the desire that was its source. Reader when you make love, stop thus. But Irene will not have it that way. Her hips thrust like a shout bursting from a throat. She moves her pelvis and belly in a circle, she arches herself, her thighs open and grip her immobilized partner's penis. In a magnificent gesture he draws back and shows her that his desire for her has not diminished: he brings out an enormous smoking prick from the convulsive nook. It is not resigned, it rises and quivers when, in the course of its withdrawal, its sensitive extremity rubs against the entrance of the pursuing den. His tired balls limply slap her cunt. Young industrious bourgeois worker and you, high official of this Republic, I permit you to cast your eyes on Irene's cunt.

O Irene's delicate cunt!

So small and so big! It is here that you are at ease, man finally worthy of your name, it is here that you again find yourself on the scale of your desires. Do not fear to move your face close to that place, and already your loquacious tongue cannot hold still, that place of delight and shadow, that patio of ardor, in its pearly limits, the fair image of pessimism. O cleft, soft, moist cleft, dear dizzying abyss.

It is in that human wake that ships finally lost, their engines now unusable, returning to the child-hood of voyages, hoist the sails of despair on a make-shift mast. Between the curly hairs how beautiful the

IRENE

flesh is: beneath that embroidery well divided by the amorous axe, the skin amorously appears, pure, foamy, milky. And the folds of the labia majora, joined at first, gape. Charming lips, your mouth is like that of a face leaning over a sleeper, not trans' versal and parallel to all the mouths in the world, but fine and long, and it forms a cross with the speaking lips that tempt it in their silence, ready for a long pinpoint kiss, adorable lips that have given kisses a new and terrible meaning, a meaning forever per' verted.

How I love to see a cunt bounce.

How it strains toward our eyes, how it bulges, attractive and swollen, with its hair from which emerges, like the three nude goddesses above the trees of Mount Ida, the incomparable luster of the belly and the two thighs. Touch, go on touch: you could not make better use of your hands. Touch that voluptuous smile, trace the ravishing gap with your fingers. There: let your two motionless palms, and your phalanges enchanted at that advanced curve, join toward the hardest, the best point, which lifts the holy ogive at its peak, o my church. Do not move, stay, and now with two caressing thumbs take advantage of that wearied child's good will, thrust downward, with your two caressing thumbs gently, more gently, push apart the beautiful lips with your two caressing thumbs, your two thumbs. And now, hail to thee, pink palace, pale jewel case, alcove a little disordered by the grave joy of love, vulva appearing for a moment in its fullness. Under the clawed satin of dawn, the color of summer when you close your eyes.

It is not for nothing, or by chance or premeditation, but by that *felicity* of expression which is like sensual enjoyment, like falling, like the abolition of being in the midst of spurting semen, that those little sisters of the labia majora have been given, like a celestial blessing, the name of nymphs which fits them like a glove. Nymphs at the edge of the fountain basins, in the heart of the gushing waters, nymphs whose rosy tint frolics beside the well of shadow, more variable than the wind, scarcely a graceful undulation in Irene, and in a thousand other, a thousand scalloped, torn effects, lace of love, nymphs who join above a knot of pleasure, and it is the adorable clitoris that quivers from the look that lights on it, the button that I barely graze, that every-thing changes. And the sky becomes pure, and the body is whiter. Let us handle it, that fire alarm. Al-ready a fine sweat beads the flesh at the horizon of my desires. Already the caravans of the spasm ap-pear in the far reaches of the sands. They have walked, those travelers, carrying gunpowder in flasks and shoddy wares in crates with rusty nails, from towns of terraces and long paths of water dammed by black docks. They have crossed the mountains. Here they are in their striped cloaks. Travelers, trav-elers, your soft fatigue is like the night. The camels follow them, carrying foodstuffs. The guide waves his stick and the sandstorm rises from the earth, Irene suddenly recalls the hurricane. The mirage appears, and its beautiful fountains. . . . The mirage is sitting naked in the pure wind. A beautiful mirage of man entering the quim. A beautiful mirage strong-limbed like a pile driver. A beautiful mirage of springs and heavy melting fruit. Here are the travelers raving mad, rubbing their lips. Irene is like an arch above the sea. I have not drunk for a hundred days, and sighs quench my thirst. Huff, huff. Irene calls her lover. Her lover with an erection at a distance. Huff, huff. Irene agonizes and contorts herself. His erec-

tion is like a god above the abyss. She moves, he flees
from her, she moves and strains forward. Huff. The
oasis leans down with its tall palms. Travelers, your
burnooses turn in the scouring sand. Irene pants to
the breaking point. He contemplates her. Her cunt
is misty with expectation of his prick. On the illusory
saline lake, the shadow of a gazelle . . .

Let your damned in hell jerk off. Irene has come.

When the leaves on the forehead of the forests have lost their green purses, when their stems have finally forgotten the circulation of sap, and that hand which said good morning to the wind closes avariciously on the gold it has stolen from the splendor of the day, the foliage, dry now, ready to run aground in the harbor of dust, takes one last look, bitter and without regret, at the universe without greenery. Skeletons of veins, wave your wisdom still disguised by the make-up of autumn. I reflect that after all there may be enough childish pranks in the world of leaves to enable a being I like to picture as the color of the sprouts waving some day the slimmest of your re-

mains to play at last on the moss with the knucklebones of the plant kingdom. It is not even the hand
of a child. Neither is it that hand whose fall, far
more moving than that of the leaves, accompanies
the death predicted to touching consumptives by
sentimental doctors who show heaven and earth in
turn, it is not the hand of the priest accustomed to
the hysterical commonplaces of death, or the hand
that waits in a seaside shop for the impatience and
drunkenness of sailors, and sometimes of landsmen,
but of all the leaves swept away to their decline by a
fateful wind, more than branches those hands should
have made the poets of the anthology delirious, those
hands which about to be recognized by a mark on
their fingers are suddenly put through train doors
by criminals in tunnels and dispersed by a great slap
of the walls into the bloody night, autumn of murderous hands. To you, elegists. Reconstruct from
these scraps which in their union were the marvelous
instrument of murder and pillage, from these scraps
in smoke and speed, the fantastic land where this
point of human resignation, this hunted and haggard
moment, is the October of an indiscernible *something*.
And taking up the problem again by the ardent hair
of metaphor reflect that autumn and its russet mira-

cles, with its sylvan metabolism, serves as an image of the man who, like fingers pressing a sponge, squeezes out the slow, terrible transformations of his heart. Let him abandon his perspectives of wounded forests: I open to him a domain where he recognizes his mute sorrows when, without a word, the telltale hands take flight at the midnight of railroad tracks. If, exhausting his nostalgia in adapting that tragedy of the shadows to his personal case, he becomes lost in the corridors of analogy, that residential hotel whose doors all bear an echo as a number, let him thank me again, I have therefore turned him away from those deplorable symbols of platitudinous autumn, I have taken him by that detached and torn hand, I have drawn him with me to a forbidden stage of perturbation. He no longer knows whether he is the hand, the murderer, or the leaf. He seeks with horrible migraine throbbings the human equivalent of the ideal cyclone that has carried him away. Of what did he complain? He cannot read that diagram, he really detests images and the complication of their labyrinths. Yet it is quite simple, child. He has never been able to picture geometry in space, how could he not go astray in the mind? He clings to the fall of the leaves, and do I know exactly what that avalanche of sparks means to him? See him pass in the wind of his thought with his fist clenched around a bouquet of female corpses. What does he want with them? The absurd comparison of his life to the course of a year does not suffice to explain that surprising and grotesque tableau in which, contrary to the laws of gravity, the poor wretch's feet, far from touching the ground, are slightly turned up toward the clouds. The contents of his pockets escape from them and there one sees an autumn more singular than that of the trees, a little pencil stub, scraps of paper, a hundred sous in change, letters from indifferent people, samples for a winter suit, ah ah joker, I was not speaking of his shroud, a piece of ribbon, a pin. Reflect on the autumn of your pockets, my friend, of your telltale pockets when, in the tunnel of images, hunted down by incomprehension, you turn them inside out at the train door, it is too late, it is your heart that flees, your heart detached from the trees of the forests, where then has the child gone who used to ask his mother for hearts with which to play at knucklebones in the night?

How a life exiles itself! The years flee and leave a man, after so many peregrinations and metamorphoses, absolutely similar, himself, on the occasion of a little moral simile, of a circumstance which makes one remember. Is it true that one loves only once in a lifetime? I have met people who thought so. I have sometimes believed it. Now I violently oppose that inhuman concept. Yet love is high enough for me. It has remained everything I love. What makes everything bend. What makes one abandon everything in the world, and it is good that this is so.

IRENE

For years I had not encountered what for me was concretely clothed in an appearance, that mirage of black water, Irene. The other image, the living one, which I had tried to efface with her—had it really disappeared? That is a harsh thought for someone who often experiences the value of eternity. It had disappeared, it had disappeared. I was madly in love with an extraordinarily beautiful woman. With a woman in whom I had believed, as in the reality of stones. With a woman I thought had loved me. I was her dog. That is my way. Then something incomprehensible arose, something like a thought dissimulated between us, and it was the cruel time of *vacation* before I had fully realized the unusual thing that was happening in certain glances. It was out of the question that we should be in the same place during those summer months. A thousand reasons. I went off into a solitude where several complications of borders and railroad networks placed obstacles between us that were barely surmountable by writing. There was no need for obstacles. I received two very brief letters in three months. Two letters. You must weigh those envelopes, and understand me.

I had taken refuge with some friends who dis-

70

played useless solicitude for me. Every day the passing of the mailman made me pale till nightfall. Evenings went by with two or three drinks. Ah that was a summer. A summer of waiting. The woman I loved, no I would not let myself go to the point of talking about her again. I see too precisely a moment in a Paris park, on her lap she had the loose sheets I had written for her at that time, it was spring, behind a café, on iron chairs. If she wants to know the image I kept of her, let her be happy: she left me the prodigious image of a death agony, and thanks to her, that too ended.

In that southern country there were none of the ludicrous possibilities of C———. The countryside, and a very beautiful torrent into which I threw pebbles. So in a pigeon house that had been placed at my disposal I took to my drug once again. I wrote from morning till night. I sometimes evoked phantoms. New ones, old ones. One day I found myself thinking of Irene, and a social idea of her, a circumstantial idea, came to me.

After that, discouraged perhaps, I never saw her again.

There is not one detail of the farmhouse in which Irene grew up that has not long been engraved in her head: she knows not only its obvious arrangement, but also the irregularities of the wall, what distinguishes one tile of the floor, the variations in color of the ceiling beams. She has developed the habit, as someone who takes great care of his body notes its particulars, of interesting herself in the plaster, wood and bricks. She lives with that house as with herself. She is traversed by its odors. She perceives the seasons as it does, by the opening of the shutters, the heaping up of the harvests. She loves that infinite gamut of the year, its limit that still exasperates her savage sensuality, betrayed by that

73

loose knot of black and tawny hair which often comes undone, and which she impatiently tucks back in place.

She is unable to refuse herself anything. She does not like others. She has never liked others. They are her enemies, she has thought so since childhood. She sometimes forgets them, motionless. It then seems that there is no longer any reason why she should awaken. Or for her sleep, the heaviest in the world. She is heavy-set and violent. Rather tall, too, and haughty. Nonchalant. If her mother jostles her she gets a vicious look in her eye. She thinks about men a great deal. As she does about all pleasures. She is sensitive to their vigor and their beauty. She is not exactly promiscuous, being too concerned with not debasing her body. Not out of virtue. It seems that she goes to bed with everyone. This is a mistaken idea. She thinks for a long time about the man she has marked with her desire. She does not give herself all at once, by surprise. There is very little taste for whimsicality in her. She takes possession of a man as water does a marsh, by a slow infiltration.

At fourteen she abandoned herself to a farmhand.

[Le Con d'Irène]

Then had him dismissed immediately. To say that she is in love is like saying it of a bitch in heat. She is not sentimental with her lovers. When it comes over her, she must be satisfied. Or good-by. There are more than one who would ask nothing better. For she is beautiful, and pleasing, and fresh. And zealous in the work of love. She does not remain foreign to it. She does not shrink from the task. She is tireless, and when she is pearled with sweet sweat she has the glitter of pleasure, she is resplendent. Carnality with her is no small affair. She expects to share it. She says that she has no sense of trickery. That is why she detests priests, most of whom have wretched habits. There is no question of her compromising herself. If people talk, they can just keep quiet. She will answer back to her mother. And the men who have given in to her, for it is not she who gives in, she does it when she decides to, have always lowered their eyes before her. She has rather thick lips, and usually turns her head away, people have a three-quarters view of her, as though she did not see them. Then her gaze plunges into their eyes like a beast of prey. Not talkative. But harsh to everyone. Contemptuous.

She knows very well that the pleasures of love are the essential part of her life. She feels herself

made for them. Everything else seems like shilly-
shallying, trivialities. She has a certain seriousness
that gives her kisses a brutal character. Money plays
little part in a life like hers. She has never thought of
living anywhere else, and here she will be, she is in
command. The affluence of the farm and its depend-
encies, patiently built up by her mother, Victoire,
leaves her, for lack of imagining or knowing, only
very simple desires, hunger, desire. Now and then a
man bores her with his words, his foolishness. She
believes that there is nothing better to do than to
leave him and take another one. A man's body has
something very strong about it that exerts a pull on
her. She gladly admits this to herself. And then what
could she do if she did not make love? Take walks?
Working in the fields would not be in keeping with
her rank, and there are enough servants in the house
for her to do something other than pretend to run it.
Some of them are old and capable. Her mother deals
with the men, and reigns. The two women hate each
other, but do not get in each other's way. They respect each other. They are very much alike.

A strange family in which for two generations
the men have been subjugated by their wives. Irene's

father died shortly after his marriage. It was said in the region that Victoire did away with him, not liking to feed a man she would be obliged to consider as an equal. Victoire's father is still there in his invalid's chair, having contemplated for forty years the women's triumph and their proud health. It was he who settled down in that countryside which was to become his whole tragic horizon. What was he, exactly? He had some money, he had seduced a peasant's daughter. He married her, bought the farm and a little land. Then when disease had struck him down, he saw his family's fortune and his progeny growing around him. It seems however that at the starting point of all this there was nothing but a bit of bravado on his part. A challenge that took substance. But the initial thought is lost. What was singular in that human wreck died before the wreck itself. A kind of unscrupulous ardor has no doubt been propagated from one daughter to the other, and mingled with their peasant savagery. All over the region, people tell stories, and dread the furious blood that flows here.

What distinguishes Irene rather sharply from

Victoire, and has moreover estranged the latter to a great extent from her daughter, is that Irene has never had the taste for women that her mother once had very strongly, and still has to such a degree that ever since she took charge of the farm not one maid-servant has been employed on it without being or becoming a lesbian. This peculiarity has made some contribution to Victoire's success. She has attached a populace of women to herself who have no other desire than the greatness of her house. The local people have a certain respect for that irregularity which does little to hide itself, and seems to be a virtue. It has done a fair amount for Victoire's prestige. Men have regarded her as an equal, and a formidable equal. It has been considered an honor to be singled out by her. There are farmers rather far away who proudly recall that she was not hostile to them. And a terrific woman, too. As her property has spread around her like a spot of oil, admiration has come to prevail over all the other feelings she aroused. Despite the priests, who are not well liked. Who do worse, and pound your ear about what is natural.

Irene, then, does not like women, even though

she has always seen women mingling in her house. Of course she tried it. It was quite simple, and tempting too. There was a big blonde, before she had had her first lover, who took her several times in her bed. She cannot say that she found it unpleasant. Should the occasion arise, if she were bored. But neither with a girl her age a little later, whom she terrorized, nor with others whom men brought to her for fun, for the region had become used to those ways and the men often turned out to like such dainty sport, did she enjoy very keenly the pleasure which eventually came, but which did not seem very different from the pleasure she could give herself, so what was the point of it? She knows all about coming. She needs a man. And to be comfortable. But then there is no time wasted. Talk about pleasure! She knows what she wants. Some men give themselves airs. She sees through them. Go on, talk, my boy. Then that's it, she respects nothing. Men. Everything you learn in town is meaningless. She doesn't like that. They act clever over nothing. First what's on her mind. They can talk about it afterward.

Victoire senses, and not so obscurely at that, that Irene does not match her in every way. It does not make her ashamed. It does not please her either. Naturally she recognizes her daughter's right to do as she pleases. She does not believe her stupid enough to condemn ways that are not her own. Yet she has asked herself the question. If Irene liked women, things would be simpler. There would not be between them a kind of uneasiness that is perhaps due to something else. Victoire remembers hardly being able to stand her own mother, but maybe it *is* due to that. She is not very sure that Irene always resists men, morally, that is. She finds her daughter lazy, and is it for a son-in-law she detests in advance that she has worked so hard! When Victoire talks to herself at night, she is beginning not to sleep so well, she is severe toward girls who fall in love with a man just like that, because he is worth something in bed, and not in the fields. She has clearly seen that her daughter does not always go to bed with the best workers. There have been good-for-nothings who have caught her fancy. This irritates Victoire. Not that she herself, she thinks, would have wanted to . . . no, and yet I think she'd have been willing, but after all, let's be sensible, Victoire is not used to being resisted. This time, this idea, she has not tried, but only because she would have come up against a disgust, a contempt. In short, let us say things as they are, there is no intimacy possible between mother and daughter under those conditions. Victoire, tired of tossing and turning, gets up and goes to the window to look at her property in the night.

For she has greatly expanded the limits of her power. She is the queen of that land. And more of a queen than a queen. Everything there is the mark of her combats. She senses in the darkness the great mass of difficulties overcome. The land and the people belong to her, by bonds that are not merely written. She has made her life and her sensuality advance together. She has not been content to acquire things, she has attached them to herself. Compared to dominating, owning is no doubt very little. She owns and dominates at the same time. She sometimes stops in front of her father and watches him slobbering. It was from seeing him that she realized that men made good servants but pitiful masters. As soon as they stop working, they drink, they yell. All they know how to do is go to the whorehouse and catch syphilis, like the old man. That has to be where he caught it, the way he looks. They like it because it's more convenient with girls who don't give a damn, and do all the filthy little things they want, and not even pretty either, skinny, pale, old. The thought of the brothel always puts Victoire in a rage. She goes back to bed.

Actually it is true that Irene looks down on her mother's vice. She does not really think it is a vice. She simply finds it vulgar. And not very intelligent. She does not deny her mother's ability however. She admires her considerably for having been able to contend so well with the peasants, who are grasping, and crafty, and for having used everything, even lesbianism, to reign in her house, and over the whole countryside surrounding it. She knows the reputation that maintains respect around the farm. She feels that her mother has played her hand well, and it is certain that she would defend her mother if someone should take it into his head to attack her. But as far as loving her is concerned, she does not love her at all. If her mother, for example, should be rash enough to stand in the way of her pleasures, she would not hesitate to do anything against her. Moreover, from several impulses she has felt in herself, she has recognized the great likelihood of the legend that has been maliciously reported to her, according to which her mother had her father killed, or rather killed him herself. This makes Victoire rather attractive to her, and wonderfully foreign. Besides, Irene is not capable of endless numbers of feelings. She says that all those nuances may be useful for men, but that women, who do not need such quibbling to deceive those who resist them, and can always find someone to satisfy their appetites, unless they are ugly, have only to enjoy themselves as much as they can, without looking for difficulties where none exist.

And the fact is that with her lovers she does not concern herself with the subtleties that they occasionally regard as an advance over the rustic love they know, because even though they are peasants they are sometimes sentimental, and curious. This is another common trait with her mother, in what is virile about the latter. Irene behaves with men more or less as men behave with girls, abominably impatient if they make plans for the future, tell the story of their life, become tender and emotional. She thinks quite forthrightly that love is not different from its object, that there is nothing to seek elsewhere. She says so, if necessary, in a direct, very disagreeable manner. She knows how to be crude and

IRENE

precise. She is no more afraid of words than of men, and both sometimes give her pleasure. She does not deprive herself of words in the midst of her sensual enjoyment. They then come out of her without effort, in all their violence. Ah, the dirty bitch that she can be. She excites herself, and her lover with her, with a burning and ignoble vocabulary. She wallows in words as in sweat. She lashes out, she raves. No matter, Irene's love is something to remember.

She is well aware of it, and when the weary beast she has just subdued is resting, she sits up with her healthy body, her long breasts, relaxed and uncon-strained in her victory, and talks about herself with vanity. Oh, not for long. Shortly afterward, if she does not pounce on him to exhaust him some more, she sends him away, she does not like him just to lie there doing nothing. And when she is alone again, really alone as she has always felt she was in the world, she looks at herself in a mirror with a bamboo frame. A beautiful face with the taste for pleasure shining from it, disdainful and avid. With that aquiline nose she got from her mother. Eyes set close together, but big, and dark, like the eyes of statues. Very high forehead, thick hair. What shows

84

her strong will is her mouth. And over everything an air that cannot be defined, in which one senses danger without any specific indication of it, triumphant sensuality and a kind of intoxicating vulgarity. She is pleased with herself. Her hands are, it is true, not well cared for, and too big for a girl. But that too seems to her one of her beauties. She plays with her hands as she does her hair up again, and their image is very white in it. Around her floats a great brunette fragrance, the fragrance of a happy brunette, in which the idea of others is dissolved.

What is a Sioux proverb? In the white and blue dance perceived amid the efforts of defecation by a man staring at the tile floor of the bathroom there is more beauty than in the pure dawn—is a Sioux proverb. A hundred francs. Everything has its price. Ah, mosquitoes.

Mirrors have over the words I use the extraordinary advantage of being made with two edges: small and jealous, for example. Thus the moon hesitates to use the sea, then bravely reflects herself in it. Which makes the value of the swarthy head-to-foot positions

of the second Republic. Which was not to be the last.
Go mosquitoes.

Why have I never in my life been able to hear
anyone speak of hazelnuts without being moved to
the point of dreaming, of, how do you say it, putting
myself, you, to sleep. Suppose that everything I say is
of a rather scientific nature. A certain imperious
control over oneself cannot, even amid favorable
circumstances, make of a man, of a well-endowed
man, an emperor. Which was not to be the last, for
example. Sighs.

It appears, it is said, or to be accurate it is insinuated, that all this will eventually make a story.
Yes, for imbeciles. It must be said that they see
novels, romantic ballads, everywhere. Some of them,
if they have encountered a gentleman wearing a pink
hat, relate it. Everything is a story to them, a little
piece of wood, an adultery, a gardenia. This constitutes a soporific stock of legends. Suppose that everything I say is of a rather scientific nature.

All this will eventually make a story for the
cream, the flower, the upper crust, the élite of

imbeciles. Arranging everything into a story is a bourgeois mania. As you wish, if you have any takers. I say this to make it clear that, under various names, I do not follow my little curve as, obeying the laws of ballistics and the Geneva Convention, a cannon ball in the air docilely follows its trajectory. Nothing could stop it, it must sign, and my God what a beautiful flourish! It's oak.

There are people who tell the story of others' lives. Or their own. Which end do they start with? In short they would summarize anything. A stair-case or a draft. They have understood of others' lives what they were capable of understanding. But even if it were like that, it would be otherwise. Anyway, enough of that. Look at a man gaping. His features come undone, they express an unknown melancholy, an immense physical despair. Yet this can have no place in a story properly speaking. Which would follow bit by bit the life of an old woman gradually led to write anonymous letters. The reflections it involves.

Arranging everything into a story is a bourgeois mania. I seem to subscribe to it, they did make a soldier of me. Yet there would be something laugh-able about it for someone who had an overall view of me. A shot of the station, with the semaphore in the background. No I am not absolutely just anyone. That I should have been a soldier is a little more revolting for an imaginary impartial witness, than if it had happened to the last dog settling down to sleep. A little more, a little less. An unknown melancholy, an immense physical despair. The same issue of *Paris-Soir* that reproduced a letter relating to a magazine that anticipated here and there my col-laboration and that of a few others and to a falsified interview with Massimo Bontempelli announced that six thousand prisoners in round numbers had left that same day for a penal colony. It is thus that, under the subtitle Natural Alkaline Mineral Water, the label of Evian-Cachat water that I have before my eyes presents against a pink background a view of the SPA just as a barouche and several strollers, among whom one can distinguish a lady with a parasol, are passing in front of the gardens. So the sun is shining. And on the royal blue and black frame around a decorative column one reads a winding streamer bearing these simple words: Approved by the Academy of Medicine. Look at a man gaping.

[*Le Con d'Irène*]

The same issue of *Paris-Soir*. I give in to discouragement when I think of the multiplicity of facts. What I embrace, compared to what I do not embrace, does not cut a good figure. Come, come, a little more humor, for heaven's sake. Another little glass of brandy. A man who, in order not to scratch himself, invincibly feels the need to drink is not ridiculous. Moreover he drinks.

Murmur, cool water of the valley of the dream. At this point where from a height of sixty-six feet six inches you fall into the smooth astonishment of the rocks it is not for nothing that the hand of man has suspended a papier-mâché belvedere. Here romanticism comes to lean, anthology in hand. Look out, Caesar, you'll fall. The nights are cool. I could not say the same of bread, Papa (I thus designate the eternal snows). The multiplicity of facts.

Where the nakedness of the rock repels the timid foot, where the discouraged plant will no longer display the seduction of its seed, where the ice-axe brings forth only sparks, I have found my pasture,

IRENE

above the blue kingdom of the flies. I am an animal of the heights. I could not say the same of bread. Let those who seek their sustenance trouble me no more with their hideous whispering.